W9-CCN-598

Alpha Prime

By Firefox

"Alpha Prime" by Firefox.
ISBN 1-58939-026-1 (softcover) 1-58939-027-x (electronic).

Published by Virtualbookworm.com Publishing Inc., P.O. Box 9949, College Station, TX 77842. ©2001 James R. Needler Jr. All rights reserved. No part of this publication may be reproduced, stored in a retrieval system, or transmitted in any form or by any means, electronic, mechanical, recording or otherwise, without the prior written permission of James R. Needler Jr.

Manufactured in the United States of America.

Chapter One

A bove the morning's reddish orange clouds High Admiral Treys Legan, Supreme Commander of the Kataran Republic's military forces, stands before his office's cinematic viewport watching the sunrise from the 385th floor of the Republic's military command center. His red rimmed eyes gazed out across the sky, taking in all yet seeing nothing.

Deep in thought, Legan turned away from the viewport and resumed pacing his office as he had done throughout most of the night. Preoccupied with the news of the *Perseverance*'s return from her 15 month unsanctioned scouting mission, and with the fate of the Human Sphere weighing heavily on his shoulders, Legan had not slept well. Pacing along the longer axis of his elliptical office, he mumbled to himself for the seventeenth time that night.

"Idiots," he said with as much pity as contempt. "They're going to get themselves killed along with the rest of the Human Sphere."

Turning about, he stood before a holographic representation of the known systems that accounted for barely one fiftieth of the galaxy as a whole. The main portion of the known region was collectively called the Human Sphere. A circular region centered on Katara, the capitol of the Kataran Republic, the Sphere encompassed the most populated human worlds with the coreward hemisphere being the most densely populated area. The Republic occupied the largest portion of the Sphere while extending beyond it rimward. Other nation-states made up the rest of the Sphere and the adjacent systems. Humans, in general, stayed within this region while nonhumans tended to keep clear of the human territories. As a result, the Sphere had become extremely insular in nature.

Over the past 150 years, the time span following the last nonhuman invasion of the Sphere, the nation-states had become belligerent and power hungry, with the result being numerous civil wars. As a result of the attrition that had ensued primarily in the past 80 years, technological improvements were rare with many industrial and scientific areas experiencing a backslide.

Weary of the endless insurrections, the past 12 years had seen a relative peace. As a result, pacifist ideologies had received fervent support from the majority of the populace, yet large factions opposed it vehemently. Thus a great debate had swept the Sphere. Most nation-states looked to the Kataran Republic for their decision, being it wise for the smaller nation-states to abide by the precedent of the dominant power in the region. Hence, the way the Kataran Republic went, so would go the Human Sphere.

Admiral Legan understood this. He understood this and a great deal more. He knew it was just a matter of time before the Sphere went back to its old ways. *Play the peace game now*, Legan thought to himself, *but eventually someone will break the self-imposed* 'fair play' *rules and the wars will start again, worse than ever*.

He sighed, then spoke aloud. "All that the past 12 years of peace have done is give the power hungry megalomaniacs time to catch their breath and rearm."

He again began to pace, his 32 years of military experience evident in his near perfect stride, hindered only by his immediate fatigue. Short, trim, bright white hair along with his extraordinarily heavy build for a naval officer showed few, if any, signs of deterioration. He prided himself on remaining physically fit, not only to naval standards, but also to the more exacting requirements of line ground troops.

As he had as a fighter pilot, he felt his skills outside a cockpit, and now outside an office, were just as important as his primary areas of expertise in keeping his combat edge. Physically stronger and more experienced than in his early years, he had not let himself go as certain officers in the fleet had.

Not that he ever could, even if he wanted to. His mind did not know complacency nor did his body. He constantly pushed his limits, growing stronger and faster every day without a hint of backslide that some of his junior officers had recently begun to show as a result of this 'peaceful' era. Most of those officers would never see another promotion for just that reason.

Legan might not know complacency first hand, but he could smell it as a predator smells its prey. His highest ranking and most closely trusted officers were well trained and did not have this or any of the other mental lapses that the populace and some of his military men and women had begun to show as a result of the pacifism movement that was sweeping through the Sphere like a plague. His 'inner circle' of trusted friends and respected leaders had managed to forestall most of the effects of the current situation from penetrating the ranks by orchestrating numerous combat simulations, both in the field and in simulators.

Effective as his combat sims were, Legan could see the gradual assimilation of his personnel to this new 'peaceful' philosophy in the near future. He knew his core element would not be affected, but the younger, more inexperienced men and women would take to the new ways.

As it was, Legan and his military forces were the focal point for the anti-pacifism sentiments, both in the senate and abroad. A visible reminder that peace is fought for and won, not a right of birth, the Kataran military was seen as the embodiment of sanity, strength, and true peace. The war about to be fought in the senate would focus around the military, with the issue of disarmament being the political battlefield.

While the military had supporters and allies in the senate that would put up a good fight, Legan knew it would be futile. A fierce political battle was being fought, but he could already see the eventual outcome in the too near future.

Pacifists are fools who refuse to believe that peace is a temporary state. Rather, they believe that peace exists as long as they don't give it up. Not realizing that peace is a mutual agreement and the actions of just one party can dissolve that peace, the pacifists will sit by in blissful ignorance as they are systematically destroyed by an aggressor that doesn't share their philosophy. This is the path of the Human Sphere that Lena Mian and her supporters would have us take.

A smile tugged at the corner of his mouth. *Fortunately, I have other plans.*

A soft tone accompanying the illumination of a communications button on his desk keypad brought Legan out of his contemplative state. He walked briskly across the room and pressed the comms button.

"Yes Lieutenant."

"Sir," responded a young female voice. "Captain Plescal is here to see you."

"Send him in."

Legan released the comms button, his fatigue temporarily forgotten. His office door quietly opened to reveal a middle aged man dressed in the traditional dark blue, close cut naval officers uniform. He wore his jet-black hair slightly longer than Legan's with just a hint of gray near his temple. He walked silently across the office to stop just over a meter short of Legan's position and executed a crisp salute.

"Good to see you again Captain," Legan said as he returned the salute. "Please sit down."

"Thank you sir. It's good to be back," Plescal said taking the rightmost of three chairs and pulling it to a more suitable position directly in front of the High Admiral's desk. Legan then seated himself before speaking again.

"Well Captain, how do things look out in the wilderness?" he said with a touch of sarcasm. "Is what we need there to be had, or did you and the *Perseverance*'s crew just get an extended vacation?"

Plescal chose not to hide his smile. "All we need and more is out there sir. The region is deserted for the most part with only a handful of inhabited worlds in any proximity to what I've designated as our territory."

As he spoke, he handed a datacard to Legan who installed it in a small input node on the top of his desk. The hologram of the Human Sphere panned out to show the local quarter of the galaxy, but with a whole new region filled in. Twice again the size of the previously filled in area, the newly scouted territory extended far beyond the boundaries of the Human Sphere out toward the rim.

"The red zone is the region that I've selected for our use, with the balance of the scouted systems in gray. The red zone is rich in resources and ripe for colonization as well as being totally devoid of inhabitation. The few inhabited systems that we came across are along the edges of the gray, but we found them to be single system nations and not part of any larger confederations. As a bonus they have little or no military forces and the majority extended welcome to our scout ships. I accepted their relayed invitations and paid each a visit to by the *Perseverance*. Albeit small, we seem to already have some friends and potential allies in the region."

"I'll look over the data later, but I'm relieved that we're going to have what we need waiting for us," Legan said as he relaxed shoulders that he hadn't realized had stiffened. "I'm glad you're back and the mission a success, because we're going to have to move up our time table slightly."

Plescal frowned. "What happened while I was away?"

"A great deal. Most importantly Mian's proposal has reached the senate and is now under debate. I've been invited, since the military is key to the disarmament issue, to be present and speak just before the final vote is taken, just a little over two weeks from now."

Plescal grimaced. "Doesn't leave us much time does it?"

"No, I'm afraid not. But it's not as bad as it seems. Even after the proposal passes it will take time for it to be effected. Still, our time grows short and I have no intention of wasting it. I saw this day coming seven years ago and have prepared accordingly. Too many people's lives depend on this gambit. We can't afford to make any mistakes." A slight smile formed on his lips. "Not that I plan to."

"No sir," Plescal said amidst a sly grin that quickly faded. "I will feel better when we're away. The Dravokian border has been far more quiet these past few years than it should have been. Now would be a bad time for a resumption of the nonhuman invasions."

"Yes, it would," agreed Legan. "But for now let's worry about the part of our destiny that we can control. First off, get yourself caught up on recent events, then see to resupplying the *Perseverance*. I'll get Senator Malcolm up to speed on your crew's families and have them set to go before the week's out. You won't be leaving that soon but I want to get things organized well before the first transport is loaded."

"Yes sir. I'll get on it immediately."

"Good, I've got several appointments before the senate vote, as well as some political appearances, mainly among the anti-pacifism factions, but also on a few neutral planets' governors' requests. Moving the timetable up will complicate things though. I'll have to roll some people out of bed early, but it can be done." Legan focused on Plescal. "Have you been home since you returned to port?"

Plescal shook his head. "I came here directly from the shuttle port."

"I thought so. Change of plans Captain. Go home and spend the day with your family. I don't think you'll have much of a chance to do so in the future. You can see to your duties tomorrow morning. And," he added more sternly, "that's an order. You've been away for over a year and I know it's been tough on your family. Continuing on with your duties without a break isn't fair to them or you. I know it isn't much time, but you're going to take it, no argument. Understood Captain?"

"Yes sir, thank you," Plescal said with a detectable wave of relief passing over his features.

"You're dismissed Captain. Make use of what little time you have." Legan stood and saluted with Plescal following suit.

"I will," Plescal said, then turned and walked across the office and out the door as silently as he had entered.

As the door closed Legan turned back to the viewport and stared at the ominous early morning sun. *Sunrise gives birth to a new day just as the present events give birth to a new era. Our upcoming 'mutiny' should make it a good day and a promising new era. I hope.*

Chapter Two

Standing behind a podium that faced a slightly tiered embankment of seats arrayed in a 160 degree arc, Colonel Alec Legan, son of Treys Legan, watched the upper access doorway slide open as his two remaining pilots entered the briefing amphitheater and took their seats. He gave them a few moments to settle in before he began.

"Alright Sentinels, listen up. Titan squadron ran the Celtis scenario and scored a squadron record high 1027. Jyce the Iceman Wilson offered up an intersquadron challenge this morning which I *graciously* accepted on our behalf."

A chorus of groans followed his revelation, and not without good reason. Titan squadron was an arrogant group of upstart fighter pilots led by the obnoxious Colonel Wilson, an average pilot with a self-image no where close to average. Most pilots avoided socializing with him and his squadronmates, but on the unavoidable chance encounters that seemed to happen far too often for Alec and Sentinel squadron, the Titans' air of superiority was all but suffocating. Jyce looked at himself and his squadron as the best unproven unit in the fleet, and had constantly hounded Alec to let the Titans and Sentinels go head to head.

Such hounding by Titan Squadron, as well as a few other squadrons looking to take a piece out of the top rated Sentinels, had prompted Alec to enact a benchmark requirement for accepting challenges. He used the Celtis run, a training simulation designed to assess a squadron's combined ability level, to deter weaker challenges. He decided that any challenge made would be automatically dismissed unless the squadron issuing the challenge had achieved a score of 1000 or better. Those squadrons who had achieved or surpassed the mark would then be able to offer challenges that *might* be accepted. It was up to Alec's discretion to determine who would have a chance to dethrone the Sentinels from their top squadron status.

Now Jyce and his boys have made the mark and offered a challenge I can't refuse.

"I know this isn't going to be much fun, but this needs to be done."

"Colonel," piped up Senjin Marquis, Alec's wingman, "our Celtis score was 1750. We'll take'em apart no sweat. What are they trying to prove?"

"I don't know Senj. Maybe after such a long history of telling others how superior they are they started to believe it themselves. But their suicidal motivation isn't our concern. We need to work on a few things, first of which is our mental edge. We need to be flying at our best even if all it will take to win is our worst. We need to stay sharp for our own sake, not just for the sure to be spectators. This challenge is part of our training exercises and will give everyone a bit more experience, even if it is just a simulation. Use this run to perfect your flying skills as well as experimenting with new tactics."

A sinister smile found its way to Alec's lips as he continued. "However, I'm rather tired of listening to Jyce boast about how great Titan squadron is. Let's show them there's more to flying than ego and hot air. They want to prove who's the best squadron. Well, I'm willing to oblige."

A hand rose up belonging to a slender woman who had her shoulder length hair pulled back into a tight braid.

"Mel?" Alec inquired.

"When does this Titan bashing occur, oh fearless leader?"

"We're scheduled for 1400 hours in SimComp B, that's a little over four hours from now." Alec looked out over the podium at the eleven other members of Sentinel squadron as a few nods and no more hands followed his response. "Alright, I'll meet you there at 1330. Let's remind them why we're the best."

Sitting in the stationary simulator cockpit, Colonel Legan launched his *starmaster*-class starfighter from the port launch bay of the sim carrier *Endurance*, feeling the accustomed light g-forces resulting from a typical launch.

In reality, starmasters carried an inertial dampening generator. Designed to counter the high g-forces of space flight, especially dog fighting, the IDF generator created an inertially neutral pocket around the starfighter just inside the near skin tight shield perimeter. The dampening field kept all but the most extreme g-forces from affecting the pilot and possibly causing impaired judgement or a blackout. In the simulator the role of the IDF was reversed, providing the g-forces that typically escape eradication under combat situations.

Alec unconsciously flinched at the burst of light that was the *Endurance*'s transition to interstellar space as it left the sim system. With the squadron moving to form up on him, the Colonel turned his fighter in the direction of Titan squadron and observed a similar view as their carrier also engaged its IS drive and disappeared from his simulator's screen.

Not possessing an IS drive, starmasters required transport between systems. Routine as it was, launching from a carrier vessel was the standard startup for most starfighter simulations. It was just one of many small adjustments that Admiral Legan had effected in the time since his promotion to Supreme Commander.

Two minutes from intercept Alec began issuing orders. "Sentinels, hold on to your torpedoes unless things get desperate. Triple our formation spacing and increase speed to maximum. Get ready to shake torpedo locks, we're almost in range. Fly through their formation on the first pass at full throttle. Set lasers for rapid fire and try to score a few quick hits on the way. Once you're through, swing back around and let'em have it. This is going to be a free for all, but try to stay with your wing man." Alec set himself before adding, "Here we go."

A moment after the words were out of his mouth, the missile lock warning light and its corresponding siren caused Alec to almost unconsciously execute a quick roll up and to the starboard. Likewise his wingman rolled to port as Alec spiraled around and back onto his original heading.

With the lock broken he began to pour blue laser splinters at the quickly closing Titan fighters. His long range shots missed wide to port, but as he closed on, then flew through the Titan formation he scored two solid hits on one of the opposing, four winged starmasters.

His first hit burned away some of his opponent's shields in addition to disrupting a target lock the Titan pilot had on one of his squadronmates. The second laser blast stripped away more of the Titan's shields but failed to connect with the fighter's hull. Sentinels Six, Nine, and Eleven also scored hits but none of the Titans' shields collapsed.

The Titans did manage to get three torpedoes off before the fighters bypassed each other. Two of the Sentinels evaded the torpedoes cleanly, but Sentinel Seven got a bit too close and as a result lost 60% of his shield power before he flew out of the blast radius.

Inverting his ship and pulling up on the stick, Alec brought his starfighter back into the fray by means of a long loop while setting his wing top mounted lasers, equidistantly spaced around the narrow fuselage, for simultaneous fire.

He snapped off a quick linked burst before maneuvering his way in behind a pair of enemy fighters that, while the same make and model of his own squadron's craft, were painted red on his viewport's tactical overlay as opposed to the green icons of his own squadron's fighters. His starmaster, which vaguely resembled a segment of pipe with four fins sprouting out from the aft section and pointing toward the cockpit, stayed with the Titan couplet as he peripherally accounted for his wingman who was following behind and slightly starboard of him.

"Two, this is Lead. I'm going to take the leader, you pick up the trailer."

"Copy Lead."

Alec let his sights trail behind the first fighter with his thumb hovering over the trigger until the fighter started to reverse its turn and come across his line of fire. He depressed the firing button, sending four neon blue bolts into the fighter's aft shields.

The shields themselves collapsed, allowing the remainder of the bolts to drill into the upper engine housing and penetrate the adjacent fuel tank. The hull plumped like an expanding balloon before the fighter exploded into a golden fireball.

Alec sideslipped to avoid passing though the dissipating explosion and now miniature debris field. A few seconds later he saw the Titan pilot's wingman suffer a similar fate.

"Good shot Two."

"Thanks Lead. Care to rejoin the party?"

"Gladly Two," Alec said. " I've got your wing."

Pursuing the pair of Titans had taken Alec and Senjin away from the rest of battling starfighters. As a result Alec had a moment to assess the situation before reengaging the remaining starfighters.

Ahead of him, too distant to see clearly, the brawling fighters were highlighted by small green circles and red triangles electronically painted onto his forward viewport. He spotted a red triangle pacing a green circle through a tight series of maneuvers that failed to shake the Titan off what the computer tagged as Sentinel Eleven.

"Two, Eleven has a tail. Let's assist," Alec said as he adjusted his flight angle to drop in behind the trailer. "Watch my back."

"Affirmative Lead."

"Eleven, this is Lead. On my mark, break up hard," Alec instructed as he adjusted his line of fire just above the weaving pair of fighters while the Titan fighter fired blue bolts that barely missed Sentinel Eleven.

"Mark."

Eleven pulled her fighter up through Alec's line of fire, soon followed by her trailer. Alec let Eleven pass through his sights, but by no means extended the same courtesy to the Titan pilot. Three of his four shots connected with the top of the pilot's cockpit, punching through already weakened shields and, had it been an actual battle, vaporizing the pilot and most of his controls. The fighter continued on its last heading a spinning, gutted craft, drifting out and away from the battle.

"Thanks Lead, I owe you."

"Forget it Eleven," Alec said while he searched the sky for targets and found just two remaining. "Just keeping my pilots in one piece."

The two remaining Titans didn't last long. Sporadic fire from Sentinels Five and Six chewed through the shields of one of the fighters before connecting with the fuselage and ending the pilot's hope of survival in a brilliant explosion. The other Titan fighter tried to make a run for it but suffered the same fate as his friend, thanks to Sentinel Four's quad-burst of laser fire.

Soon after Four's kill, Alec's screen blanked then reappeared with his stats from the engagement. He ignored them and popped the hatch on his simulator's cockpit. Pulling himself up and out of the simulator, he joined his squadronmates at one corner of the room opposite the knot of Titan pilots, one of which was red faced and looked to be barely in control of his temper. That same pilot strode over and addressed the group of Sentinels as the spectator gallery quickly emptied.

"Have you no honor?"

At that comment shocked and bewildered expressions crossed the eleven faces around Alec. His face alone was set in a stone mask, not revealing his surprise. *What are you up to now Iceman? I wonder what kind of excuse can alleviate the embarrassment of a 12-0 rout.* Alec mentally laughed. *Should be interesting to find out.*

Alec stepped forward. "Alright Jyce, what's the problem? You got your challenge and the opportunity to prove who the best squadron was. Personally, I think you did a good job of clearing up any ambiguity."

Jyce's eyes became molten fire with his voice a low growl. "It certainly proved who was the most dishonorable. I don't know which of you shot me down in the middle of my duel with another of your pilots, but that person should be booted out of the fleet for such a breech of honor."

Alec looked to his pilots and got only confused expressions in return. An expression he shared.

"Jyce, the only duel was 12 on 12, there are no 1 on 1's in combat."

"There are *only* 1 on 1's in combat," Jyce responded vehemently. "All battles result from individual duels won or lost with the superior pilots prevailing. The backstabbing tactics that took me out have no place in civilized warfare."

Alec looked at Jyce with disbelief. *Can he really be this naïve?*

"Jyce that's ludicrous. Wars aren't civilized. There are no rules. If our enemies were as *civilized* as you suggest then they wouldn't be our enemies. War isn't some gentlemen's dispute, it's a fight to the death. Protecting our squadronmates and defeating an enemy in battle, by whatever means, is not dishonorable." Alec shook his head and sighed, letting his frustration dissipate. "I would not be honorable if I let one of my friends die when I could have saved him."

Jyce casually waved away Alec's words. "Justify your dishonor as you will, but it changes nothing. Unlike you Sentinels, Titan squadron is a group of honorable warriors."

"Yeah, dead ones," said Jett Anderson, Sentinel Seven. "Honorable or not, right now you're all floating debris in simspace."

"Perhaps so, but next time we will be ready for your cowardly tactics."

With that final word, Colonel Wilson turned and strutted out the door with his squadron following in his wake, leaving the Sentinels alone in the SimComp. After a moment of stunned silence Senjin started laughing.

"You gotta admit, that was pretty good speed work. He had what, a minute and a half, assuming he was the one Alec shot off Mel's tail, to come up with a cover story for their failure to defeat us as promised before hand. Seeing as how he's not that much above the intelligence of a rock, that little feat must have cost him a lot of brain sweat."

The other members of the squadron laughed at that last caveat and even Alec had to smile.

"Ok everyone, I think that we all agree that Jyce and his goon squad got what was coming to them. Even though the exercise was shorter than I had hoped it would be, a clean sweep with no casualties on our part is ample compensation for lack of competition. Consider yourself at liberty for the rest of the day. Report back to the briefing room tomorrow at 0800."

Muted cheers accompanied his declaration and the room quickly emptied as the pilots hurried off to enjoy the rest of the day, free of training simulations. A welcomed rarity.

Soon the room was empty, save for Alec and Melanie Cindel. "Well Colonel, care to get a bite to eat. I'm buying."

Alec eyed her questioningly. "Why so generous?"

She shrugged. "I owe you for vaping Jyce. If you hadn't I might have ruined our clean sweep."

"I though I told you to forget it," Alec admonished.

"I know, but I pay my debts. I'd appreciate it if you'd let me pay off this one," she asked a bit too persistently.

"Very well, but just this time. From now on Sentinels owe each other enough that we don't keep score. Agreed?"

"Agreed. So, where do you want to eat?"

"You're buying, so you can choose. Just make sure it's not anywhere close to any Titans," Alec added.

"Will do Colonel," Mel said after a quick laugh. "I don't like eating with whiners."

Chapter Three

S tanding before the full-length mirror in her opulent
senatorial quarters, Lena Mian studied the pure white
gown that flowed gracefully along her petite figure. Made
for the explicit reason of drawing attention, it had accomplished
its task quite well over the previous year as she traveled across
the Republic, creating herself as the principle symbol of the
pacifist movement that had spread like wildfire across the
Sphere.

She had developed the proposal herself, starting the
movement for disarmament and creating the plan for the
restructuring of the Kataran Republic into her idea of paradise.
Or at least that's what everyone thought. Her true motivation was
more ambiguous, with only her closest advisers aware of her real
plans.

So far everything was going well. The senate had taken
to her proposal favorably and looked to confirm it without the
usual arm-twisting. The populace had embraced the message of
peace and tranquility for all vigorously, with only a small
minority in opposition.

But it was a troublesome minority. Led by several key
figures, principally Senators Malcolm and Jaxsen, but also by
High Admiral Legan, who stood tall and proud as a reminder of
the past. She admired his uncompromising position. Outside of
politics, yet always in view of the politicians.

*Yes, if there is to be any true opposition it will come
from him and him alone. He has allowed the mantle of the
opposition to be placed solely on his shoulders. Just like me, he
is a figurehead to which supporters cling. He intends to fight,
and has moved the battle from the public to the two of us.*

She smiled seductively. *If he wants to get personal, so much the better. Politics are my forte, not his.* She considered. *However, I will not underestimate him. He is accustomed to fighting impossible battles and winning by the most unusual of means.*

A fresh wave of embarrassment nearly overwhelmed her as she remembered the *Goliath* project, but she fought to regain control and quickly succeeded.

Legan may have outmaneuvered me once, but never again. I will be prepared for his irritatingly persuasive demeanor. He may have won a small victory by means of his war hero status, but he will have to play my game this time. Only a politician will win this war. Between the two of us, I am clearly superior in the political realm.

Frowning at her image, Mian called to her attendant. "Jenna, bring me the golden amulet."

"Yes highness," the attendant answered in a small voice.

Mian smiled. If her colleagues ever heard her addressed as Highness, Excellency, or any of the other titles her staff were instructed to use they would probably sternly disapprove. Eventually there would come a time when all would address her in a similar fashion, but for now she would have to settle for her staff's indulgence.

Carrying on a royal blue cushion a golden circle with a multi jeweled center icon, her attendant appeared at Mian's side. Lena removed the amulet and held it up to the light as her attendant disappeared into an adjacent room. Today would be the first public appearance for the amulet and the royal crest it contained.

Descended from one of the ruling houses of the long dead Anteron Federation, Lena Mian had inherited the amulet as an heirloom before discovering her true ancestry and the significance of the symbol to which she now lay claim. The day she had discovered the truth of her lineage her life radically changed. She had vowed to resurrect the Federation and put House Mian back in its rightful position of power with Lena ruling as Empress. The other four inferior Houses that had ousted House Mian no longer existed and would pose no threat as Lena reestablished the Federation from the ashes of her birthright.

She fastened the amulet chain around her neck, then stepped back to get a better view of her royal splendor when the door chime softly sounded. A different attendant stepped to the door, admitted Senator Thorbin, then showed him to the room where Lena Mian waited.

"Senator Thorbin, thank you for seeing me on such short notice."

"My pleasure, Senator Mian."

Both smiled at the unnecessary use of their titles.

"Trevel, I hope you're not adverse to a short walk. I'm due at the High Council shortly and it would give a bad impression if I'm late."

"No, of course not. I wouldn't dream of making you late for such an important meeting."

"Thank you," Lena said as she began to walk with Thorbin keeping in step with her. "I wanted to talk to you about Legan. I'm afraid he will be something of a nuisance," she said as they stepped out into the hallway through the door opened by one of her attendants.

"Perhaps, but a small one I think," Thorbin said as his brow furrowed in concentration. "He has the support of approximately 10% of the senate at present, and I could possibly see that number swelling to 15%. But that leaves us at worst a 10% margin of victory."

"I agree. But it's the thought of him refusing to step down that worries me," she said with a touch of muted fear. "All of our efforts would be for naught and the peace that everyone wants so very much would be replaced by a military dictatorship that would restart the civil wars that have harmed our people so much in the past."

She finished in a meek voice and even managed a small tear that Thorbin quickly wiped away.

"Don't worry my dear, all will be well. Treys Legan is an honorable man. I trust in him to do what's best for the people. When the peace proposal passes, I'm sure he will abide by it." Thorbin gave Mian a very grandfatherish look. "Now put to rest these fears so you can concentrate on the task at hand. The High Council needs you to steer them on the right path. Focus on the part of your destiny that you can control and let the rest worry about itself."

Despite the nauseating tone in his voice, Mian gave him a hearty smile. "I'll do my best."

The High Council was a distillation of the senate proper. Though having no ability to pass any sort of regulation, the council was fashioned as to let the senior members of the senate discuss and modify important pieces of legislation before any vote was taken. The operating structure was twelve seats, each representing one of the 12 districts of the Kataran Republic. Each of the members were appointed to the semiformal post by the other senators from their respective districts.

Seated at a raised semicircular bench that focused on a slightly less raised section of floor, the twelve members watched closely as Senator Mian was escorted to the inner raised platform by the doorway sentry.

Her tightly trailing robes settled quietly around her feet as she bowed slightly, causing the council members to take a closer look at the amulet as it hung from her neck. It sparkled from the sunlight coming in through the enormous crystalline skylight overhead, refracting off the rubies and emeralds that made up the once infamous ringed 'M'.

When she spoke she did so softly and patiently, forcing the senators to listen closely. "My fellow senators, I was told there were some discrepancies that I needed to address. Please enlighten me."

Senator Jaxen spoke first. "They are not so much discrepancies as they are clarifications. Foremost of which is the military. How do you propose we go about disarmament?"

Mian intentionally hesitated before answering. "I have consulted with many people wiser than myself on this subject and after discussing peaceful disarmament with them for hours upon end we reached a consensus of sorts. The main problem we faced was what we should do with the extremely high number of lost jobs. It was suggested that special programs be enacted to train some of the military personnel as Peace Core officials, thus turning soldiers into policemen."

"And if they don't wish to become part and parcel of Peace Core, what then? We just turn our backs on the people that have defended us time and again from all manner of threats. That would be highly disrespectful to the sacrifices of time, effort, and sometimes life made on our behalf," Senator Carson shot back.

"The Peace Core proposition is an offer to our military men and women, not the entire solution in itself," Mian responded coolly. "The suggestion that I and my colleagues have is to take disarmament slowly over the course of a few years. All military personnel will receive pay for those years as they search for new positions and lives within the new peaceful society. The military would be disbanded a piece at a time instead of a complete and sudden shutdown. Our military people will not be abandoned. We will help them all we can in the transition to civilian lives."

"But what of the persons who have made a career out of the military?" questioned Senator Malcolm. "These people are too far along in their lives to start over again. What would there be for them in this new peace loving society?"

Mian held her temper. "Senator, I do not believe there is a scenario possible that would work for every single individual. If there is please enlighten me."

"The good of the many speech doesn't need to be repeated here, Senator Mian. The fact is your proposal will cause a great deal of pain and suffering for our military personnel. This I do not see as acceptable."

Mian silently counted to five before responding. "I'm sure there are plenty of resources at our disposal to alleviate the majority of that pain and suffering. But if we do nothing we cause pain and suffering to the trillions of people looking for a better way of life, looking to us to show them to a peaceful future. Loss of hope can be the most painful of all."

"We are experiencing the birth of a new order. Of course there are going to be pains in the transition, there always are. We can help each other through the changes, but to shy from making the transformation our society so desperately needs can and will be more harmful in the long term."

Senator Morrison was next to speak. "I agree that we are about to head into a new era and there will no doubt be problems to overcome. My question is not about the personnel, but rather the equipment left behind after disarmament. What will we do with all the weapons?"

"The weapons will be destroyed and the parts recycled into useful products for a peace driven society," said Mian with a touch of relief at finding an ally.

Jaxsen immediately interrupted. "I find that very frightening Senator Mian. Would it not be wise to store these weapons in a safe place in case they ever be needed in a future emergency?"

"What kind of emergency do you refer to? The need to seize another's realm. The necessity of killing billions to add a planet or two to your collection. What about the need to back up your cowardly words with violent acts." Mian suppressed a smile. *Now I have them where I want them.*

"No, there is no need to keep alive the instruments of war. Peace begets peace. If we result to violent solutions to problems we only create more violence. The key is to remain at peace. If we pose no threat, we will not be threatened. Pacifism is the next step that our society needs to take. There's no reason to leave the toys of war around to entice us to step backward."

After two more hours of heated debate, Lena Mian left the High Council wearing a triumphant smirk. Maintaining her cool while her opposition made no attempt to control their anger had aided her immensely. The two neutral senators on the counsel had long been a concern, but not anymore. Both had quietly given her their support in the final hour of debate.

Now the only obstacle in the road to pacifism was Admiral Legan and whatever wildcards he might throw out. But at the moment that was of little concern. She had just won an important victory and needed to use it to her full advantage. A few more attitude adjustments here and there and the proposal would be all but locked in.

As she walked across the transparent walkway between the senate building and the senatorial apartments an idea struck her. A way to subdue most of the hard feelings between herself and the military, save for the High Admiral of course. His attitude was beyond adjusting.

Yes, she could praise them as the guardians of a past era, implying that violence may have been a necessary part of life before, and that the military men and women were once essential to the Republic's very survival, but no longer. *Though obsolete now, they will still be honored for their past heroics. However, it will be known that that way of life is over and that the new era of peace has begun.*

Laughing lightly, she stepped into the lift that would take her to her quarters' level. Options poured through her mind like the sand in an hourglass, but slowly one rose above the others in her mind's eye.

She would arrange a semiformal gathering at one of the Republic's remote resorts, honoring the top military officers and offering the soldiers and politicians a chance to mingle and sooth some of the tension between the two groups. She would even see to it that medals of honor were presented to the officers for their long years of service on the final day of her honorary summit.

Her triumphant smirk returned as she exited the lift and headed back to her quarters to start the ball rolling. She knew exactly when she would extend this 'olive branch' to the military.

She would announce the summit at her press conference following the senate's confirmation of the peace proposal.

Chapter Four

S itting at his desk looking over the current market prices, Gregory Nartalo sighed in utter defeat.

It's just a matter of time now. I've lost too much business to this infernal peace plan. Even with my reserves, I'm not going to be able to keep from laying off people for much more than a year. Even then I know I won't lay off anyone, not that it would help me much anyway. The business just isn't there. I'm selling my surplus for less than half what it's worth just to stay above water. If I can't find a way out of this soon, Nartalo Enterprises is finished.

He looked over at the holographic map of his mining sites and laughed in spite of himself. *After all this time, all those years of slowly expanding my inheritance, my operations will be destroyed, not by the competition, or mishaps, or even by invasion, but by peace.*

Nartalo slammed his fist down on his cluttered desk, and hard.

"That's one way to deal with annoying paperwork," Admiral Legan said as he stepped into Nartalo's office. "But I'd not recommend it's long term use."

"Who are you?"

"I am High Admiral Treys Legan, Supreme Commander of the Kataran Republic's military forces." He smiled slightly. "I believe I have an appointment."

"Oh…Yes of course. My apologies, I'd forgotten. Please sit down Admiral," Nartalo said as he waved Legan to a nearby chair.

"Thank you Mr. Nartalo. I heard business has been down as of lately."

"Call me Greg and yes, business is down, so far that I may not be able to recover. I've been forced to sell off some of my reserves just to break even, and the market prices for Duridiem, Scential, Renzin, and the other ores I mine are falling and falling quickly. This new found era of peace is more destructive than the past three civil wars I've lived through combined."

"Yes indeed. That is, in fact, why I have come to talk to you. I need your help."

Nartalo perked up slightly. "That depends on what kind of help you need. I'm eager for new business, but with your apparent disarmament I don't think that's why you're here."

"On the contrary, that's exactly why I'm here. I need you and your *entire* organization to work for me."

Nartalo was taken aback. "What are you talking about?"

"I'm offering you and your men and their families a chance to work for me without having to worry about money or losing their jobs. Everything they need will be provided for them so they can focus on doing their jobs safer and more efficiently than ever before." Legan raised an eyebrow. "Interested?"

After a moment of shock Nartalo laughed out loud.

"Follow me," he said, getting up from his desk and heading for the door.

Legan followed him silently as he walked down a hall and opened a wide door to reveal a transparent lift. Legan entered the lift behind Nartalo and after the door closed behind them they began to rise along the outside of the space station.

The view was spectacular. All manner of asteroids floated in prescribed orbital sectors as small craft slowly cut them into smaller pieces, which they transferred to each asteroid's adjacent ore processing machinery. The ore processors separated the asteroid's constituent metals and ores and molded the molten material into meter wide cubes that were loaded onto transports which would take their precious cargoes to the nearby moon base for storage. In the far distance, Legan could just make out a small flotilla of space tugs shepherding a large asteroid into a vacant sector where the awaiting ore processor station and its debris extractor craft would begin their work anew.

After a short ride, Nartalo and Legan arrived at their destination: a large observation tower at the top of the administrative station. Nartalo walked to one side of the 360-degree circular viewport and waited for the Admiral to come around and stand beside him before speaking

"Look out their Admiral, this is my life. Mining. Ever since I was a young boy and my father took me on a tour of my grandfather's underwater mining operation on Talus 7, I knew what I wanted to do with my life. Mining had always flowed in my blood. It was then that I realized it was also in my heart. My employees are friends and family and they look to me for direction and hope that I will find a way out of our current dilemma, but I haven't. I have sought out every option that I could think of and come up dry. At best I can delay my company's collapse, but not prevent it."

A small tear formed in the corner of his right eye, but very little emotion entered his words. "Now you offer me an opportunity to save my friends and family from certain doom and give me a chance to do what I love to do without all the hassles. My first thought is that it's too good to be true. Please tell me I'm wrong."

Legan took that as his cue. "It's true Greg. What I have planned is very risky and will require you and your people to leave their homes and travel a great distance, but money will never again be a worry. You will work for me and I promise the work will be for a good cause. I'll need your answer before I go into more detail, but I will tell you that I'm on something of a short time table. If you decide to accept, I'll need your answer in the next few days."

"You'll get it now," Nartalo declared. "There's only one choice that I can make, only one choice that I want to make. If all you said is true then yes, we're with you."

He extended his hand and Legan took it with a firm grip.

"Glad to have you aboard."

Legan released his hand and fished into his pocket until his hand came out holding a small datacard, which he gave to Nartalo.

"This is the survey of the worlds we expect to be deploying you and your men on, in addition to other mining units that will be under your command. I'm making you Administrator of all mining operations soon to begin in the region outlined on that datacard."

To Legan's surprise Nartalo pulled a datapad from his pocket and inserted the datacard. After a few minutes examination he looked up at Legan, wide eyed.

"How many additional units were you referring to?"

"About three times the size of your organization cobbled together from other companies and corporations that were in a similar condition to your own. The data card doesn't give the exact location of our new home, but it's a little less than a month long trip at transport speed rimward. How long will it take to mobilize your personnel and equipment?"

Nartalo considered. "If you can supply additional transports we should be able to pack up in about two weeks once we get the word."

"That's faster than I would have expected. How large of transports are you talking about?"

"Nothing smaller than a *Nebula*-class frigate I'm afraid."

Legan nodded. "Shouldn't be too much of a problem. Better start preparations to mobilize, the word will be coming soon."

"If I might Admiral, what exactly is going on?"

Legan unconsciously straightened. "The senate will soon pass, despite my objections, Lena Mian's peace proposal which calls for disarmament and a make over of the governmental system to suit a pacifist society. In my best judgement, these events will destroy the Human Sphere in one form or another. I do not intend to be here when that happens. I'm taking the military, as well as a good number of civilians who are of like mind, out beyond the Human Sphere to the newly scouted region on the datapad in your hand. It is my hope to build a small empire, absent political influence, that could some day return to the Human Sphere and save what little will be left of it."

He looked at Nartalo. "You and your men will mine the basic materials to create that empire after we have successfully left the Sphere behind."

"If what I see on my datapad is correct, we should have no problem getting you the materials you need. In fact, I'm already anxious to get at these deposits. Your data indicates that the region is deserted and the ore fields marked have not yet been touched. If this is so, we should be able to use the raw materials to expand our current mining capabilities tenfold, absent the monetary restrictions. Does this datacard contain the names of the other mining organizations you've put under my control?" Nartalo asked.

"No, but I can arrange a personal meeting in the near future. I would also ask that you leave out most of the details concerning my plans when you tell your people. Tell them that you've found a way to keep the corporation alive and that they will have to move a great distance, but don't tell them much more unless you have to. Also, keep that data safe and only show it to your most trusted people, if anyone. As I said, this is risky and we can't afford any mistakes. I have every intention of succeeding, but I don't want to make things harder than they have to be."

"Understood Admiral. There won't be any leaks from my people."

"Good. Now I need you to start assembling an advance unit to set up preparations for the main body of equipment and personnel. I want the area organized and ready to accept the incoming transports as quickly and efficiently as possible. I also want you to be set up and be somewhat operational when the main convoy arrives so you can immediately start the incoming personnel on their new assignments. Nothing's worse than having people sitting in transports waiting to be given the go ahead to start their work."

"I agree. When do you want this advance unit ready by?" Nartalo asked.

"As soon as possible. The senate will vote on the peace plan two days from now. After they pass it into law things will begin to heat up. I may have to make some snap decisions and I'd like to have you as ready as you can be."

"I'll start on it right away. We have special equipment packages designed for fast implementation. I'll assign my best people to seven of those units and be ready to move in your two days Admiral."

"Hopefully we will have more time than that, but I like to be prepared for the unexpected. I'll also need an inventory list of all your equipment as well as a personnel list in the near future. Getting the supplies for the trip won't be difficult, but I need accurate numbers for vessel assignments in addition to keeping track of everyone once we're on location. I'll fill you in on the transportation details when the time comes. In the mean time, I'll arrange the meeting with your new mining units and I want you to handle their inventory and personnel lists as well. From then on they'll report to me through you. Would tomorrow morning be convenient? I can have a holo-conference set up."

"That would work well, it's best if I don't leave my operations in the near future. I'll get the other companies organized and under my control shortly. Most are probably owned by old friends so it shouldn't be much trouble to reorganize if you can handle the transportation."

"I'll have the ships soon enough, just tell me what you need and you'll have it. On the datacard is the means by which to contact me. If you have any problems let me know as soon as possible. If I'm not available, talk to my aid Tanner and no one else. He should know what to do in most cases. If not, he'll know where to find me."

"Understood. I'll try to get those lists to you by the end of the week. And Admiral, thank you for what you're doing," Nartalo said hesitantly. "If not for you we would all be out of a job in short order."

"No thanks are necessary *Administrator* Nartalo, we're helping each other out. And if you'll kindly show me the way out, I'll let you get to work."

After escorting the Admiral to his shuttle, Nartalo returned to his office to begin the tremendous effort ahead of him. Sitting at his desk, now cleared of paperwork that had mysteriously ended up in a recycling bin, the newly appointed Administrator of Mining contacted his second in command out in the asteroid field.

"Johnson, get to my office. I don't have time to explain now, but things have changed drastically. I'll fill you in later. Right now we have a lot of work to do."

Chapter Five

G azing out the viewport in his personal quarters onboard the *Rogue*, his flagship, Legan patiently counted down the minutes until he would make his appearance in the senate and try one last time to dissuade its members from voting for the suicidal peace plan. Some senators would hear his words and be convinced of their foolishness, but not nearly enough.

After tonight he would no longer be a part of the Human Sphere. When the peace proposal passes, Legan's last link to the Kataran Republic will be severed. Officially he will still be Supreme Commander for the duration of the disarmament, but it would be an empty title. Those few years would be nothing more than the tearing apart of what he had worked so hard to build.

The Republic was turning its back on him, yet for some reason he felt relieved. After this vote he would be free to operate as he chose. There would be no more political strings pulling him away from how he wanted to run the military. No more squabbling diplomats to deal with. He would be alone and in charge of his own destiny, the thought of which was a breath of fresh air to his politically suffocated mind.

Suffocated from years of having his autonomy dissected down to practically nothing. From years of having to scrape together every bit of political influence that he could gather to be able to do the smallest of things. Save for his one political victory that allowed him to create the *Goliath*, the soon to be finished new flagship that had every other vessel in the Human Sphere out gunned at least two to one. But even the *Goliath* was not that all he had wanted it to be. Legan's hands had been bound for so many years and tonight they would finally be untied.

He had chosen to wear his original High Admiral's dress uniform. One of a kind, the bone white uniform worn with calve length glossy black boots and decorated with golden embroidery on the shoulders and outer sleeves, had only been worn by him and no other. Given to him by the late President Brendall, the uniform had been a symbol of the President's trust in him and his judgement. Wearing it tonight would contain a double meaning. The older senators would remember the uniform and the reason it was given to him, possibly moving them to support his stance. The second reason for wearing the uniform was because it had been given to him as a symbol of his independence from political influence, as was prescribed in times of war by an old regulation passed years ago that was recently discarded by the senate. Wearing the sparkling white uniform seemed appropriate now that he was about to leave behind all political influence *permanently*.

The clock above his doorway turned over to 1800 hours accompanied by a small chime and Admiral Legan resigned himself to this one last battle. He walked out of his quarters and headed to the shuttle bay, realizing that after these next few hours his time here would be over, and whatever future that awaited him would begin.

Lena Mian shared his revelation, although with a slight twist. She wasn't leaving. She was staying. And after tonight she would finally be rid of the troublesome military and her only opposition would be the soon to be defenseless politicians. She smiled to herself. *Candy from a bunch of whining babies*.

In her quarters, preparing for the final round of debate and the long awaited vote in the senate, Mian felt none of the nervousness she had expected. The outcome wasn't in question, even taking into account any surprises from the High Admiral. It was time to take the nest step on her long road to power. With tonight's vote and the subsequent changes in government, her full range of plans would begin to take effect. Soon after the military was disbanded and their weapons destroyed, Peace Core, which was under her control, and her personal army would have no problem stepping in and seizing power. Then her destiny would be fulfilled as she proclaimed herself Empress of the resurrected Anteron Federation.

But she was getting ahead of herself. Much still remained before that day would come. Setting her mind to the task at hand, she prepared herself for whatever tricks Legan might have up his sleeve.

The senate was unusually quiet as Legan strode to the central podium. After two hours of debate, his speech was the last event on the schedule, save for the vote itself.

Stepping up behind the podium, he eyed the crowd unflinchingly. He wanted them to see in him all that had been obscured by the pacifism philosophy, principally uncompromising strength. *At the heart of pacifism is the idea that all people live in harmony with each other. Pain, conflict, and dissent are conveniently forgotten by those who wish for a perfect society.* Legan intended his appearance to vividly remind them.

"I am High Admiral Legan, Supreme Commander of the Kataran Republic's military forces. I am here at your request for my opinion on what essentially is a debate about the necessity of maintaining a military. I have agreed to be here because I do not believe you understand what is being proposed in this peace plan. As I am the most knowledgeable individual in the affairs of war and peace, I gladly accept your invitation to speak in hopes of clearing up any ambiguity," Legan said, then pausing before continuing.

"The reason behind the creation of a military force is not as obvious as it seems. The main purpose is defense, which is broken down into four constituents: Interior, exterior, known, and unknown. Interior defense is the defense against insurrection, protecting the legally elected governmental body from being ousted by a rebellious faction of our own people. Exterior is the defense against the enemies we have at present. We know where they are, what borders they have, where their capitol is located, and the strength of their military. Known is the defense against the possibility of neutral nations or even our allies turning against us and becoming enemies. Unknown is the possibility of threats that we do not know exist but cannot prove do not exist."

"These are the four principle reasons for establishing and supporting a standing military. Basically the military watches over the civilians while they live out their lives as they choose, without worry. A shepherd watches after his flock day and night with the purpose of driving off or killing any lions looking to make a meal of his sheep. But without a shepherd the sheep are defenseless and no matter how much they wish away the lion, he is still there. In the last moment before the sheep is killed his eyes are opened and he realizes his mistake, but it's too late. The lion kills him, has his meal, then moves on to his next defenseless victim. The military is the shepherd to the flocks of citizens under our protection and is necessary to the continued survival of our people. Humans are not alone in this galaxy, we know not how many lions lurk just beyond the horizon."

On impulse, Legan moved in front of the podium and stood, feet spread, arms crossed over his chest in a defiant stance and addressed the senators directly.

"I know that most of you do not understand or believe me," he said, raising his voice and chin at the same time. "Come. Ask me your questions. Let me help you open your eyes to the truth."

A not so subtle murmur accompanied his unorthodox behavior. At long last one of the peace loving senators stood.

"I have a question for you, High Admiral."

"What is your name Senator?" Legan asked before he could continue.

Taken slightly aback the senator answered. "I am Senator B'tol, representative of the Nargolian system."

"Very well then B'Tol, ask your question."

"My question for you is this: Why must violence be used to solve disputes? Why can't a peaceful resolution be found to settle differences of opinion?"

"Sometimes a peaceful resolution can be found, but some things can only be settled by fighting. However, fighting itself is not evil, nor is it good. I ask you, is a simple task such as lifting a glass of water," he demonstrated by picking up his water glass from the podium, "and setting it back down again good or evil?"

He paused for a moment after his rhetorical question. "The answer is neither. It is an action, or you might say it's a skill. Fighting is also a skill, often employed by evil men, but also used by the forces of good to destroy the forces of evil. We do not attack friends, only enemies. And when we do fight, it is for more than just a simple dispute. I fight to defend the defenseless against the forces of evil. I fight for life. My life, the life of the men and women under my command, and the lives of the people under my protection are my motivation, not greed, vengeance, or petty disputes. You people are not warriors. I do not expect you to fully comprehend what I am saying. I am the one who must understand. I am the defender and you are the defenseless. And the defender doesn't need the defenseless telling him how to defend them."

After a short pause he added, "Does anyone else have a question?"

Lena Mian then stood. "If I may, Admiral, what you are saying is that war is your area of expertise, not ours, and that we should trust your judgement?"

"Not just war, but the maintaining of peace through preparation for war."

"But why prune a plant that grows straight? The Human Sphere is now a peaceful society with none of your lions about to devour us sheep." Light laughter accompanied her mocking of the High Admirals metaphor.

"Is it not wise to have a shepherd tending the flock in case a lion might appear some day in the future, or, in the case of the plant, keep the pruning shears close at hand should the plant ever begin to grow crooked?" Legan deftly countered.

"Such safeties are not needed when lions are extinct or when plants no longer have defects. There are no more threats about. High Admiral, you have served us well in the past but your kind are no longer needed. Warriors are soon to become like your lions: extinct."

"Why Senator Mian, because you say so?"

Mian's face burned red at his comment.

"Your wishful thinking does not replace reality. How can you be sure there are no more threats? And how can you be sure no more will arise in the future? The galaxy's a big place, and no one knows what the future holds."

"As far as warriors becoming extinct, I wouldn't count on it. Warrior isn't an official title bestowed upon one by a government. Rather, it is a type of person. Some people are born warriors, others become so through training. But they do *not* exist at the pleasure of the government and I would remind you that sheep cannot kill lions."

"I'm sure that you believe what you're saying is true, but the vast majority of the Republic believes otherwise." Mian said, now back under control.

"Truth knows no majorities. Reality carries no opinions. What is, is. And what isn't, isn't." Legan responded as Senator Malcolm stood and spoke.

"Admiral Legan, you have explained to us the necessity of maintaining a military quite well, as far as I'm concerned. Would you please give us your recommendation on how we should deal with the peace proposal currently before the senate."

"I would be glad to Senator," Legan said as he nodded in Malcolm's direction. "In my best judgement, this peace plan is a foolish notion derived from wishful thinking. There will always be threats. One cannot simply make them disappear by looking away. They will only stab you in the back. The Kataran Republic must remain militarily strong in order to survive. This plan will strip away that strength and leave us vulnerable. It will only be a matter of time before someone strikes us down, then it will be too late to fight back. It is better to be prepared and have nothing happen, than to not prepare and have something terrible happen."

"In all my years of military experience, I've seen nothing as dangerous as what you now propose to do. We will die by our own incompetence and do so willingly in the name of peace. True peace is worth fighting for. Sometimes the best shepherds are friendly lions. And only a lion can truly understand how another lion thinks. Take it from this lion. The path you seem determined to follow will lead to your willful destruction. Avoid that path at all costs, before it's too late."

Chapter Six

Thee time allotted for the vote on the peace proposal was two hours in length, but not a minute of it was dull. From the beginning of the two hours down to the last few minutes the debate was furious. Senators moved about, discussing this and that with colleagues then moving on to other conversations. Some senators approached Legan with serious questions, which he answered graciously. One senator would finish only to have another approach him with a different question as others listened in.

As it turned out, Legan was encircled by a small group of anywhere between 20 to 30 senators asking questions the entire two hours until President Morton called the senate to order. When all the senators were seated the vote was called for. After all the senators had locked in their final votes the results were displayed on a two story high and equally wide viewscreen behind the President's podium.

Cheers of joy and, to a lesser degree, roars of disbelief consumed the senate when the viewscreen displayed a three-barred graph showing 1073 ayes, 273 nays, and 34 abstentions. Not surprised the least bit, Legan looked on as the ecstatic pro-peace senators gathered around Lena Mian and hoisted her to their shoulders. They proceeded to carry her up the isle and out into the hallway, on their way to a subsequent holonews conference where Lena Mian would cheerfully announce the results and proclaim a new era of peace for mankind.

The senate quickly emptied, save for most of the senators that voted against the proposal, who were now gathering around Legan. At long last the day that he knew was coming was here, the moment of truth was past. The last of his ties to the naïve government finally severed. Legan felt like a great fog had lifted from his mind, and his hands, bound for so many years, had just been untied.

Legan saw Malcolm heading toward him and met the senator halfway. "I want you to make a list of everyone who voted against the peace plan and offer to take them with us," he whispered in Malcolm's ear. "The clock is running, let's not waste any time."

Legan then raised his voice to address the crowd of concerned senators. "Listen all of you. Mian and her followers think they've won, but they haven't. I want you all to get in touch with Senator Malcolm. He'll let you know what needs to be done."

After her press conference, Lena Mian was escorted by a throng of jubilant senators to a large victory celebration, then to a private dinner with several important governors and more senators before finally returning to the comfort of her quarters.

Reclining in one of her wave massage chairs, she set the controls on gentle and let the low vibrations sooth the aches and pains resulting from being bodily carried out of the senate. She relaxed and let a smile touch her lips. *Everything is working just as I planned. Legan's efforts made the vote closer than I thought it would be, but no matter. It passed and I'm all that much closer to becoming Empress*, she thought to herself as the soothing waves traveled throughout her body, eradicating all evidence of her despicable treatment.

She had let them carry her, smiling all the way, but inside she despised every second of it. Had she already seized power and revealed who she truly was the insolent senators would have knelt before her, never daring to touch her. Let alone carry her on their shoulders.

I will have to excuse such inappropriate behavior for a little while longer, but the day is soon coming when I won't need to put up with these pathetic souls. Once the military is gone I will have no trouble with these fools as my armies conquer the Human Sphere and restore me to my rightful position.

Now that her muscles were cleansed of the senators' maltreatment, Mian reluctantly got up out of her wave chair and headed to her communications terminal. From there she contacted General Dyson, the commander of her personal military, the majority of which was now scattered throughout various nation-states, beyond the borders of the Kataran Republic.

"General, the peace plan has been passed and the time is near. Begin planning you assaults for a one to two year timeframe. I presume Admiral Legan will delay the dismantling of his fleet as long as he can, but he can't put it off forever. I want you to be ready to seize his ships once he relinquishes them, or at the very least the scrap metal," Mian instructed.

"Yes Excellency, I will begin preparations immediately."

"See to it carefully General, I want no mistakes," she said as she signed off.

Opting to not return to the comfortable wave chair, she proceeded to her bedroom where she removed her worn out clothing from a very eventful day. Stepping into the warm bubbling waters of her whirlpool, Mian felt the heat rising upward through her body far more relaxing than her chair and thanked herself for making the right choice between the two. She let herself slip beneath the unusually deep waters and let them burn away the weariness that she had accumulated throughout the day.

Utilizing a remote keypad, she turned off the room's lights and exposed the ceiling skylight to the night sky. She lay there in the warm rolling waters and watched the nighttime skylane traffic above her apartment complex. The hover cabs and repulsor limousines moved about along the proscribed, block like traffic patterns. Here and there she would see a cargo transport fly high above the skylanes, probably from the nearby Katara Central Spaceport. She followed one in particular as it made its long, slow journey up into the stars and disappeared. She remained staring at those stars, wondering which ones were which and how long it would be before she controlled them all.

Lena Mian sank further into the bubbling warm waters and closed her eyes. Dreams of long awaited glory soon followed.

When Admiral Legan left the senate he did not go to his quarters, but rather to his office. He had many arrangements to make and plans to set in motion. But before he began, he took a moment to consider what lay ahead of him.

When he walked to the viewport he too watched the skylanes and he too traced the path of the cargo transport before it disappeared into the starry sky. He was left looking at the stars. At the stars he would soon be leaving behind. One might think his plans crazy or even foolhardy, but he knew they were anything but.

This is what needs to be done and I'm the only one who can do it. Millions of people are going to be depending on me to lead them to a new home and a new way of life. I can afford no mistakes. These people have put their lives in my hands and I do not intend to let them down. This whole scheme is risky, but I know I can pull it off. I am a High Admiral, and that's no honorary title. Time to show these politicians what a true leader can do with good men under his command. Hopefully a lot more good men.

Legan had not yet revealed his plan to all of his officers, only a few highly trusted individuals like Captain Plescal and Treys's son, Alec. He had not yet decided when to break the news to his men, but he knew it would be soon.

His time in the Human Sphere was running out. He had to move his people out before the disarmament began or he would draw suspicion on himself. One might think as Supreme Commander he had little to fear from unarmed politicians, but Legan didn't want to risk any surprises. *Though they claim pacifism as their way of life, I have no doubt some of them would kill for their nonviolent philosophies.*

Thinking back to the senate and the willful disregard they had for the truth, an image he had seen returned to his mind. Lena Mian wearing an amulet. A very familiar amulet. In fact, now that he thought of it, he remembered the pattern from his studies into Anteron archeology.

Yes, now he remembered. The symbol was that of one of the five Ruling Houses. He thought hard.

Of course, House Mian. She must be a descendant of that House. I wonder why she wears it. House Mian was a ruthless body of would be tyrants that forced the Overlords to disband the Federation and split the territories between the five of them in order to maintain control, hardly an appropriate symbol for peaceful ambitions.

Fearful that the corruption that had slowly been infecting their armies and navies would cause the Anteron military units to turn upon each other and begin a bloody civil, the Overlords, the warlords of the Federation, divided the Anteron Federation amongst themselves with each Overlord crushing the rebellious factions in their respective territories.

They maintained the peace until the last of them died, with the bloodiest civil war in history quickly ensuing. The result was the Human Sphere of today, though it is believed that the original boundaries of the Anteron Federation exceeded those of the Human Sphere and that those lost territories were destroyed during the wars or abandoned. But there was another small piece to the legend that interested Legan.

When the Overlords divided the military between them they did not divide Crestanya, the armory world. They divided the key to the world into five parts and each took one of the key pieces in case that some future doomsday situation would require the opening of the armory. But they had primarily split the key in the hopes that the rebellious factions would not have access to or even knowledge of the armory.

Legan had found the legend intriguing, but had always thought it wishful thinking on the part of historians until 12 years ago when he was on an archeological dig in the ruins of Drakoris, an ancient city on a deserted planet in the Belcosian Confederation, and discovered an artifact that he later confirmed to be one of the missing key pieces.

After that find he had searched off and on for the four remaining keys until he intercepted a Peace Core intelligence communiqué that vaguely referred to 4 of 5 unnamed, undescribed objects being acquired. Legan knew the possibility that these were the other four key pieces was remote, but he had a feeling that it was just so. His operatives had failed to penetrate Peace Core's headquarters, the most secretive and highly secured facility in the Sphere, so he had never been able to find out the truth.

Legan walked over to his wall safe, hidden behind his holoprojector plate and proceeded to open it and take out an irregularly shaped artifact. He turned it over in his hands several times, as he had so many times in the past year. He knew not what treasures the armory might contain, or even if it still existed, but he decided it was worth finding out. In that moment, Legan made a snap decision to see an old friend about some help in that department, even if he had to swallow his pride to do it.

If the armory could be found it would help his efforts beyond measure. So much technology was presumed to have been lost during the bloodbath that followed the death of the last Overlord that the Sphere had yet to reach an equivalent level of development, or so the theory went. Many believed that just another part of the legend, but if it were true, what the armory contained could advance Legan's soon to exist RnD department beyond those in the Human Sphere by light years.

He thought it was worth finding out, even if it cost him a headache in the process. Jace Starfield was not the easiest man to get along with. Though close in their youth, they had not spoken to one another in years. In fact, officially Jace was considered dead. Only Legan and a few others knew otherwise.

Placing the artifact back in the safe, Legan sealed it and walked over to his desk, where he sat down and closed his eyes, absorbed in thought concerning the enormous task ahead of him. So much responsibility now fell on his shoulders, but he wouldn't have had it any other way. Though wishing that the actions he was about to take need not be necessary, he looked forward to the work ahead. He had long wondered what he could accomplish without political influence and monetary restrictions.

Soon he would be able to find out. After he successfully evacuated the Sphere with his men and a large number of civilians, he would be able to focus his full energies on the task of building an empire from scratch.

He welcomed the challenge. However, there was much work to do before his hodgepodge fleet left for, what the Sphere considered, the wild regions of space. First he had to find out how many of his subordinates were loyal enough to be willing to follow him. Also, he had to secure ample transportation for all the personnel and equipment that would be making the near month long journey. This was a one way trip only, everyone had to leave at once. There would be no return trips.

Legan also had to finish the arrangements for the vast number of supplies needed for the trip and afterwards on the new capital planet, code-named Alpha Prime. He also had to arrange pickup for his men's families, the numerous civilians wishing to be no where near the Sphere when the peace plan took affect, and the technicians along with their families. All had to be assigned to specific transports and designated landing zones for pickup.

The rendezvous point had to be secured, and its coordinates downloaded to the convoys that would gather at other rendezvous points inside the Sphere. The convoys would then check in at the principle rendezvous point outside the Sphere, then be sent on their way with escorts guiding them to their new home. Other smaller details had to be taken care of and even though Legan had most of the preparations completed, the balance would be a challenge to complete in the short amount of time that remained.

He looked at the progress reports and vast lists of soon to be refugees that were contained on 20 or so datacards on top of his desk, each of which were palm size. He picked up the first and placed it in the input slot on his desktop keypad and punched up the first progress report.

He had a lot to do, and it was time he got started.

Alpha Prime

Chapter Seven

Alec waited for the last Sentinel to cram herself into his and Senjin's quarters before he shut and sealed the door. Touching a small button on a palm-sized cube, he activated the bug jammer his father had given to him. Emitting a signal covering a 15-meter radius the jammer interfered with all audio, visual, and holo-recording devices. Though the possibility that someone was eavesdropping on their meeting was slim to none, his father didn't want to take any chances.

Maneuvering his way between and over his squadron mates, he sat down at the foot of his bed, one of the few empty places remaining in the small room.

"My father asked me to have this meeting in order to gage where all of you stand in the pacifism debate which now happens to be the law. None of what is said here leaves this room." He hefted the bug jammer to emphasize his point. "Nothing."

Looking at each person with one sweeping glance of the claustrophobic room, Alec smiled. These were his squadronmates, the best pilots the fleet had to offer, and his friends. Some were seated on his and Senj's beds, some on the floor, some leaning against walls, all looking expectantly at him. He had not told them what this meeting was about, yet here they all were, without an order having to be given. They trusted his judgement and looked to him for leadership, even though each of them was perfectly capable of commanding a squadron of their own. They had been his family for the three years since he had taken command of Sentinel squadron. He hoped he wasn't about to loose any of them.

"I want your honest opinions, not even my father will know what takes place in this meeting besides that of the final outcome. So, speak up. Where do we all stand?" Alec asked as a slight trickle of fear ran through his gut.

"I don't know about the rest of you," Senj said first, "but this whole pacifism deal sucks. How stupid can the senate be? Don't they see this will solve nothing."

"It's worse than just naivete, this is an attack on us directly," said Wes Scott, addressing first Senj, then the squadron as a whole. "They believe warriors are evil, and we as warriors will be destroyed one way or another."

"Say again Wes?" a confused Mel asked.

Wes took on a contemplative look that would have been humorous save for the grave tone to his voice.

"We, as warriors, are a threat to their beliefs. As long as we exist, we are living proof that warriors can be good, not just evil. Their whole philosophy crumbles in our presence and they do one of two things." He counted the points off on his fingers. "The first is to ignore us, disbelieving that we really are warriors. They will refuse to believe warriors do or even could exist." Wes raised a second finger. "The other way they deal with threats to their beliefs is to change them. They will see us as mentally ill or emotionally distressed because no good person in their right mind would be violent. They would have us undergo psychological treatment to remove this ability to harm others. If we would not bend to their will they would lock us up as lunatics or declare us a threat to the state and have us eliminated." He paused slightly. "If that ever becomes the case, I would die fighting, taking with me as many of those hypocrites as possible. Real pacifists do not harm or try to change others. They themselves are content with not fighting and do not try to oppress anyone or anything. My parents were like that. I respected their choice even though it got them killed in the last civil war. They were true pacifists, not these imposters. All these people are or will soon become is tyrants and murderers, the only difference is they smile."

Wes let out a breath and let it take with it the frustration and pain of old memories that had resurfaced. Mel slid over and put a hand on his shoulder. He gave her a slight nod, but let her hand remain.

"I don't like what Wes just said, but thinking about it I can't disagree," said Senj. "We're in danger, if not now, then sometime in the near future I think."

"I've always wanted peace," said Tyler Rico, "but true peace usually has to be fought for." He shook his head. "Peace isn't a birthright."

"You're right Ty, it isn't." Mel agreed. "But there are more important things than peace. We should live our lives as we see fit, not always trying to fit under the mantle of peace. Personally, I'd rather be fighting the enemy than living in peace. I'm a warrior, so peace isn't important to me. It's just a time to rest between battles. I live for truth and justice, not peace."

"No kidding," Rachel Hanson spoke up, "I'm tired of hearing about peace, I'm ready to kick some butt. I'm fit to bash people's heads in when they say violence is wrong. Sorry, but that just really gets under my skin."

"Well, we've heard from our amazon women," Alec said playfully. "What about you Brett?"

Brett Pegatt was slow to respond. "I welcome peace, but I also know there are times when one must fight. I think the government's position will eventually lead us all to self-destruction. There are too many conflicting personalities out there. Conflict is inevitable. The fighting will start again, only there will be no one to stop it this time."

Alec looked to Lieutenant Anderson. "Jett?"

"I welcome the day when war will be unnecessary, but for that to happen all evil has to be destroyed. I don't think that's going to happen any time soon."

"Derrice?"

"I never liked politicians, and I like even less them telling me how to run my life. I say forget them. Warrior now, warrior forever," declared Derrice Matrix. "If they want me, let 'em come and get me."

"Jax?"

"I'm with you guys," agreed Nevir Jackson. "This whole peace plan is bogus. No way I'm going to lay down and die. Like Derrice said, 'let 'em come and get me.'"

"Eric?"

"I don't like the idea of us disarming, it can only lead to trouble. We have a responsibility to defend the people under our protection. We can't do that if we aren't armed. They're not going to get my Starmaster," promised Eric Cremelian.

"Nevel?"

The last to speak, Nevel Kesimir, made the sentiment unanimous. "I'm not going to sit by and let my planet and people be destroyed. I'll fight back in whatever way I can."

"Good," Alec said, "then I don't think you'll be objecting to my father's somewhat devious plan."

"Which is what?" Senj asked hopefully.

Alec smiled. "We take the military and all the willing civilians we can outside the Human Sphere where my father will go about building and empire that will someday return and save whatever pieces of the Human Sphere are left standing."

Expressions of surprise and shock appeared on everyone's features, except Eric's. "I knew it. I knew your father wouldn't let us down," he said enthusiastically. "What do you want us to do?"

"Right now I want your opinions and questions. Give me whatever feedback you can. That's what my father wants. He wants to know how you think the rest of the military will respond."

"I think most of the other pilots, even Titan squadron, feel as we do," offered Mel. "When exactly does all this take place?"

"There are no fixed dates, but it will be soon, very soon indeed."

Rachel raised a hand. "What exactly are we going to use to build this empire. And where exactly is it going to be?"

"My father saw this day coming and began preparations over seven years ago. He has gathered equipment and allies as well as a great many civilian connections that are allowing us to assemble all that we need to start industries, farms, shipyards, and the like. We will soon have the last pieces in place and when we do we'll leave rimward to a region that Captain Plescal of the *Perseverance* has recently surveyed. It is a deserted area of space that has all the natural resources we could ever need and then some."

"Are there any nonhumans in the region," asked Jett.

"Only a handful of planets on the edge of the survey area, all of which welcomed the presence of the *Perseverance* when she was passing through."

"So we already have some allies," inquired Wes.

"So it seems, but none of the planets had a significant military force. Allies they might be, but not for the purpose of self defense I'm afraid."

"How many people are we talking about moving?" asked Rachel.

"Combined military and civilian, over 300 million people and all in one trip. Everyone leaves at once, hopefully before anyone can try to stop us. Plans have been made for ships to pick up people from various planets and form into seven different convoys that will meet up at a rendezvous point outside the Sphere before heading to the scouted region which, by the way, is about a month's journey at transport speed."

Senjin's brow furrowed. "Where are we going to get or rather, where did we get enough ships to carry all those people?"

"In addition to military vessels, several civilian corporations have decided to leave with us and have a number of vessels to donate to the cause. Also, my father is in the process of restoring and activating all of the Republic's mothballed ships. The combined number of vessels will be staggering once they leave for the rendezvous point, which also serve as a checkpoint to make sure all vessels are accounted for before the last wave of ships leave the rendezvous point for our final destination. A planet code-named Alpha Prime."

"I hate to ask this but what happens to the people we leave behind?" asked Tyler.

"Most of the people want this new era of pacifism, so we'll let them have it. But the others left behind will be on their own. Once we leave we can't come back until we're ready, lest someone find out where our new home is. The only hope we can offer is the promise that we will one day return and put things right."

"But how do we keep people from following us anyway?" Wes asked.

"That's the reason for one convergence point for the convoys. After they reach that point, any ships not our own will be convinced to stay away by our contingent of warships that will be serving as escorts. The warships will keep them back until the convoys are out of sensor range and then each will take a separate route, outrunning any pursuit, to our new, secret home."

"How much of a warning are we to expect before we pull out?" Brett asked.

"Honestly I don't know. My father hasn't given me an exact date. We're the first line unit, outside of the *Perseverance*, to know of his plans but I myself am not privy to all of them. We will however take any and all of your family members that wish to go. My father already has a list of names and locations, all he needs is the go ahead. Discreetly tell your families what is happening and ask them what they want to do. Oh, and by the way, this evacuation is not being ordered. Any of you can stay behind if you wish. Do any of you want to stay behind?"

All the pilots in unison shook their heads no.

"We're with you Colonel. All the way to the end."

The trickle of fear in Alec's gut finally disappeared. "Thanks Jett. I appreciate it." He let out a sigh. " I know there isn't much time, but get in contact with your families as soon as possible and communicate through me who's going and who's not. If you want to add a few names to the list you can, no problem. A lot is going to change very quickly so stay on your toes. If there aren't any more pressing questions, go find a terminal and contact your families now, unless you want to wait and talk to them in person, but I'm not sure if you'll have the time. Whatever you decide to do, do it quickly. No more questions? All right then, you're dismissed. Get going while you still have the time."

Sentinel squadron exited Alec's quarters as fast as their tightly packed bodies would allow. Everyone left to send messages to families or close friends leaving Alec alone with Mel. He raised an eyebrow in her direction and she caught his unspoken question.

"I'm an orphan, I don't have any family members to talk to."

"That doesn't explain why you're still in my quarters."

"I have a question to ask you."

"Shoot."

"Why are we leaving instead of seizing control. Surely we're strong enough to overthrow the senate. They're just politicians, they wouldn't have any means to fight back." She hesitated before continuing. "I trust you father's judgement, I just don't see his reasoning."

Alec took a moment to consider before speaking. "We could overthrow the senate and take control of the government, but our forces would have to be spread thin to maintain control. We would spend years trying to hold together rebellious fragments while the accumulated attrition would eventually destroy us. We don't have the resources or the monetary support here to do what we need to do. How my father explained it to me was this. We can stay here and hold the pieces together indefinitely, or we can leave and rebuild ourselves into a dedicated, focused, well trained military unit with all the resources we need at our disposal to one day return to rebuild the sphere anew, rather than rule over the rubble. Leaving is necessary to refocus our energies as a people and excel beyond our current mediocre standards in order to prepare for future threats."

"You're not referring to the nation-states are you?"

Alec smiled to himself. *She's quick.*

"No, I'm not. Sooner or later the nonhumans are going to resume their aborted invasion with weapons and tactics we've never seen the like of. We have to prepare for an enemy better trained and better equipped than us. We've been far too complacent in the past, according to my father. We've not tried to improve, settling for more of the status quo." Alec shook his head and smiled. "When we get where we're going, my father is going to send a jolt through our society so strong it will wake them from their stagnation rather violently. He's going to push us farther and harder than ever before as only he can. When he's finished, it's going to be some sight to see. I just hope we make it there so he can make his vision of our future come true."

"Don't worry Alec. Your father is the best there is. He'll pull it off, and when he's through, we'll all stand back in awe at what we've accomplished under his leadership."

Alec smiled sheepishly. "Yeah, I know."

Chapter Eight

"**A**dmiral," Legan's secretary's voice came over the comm, "your son is here to see you."

"Send him in," Treys ordered, sitting at his desk holding a holo-message cube in his hand. His office door slid open to reveal Alec Legan, resplendent in his dark gray pilot's uniform.

"You wanted to see me Pops?"

Treys stared at his son for a moment. "I don't think 'Pops' is the correct way to address a superior officer. In fact it's a breach of regulations."

"When have I ever been one for following regulations?"

"These regulations have been around longer than either one of us has been alive?"

"Then I think it's about time you retired them."

"You never quit do you?"

"Nope, that's why I'm the best."

Treys smiled at that. "True. But to the business at hand."

He gestured to the holoprojector unit on his desktop, not the wall mounted unit displaying a schematic of the Human Sphere, and inserted a message cube. A 34 centimeter tall figure appeared above his desk, wearing a long white robe and a familiar amulet around her neck.

"Greetings Supreme Commander, I am Senator Lena Mian. Today is the beginning of a new era of peace and harmony for the Kataran Republic and perhaps one day for the Sphere as a whole. But the people of the Republic will not forget the efforts of you brave warriors who have defended us from our enemies and secured our freedom in the past. If not for your past efforts this day would not have been possible. Therefore, I invite on behalf of the senate, you and your senior officers to a two day retreat at the Northwood spa, located in the forests of Rancoon, where you will be honored for your past heroics. The senate and I do hope you will be able to attend and enjoy a relaxing weekend of celebration. Details and arrangements are also included on this message cube. Thank you for your time High Admiral."

After a short bow from Mian the holoprojection disappeared into Legan's desk, leaving Alec not the least bit confused.

"Pop, you're not going to go are you?"

"As a matter of fact I am."

"But doing that will play right into their hands. They want to dispense with the hostile feelings toward them from the military. This celebration is just another one of their little schemes."

Alec hesitated, looked at his father's almost straight face, then theatrically smacked his palm against his forehead. "I'm so stupid. You have no intention of playing into their hands. So, what have you got planned?"

"Not bad, a little slow, but not bad at all." Treys laughed slightly. "Lena Mian isn't going to get the happy party guests she expects. After all this talk of peace and all the promised joy, relaxation, and painless living, I think a few days hike through the Rancoon wilderness will do our officer core some good. It will let me vividly remind them that life isn't as peaceful as everyone is claiming it should be. By the time we reach the reception, any influence the politicians might have had will be severely diminished or destroyed. Besides, some our Admirals have gotten a little soft around the middle. I think a lesson in the necessity of remaining physically fit would do a few select individuals some good."

Alec laughed out loud. "It must be inherited, you never quit either."

"No, I don't."

"Will I be part of this expedition to reality or was there some other reason you called for me?"

"No, you're not going. I have more important work for you and Sentinel squadron." Treys looked at Alec questioningly. "That is if they're with us. How did your meeting go?"

"Very well, the consensus was unanimous. They're in it to the end."

"Good, very good. Then prep your squadron, you'll be leaving within the next 10 hours."

Alec's eyes widened. "You care to explain that?"

"I see you look a little bit shocked. I'm sending Captain Plescal back with a convoy of personnel and equipment to ready Alpha Prime for the influx of refugees in the near future. I'm sending Sentinel squadron with him."

"What kind of readying are you referring to?"

"I'm sending earth movers, prefab housing, temporary fast grow greenhouses, and all other equipment needed to establish a network of temporary settlements which will be used to accept, sort and assign people to their new homes until we can bring our industry online and start building permanent facilities."

"Why is our presence necessary, isn't there work for us to do here?"

"No, I need you out there to take command of the fighter core. In addition to the *Perseverance*, I'm sending the *Liberty* and the *Indomitable* along as escorts for the convoy. You are to take command of their starfighter squadrons and secure the area. There will also be a class III command space station being moved in bits and pieces to Alpha Prime. Once there, you're to move all fighter squadrons, save one per vessel, onto that station and use it as your base of operations. I want constant patrols and simulator exercises. Keep them at a high state of readiness. Captain Plescal will move onto the command station and coordinate the planet's preparations from there. He and you will work out a system to organize and escort into orbit the rather high number of transports that will be entering the system, utilizing the fighter squadrons under your command. I want Alpha Prime ready to accept the 300 million plus people in an organized fashion. How you do it will be up to you and Captain Plescal, but get it done right. I don't want to find chaos when I arrive with the fleet."

"As you wish, but I was hoping to get into some action, and I don't think we'll find much on a deserted planet."

"What makes you think you'll see action if you stay?" Legan asked Alec.

"Oh, gee, let's see. We take the fleet away against the senate's mandate to disarm as well as taking a good portion of the civilian opposition with us, all the time thumbing our noses at Lena Mian and the rest of the senate saying, 'Oh yeah, make me.' Don't you think someone will try to stop us?"

"The thought has crossed my mind."

"And?"

"And I'm prepared for opposition. I've assigned escorts to all of the convoys and will have additional forces at the rendezvous point in case anyone decides to follow them. I don't expect much, if any, opposition, but I've made contingency plans just in case I'm wrong. We'll be able to get by without Sentinel squadron. What we can't have is panic and confusion when we arrive at Alpha Prime, the whole operation depends on an orderly planetfall and integration of personnel and equipment. I'm trusting you and Plescal to that job, so don't take it lightly."

"Just wait, you'll get into combat before too long. There are bound to be numerous nonhuman threats outside of the survey area. I wouldn't put my money on them leaving us alone forever. And even if they do, we will still do some housecleaning of the region. There's always some would be evil tyrant that needs smashing. Don't worry, there will be plenty to do. The galaxy's not a safe place, there will always be threats somewhere."

"But until we get our base of operations set up, none of that's going to happen. If we don't do things right at the start we won't survive very long. We have ample supplies but they won't last forever. We have to get our own facilities up and running to produce the foodstuffs we need. After we have our food supply stabilized we can begin construction on other planets as well as get our shipyards going. The more we grow, the larger we will be able to grow. Within a few years we will have permanent colonies established and we can focus all our energies on not just rebuilding, but creating a new military. One that can hit harder, faster, and more efficiently than any unit in existence. We'll build a force that can someday return and rest control of the Human Sphere from its incompetent rulers. But none of that will happen if you don't complete your mission. Because it's that important is why I'm sending Sentinel squadron. I'm not trusting anyone but you guys to go the job right. Now do you understand why I'm sending you?"

"Yeah Pop, I got the idea two minutes ago. Thanks for the expanded explanation, but I'm not one who has to be led around by the nose. You could have just said, 'I need you there', and that would have been enough."

Treys sighed in defeat. "You youngsters don't have any idea what respect means do you."

"Sure I do. There was a lecture on the subject at the academy. I listened for a full three minutes before falling asleep."

Treys laughed at that. "You're unorthodox methods aside," he said sobering, "I need you and Sentinel squadron to take care of this end of the operation."

"No problem Pop, you can count on us."

"I wouldn't expect any less. Now, the convoy you'll be taking with you will have the start up elements for agriculture, aquaculture, mining, industry, both on planet and orbital construction, and material synthesis units, plus a few others. The administrators of all these areas are going with you on the first trip to oversee the initial setup and start production. Let them handle their part with as much autonomy as possible, but you're still in command, second to Plescal overall. Between the two of you, I expect things to be running smoothly by the time I arrive with the main body."

Alec thought through his new mission for a moment. "I'll have to talk things over with him, but there shouldn't be any problems in implementation. The arrival of the civilian fleet is what bothers me. I don't want ships jumping on top of one another. We'll have to assign various drop points for the convoys to come out of IS space at, preferably away from the planet. That way we can bring in a few ships at a time without worrying about them bumping into each other."

"A good precaution. How far out do you want them?"

"At least an hour from orbit. Let's do this. Draw a sphere around the planet with a radius the distance of one hour at sublight cruising speed. Then divide the two hemispheres into quadrants, giving us eight regions. Divide each of those regions into 64 segments. Assign your ships as you choose, but spread them out into all the segments, even on the far side. They may have to make some secondary jumps but it will be worth it. This way I won't have to know what ships go where, I can just call in a sector at a time to give them an orbit slot and let them unload. Those ships that are capable of grounding, I'll put down at some temporary spaceports that I'll have built, though they won't be much more than a gridded field with a command post in the center."

"Good idea. I'll assign each ship one of your sectors before they leave the rendezvous point, probably even before that. Make sure you get the communication satellites up and running so you can query the ships. They will all have cargo manifests and personnel lists attached to their identity transponders. That should make it easier to decide which ships to send where."

"Ok, that'll work." Alec pulled a datacard out of his pocket. "By the way. Here's the list of Sentinel squadron family members and friends that want to go along and their current locations."

"I'll see to it that they make it onboard their respective ships. Did anyone elect to stay behind?"

"No, everyone's immediate family is coming, as well as a host of aunts, uncles, grandparents, etc."

"I'm glad the Sentinels are not going to have to leave family behind. Having family around will help them adapt to their new situation better."

"Everyone except Melanie Cindel, she's an orphan with no family or friends to take along."

"She's got you, doesn't she?"

Alec reddened slightly. "I'm her commanding officer and friend, nothing more."

"You sure about that?"

"What, do you know something I don't?"

"No, it's just that the two of you spend a lot of time together. I assumed that when you have dinner with a woman regularly there's something more there than friendship."

Even redder, Alec all but shouted. "Yeah, well you assumed wrong. What do you do anyway? Have Midnight Star agents spying on my personal life."

"I thought you said there wasn't anything personal between you and 'Mel.'" When Alec failed to come up with a response, he continued. "I just would like to have some for forewarning of any future announcements," he shrugged innocently.

"Believe me when I say you're going to be waiting for a very long time. I have no interest in anything but flying and fighting, and Mel is the same way."

"I think that's a good sign, don't you? Besides, how could she ever turn down a General."

Alec started to say something but stopped short. He stared at his father as if he had heard wrong.

"Yes, I said General. I know that's skipping a couple of ranks but it's deserved. I no longer have to abide by promotion regulations. I'm making Plescal an Admiral as well. Think of it as a sign of my trust in the two of you to complete your mission and have things in order by the time I arrive at Alpha Prime. No arguments, you're stuck being a General now. I won't accept a declination. You're the best we have and your rank might as well show it."

"Thanks dad, I won't disappoint you."

"All respectful now are we?"

Alec smiled broadly. "Sorry Pops, lost my head there for a minute. Do I still retain my position as Sentinel squadron commander?"

"Yes you do, unless you want to leave, which I doubt. You will just be given other duties in addition to your squadron command. First of which is your current assignment. You don't have much time, so find your squadron and get them prepped. Then fly up to the *Perseverance* and talk with Admiral Plescal. You can give him the good news as well as this message cube, verifying his promotion," Legan said tossing the cube to Alec who deftly snatched it from the air. "You two have a lot to discuss on the trip, but make sure you two have everything you need before you depart. You won't be seeing the Human Sphere again for a very long time."

"Alright, I'll get on it at once. See you again at Alpha Prime. Try not to do anything stupid while I'm away."

"I won't. See you on the other side." Treys crossed to where his son stood and gave him one of his rare hugs. He released Alec only to loop his arm around his neck in a stranglehold. "We both have important work ahead of us. We each do our part and things will move smooth as clockwork."

"You worry about your own end, this General has his covered."

"Very well then, General. How about we show these arrogant politicians what can be accomplished when you have warriors leading the way."

"Fine with me Pops, just promise me one thing."

"What's that?"

"When all this is over, have someone design more comfortable officers uniforms. I feel like I'm wearing a suit of armor."

Treys laughed. "With the recommendation coming from *General* Legan, I don't think it will be much of a problem."

Chapter Nine

A dmiral Legan leaned over and tapped Davis Chensir on the shoulder. "You up to this General?"

A quizzical look crossed the General's face. "Of course I am. Having lead training missions through the swamps of Tescril with 50 or so cadets makes this little operation look like a picnic."

Legan laughed lightly. "Well, this time it's a trek through the forests of Rancoon on route to a political conference with forty some Admirals and Generals. You might have been better off with the cadets."

Chensir smiled. "Perhaps, but you're in command of this bunch, not me. I'm just along for the ride."

"Lucky me."

The pilot of the shuttle that was flying Legan and half of the officers he had asked/ordered on this trip turned around. "Admiral, we're two minutes out from the landing zone. If you would, have your men prepare to disembark."

Legan raised his voice. "Alright, you heard the Lieutenant. Strap on you chutes and make sure you have your equipment bundles secured to your quick release hooks. Then connect your parachute pull lines to the center bar overhead. Remember. Give each other enough spacing on the jumps so you don't get tangled up with anyone."

The twenty some Admirals and Generals in the first of two shuttles with Legan proceeded to check all their equipment and nervously attach their chute hooks to the auto pull bar that would release their parachute the moment they stepped from the shuttle. The Admirals were a bit more nervous than the Generals who had made numerous jumps previously in their lives, even if it had been a while since their last jump.

Legan made it a habit to periodically train with his ground troops and was well acquainted with these kinds of jumps. The shuttle would fly over the landing zone at a low altitude but high enough for the jumpers to maneuver once they left the confines of the troop shuttle.

The pilot then gave the one minute warning.

"Get ready everyone. General Chensir, care to be the first one out?"

"Gladly Admiral."

Chensir then moved to the front of the line of jumpers and attached his chute hook to the appropriate rail above his head. Admiral Legan took up position at the end of the line and attached his chute hook as the pilot opened the wide aft shuttle doors, one half moving up, the other moving down to provide something of a crude ramp that Chensir immediately steeped to the edge of, directly across from the jump master who would soon give him the go ahead.

Legan checked all his straps and hooks for the third time before his attention shifted to the countdown clock directly above the open doors. He watched it count down to 20, then 15. *10, 9,* he silently counted down with the clock, *8, 7, 6, 5, 4, 3, 2, 1, mark.*

A green light illuminated on the jump master's console. He immediately gave the General the go ahead, and Chensir casually walked off the edge of the ramp and out of view.

Legan caught the view of the top of his parachute before it too disappeared and the second person inline was signaled to go by the jump master. He patiently waited as the overhead clock read –5, –10, -20, then turned over to –25 as the jumpmaster signaled to him. Then he stepped off the shuttle's ramp into freefall.

It didn't last long as his chute deployed and slowed his descent. Legan could see a large clearing nearby that twenty some diamond shaped chutes, long points fore and aft, were centering on. He steered himself onto a sloping line of descent that would land him in the center of the clearing when he heard and caught sight of the second shuttle as it began to disgorge jumpers.

Within 50 meters of the ground, he let go his equipment bundle, utilizing the quick release attachment. The pack hit the

ground with a muffled thud and Legan pulled down on his handgrips, slowing his descent suddenly to land somewhat softly 20 meters from his bundle. He jogged forward to keep from being covered by his chute and laid it down behind him like a long cape. Unhooking the chute pack safety straps, he took the pack off then turned around, spotted his bundle, then began to repack his chute into its pack with an instinctive haste developed from a number of past training exercises.

All around him the others did the same, albeit a bit more slowly. Overhead he could see the second shuttle's jumpers making their final approach. They too cut their bundles loose and managed to land in some semblance of order.

He finished packing his chute and slung the pack over his left shoulder by a single strap, then retrieved his bundle and slung it over his right shoulder. Then he proceeded to the place where the other jumpers were gathering. It took him a few minutes to navigate the waist high grasses before he reached a dry, gravel covered streambed when Chensir noticed him and waved him over.

"Still in one piece Admiral?"

"Yes. I *have* done this before you know."

The General shrugged. "Never hurts to ask."

"No, it doesn't. Everything seems to have gone smoothly for our group. Did you notice any problems?"

"Aside from a few Admirals hitting the ground a little harder than they planned to, no. They'll be sore for a couple of days, but it will remind them to pay more attention in the future," Chensir said as the last of the second group hit ground.

Legan waited quietly until the last of the second group had joined them in the streambed. He did a quick head count and came up with 43, with him making 44, which meant everyone had made it.

"Ok everyone, we leave our chutes here. Another shuttle will be here in a few hours to pick them up. As for us, we have 50 klicks to cover in a little over two days so let's get moving."

Legan tossed down his chute pack into the middle of the rough circle that the top officers in the Kataran military had outlined. They followed his lead, forming their packs into a small mound in the dry streambed. Legan hefted his bundle and pointed over his left shoulder.

"We head east for about 20 klicks until we come to a ridgeline which we follow southeast until we hit the compound. We have about five hours of day light left and I intend to make the most of it. Travel two abreast as long as the terrain permits. General Chensir and I will take lead. The rest of you form up behind us. Any questions? No? Then let's move out," Legan said as he started walking to the edge of the clearing, half a kilometer in the distance.

Chensir fell into step beside him as the others complied with his order and formed a column two wide and 22 long. As one they marched across the clearing, then an unusually dense area of forest which, at times, had restricted the group to single file.

Chensir ,in the lead, pushed back a low branch and held it until Legan grabbed hold and he, in turn, held it for the next person as the now common trend continued down the line with only a few misses in the past four hours resulting in some nasty facial bruises for a few careless individuals. Following a stride behind, Legan finally broke the hour long silence that was the result of fatigue and lack of conversation.

"General, start looking for a place to make camp. This cloud cover is going to force us to stop early."

"I was wondering when you were going to call it quits."

"Getting tired are we?"

"I'm afraid I must admit to a little fatigue myself, but I was mainly thinking about the others. Most aren't up to this sort of physical activity."

"All the better to jolt them out of their complacency." Legan smiled. "Wait till tomorrow morning. Some of them will wish they had never been born."

"Approximately 15 minutes later, General Chensir spotted a level bit of cleared ground at the top of a small rise. Covered in the same long grasses as had been their drop zone, the clearing was big enough to snugly fit 44 small dome shaped tents. They were grouped together in 4's encircling a total of 11 campfires that were used to warm up and rehydrate rations utilizing the water from a small stream some 450 meters to the northeast.

Wore out from the day's trek, the officers had retired early after getting some food and exchanging complaints and questions about this unexplained trip. Some of the Admirals and Generals thought Legan was just trying to make their lives difficult. Others believed this was a last act of defiance against the victorious pacifists, one last time for the military officers to be themselves before they were put out to pasture. But gazing up at the stars from a prone position on the grasses outside of his tent, Admiral Legan knew better.

This expedition was going to be his opportunity to address the officer core as a whole about his plans. It wasn't a last grab at their past, it was the beginning of the future. Tomorrow night, after two days of wilderness travel had brought them back to the painful reality of life, he would reveal his strategy and hope for the best.

He assumed most of his officers would follow him, but he couldn't be sure until he asked them straight out. He had planned this whole trip for just this reason. The idea of this being a countermeasure against Lena Mian's celebration was merely a smokescreen to hide his true intentions.

Looking up at the stars through a crystal clear sky, he rested as comfortably as he could on the rough ground. He found the aches and pains, minimal as they were, that he had gained from the day's journey refreshing and revitalizing. With his plans foremost in his mind, he had had little time to concentrate on his physical shape. He had not allowed himself to deteriorate, but not pushing his limits was something that nibbled at the back of his mind. The day's trek had stopped the nibbling for the time being.

After all this was over he would have more opportunities than ever to train. He was even considering waking up his long dormant pilot skills. Legan had never been one to sit by and let time pass. He was always in motion, physically or mentally, working on bettering himself or those under his command. Even on occasion he had visited with the engineers that designed his starfighters and warships, giving advice on how to improve upon the original design.

Now was one of the rare moments that he let everything go and truly rested. All schedules and appointments forgotten, he let the sounds and smells of the nighttime forest soak into his senses as he closed his eyes and let the galaxy beyond his current position seize to exist. The coolness of the ground penetrated his combat jumpsuit and sent a shiver up his spine. The scent of dying campfires drifted on the air where he lay. The smoky scent mixed with that of sap dripping from nearby trees produced an oddly pleasant aroma. It had been years since he had felt like this. For the moment, he knew true peace. Tomorrow morning the pressures of humanity's continual survival would lay heavily on his shoulders but tonight they were nowhere to be seen.

He lay in peaceful contemplation as he heard footsteps approach and stop about two meters to his left, he guessed. Opening his eyes and sitting up, he saw General Chensir standing approximately where he had mentally placed him.

"What can I do for you, General?"

"I'm sorry to interrupt but I had hoped I could talk with you for a moment, if it's not too much trouble."

"No trouble, have a seat."

Chensir sat to Legan's left in front of his now dead campfire. "I was wondering why you ordered this trip. There are easier ways to get to Northwood."

"I know, but I though we needed this. Too much time has been spent discussing peace that some of us have forgotten what pain and hard work are like. I though a reminder appropriate before we are absorbed in another round of discussion about peace."

"Makes sense. I think most of us are getting the message, but is that the only reason?"

"No, it's not. Tomorrow night I plan to call a council of war to discuss the current situation." Legan looked Chensir straight in the eye. "I'd appreciate it if you kept that to yourself."

"No problem, but isn't a council of war overkill for a discussion about peace?"

"If it were a discussion on peace, then I would agree, but that's not the main topic." Legan smiled as he eyed the General. "And that's all you're going to get out of me till tomorrow night."

Chensir sighed. "Can't blame me for trying. By the way, how far do you think we'll get tomorrow before we stop?"

"I expect we'll be within 10 klicks of Northwood by dark. We'll finish the rest the next morning then check in at the spa. We'll have the rest of the day to prepare for the reception."

"What do you think the politicians have up their sleeve this time? We all know they have no respect for warriors, so why the whole honorary ceremony?"

"Best guess is to eliminate some of the hard feelings between the military and the senate. They're probably afraid we'll overthrow the government or something when they call on us to disarm." Legan said casually. "This gathering is just a precaution against us doing anything rash. They don't want us spoiling their hard fought for peace. After all, we're just a bunch of blood thirsty savages out for war who know nothing about true peace," Legan said sarcastically.

"Are we going to overthrow the government?" Chensir asked a little too expectantly.

Legan Laughed. "My lips are sealed, but I promise you won't be disappointed."

"So there's still hope?"

"There's always hope."

"Good. Then I'll leave you to return to your restful pose, however you manage it here, and I'll get some sleep dreaming hopeful dreams all the way till dawn."

"Carry on General and good night."

"Good night Supreme Commander," Chensir said, then disappeared into the night.

Legan elected to move inside his tent and get some sleep as well. He had an important mission to accomplish tomorrow, and he needed to be well rested.

Slipping into his thermal sleeping roll after securing the zippered door, Legan took a quick look at his chronometer.

2300 Local time. In just over 21 hours he would potentially face the most important discussion in his life. He had to convince his own officers to join him in an illegal action against a legally elected government.

Legan smiled to himself. *Sounds like fun.*

Chapter Ten

"Y ou wanted to see me, Admiral?"

"Yes General. Please be seated," Plescal said pointing to a chair adjacent to his in the *Perseverance*'s conference room. A rainbow of color, typical of IS space, flowed by the port viewport and silhouetted Admiral Plescal amidst the darkened room. Before Alec could ask about the lack of illumination, Plescal touched an activation keypad and a galactic holo sprouted above the lengthy oval table at the head of which both of them now sat.

"I've been meaning to discuss our joint mission with you but ship-wide duties have kept me from it till now." Plescal pointed to the map with his right hand while he used his left to zoom in on the newly scouted territories that the *Perseverance* was now on route to. "This is our destination, Alpha Prime. Chosen as a temporary capital due to its proximity to the dozen other Alpha worlds, it will serve as a supply depot, refugee camp, and base of operations until the other worlds are constructed to specs. These specs are even now being drawn up by the Supply Core Administrators and our delegated engineering staff. Alpha Prime will become a starting point consisting of every improvisation possible to make ends meet. No design specs are being made for Alpha Prime as yet. The other prime worlds are being left alone until permanent facilities can be established according to a planet-wide design schematic. The same goes for the 127 secondary systems necessary for our long term survival and growth. Nothing will be constructed outside of Alpha Prime unless it's a part of the long-term plan. All short term necessities fall to Alpha Prime, which eventually will be reconstructed into a long term colony once all the temporary structures have been abandoned."

Hitting another button on his keypad, Plescal brought up system designations for the new territories that now covered the length of the table. Supply lines ran gold between points of red, green, and blue with the colors determined by the systems' worth. Alpha worlds flared red, secondary worlds green, and all other potentially beneficial systems were pinpricks of blue among the dull gray points that highlighted the remainder the newly cataloged systems.

"I've drawn up a priority map based on my scouting missions. The supply lines are what I see as existing five or so years down the road. Here," he said as the computer highlighted a ring of systems yellow at his touch, "are what I think would be the best position for border worlds. Assuming we will face invasion sometime in the future, I have assigned sector headquarters, patrol zones, and probable outpost locations in what I think are the most defensible positions available. These," he said as seventeen orange dots appeared, "are where I would put our shipyards. They all have nearby access to planned mining and industrial material synthesis sites as well as being well with our perimeter defenses. I've separated our selective territories into 327 sectors that will serve all military and civilian purposes. In addition I have marked off the remains of the scouted territories into 1537 sectors purely for navigational use. I don't think we will need go beyond the marked boundaries, there are more than enough systems in the prescribed region to meet our needs." Plescal looked to Alec. "Your thoughts?"

He considered a moment before answering. "Well Admiral, from what I see here we should be able to do quite well for ourselves. The system tags indicate a great amount of natural resources located at numerous positions throughout the region. The boundaries you have marked off appear to make sense, though I do have a question about the border along sector 237. Why isn't the boundary expanded to include this dense cluster of star systems?" Alec asked thrusting a finger at the map. "It would seem logical to secure such a region just for the sake of denying any future enemy such a multitude of worlds to choose from for a forward base, let alone the close proximity of the natural resources and habitable worlds I see tagged. Why did you exclude this particular cluster?"

"I didn't want to extend the border that far rimward, but you're right. If the cluster is going to be on the border it might as well be on our side. I'll redraw the map later. You see any other oversights on my part?"

"Not at the moment. But I would like to take a closer look at the boundary regions' systems individually. I might be able to tweak the lines a bit or at least confirm your selections."

"Good idea. I'll have a copy sent to your quarters later on."

"If I might, there is one thing I would appreciate if you would clear up. On this map I can see that Alpha Prime is well rimward of the center point. Would not a more central or coreward system be preferable as our initial base of operations?"

"We considered placing our base of operations on a coreward planet, but decided otherwise because the systems we initially plan to excavate and colonize are rimward. Therefore our supply lines will be shorter if Alpha Prime is rimward itself. The fleet *will* have to travel further, but the extra distance will be worth it in the long run. Does that adequately answer your question General?"

"Yes, thank you. I don't spot any other problems at this time, as far as planning goes. The reality of our mission requirements is something else entirely."

"I agree. Our mission is all but impossible. I want everything that *can* be decided on route to *be* decided before we reach Alpha Prime. We have very little time and I want to make the most of every minute. Between the two of us, we have to create a system to handle all incoming transports from scratch. Not only do we have to coordinate the arrival and unloading of transports, we have to organize the ground based sorting and processing of personnel and equipment, plus facilitate their integration into the startup operations. All in all, not an easy assignment."

"No Admiral, not at all. I think my fighter squadrons can herd the transports into position and keep the unloading somewhat orderly, but we need to assign ships and cargo to specific orbits and drop zones before they arrive. If we try to do it on the spot we will have chaos. Every last detail needs to be planned out before they arrive if we're to pull this off."

"I agree. We also need to assign land zones to the various industrial and agricultural units that are with us now and will be deploying when we arrive."

At a motion of his hand, the holographic map of the newly scouted territories telescoped in on Alpha Prime until the planet alone hovered above the table. Grid lines dissected the planet's surface. On the second largest continent in the southern hemisphere, a small area was blocked off into tiny red squares. The map again telescoped down to show the particular continent and the highlighted area.

"This is a preliminary sketch of what will be our base of operations on the ground. The red areas are where we're going to put the bulk of our equipment and house our people, but no specifics have yet been arranged. That falls to us."

"Lucky us."

"True, but it's a job that needs done on a strict timetable. Who else could handle such an enormous project in such a short timespan?" Plescal asked mirthfully.

"Is that how my father stuck you with this assignment or did you just volunteer out of the goodness of your heart?"

"Both actually. Being as how I am the only senior officer to have firsthand experience in the region I was the logical choice and I agreed to lead this expedition when Admiral Legan asked me to. Besides, I'd rather be out of the Sphere before things start heating up. I don't expect the mass desertion to go unnoticed. I don't know what the politicians will do or what they can do but they're bound to be somewhat ticked off."

"You have a point Admiral. The latter group is going to be much larger and have a lot more trouble leaving than we did. We need to have things ready when they get there. To that end I have a few suggestions, if I may?"

"By all means General, proceed."

"The arrangements we're going to make are going to be complicated for sure, but they don't have to be anything fancy. On the ground, let's divide the selected area into one klick squares and divvy them up as we please. I think it would be best if we have the temporary shelters set up on and around this plateau in the south," Alec said pointing to the appropriate spot on the map. "The general headquarters can be located in the center region with multiple spaceports ringing it. The main industrial structures can be set up in the Northeast quadrant and the Northwest quadrant can contain all agricultural buildings. Both industrial and agricultural units can spread out farther to the north as needed and won't interfere with the temporary refugee camp. We can section off the areas directly east and west of the center point for storage and miscellaneous buildings. We can have the Supply Core Administrators and their staffs draw out basic plans for the layout of their facilities that we can look over and make changes to, if necessary, before we arrive at Alpha Prime."

"Excellent ideas General. I might add that the portable shelters be arranged into small camps that be given recognizable names as a means of navigation, rather than just serial numbers attached to buildings arrayed in block formations. Adjusting the arrangement according to the terrain and unitary support facilities would be preferable to the great deal of landscaping that would need to be done for the monotonous block grid layout."

"That would be beneficial in the long run. How long do you think we'll be confined to this megacamp before permanent facilities are built on other worlds?"

"I would guess a year and a half to two years before any appreciable number of people are moved off planet permanently."

"In that case I suggest we add some communal buildings for each of our little camps. Entertainment facilities, sport fields, meeting halls, anything that will give a sense of identity to our people during this transition period will help alleviate the feelings of being away from home and begin to help people make their new homes, even if they are temporary ones, on Alpha Prime."

"That could be arranged rather easily. A few structures made from scratch would be no problem for our construction crews. Once they're in place and the refugees are settled in we could organize intercamp competitions. Sports can be a powerful distraction to panicky people. And panic is the last thing we need in this critical stage."

"Competitive sports are a good idea. They'll help put nervous energy to productive use and give the people a sense of identity through their local teams. But before we get too concerned about life on the ground we need to make sure we get everyone down to the ground safely. That leaves us with the task of assigning orbital slots and creating a landing schedule. The far orbit grid my father and I agreed on for the initial organization of vessels coming into the system can be used for near orbit as well, but in a different arrangement according to priority instead of entry vector. But that still leaves us to draw up a landing schedule and to organize our own convoy's deployment when we arrive. I hope we'll just be able to point the administrators to their areas and let them handle their construction and deployment of the startup machinery on their own."

"I would think them able to handle their own operations with minimal interference from us General. We're mainly the overall architects of the base camp and facilitators of the implementation. Your father picked good men for his administrators, I don't think we'll have to hold any of their hands along the way."

"That's good to hear. I think that pretty much takes care of the big picture, now we're down to the details of the orbital slots, landing zones, landing or offloading schedules, spaceport construction, and probably a dozen other problems waiting to be solved that I've overlooked. Do you have the cargo manifests?"

"Yes, both our convoy's and the main convoy's."

"Good. If we get the bulk of this done now, we can spot any problems in the system before its implemented. This is an enormous task before us. My father is counting on us to get this job done right and I don't intend to disappoint him. If you will Admiral, pull up those manifests and we'll get started on the vessel assignments."

Three hours and 17 minutes later, Alec left Admiral Plescal's office and headed for one of the *Perseverance*'s hanger bays. The majority of the landing schedule had been written out, save that of the initial orbits of the vessels. While the Admiral had delegated the task of orbital coordination and thus the headache of the command station's construction schedule to himself, he had let Alec choose the orbital sector arrangement since it was his fighters that were going to be handling the incoming traffic.

Tired from the long meeting but none the less determined, he caught a nearby lift and took it all the way to the port side hanger where his starmaster was stowed. He crossed the deck, nodding to the few techs working on this or that around the hanger bay, nothing that really needed to be done, just extra maintenance work to keep themselves occupied.

Alec climbed the access ladder to the dorsal hatch on his four winged starfighter, which rode directly in front of the top vertical wing that angled forward slightly but not enough to crack his skull on if he ever needed to eject from the starmaster.

Hopping on top of the craft, he pulled the access lever and the hatch popped open with a slight hiss resulting from the equalization of air pressures between the hangar's atmosphere and the starmaster's self-contained, continually recycling atmosphere. Alec slid into the shadowed cockpit and closed the hatch behind him.

With a touch of a button, he brought up the internal illumination far enough that he could read the datapad that he had slipped from a knee pocket on his combat jumpsuit. Settling in to his favorite place to think, he activated his datapad and concentrated on assigning orbital slots to the transports that he would be responsible for in the not too distant future.

Chapter Eleven

A fter a long, hard day of hiking, the Kataran military's
officer core settled in for the night in a wide, tree-
covered valley bisected by a fast moving, shallow river.
Their encampment was 50 meters to the west of the southward
flowing river and was centered in a small clearing surrounded by
thick-trunked trees sprouting 30 meter high masses of greenery.
A small patch of cloudless night sky, resplendent with bright
white stars, was the only gap in the vast forest canopy.

It was under this break in the trees, created years ago be
a long since decomposed deadfall, that a lone campfire burned at
the center of a ring consisting of 43 Admirals, Generals, and a
few highly influential Captains that waited for the lone High
Admiral to tell them why they were gathered here in the calm,
cool night air instead of sleeping in their almost comfortable bed
rolls.

Some officers thought they knew why Legan had called
this meeting, others speculated quietly amongst themselves while
still a few others waited patiently for the High Admiral to begin,
curious, but making no assumptions.

Here they all are, save for Plescal and Alec, Legan
thought to himself. *My most trusted officers and supporters for
the past fourteen years, some of them for longer than that. They
are the true core to this military. If I don't have them at my side
things will become much more difficult. I won't give up, ever, but
I do need their help if I am to succeed in my true mission.*

He looked around the circle once before standing up, an
action that stopped what little conversation remained. After
looking each and ever one of his officers in the eye, he began the
discussion that, little did he know, would decide the fate of the
galaxy in the distant future.

"All of you, I'm sure, are wondering why I called for this gathering and even why I organized this cross country trek. The reason is simple. I brought you here for a council of war."

Looks of disbelief, shock, and most abundantly hope, spread across the men and women dressed in civilian clothes and sitting casually on the dirty ground around a small bonfire. Hardly the ideal situation for an important meeting, but it was a deliberate one. Admiral Legan had wanted a situation that would leave behind all formality and obligation to the Republic, and now he had it.

"We are responsible for the safety and well being of trillions of people across the Human Sphere. Our obligation is not a legal one. We are the defenders of the people because of who and what we are. Law cannot give to us nor rescind from us that duty. Sometimes that duty requires us to operate illegally, and now is one of those times. Laws come and go, but truth and justice are constant. This peace plan is a danger to us and those that we defend. If we let ourselves be destroyed, then there will be no one left to defend the defenseless. I'll die before I fail to defend my people, but this time is different because the threat comes from within. The government is becoming corrupt; therefore we will no longer serve beneath it."

"What is going to happen is this: In the near future I will be taking the military and a number of civilians beyond the Human Sphere to a region mapped out by now Admiral Plescal. He is now on his way back there with men and equipment to prepare for our arrival. I have arranged for all necessary supplies, equipment, and personnel to be taken with us in order to establish colonies for the 300 million plus people we're taking with us. All but a few last details have been taken care of previously. We're all but ready to go. I know a council of war is meant to determine what action is necessary and that I've already decided the course we will take, but I value your input. Give me your professional opinions of the current circumstances and your assessment of my plan."

"Admiral," Captain Nardeu of the *Determination* spoke up first after a brief moment of silence. "I must say this revelation is unexpected, yet I'm not surprised. You've bent the rules to get things done before and I agree that the rules need not be followed any longer if they serve no purpose. But I am somewhat confused. Do you mean to abandon the Republic?"

"Yes, I do. I believe the best way to protect the people is to leave for many years, long enough to build up a force that can return and remove all threats, internal and external, from the Sphere and eliminate any hindrance to the defense of our people. I know many of you are pondering the same question: Why leave at all? We can overthrow the government and won't have to abandon our people. I have thought long and hard on this argument and have come to one conclusion. We *can* overthrow the government. We have the manpower and firepower to do the job, but we don't have the resources to gain full control or to even maintain control. We would stretch ourselves thin and be unable to do anything but maintain possession of our systems."

"To put it simply, we would be fighting the planets under our control plus outside forces, and we don't have the resources to be able to achieve anything but a stalemate in that situation. Eventually the physical and mental attrition would wear us thin and we would fall apart. Then the worlds under our protection would fall prey to the other worlds we failed to control. We could selectively choose worlds in order to minimize the attrition, but that would only delay the inevitable. We have to build first, then conquer. If we try to do the reverse we will fail and our people will have no hope for the future. Without political influence we can build a strong nation, ruled, but not oppressed, by the military. We will then be able to defend our people without having our hands tied behind our back by red tape. When we return, the resources of our soon to be colonies will sustain us while we gain a firm hold on the Human Sphere, not a fleeting hold that an overthrow would gain us. We are the only *long-term* hope for our people and we must leave so that we have the opportunity to grow larger and stronger than ever before. Then and only then will we be able to truly help and defend our home systems and all others under our irrevocable protection."

"I'll be blunt. Our people are going to suffer. If we stay we can delay but not prevent their suffering. Dissident elements of the population are going to cause the Sphere to self-destruct and destroy us if we do not leave. Stay and be destroyed or leave to become a hope for the future. I choose the latter."

Admiral Dravcus cleared his throat. "I don't like your assessment of the situation, but I'm forced to agree. If we stay here, we *will* be destroyed by the pacifism movement. I'm glad one of us had the forethought to prepare for this day. If not for your initiative Admiral, all would be lost."

Legan smiled grimly. "That comment may be premature. We're not out yet."

"Can we get out?" asked General Mastrick. "It seems impossible that such an endeavor could succeed."

"We'll have our hands full to be sure, but we'll also have civilian corporate assistance in some areas. I assure you, all has been planned carefully. I do not intend to fail."

"I have no doubts that you will succeed sir," Admiral Senxir, one of only three female officers present, confidently proclaimed. "Your only opponents are politicians, while you are an experienced warrior and a true leader. My question is what do you mean by 'building'? What plans do you have for us once we reach these new territories?"

"First of all, *our* opponent is time, not politicians. And second, a leader can only do so much without competent people under his command. As for my plans, I have not made any firm decisions as yet. Much will depend on what technologies our soon to be RnD department develops. I hope to field all new equipment based on combat environments instead of monetary restrictions. New tactics will be developed, the military will be reorganized, and training programs radically altered. When I'm finished we will have created a military the likes of which has never been seen before. It may take a number of years, perhaps decades before we're ready to come back. But we will, and stronger than ever."

"What of the people we leave behind?" asked Admiral Termel. "Can we do nothing to help them?"

"Very little I'm afraid. I've made arrangements with certain high placed officials on backwater worlds to provide sanctuary for political malcontents, but all of our people are leaving. We don't have anyone to spare nor do we have the resources. We need everything and everyone we can get on Alpha Prime, our soon to be base of operations in the new territories. I wish there was something that we could do for the masses of people that we leave behind, but there isn't. They'll be on their own until we come back."

"When will we be back?" Captain Asande asked.

"Whenever we're ready. If things go smoothly we could be back within 20 years, but my best guess would be 30 to 40."

Muffles gasps followed his timeframe and he sympathized. "I know that is a long time, but building a military takes time and can't be rushed. The Human Sphere will tear itself to pieces before we return, but if we don't do this right the Sphere could be ravaged by civil wars for centuries or worse yet conquered by a nonhuman invasion. One way or another, we are all that stands between the Human Sphere and complete destruction. And in order to save the Human Sphere we must first abandon it."

"How do you plan to support 300 million plus people?" asked General Chensir, "That would call for an unbelievable number of supplies, and eventually the supplies would expire. By what means will we acquire new supplies?"

"Admiral Plescal is on his way to Alpha Prime as we speak. With him is an advance expedition that will construct the beginning structures of our agricultural mechanism. When we arrive the fast grow crops should already be producing minimal amounts of foodstuffs that will replace our supplies when they expire. By that time the normal crops and animal herds will be firmly established and we can start drawing off of them for supplies. Eventually, the agriculture unit will expand greatly and provide us with a large surplus, even as our population grows. If all goes as planned we will never be wanting for foodstuffs."

"What will happen when we reach Alpha Prime initially?" Admiral Conel asked.

"Once we reach our destination, the transports will begin unloading equipment and personnel to the surface. The transports will then be parked in high orbit for temporary storage. The people will be quartered in temporary shelters that will already be set up by Admiral Plescal. Also, he will have overseen the setup of our agricultural and industrial units. Part of the population will be able to begin working a day or so after arrival. The others will wait until they're needed in the encampment of temporary shelters along with the military personnel's families. Until permanent facilities are created the temporary shelters will be home. The bulk of our navy will be centered around a class III command station that Admiral Plescal is also taking with him in segments. Our quarters will be on that station as will be those of the rest of the officers not assigned to a military vessel, but I hope to have new facilities built in short order. Our construction units will be onsite by the time we arrive, as will be the key elements of the mining units. Once the final pieces arrive with us, the whole operation should take off at an amazing rate. We have all the resources we need in the region, all we have to do is go out and get them."

"Admiral, are we going to be alone out there or will we have nonhuman populations to contend with?" Captain Huesky asked.

"The region is, for the most part, deserted. There were a few nonhuman systems found by the survey team, but they are all on the fringes of the scouted territory and far from the space we have designated for our purposes. Also, none are a military threat by any stretch of the imagination. From the information I have, they're independent colonies with what barely suffices as a police force, but none of them have a standing military. Our survey team was graciously welcomed when they passed through the area so we may have something in the way of allies, but not on a military basis. As for the space we've claimed, or rather will claim for ours, it is completely devoid of humans and nonhumans alike. The mineral deposits have not been touched as far as we were able to tell, so our miners should have little problem finding the necessary materials."

Legan looked around the circle of officers as no more immediate questions arose. "I want all of you to know this is a volunteer mission. I'm not making this an order. You can stay behind if you like, but I really do need your military expertise. The choice is yours, as it will be for all military personnel. I know this isn't much forewarning, but I need to know where all of you stand here and now."

Legan then went around the circle asking each individual for his or her decision with the consensus being unanimous. They would follow Legan wherever he led. Only Admiral Termel was of a different mind.

After the council of war was disbanded Termel approached Admiral Legan who sitting before his newly made campfire warming up some cold ration bars.

"Admiral, could I have minute?"

"Sure. Pull up a piece of ground."

Termel did sit down and flinched as the cold of the ground soaked through his clothing. "I wanted you to know I'll follow whatever orders you give me, sir, just as I said before, but I think I could be most useful if I stayed behind." When Legan didn't comment he continued. "As you've said yourself, the Human Sphere is going to tear itself apart, and I think someone should stay behind and help our people in whatever way they can. I think that person should be me."

"What exactly did you have in mind?"

"My family is rather rich. We own several megacorporations as well as stock in numerous others. No matter how badly the Sphere battles itself, I'll have assets somewhere to utilize. My thinking is that I can establish a base of operations on a fringe world, preferably outside of the Republic, that I can make as a haven for refugees from whatever wars break out. I could also, if I had the men and machinery, pacify a small region and hold onto it until you and the rest of the military eventually returned."

Legan's brow wrinkled slightly as he thought. "You would create for yourself a small empire into which you would welcome refugees, and you would fight off anyone who came after the refugees. Correct?"

"Yes sir."

"In order to do that you would need a sizable fighting force and a way to replenish your supplies. You've accounted for the latter so I guess I can account for the former. I'll let you keep your current battle group and throw in a few other warships staffed by those military men and women that wish to stay behind, provided that you move their families to your new empire and not try to take control of more systems than necessary. Hold onto your empire as long as you can. Don't provoke anyone, but also don't hold back if they come after you."

"Thank you sir," Termel said with obvious relief. "I won't disappoint you."

"I know you won't Admiral, I'm counting on it."

Chapter Twelve

S tanding on her suite's balcony, which was large enough to easily hold 20 persons, Lena Mian solitarily looked out across the vast forest that surrounded the spa on all sides. The only access to the Northwood spa was a small, elegantly designed oval landing pad with a large 'NW' accentuating its center.

Only a few minutes ago a luxury class shuttle had arrived, dropped off its single occupant and his luggage, then made for orbit as quickly as it had arrived, all of which Mian viewed from her current position. It was then no surprise when she heard faint footsteps across the wide balcony that came to a stop a few meters behind her. She turned about and bowed slightly to the gray haired man dressed in civilian clothes.

"Welcome Senator Trir. I would have thought checking into your suite would have taken more time. I didn't expect you so soon."

The slightly taller senator returned her bow. "I had the valet take my luggage to my suite, I wanted to talk to you before the other senators' arrival."

"You needn't have bothered. They won't be here for a few more hours, I checked their scheduled arrival times."

"Well then it appears we have ample time to talk. How goes the Peace Core agents' work?"

"Quite well actually. We have the majority of the hot sheets completed. There should be little trouble rounding up the antipacifists when the time comes."

"You can speak plainly Lena. Save your pacifism rhetoric for the public, I do not need to hear it."

"Sorry," Mian said apologetically. "I guess after so many years of spreading the word of peace that I've started to believe it somewhat myself." She laughed lightly. "There can be no peace without a strong hand pacifying the region. These foolish people have allowed me to convince them that pacifism and disarmament are the answers to our endless wars. Nothing could be further from the truth. Such a diverse group of people can't help conflicts from occurring, it's their basic nature to fight amongst each other. Many a nation has tried to control this infighting and not one has truly succeeded. The idea that we all put down our weapons and be friends is absurd, but that hasn't stopped the masses from embracing the message of 'true peace'. It will make it that much easier to subdue them when the time comes."

She looked to Trir. "As you asked, Peace Core has nearly compiled the list of our soon to be political prisoners. When they finish we'll be able to seize the majority of the people opposed to us before they have a chance to act."

"Does that list include High Admiral Legan and his officers?"

"Of course, we can't have a vengeful warlord running around loose inciting rebellion, now can we? Legan and his supporters will be the first people that the Peace Core officials arrest, but not before they've been disarmed. We can't risk them turning their forces on us so we must wait until those forces are scrapped in the name of universal peace. Then and only then will we be free to take control of the Kataran Republic and reestablish the Anteron Confederation."

"Don't overlook the possibility of Legan taking preemptive action. He's by far the most dangerous of our enemies. If he finds out what we have planned, he'll come down on us so hard that we'll loose everything we've worked for and end up in prison before we know what's happening. That is if he doesn't kill us outright."

"Surely you must be crazy. The thought that Legan would take matters into his own hands is ridiculous. He'd only act on word from the High Council or President Morton. He's a man that serves the people and plays by the rules. If he found out what we were planning he'd destroy us, but through proper procedure. The military is far more strict about rules and regulations than the senate, and Admiral Legan is nothing if not a stickler for order. If we were discovered, he would obey the dictates of the civilian government and not come after us personally. That's assuming he did find out and I don't expect he or anyone else will discover our plans until it's too late to stop us."

"Do not underestimate Legan's initiative. His grandfather had a reputation for bending or breaking the rules when the situation deemed it necessary, and I've seen nothing in Admiral Legan to suggest the trait didn't breed true. I suggest you not underestimate how far he will go when he thinks he is right. Also, there need not even be a leak from one of us to alert him to something amiss. He may discover that for himself. I don't know exactly how he does it, but he has the bad habit of finding out things that he has no right to know about or even reason to look for. He may uncover our plans somehow or at least feel we have something planned and move to circumvent our threat to the nation under his protection."

"That is why we must stay hidden until his weapons are destroyed. Then he will have no means to stop us even if he discovers our true plans."

"I fear Legan to be more clever than you think. What if he conveniently misplaced a few ships on the active duty roster or calls up reserve vessels and hides them away during the dismantling only to reveal them when we seize control. I would expect no less from the man. He is not an enemy to be taken lightly."

"I have no intention of taking anyone lightly. All the necessary preparations have been made to insure secrecy. Everything has gone smoothly so far and I don't expect a change. Admiral Legan fought us for the last time in his senate speech. He did better than I expected and caused the vote to be somewhat closer than projected, but I believe the overwhelming number of senators supporting the peace proposal in the final vote killed any of his hopes for stopping disarmament. I think he will humbly cooperate with the senate concerning the scrapping of his military and make sure his men are not overlooked in the process. Being the honorable man that he is, he will abide by the peace proposal because it was legally confirmed and it's what the people want. But I still don't intend on taking any chances. This honorary celebration is meant to quell any rebellious feelings Legan or his officers may have. By honoring them as past heroes we bring them onto our side even if it is reluctantly. They won't oppose a government that honors them."

"An interesting idea. It may well prove to be as you say with Legan's officers, but I doubt the High Admiral will be as easily swayed. He's old school and doesn't care for politicians giving warriors orders."

"Too bad for him because warriors are soon to be extinct, or so everyone believes." Mian smiled. "Won't the senate be surprised when we arrive at Katara with a full armada of warships? I'm glad I'll be there to see the look on their faces." Mian's expression became more serious. "Have you acquired the ships on the list that I sent you earlier?"

"Some but not all. The Arcolus League has been reluctant to seed us its mothballed warships. We do now have seven carriers salvaged from the Levonian Confederation orbital junkyard and are now refitting them at the Lycosian shipyards. All under false ID's of course. As for the majority of the ships on the list, I believe I can acquire about 60% of the remaining vessels but I don't believe I'll be able to get them all."

Mian waved away his comment. "Those ships aren't necessary to our plans. The only reason I wanted you to try to get them was so we could display a more imposing image over Katara, but the exact number is irrelevant. There won't be any military vessels left to stop us. Perhaps some loyal civilians will oppose us in their armed personal vessels but they will easily be destroyed by our fleet. General Dyson has done a good job training our military and once the Kataran vessels are destroyed we will be able to handle any other nation's forces with ease. I believe we could even handle a coordinated joint offensive by all the nation-states, but it won't come to that. Our agents outside the Republic will make sure the civil wars begin anew before anyone thinks about jointly trying to destroy us. You see Senator Trir, I have taken care to anticipate every possible problem and adjusted my plans accordingly. No one will stop us from realizing our destiny. I guarantee it."

"I hope you are right." Trir walked to the rim of the balcony and looked down over the edge onto the crystal dome that covered Northwood's oversized swimming pool. Beyond that the compound extended across a grassy plain to a short wall that surrounded the entire compound. He gazed at the forest and river beyond as a disturbing thought occurred to him. "I hate to bring this up now, but have you ever considered the possibility that descendents of the other Houses might still exist?"

"I find that highly unlikely. Houses Tregata, Cronomi, Ysameis, and Aesynar are all extinct due to their own infighting, according to the few records I have. House Mian was also thought to be destroyed but somehow my ancestors survived while the other Houses did not. No, I am the only descendant left from the five Great Houses. I've checked every database that Peace Core has access to and I've found no other links to the Great Houses besides my own."

"I didn't think it was likely but I wanted to bring it to you attention just in case."

"You always have kept me on my toes Senator. Anything else you would like to concern me about?"

"You should be careful to watch Legan, apparently he hasn't given up the fight yet."

"Why do you say that?"

"Look towards the west and the river," Trir said pointing slightly to his left. "See those people crossing the river?"

"They're wearing combat gear. Does Legan mean to take us prisoner?" Mian asked, fear filling her voice.

"No, no. That's not combat gear, it's camping gear. And those men are the officers that you invited here." Mian looked confused so he continued. "I heard rumors that Legan and his officers had parachuted into the forest some distance form Northwood and chose to hike here as some sort of exercise. Until seeing them now I had thought it just rumor, but it appears Legan isn't going to fade into the sunset as you thought."

Mian regained her composure. "Apparently I was wrong, but I would not be too concerned. This only means the High Admiral will protest the disarmament to the end, but that end will still come. If he's still playing political games it means he won't openly rebel against a peaceful government and will reluctantly allow the disarmament. He can't do anything else. Let him protest as he likes, in the end it will do him no good. I'll seize control of the government and there won't be a thing he can do about it from inside a prison cell. Then the Anteron Confederation will rise again and at last I will fulfill my destiny."

After showering and settling in to their suites, Legan and his officers reluctantly joined the newly arrived politicians for the evening meal and some polite discussion. High Admiral Legan, General Chensir and Admiral Senxir stood off to one side discussing the new era of peace with a group of 11 senators.

"I have no bloodthirst driving me to war senator, I welcome peace as much as the average citizen does, we just disagree how to achieve that peace," Legan answered politely.

"But why maintain a military when we have no one to fight. The funds and resources could be used for more constructive projects in a peaceful society instead of maintaining mechanisms of destruction."

Legan managed to keep from rolling his eyes. "There will always be threats somewhere. Even if we purge the galaxy of all the enemies of the Kataran Republic, there is nothing to stop new enemies from arising. An ally could even become an enemy in the future. We cannot eliminate all the threats to our nation. We must constantly be on our guard for we never know when a new threat may present itself. Burying our heads in the sand won't make the bad guys go away, it just gives them an easier target."

Polite laughter accompanied his not so humorous remark, not that he intended for it to be funny. He wanted to jibe some of the senators and make it look like he was somewhat upset but still hopeful that he could convince them of their folly. He needed everyone to have the impression that he didn't believe that the political fight was over and that he would continue his efforts to convince the senate to repeal the peace proposal before it was too late. That way no one would suspect he had anything else planned and that nativity would give him the time he needed to accomplish his mission.

"Admiral, many of us are of the opinion that if we disarm and pose no threat to others that they will leave us alone to live in peace. Don't you agree?"

"Not at all. Is a thief dissuaded from breaking into your home by the absence of weapons? No, of course not. It makes his job all the easier. Pacifism will not deter our enemies and the thought that we simply won't make any enemies is suicidal because you're forgetting one important thing. Someone else can declare you to be their enemy for no reason what so ever and you have no say in the matter. It takes two to be allies but only one to be enemies."

"Still Admiral, even if there is a *possibility* of new threats arising, we know that won't happen. Why bother with precautions that are unnecessary?"

"I don't see them as unnecessary Senator. Whose judgement are you going to trust, a civilian's opinion or the opinion of a military officer whose area of expertise is defending civilians?"

"Why don't you trust us to do our jobs?" General Chensir interrupted. "We're the one's who have been trained to handle these matters. The senate's job is to administer the Republic, our job is to defend it. We don't interfere with your job so why do you try to tell us how to do ours?"

"The military is subordinate to the civilian government. Its job is to serve the people and the people elect the senate. The people, though the senate, called for disarmament and it's the military's obligation to serve the will of the people, even if that means standing down so a new era of peace can begin."

Such conversations continued for several more hours before everyone retired for the night. When Admiral Legan finally reached his luxury suite he had a mild headache and a desire to smash something. *I still need to delay them as long as possible, but I'm glad that's over. Tomorrow we can stop playing nice and get down to business. When we leave Northwood, political influence in the Kataran military will be at all but an end and I'll no longer have to play subordinate to these morons, save for the High Council.*

Legan made his way to his large bedroom and relaxed on his repulsor cushioned bed. *Soon the reigns will be off and I can stop running and hiding from these people. I will finally be free to deal with things in my own way and on my own schedule.*

Treys smiled to himself. *Watch out galaxy, here I come.*

Chapter Thirteen

A dmiral Legan led his contingent of 43 military officers, all wearing dress uniforms, into the large meeting hall at the Northwood compound. Akin to many of the other buildings at the spa, the hall was capped by a crystalline dome through which the morning sunlight refracted into a rainbow of color that bathed the already seated senators.

Standing in the center of the 360 degree arc of tiered seats stood Senator Mian, slowly revolving on the central dais that would allow her to face each person in the audience at some point in her rotation. She waved Legan toward a front bank of seats, the only ones available in the packed chamber.

He responded by walking down the nearest isle and taking the farthest front row seat position, but he remained standing until all of his officers were also standing in front of their seats. Then in unison they took their seats.

The senators each wore their planets' individual robes, all of different styles and materials, looking as diverse as a group can be. In sharp contrast, the 44 military officers sat in a block of seats wearing the same style and cut of uniform, the only difference being the colorations and rank insignia. There were 13 gray Generals uniforms present, 30 dark blue naval uniforms, and one bright white High Admiral's uniform. Each and every one of Legan's officers looked like the elite military commanders they were.

Sitting beside him, General Chensir whispered softly. "They look real happy to see us."

"I'm sure they are," Legan answered as Mian looked through her notes, "considering they were all but dragged here by Senator Mian and her allies at such an early hour. I've heard that some particular senators view getting up before noon as sleep depriving."

"I don't doubt it. It looks though that Senator Mian woke up fairly early judging by her hair," Chensir surmised.

Legan looked toward the podium for the first time with his full attention and noticed a number of microbraids, braids consisting of only five to ten hairs each, and marveled at the intricacy of the design. Mian's long dark hair lay just above her shoulders in a veil-like weave that started just forward of her ears and continued around the back of her head. The reversed veil was outlined and bisected by braids of greater size and strength, with the outlined interior filled in by a patchwork of continuously smaller braids until the smallest sections were filled with microbraids while other microbraids held her hair structure together with the help of all but invisible braid ties. Legan wondered how many hours and hairstylists it took to complete the extravagant hairstyle.

"Judging from the looks of her hair, I'd guess that she woke up long before we did, if she slept at all," Legan said.

"Seems like a waste of time to me," Chensir said. "Especially since she's trying to impress us."

Legan nodded his agreement as Mian prepared to speak. He settled into his seat and waited to see what she would have to say.

"Today we have gathered here to honor these members of our military for their past heroics as we usher in a new era of peace. But first I would like to thank the Northwood administrative staff for graciously allowing us to use their facilities for this summit."

Applause broke out for the Northwood senior staff, who were seated in an upper tier, by everyone except Legan and his officers, as per his instructions. Senator Mian noticed their indifference but continued undaunted.

"The military officers we have invited to join us here are the best and the brightest that we have. On numerous occasions in the past they have saved the Kataran Republic from ruin. For those of you who don't know of their storied past let me indulge you in a few tales of their exploits. The most recent was a little over 13 years ago. The Zarconian Empire launched an invasion against our coreward systems. They struck with such swiftness that many of our systems were captured before word of the invasion reached Katara. By the time High Admiral Legan arrived with a fleet of warships, the enemy had fortified the stolen worlds and stood ready to repel our forces. Out numbered and outgunned, Admiral Legan took his fleet and went about the seemingly impossible task with unimagined ease. He and his fleet decimated the enemy force on a number of the captured worlds before the Zarconians sued for peace."

"During that same campaign, then Commodore Chensir led a task force into the capital city on Danovir, one of the captured worlds, and proceeded to send the enemy reeling despite being outnumbered three to one. He cleared out the capital then chased the remainder of the enemy troops off planet."

"Three years before that, the Levonian Confederation launched an attack on one of our shipyards near their border. Then Captain Senxir succeeded in repelling the attacking forces with only minimal damage to her ships, and she also managed to keep the ships under construction out of harms way. The Levonian Confederation never again dared attack us thanks to Admiral Senxir's actions that day."

"One last exploit I want to make you aware of is that of the young Colonel Legan and his then infamous Scorpion squadron. Responding to a distress call from the Kataran frigate *Courage*, Colonel Legan and his fighter squadron took on a Malcosian warship and against all odds severely damaged the enemy warship, buying enough time for more reinforcements to arrive. Due to their heroic efforts, the *Courage* was saved and is still in service to this day."

"These are but a few of many examples of the unending dedication these men and women have shown to the Kataran Republic throughout their long years of military service. They have been vigilant every moment they have worn the uniform of the Kataran Military and made a career of defending our sovereignty and at times our very lives. Excelling in all areas of warfare, these officers had made the Kataran Military the unquestionable master of the stars. Today we are here to pay tribute to these men and women who we owe so much to."

"It is now time that the stars know no master and all peoples live in peace. But we will not forget the people who have put their lives on the line to make this day possible. They are the reason we have our freedom. They are the reason citizens can live their lives without fear of unjust government and maltreatment by tyrannical rulers. Every aspect of our daily lives is in some part due to their unequalled sacrifices, both those men and women seated here tonight and the thousands of warriors who traded their lives so we can stand here today free from oppression. We owe everything we have to these warriors. If it had not been for their past efforts, most, if not all of us, would likely be dead or enslaved by our enemies. Now that these brave warriors have cleared the stars of threats to our freedom and past enemies have become friends and allies, the military will stand down and it's men and women will finally be able to rest and enjoy the fruits of their efforts. They will be forever remembered for their epic struggles in the name of freedom, and for as long as they live will be treated as the heroes that they are. I would now ask that High Admiral Legan and his officers to join me on the central dais."

At her request Legan rose from his seat with his officers following suite. He paused a moment to straighten his uniform before mounting the slowly moving circular platform that Mian had stood upon throughout her speech. He took up a position to Mian's right while his officers arrayed themselves in two lines, one front and one back, a step behind Mian and Legan. She waited until all of the 44 military men and women stood at attention before continuing.

"It is my proud honor to introduce to you the men and women of which I speak so highly. The man standing beside me is High Admiral Treys Legan, Supreme Commander of our beloved military forces. He and he alone has commanded our forces during the longest period of peace ever recorded. He and his forces have secured this peace and quite frankly put themselves out of a job. We owe much to these people standing before you now and it is only right that you know each and everyone of them by name."

Mian proceeded to read off the 43 names of Legan's officers alphabetically. As each name was called the respective officer came forward and reformed the ranks off of Legan's left. The first person called was the rightmost of the back line. He came forward and stood directly behind Legan. The next officer in line, matching the next name called, began to reform the back row with each successive officer taking his or her original position only this time with Legan included in the ranks. When Mian had finished there were two neat rows of 22 officers, each standing at attention before the assembled senate members.

"To these men and women we owe our lives, our children's lives, and our children's children's lives on down through future generations." Mian turned to face the double ranks of warriors. "We forever owe to your our future."

She initiated a round of applause that swept through the chamber and sending an involuntary shiver through Mian's spine. Legan turned his head slightly to receive almost imperceptible nods from his nearby officers. They were ready.

While the applause continued four attendants each carried a box containing eleven medals of valor which they proceeded to hang around each officer's neck. When each officer was wearing a medal and the applause had subsided, Legan took the podium at Mian's gestured request.

Taking a moment to view the portion of the crowd, which the moving podium now faced, he gathered his thoughts then began to speak. "You have brought me and my officers here to receive medals of valor for our long years of heroic military service. You claim that we were entrusted with the lives of the people of the Kataran Republic and that we saved those lives time and again. We are the defenders of the people, you say, and you are correct. We are the defenders of the people, but if we willingly let ourselves be decommissioned then we will have failed in our duty."

Legan took off his medal from his neck, as did his officers, and as one they dropped them unceremoniously to the floor.

"Our duty is to protect our people from any and all threats posed against them. It is a lifetime commitment that we proudly accepted and will never rescind."

Legan turned to the nearest isle and swiftly walked out of Northwood's meeting hall with his loyal officers following at his heels. One by one they left until only the stunned senators and the furious Lena Mian remained.

After an awkward exit from the meeting hall, Mian returned to her suite with Senator Trir soon joining her.

"How dare they! How dare they do that to me? I bring them here to honor them and they walk out on me, on *me*! I've never been so disgusted in my life."

"Lena please calm down, it's not as bad as it seems. My guess is that this was Admiral Legan's last attempt to disrupt the peace plan. He knows there is nothing he can do to stop the military's disarmament but he has to try. That's the kind of man he is. If he's going to lose, he'll go down fighting. This was a planned attack on you and your peace proposal but it was also a notice to the senate members that the military will not go willingly. The senators may have been shaken up a bit but not nearly enough to cause them to repeal the peace plan. It's been passed, your plans are going smoothly, and this will not disrupt any of our operations. Legan may have discredited you in some of the senators minds, but their opinions no longer matter. The peace plan has been passed and disarmament confirmed, the senators are unimportant now. Legan would not have pulled such a stunt if he had other plans. This was an attack on the pacifist philosophy in a last ditch effort to sway the senate, but it won't work. You've already won. Legan's actions may sting your ego but this was his last act of defiance, his last battle, his last hope. It's over for him now."

Mian had slowly regained her composure and finally forced herself to laugh. "You're right. He's fought his last fight and now there is no one left to oppose me. Legan will be forced, although reluctantly, to stand down and disarm. He can't stop it so it's only a matter of time before we seize control of the government. Soon no one will dare treat me with such disrespect. If Legan's little tantrum was the price to pay for fulfilling my destiny then so be it."

She walked across her suite's central room and all but collapsed into a self-conforming chair, her body going limp from the emotional firestorm that she had just passed through. She closed her eyes and let some of her frustration bleed off before looking Senator Trir in the eye. "What would I ever do without you Mik?"

He smiled. "You'd probably have a few gray hairs by now but you would manage alright." His tone sobered. "Don't worry about Legan. I don't think he'll cause much more trouble, if any." He stood and headed for her suite's door. "I think a warm bath and a long nap would help relieve a lot of your stress, but what you do is up to you. Just try not to break anything expensive," he said as he left Mian to her thoughts.

He's right. I need to relax and get Legan off my mind.

To that end she called her attendant and ordered her to ready her bathing water, then went over to her opulent dresser and pulled a small device from the top drawer and pressed the button marked release. When she did the small ties that held her hair together unclasped and fell to the floor. She ran her fingers through her hair to loosen and undo the numerous braids until her hair rested softly on her shoulders.

She looked at her image in the mirror and sighed, letting even more of her tension escape along with her breath. She focused her thoughts on the future to relax herself, as she had often done in the past. Imagining herself sitting on a multi-jeweled throne with ultra-fine silk upholstery, she pictured the ranks upon ranks of Confederation soldiers marching past her in a war day parade. Starfighters flew across the sky in perfect formation as mobile assault vehicles floated above the marching troops. She envisioned her advisors bringing her progress reports of far off military campaigns, informing her that she had new territories to add to her nation and spoils of war returning from the conquered planets on the next wave of transports. Enmeshed in her vision of the future she barely noticed her attendant's small voice.

"Highness, your bathing water is prepared."

She vaguely acknowledged the attendant as she walked into the bathing chamber and felt the steam roll across her face. *You were right Mik, I need to relax and let this tension bleed away.*

Mian stripped off her robes and left them in a puddle at her feet as she stepped into and slowly sank down beneath the surface of the comforting waters. *And I think this bath will go a long way to meeting that end.*

Chapter Fourteen

S itting in his ready room aboard the *Perseverance*, Admiral Plescal tediously checked and rechecked every detail of the system that he and General Legan had created some two weeks earlier to sort and organize the convoy vessels that would soon follow them and their advance party to Alpha Prime.

The system was relatively simple on its face. The convoy ships would come out of IS space in prescribed high orbit sectors. Then General Legan and his fighter squadrons would escort the vessels, individually, to their assigned low orbit sectors as they arrived. When the first ships on the priority list made low orbit they would either start to disgorge shuttles carrying their cargo or, if the ships had the capability, land on the surface for unloading. One by one they would unload, each vessel according to its position on the priority list with the cargoes that would be utilized immediately after they reached the ground receiving top priority.

The remainder of the equipment would be brought down to the planet and placed in large storage facilities until it was needed. The personnel transport vessels were also on the same priority list as the cargo transports. Transports containing personnel that would be put to work immediately upon arrival, such as the bulk of Nartalo's miners that hadn't accompanied Nartalo himself, who was currently aboard the *Perseverance*, would be given landing priority over all but the most essential of cargoes. Eventually all materiel and personnel would be transported in some form to the planet. The transports would then be individually guided by General Legan's starmasters to permanent mid level orbital parking zones until they were needed again in the future.

A small chime alerted Plescal to the presence of someone outside his door. "Come in," he spoke loudly enough for the sound of his voice to be heard outside his quarters.

The door quickly opened to reveal a young man in a naval captain's uniform. "What can I do for you Captain Veske?"

"Sir, we're three hours away from reverting to realspace and I was wondering if you might be able to give me an idea of what we'll find at Alpha Prime."

Captain Veske had been transferred and promoted to fill the captain's vacancy left when Plescal had been promoted to Admiral. While the *Perseverance* was still under his command, Plescal was no longer her captain, or so Veske thought. The *Perseverance* was Plescal's personal ship no matter what rank he held.

"I expect to find nothing but a deserted planet ready for us to make our own. No one knows where we are or where we're going. As for the native populations in the region, there aren't any. Alpha Prime is an empty planet in the middle of an empty region of space mapped out by no one in the Human Sphere save for us. So what exactly is it you think you might find Captain?" Plescal asked with a hint of steel in his voice.

"I wasn't expecting to find anything. I just don't like making a jump into an area I'm not familiar with."

"Don't concern yourself too much, I'm the one who scouted out this region in this ship and with this crew. Everyone else aboard ship knows what lies ahead."

"I know and I don't like it a bit. I'm the captain of this ship and have not, in my opinion, been given enough information about what awaits us. I have only your word that there are no hostiles in the area. For me to be denied the information that I need puts this ship at risk."

"This ship is *my* ship Captain, and it will always be my ship. You may sit in the Captain's chair but I am still in command. You don't need to know everything because I do know everything there is to know about Alpha Prime. Now, if there's nothing else, I have work to do. You're dismissed Captain."

"Yes sir," Veske said between gritted teeth as he left Plescal's quarters and nearly ran into General Legan.

"Excuse me sir," he said and walked on towards the nearest lift.

Alec walked into Plescal's quarters through the still open door. "Did I come at a bad time?"

"No, please come in General. Captain Veske is a good officer but he tends to forget that this is my ship and not his. I have to remind him of the order of things every now and then."

"Personally, I'd not want to be on the receiving end of such reminders."

"No you wouldn't General. Then again I'd imagine you'd be sufficiently challenging opposition if we ever had a disagreement. Let's make sure that never happens."

"Agreed Admiral, my mission isn't to fight with you, but to work with you to prepare Alpha Prime for the mass exodus from the Human Sphere. To which end I have prepared some contingency plans," he hefted his datapad for emphasis, "in case we run into any problems."

"A wise precaution General. It never hurts to be prepared. Speaking of which, I want some, if not all of your fighter squadrons to provide escorts for our small convoy after we enter realspace. I don't believe we'll find any trouble, but escort duty should do your pilots some good after being out of the cockpit for nearly a month. I don't want to have rusty pilots screening for my ships if we should encounter any opposition in the near future."

"I'll get a signal out to our sister ships and have them prepare their squadrons to launch after we revert to realspace. Getting a chance to stretch my wings again will feel good after all the mind-numbing manifests and personnel files we've been looking through."

"You'll be flying yourself?"

"Of course, what did you expect?"

"I thought you might prefer to be on the bridge when we enter the system."

"Nope. I may be a General but I'm still a fighter pilot. My ship may be a single seater, but no one is going to take her away from me either."

"Understood. Is there anything else you wanted?"

"No, I just wanted to give you a copy of these contingency plans." Alec pulled out the datacard that was inserted into his datapad and dropped it on the only clear spot on Plescal's desk.

"In that case I think I'll head on up to the bridge and let you prep your people for launch. We'll arrive at Alpha Prime in just under three hours. Make sure your squadrons are ready to launch before then."

"My pleasure Admiral."

When Alec reached the hanger bay where his starmaster was kept he saw a completely different sight then had had the few times he'd visited the hangar during the long trip. Tech's swarmed about the bay checking and prepping the three dozen starmasters parked in tight, neat rows along the walls, keeping clear the deck immediately in front of the massive stasis field that kept in the ship's atmosphere but allowed the starfighters to pass through unharmed. The large hangar bay doors that normally covered the outside of the stasis field where already open.

Alec almost lost his balance as the brilliant colors of IS space flashed by faster than his eyes could follow. He took a moment to steady himself before he headed across the crowded bay towards his gray starmaster.

After climbing the access ladder to the top of his ship he slipped into the cockpit through the hatch held open by a tech standing on an opposite ladder. Once inside, the tech sealed the hatch and pulled both ladders away from his ship. After fastening his restraining harness and donning his helmet, Alec went through the standard startup procedures.

First off he activated his craft's computer systems by means of a keypad to his right. With a flick of an overhead switch he activated his cockpit's secondary monitors then another such switch brought up his tactical overlay. He brought his cold engines slowly up to half power before enabling his weapon systems and shield generators. Three green spheres appeared on an upper right monitor, two of which read 100% and the third read the number 8. In addition to the status lights for the shields, lasers, and torpedo complement respectively, a fourth yellow ball, indicating engine power turned green as Alec brought his engine power up to full stand bye.

He then activated his comm unit and sensor screen, which would remain blank until he left the ship. Through his circular forward viewport that the tactical overlay was now superimposed upon, he could see his squadronmates just arriving and climbing into their fighters. Soon they would all be up and running, waiting for the reversion to realspace and their launch signal. The other two squadrons similarly prepping for launch in the hanger were also under Alec's command, as were all fighter squadrons attached to this mission.

Lancer, Nova, and Striker squadrons were also prepping for launch in the *Perseverance*'s other hanger bay on the opposite side of the ship, presumably going through the same startup procedures. The techs in Alec's bay gradually filtered from the main deck into clear bunkers designed to protect them from any launch mishaps. Not long after the deck was cleared, the colorful lights outside the warship suddenly shrank back to mere pinpricks of light from the local stars in the region. The deck officer's voice suddenly flooded over the comm channels.

"Sentinel Squadron you have clearance to launch."

A host of guidance lights illuminated on the hangar ceiling above the stasis field and began to guide Sentinel squadron out of the hangar bay one by one.

"Give me the count Lieutenant," Admiral Plescal ordered the helmsman.

"Reentry in eleven, ten, nine, eight, seven, six, five, four, three, two, one, mark."

The *Perseverance* then dropped out of IS space near Alpha Prime alongside her companion vessels *Liberty* and *Indomitable* with the rest of the convoy following shortly.

"Launch all squadrons. Sensors, give me a scan of the system. Communications, have all ships in the convoy advise us of their status and instruct the *Liberty* and *Indomitable* to launch their fighters if they haven't already done so."

"Sir," the sensor officer answered, "the system is clear. Only the *Liberty*, *Indomitable*, and the convoy vessels appear on our scopes."

"All vessels report nominal status," sang out the communications officer.

The sensor officer again spoke. "*Liberty* and *Indomitable* are now deploying fighters. Squadrons are flanking the convoy, moving into escort position."

"Very well Lieutenant. Communications, patch me through to General Legan's starmaster."

After a short delay the comm officer signaled for him to begin. "General Legan, the system is clear. Begin grounding the transports. I'll supervise the unloading in orbit while you take command on the ground."

"Understood Admiral. Heading to ground now." There was a small click of static as Alec broke the communications link.

"Captain Veske?"

"Yes Admiral."

"Take us into low orbit just above the orbital lane designated for the command station."

"Aye sir." Veske said, then began issuing orders to the helm.

Plescal felt a slight jolt as the ship began to move and the inertial compensator kicked in. "Comm, signal the convoy vessels carrying the station components to move to their assigned orbital sector and begin assembly."

"Sentinel Two, we're going to run these transports to the landing zone then we're going to ground ourselves and coordinate things dirt side."

"Copy that Lead."

"Sentinel Six, Two and I are going to ground so you'll have command of the squadron. Continue escorting ships down until every ship that is capable of grounding does so. Understood?"

"Will do General. Have fun on the ground. Six out."

Have fun indeed. Alec would much rather be flying than playing traffic cop, but Admiral Plescal had given him the duty and, like it or not, he was stuck with it.

"Sorry to drag you down with me Senj, but I really do need your help."

"Not a problem, Alec. I'm your wing, so if you need me I'm there."

"Thanks Senj, I appreciate it."

Both Alec and Senjin flew escort for a rather large and intricate mobile command center provided by one of the many corporations moving out of the Human Sphere with Admiral Legan and the main convoy. They directed the mammoth vessel, almost too large to be landing capable, to a large basin guided by a homing beacon left behind on Admiral Plescal's last visit.

Alec waited until the large ship was well immobilized before setting his starmaster down next to its bridge landing ramp that was already in the process of extending. He quickly ran through the deactivation procedures for his starmaster then waited at the foot of the ramp until Senjin joined him. Together they walked up and into their new command post.

They made their way past a pair of security guards and onto the bridge where Alec immediately took command. "I'm General Legan, your new superior officer. This is Lieutenant Marquis, my second in command. From here on we'll be running the entire land based operation, so we might as well get started. Give me the holographic display."

On his word one of the techs punched a series of commands into his terminal and activated the holographic map of the immediate area. The hemispherical map appeared in the center of the circular command center and highlighted the incoming ships.

"Give me a surface grid."

The tech punched more commands into the map controls and a 60 km wide grid centered on the mobile command center appeared at the base of the holographic map.

"Alright. Split the grid into kilometer wide squares and number them off."

The tech did as bidden and sectors labeled 1 to 3600 filled the grid.

"Now, color in all empty sectors green and occupied sectors red." 3599 green squares appeared with one lone red square marking the position of the command center and the two starmasters.

"Color our airborne fighters blue and the transports yellow. Begin assigning sectors starting at our position and expand outward. When a transport has received its assignment and gives confirmation of the coordinates change it from yellow to red. Senj, you and I will be handing out assignments and these men will assist us with the communications and equipment. You ready?"

"I was born ready General."

"Good, let's get started."

24 hours later all ships capable of grounding were parked in one of the 3600 sectors. The ships in orbit sent their cargoes down by shuttlecraft and they were now spread out across the basin, each assigned to designated sector alongside the grounded ships.

After 17 hours of traffic control, Alec and Senjin found quarters on the mobile command center and fell asleep moments after they each hit the sack. Meanwhile, the well-rested Supply Core administrators began assembling their workforce. Setting up base camps in the areas prescribed by Plescal's and Alec's detailed plans just over 20 km from the gridded landing zones, the Supply Core techs and engineers assembled the machinery that would allow them to begin their work, whether it be mining, materials processing, agriculture, aquaculture, etc. Before day's end most of the Supply Core units would be marginally operational and begin expanding their facilities along the guidelines that the administrators drew up on their trip to Alpha Prime.

The orbital command station was assembled in less than ten hours and operational a few hours after that. Admiral Plescal had moved most of his command staff onto the station and all squadrons had returned their starfighters, save Alec and Senj's ships, to the three warships or moved them to the command station itself.

Plescal himself transferred his command to the station but left most of his personal effects on the *Perseverance* since he knew he would be returning to her when Admiral Legan arrived and took command. From the command station he oversaw all aspects of the ground-based operations and the few orbital platforms that would soon be constructed.

After seeing to the initial ground operations and getting some sleep on the mobile command center, Alec and Senjin moved into quarters on the station. Alec had his 18 fighter squadrons on patrol 24 hours a day with no less than two squadrons on patrol at all times. He knew there was little strategic justification for the patrols but he wanted his pilots to continue to log flight hours and remain as sharp as possible. It would probably be many years before he and his pilots saw combat again, but he wanted to keep their minds focused during what promised to be a dull next year or so before they would fully resume combat training again. He would, in addition to the patrols, run his squadrons through some mock combat exercises so they wouldn't loose their combat edge. If any surprises were to occur in the near future, they would be ready.

Chapter Fifteen

S tepping from his hovercab onto the pedestrian walkway in front of the main entrance of the Kataran Historical Museum, a large 173 floor building in the center of the Republic's capitol city of Katara Prime, a building that he visited often. Legan, dressed in civilian clothing, climbed the terraced steps and entered the enormous building through two imposing 16 meter high doors that always remained open during public hours.

He promptly made his way to the nearest lift cluster and pressed the large signal button, which rerouted the nearest lift car to his position. A soft tone sounded and one of the six lift doors opened to reveal an empty lift car. Legan stepped into the lift and selected the 3rd quadrant of the 107th floor by means of a not so small keypad located just below the red emergency stop pull down lever on the lift wall.

Utilizing internal dampening technology, the lift car was able to travel at high speeds throughout the network of lift shafts in the building. Legan never felt the extreme acceleration, deceleration, and sharp turns the lift car made during its 27 second journey.

Leaving the lift car behind he walked casually around the 107th floor, occasionally stopping to look at an exhibit as he made his way to restroom #17. After entering the restroom, Legan walked over to a nearby mirror and used his fingers to comb through his hair superficially as he studied the nearby stall's empty/occupied indicator light reflection in the mirror. Turning about he entered the seventh stall then closed and sealed the door.

He touched a hand to the intricate pattern of seemingly random nubs and depressions decorating the stall's walls.

Pressing and holding his right thumb against a particular depression he waited patiently for the small indicator light imbedded beneath the nub above his thumb to illuminate. Still holding his thumb against the depression, he used his other hand to depress another nub half a meter to his left.

Soundlessly, the tiled floor beneath his feet began to give way prompting him to pull his hands off the decorative wall. The floor lowered him into a small chamber that rose again as he stepped off. When the section of floor returned to its original position, the stall door automatically unsealed itself when its motion detection sensors signaled the immediate area was clear.

Legan crossed the small room in two strides. He entered his identification code into a hidden wall keypad that opened the door on a one-man lift car when his code was confirmed. He stepped into the claustrophobic vertical cylinder and pressed the only button on the wall.

The lift car traveled down a straight shaft past the 1st floor and descended below Katara's surface well into the planet's bedrock. The lift's lights cut out as the door opened into a similarly dark room save for a bright overhead tubular light shaft that illuminated a small circular patch of floor in front of him but left the rest of the room pitch black. Legan then stepped out of the lift and into the lighted circle.

"Legan. Alpha 476, Omega 279," he spoke his verbal ID code.

The overhead light disappeared plunging the entire room into darkness for a moment before the primary lights illuminated the entire room, revealing six armed guards where the shadows had been. The room's only other door opened to reveal a long, well lit hallway which Legan strode down without hesitation.

He passed by numerous doors before coming to the end of the hallway. A large metal door split into two sections that slid into the wall as he approached. He passed through the automatic door and into Midnight Star's operational command center, a large cavern like room studded with workstations, all of which were centered on a 15 meter high, 20 meter wide viewscreen that currently showed a schematic of the Human Sphere. Analysts, techs, and agents moved about in a controlled frenzy typical of the past few months. Preparations to pull out and concluding current operations kept Midnight Star's personnel busy around the clock.

Legan walked over to the central control platform, acknowledging a few hurried greetings from passing command staff. He walked up beside a man in a black waistcoat with a single white star over the left breast which bore the Midnight Star insignia.

"How are things going Arky?"

"Fairly well sir," Legan's second in command answered. "Most of our field operatives have been recalled and are now moving to the designated pickup points where they'll board the civilian transports under their forged IDs for the trip to Alpha Prime. The few agents we have left in the field should be able to complete their assignments and infiltrate the civilian refugees before the convoys leave."

"See to it that they do. I don't want anyone left behind."

"Yessir."

"Did you receive my message?"

"Yes, the agents you specified for the *Goliath* mission are down in the lounge and Agent Venture should be arriving in the next five minutes or so."

"Send the *Goliath* team to my office. Hold agent Venture until I'm through briefing them, then send her in."

"Understood."

Legan climbed a wall-mounted staircase and walked a short way down another hall before coming to his personal office. He sat down in his chair behind an intimidating desk and waited for his operatives to arrive.

He didn't have to wait long, barely 30 seconds later five men wearing black combat jumpsuits carrying the Midnight Star insignia entered his office.

"You called for us sir?"

"Yes I did. Please sit down gentlemen," Legan said as he pointed toward a row of five chairs facing his desk. "I have a mission for the five of you. The newly constructed warship *Goliath* is currently moored at the Xenarin shipyards. As you know, the Xenarin shipyards are civilian owned and operated, therefore I do not control them or any of the personnel on the inside. The *Goliath* is the largest and most heavily armed warship ever constructed in the Human Sphere and I don't want it left in anyone hands but our own. I also don't want to see it scrapped, so you five are going to get it out of Xenarin hands and into mine. The timing on this mission is going to be tricky. You have to seize the ship at the same time I have the fleet move out so neither action compromises the other. You'll have to evacuate the ship of all personnel or dump them off on your way out because after you take control of the ship and leave the system you'll be taking *Goliath* to the convoy rendezvous point outside the Sphere. Agent Cerus, you're in command and I'll leave the specifics up to you. Your mission is to evacuate and seize control of the *Goliath*, remove the ship from the Xenarin shipyards, and deliver it to the rendezvous point. How you go about it is up to you. All data and equipment you need will be in the mission prep room. The exact time of the fleet's departure hasn't been decided yet but I can guarantee it will be in the near future. Any questions?"

"A few. Does the shipyard have any warships guarding it?" Agent Cerus asked.

"Warships no, armed patrol craft yes, but the *Goliath*'s shields will be able to shrug off their laser blasts with ease. The problem will be the base mounted weaponry. The shipyard where the *Goliath* is being held is armed with warship grade weapons and a lot of them. In addition to omnilasers, the command center of the shipyard is equipped with plasma torpedoes and Nevarian cluster missiles. The base is also equipped with a large number of tractor beams in addition to the ones currently mooring the *Goliath* to the shipyard. You'll need to disable the weapons systems and deactivate all beams before you board the *Goliath*."

"Understood sir. Just how exactly are we supposed to evacuate the ship?"

"Any way you can. Best way would probably be to simulate a reactor core overload and signal the evacuation alarms. The shipyard command staff might even try to tractor the ship away from the station before it explodes, so you may want to place explosives on the tractor beam generators that you can remotely signal once you're aboard ship. It would be better if you could find a quieter way than explosives but complete the mission however you see fit."

"What are our operating rules regarding base staff?"

"You'll have access to any weapons you deem necessary, but don't kill anyone unless your own lives are in danger. I want you all back alive. That shouldn't be a concern if all goes well. If you do it right, you'll be gone before they know what's happening. Anything else?"

"No sir."

"Then get down to the prep room and start going over the schematics of the *Goliath* and the shipyard. If you decide you need anything special in the way of equipment, just ask the tech on duty, you've been cleared to use any and all equipment we have available. Plan carefully Agent Cerus. I want that ship and the five of you alive at the rendezvous point. Be aware that if you fail to gain control of the *Goliath* or are late to the rendezvous point, you'll be left behind. I'll wait as long as possible, but when the last transport pulls out so do I. Make sure you time your raid accordingly."

Agent Cerus nodded. "We'll get the job done sir. You won't have to wait up on us. We may even beat you there."

"I hope so. Good luck to you all. Now get down to the prep room and start planning your raid."

"Yes sir," Agent Cerus said before leading his squad out of Legan's office to the mission preparation room where they would begin devising plans to steal the *Goliath*.

Technically, the *Goliath* was part of the Kataran military, but it had yet to be taken possession of. The senate's actions had delayed commissioning the vessel until the peace proposal was accepted or rejected. Since it had been accepted, the newly built *Goliath* waited to be turned into scrap and Legan didn't want that to happen.

A soft knock on his open door brought his attention to the petite female agent standing in the doorway.

"Come in Agent Venture. Please sit down."

Cara Venture quietly closed the office door behind her before appropriating one of the seats that Agent Cerus's men had vacated.

"I'm going to be honest with you. You're the best agent we have and I have a dangerous mission that I believe only you can accomplish. I want you to infiltrate the Kataran Historical Archives and download as much data as you can, hopefully all of the records in the Archives. Those records are the most heavily

guarded secret the Kataran Republic has. Even as Supreme
Commander I don't have access to all of them. The Archives are
more military installation than library, with armed guards on
constant patrol inside the facility. There are numerous security
systems throughout the building, some we know of and probably
more we don't. It's only fare to tell you that two years ago one of
our agents failed to penetrate the security measures and barely
escaped alive. The guards will not hesitate to fire on
unauthorized personnel. They have been specially trained to
protect the archives and maintain a high level of alertness. They
immediately investigate any irregularities and don't believe in
system flukes. You'll have to be at your best to get in and out
undetected because one slip up could cost you your life. Due to
the extreme danger of this mission I'm asking, but not ordering
you to except it."

"What's so important about the records that would
require such high security?"

"We don't know for sure, but our analysts speculate that
the restricted portion of the archives holds data on highly illegal
government programs and agencies. We want both the restricted
and nonrestricted portions of the records downloaded so we can
take them with us when we leave the Human Sphere. The data
could be highly useful in our future operations. The classified
portion of the records will probably be encrypted so if you
manage to come across the decryption key during your mission
please download it as well, but if it's not apparent don't go
looking for it. Our people can decrypt the records without it, it'll
just take some time. Our basic reasoning is that if they guard
these records this closely then they have something important to
hide."

"Makes sense. I'll probably need some of Johnson's
new equipment to get in though, if you can talk him out of
further equipment tests."

"He's already been instructed to give you whatever help
you need and knows the severity of your mission. He even said
he was working on something special just for you."

"This mission must be nearly impossible if Johnson's
taking a special interest in it. On the other hand he might just
want to field test some of his new toys. Either way I need all the

help I can get, if what you said is true about the archives. I assume I'll be operating under non lethal procedures?"

"No, you are free to use whatever force necessary. Unless sedation is preferable, shoot to kill. Hopefully you will be able to access the files without alerting security, but there are sure to be a guard or two in the file access room that you'll have to eliminate. These guards are efficient killing machines so don't hesitate to put them out of commission if necessary. These files are important to our future operations outside the Human Sphere, but they're not worth your life. Don't take any unnecessary risks. Get in, get the files, and get out. If you can't get in quietly, then abort the mission. That is assuming you volunteer. Want a crack at the Archives?"

She nodded. " I'll take the mission. How much prep time do I have?"

"You have three days to plan your insertion. We have the basic building blue prints but our previous agent who tried to get in tells us they've done some considerable remodeling, so you'll have to play this one by ear."

"Understood. I assume I'll be going in alone."

"Yes, we believe a lone agent has a better chance than a pair or a squad. You should be able to penetrate security easier if you're alone."

"How am I supposed to break into the files, presuming you don't already have the access codes."

"No I don't, but Johnson has developed an advanced code breaking unit that should be able to get you into the records. We don't know where the file access room or rooms are. Our other agent never got that far so you'll have to find it on your own. Once you do, secure the room and download the data as fast as Johnson's equipment will allow, then get out of the building before they have a chance to discover your presence."

"I understand. Was there anything else?"

"No, that about covers it."

"Then if you don't mind sir, I'll start going over the building's blueprints."

"Very well Agent Venture. Good Luck."

"Thank you sir," she said before exiting her office.

He stared at the door she just walked out of, hoping this wouldn't be the last time he saw her alive. The mission he'd given her was no easy assignment. In fact, the mission was so difficult that none of his other agents would be able to pull it off. Only agent Venture was skilled enough to have a chance at successfully completing the mission.

Legan looked down at the stack of datapads on top of his desk and let out a sigh. It had been quite a while since he'd been to the Midnight Star complex and the mission progress and after action reports had accumulated while he was gone.

He picked up the first datapad and began to review what had happened while he'd been away.

Seven hours later Legan, still dressed in his civilian clothes, walked out of a stall in a restroom at the Kataran Central shopping mall. He washed his hands in the nearby sink and looked at his slightly red rimmed eyes in the mirror. He then left the restroom and joined the flow of pedestrians in the large hall chamber that spanned three floors.

He passed by an intricate system of waterspouts that created an arched wall of water over his head without a drop falling to the floor. He continued to weave his way through the seemingly endless system of halls before coming to an exit where he climbed into one of a number of hover cabs patiently waiting for passengers.

He instructed the driver to take him to a nearby spaceport where he switched cabs. The second cab took him to the Kataran military's command building where he took the elevator to his office on the top floor.

Walking past his secretary's desk and greeting her with a small smile he entered his office to find a gray haired man dressed in civilian clothes of the same cut as Legan's sitting in his chair behind his desk looking out his window at the setting sun.

"Please excuse me for a moment while I change," Legan said to the man.

"Take your time. I'm in no hurry."

Legan crossed his office and into an adjoining room that served as his temporary quarters when he was working late. The small room contained a bunk, kitchenette, and connected to a personal bathroom. He opened a small closet and took out a daily, white High Admirals uniform, a slightly less decorative version of his dress uniform.

He stepped into his bathroom and dressed in short order. He placed his civilian clothes into a small chute that would take them to the downstairs laundry that served many officer's permanent quarters on lower floors. Legan's personal quarters were situated in a different building and much more opulent, even more so than Northwood's suites. Rank did have its privileges after all.

Legan used his fingers to roughly comb his hair into order. Blinking fatigue from his eyes he stepped into his office proper and walked to his desk where the man sitting in his chair seemed oblivious to his presence as he continued to stare out the window. Only when Legan walked to the window and stood beside him did the man seem to take notice.

"You dress quickly Admiral. Long day?"

Legan smiled. "Lately everyday seems to be a long day, but apparently today isn't quite over yet. Did you come all the way over here to sit in my chair and watch the sun set, or was there something you wanted Senator Malcolm?"

Chapter Sixteen

"I wanted to talk to you about the civilian arrangements even though the view is quite magnificent."

"Is there some sort of problem?"

"Possibly. There have been concerns expressed to me about people being left behind if they're a few minutes late to the check point, grumblings about having to leave belongings behind, worries about family members being separated, and accusations of preferential treatment as far as transport assignments are concerned. Basically normal reactions from a group of nervous people that are beginning to panic. I have a meeting scheduled four days from now with the planetary governors, corporation heads, and other influential people. I was hoping you could give me some words of wisdom to pass onto them."

Legan chuckled. "Of course Senator. Tell them on my behalf that the transports have a list of each and every person assigned to them and won't take off until everyone is aboard. If some people fail to arrive the captain will wait as long as he can but will eventually have to leave them behind when his time window expires. Tell them that if they're on time or early, and emphasize *early*, that they need not fear being left behind. Family members will be assigned to the same transports and be kept together as best as we can manage. Remind them to wear their wrist ID tags so that if anyone gets separated from their families they can be reunited in short order. If they're not wearing their tags things will be much more difficult. Be sure to drill it into their heads to make sure their people wear their tags. As far as belongings go it's fairly simple, they can take with them whatever they can fit in the meter wide cubicles given to each person and no more. We only have so much space aboard the transports, and we can't afford for people to bring everything they own with them. Express to them my apologies, but cargo space dictates that limitation, not me. And when they complain about preferential treatment remind them that I will see to it that everyone is taken care of. Also remind them that all people are not equal and I've assigned personnel with similar skills to the same transports. But also tell them that this is my operation and I'll give preferential treatment to anyone I choose. If they don't like it they can stay behind."

"Thank you Admiral, I believe that will clear up most misunderstandings."

"But not all?"

"No, there are still many questions being posed to me about what will happen when we arrive at our new home. I've told them time and again what you've told me. That once we reach Alpha Prime the populace will move onto the planet and live in temporary structures until permanent facilities can be constructed. They ask how they're supposed to make a living and take care of their families, what currency will be used, how will the new property be divided, what form of government will we have, or when will we hold elections to decide that. I've answered their questions as best as I can but whenever I give an answer I get three more questions."

"Then tell them that I personally will resolve all ambiguity once we arrive at Alpha Prime, but until that time they will simply have to trust my judgement and accept my word that I will take care of everything. They need not concern themselves with anything besides packing up their belongings and getting to their transports when the word is given."

"I'll give them the message, but I was wondering if you could explain to me what you have planned. I trust you to do what's best. I'm just more than a little curious about how you're going to play this."

"Of course Senator Malcolm, I'll tell you what I have in mind as soon as you get out of my chair."

"Oh, sorry," Malcolm said, vacating Legan's seat and grabbing another chair for himself.

Legan sat in his own chair and began to explain his intentions. "First off, my main priority is to save the military, both personnel and equipment. If we're destroyed, even by our own hand, there will be little or no hope for the future."

"I'm with you so far."

"In order for the military to survive it needs two basic resources: materiel and personnel. When we arrive at Alpha Prime, Admiral Plescal and my son should have the basic elements of our agricultural and industrial units operational, ready to begin expanding their operations with the mass of equipment and personnel we're bringing with us. Once we arrive our Supply Core will be born. In short order space born mining operations will begin to collect and refine the building materials that will be needed to make more mining equipment which will in turn collect and refine more ore. The process will snowball down the line, starting with mining operations then continuing on into materiel processing and syntheses, all the way down to construction units."

"When Supply Core's industrial branch reaches sufficient size we will begin to transform three other worlds, Alpha 2, Alpha 4, and Alpha 7. On Alpha 2 we will begin construction on permanent colonies for our civilians to reside in based on a planet-wide design schematic already in the final stages of development which should be completed in the next few months. The engineers and architects are already on site with the help of Admiral Plescal's small fleet, finalizing their designs. Rather than a number of individual homes, large city-buildings will house most of our population in spacious quarters twice as large as the average homes on Katara. Instead of building sparse structures for the populace to get into quickly, our construction units will slowly build to detail the structures as our designers envisioned. Each city will be one massive complex rivaling any structure in the Human Sphere. As each new city-building is constructed portions of the population will move into their permanent homes. Five such structures will be able to house all of our 300 million plus population, but further construction of the entire planetary design will continue at a highly decreased rate after they've been completed. When construction begins on the CBs, orbital habitats that will house miners and their families will be a constructed around the planets nearest the mining sites whether they be on planet or off."

"At the same time Alpha 7 will begin a transformation based on another planet-wide design into a planet sized greenhouse. The entire planet will be reshaped by construction units into a patchwork of agricultural and aquacultural farms. Kilometer long grain fields and terraced valley gardens will first be sculpted by the construction units, then permanent facilities will be built. The agricultural branch of Supply Core will begin seeding each new field or facility as they are built. Once completed many years later, the planet will be filled with plant growth, both in outdoor fields and indoor hydroponic facilities. Millions of square kilometers of grassland will be host to numerous herds and flocks of nearby every type of domestic animal present in the Human Sphere, the beginnings of which will be brought in the main convoy. Artificial lakes and reconstructed natural ones will be host to expansive aquacultural farms which, in addition to the agriculture portion of the planet, will produce all the foodstuffs our people could ever want and then some. All of which will be stored in massive facilities located on or near the equator designed for just that purpose. The food processing and packaging facilities will be located at each pole of the uniseason planet, which is due to the negligible tilt of its axis. The equatorial regions are tropical in nature with the poles having a temperate climate. Eventually the planet will produce enough supplies for not 300 million people, but more than 300 billion. Alpha 7 will be transformed into the bread basket of the new territories."

"You still with me?"

"So far."

"Good. Now Alpha 4, at the same time as Alpha 2 and Alpha 7, will be transformed into one enormous supply depot for the industrial branch of Supply Core. Massive storage facilities will be built, both above and below ground, across the planet along with materiel processing facilities. Countless factories, mostly automated, will fabricate every type and make of material needed in the new colonies. The materials will be used in factories orbiting Alpha 2's three moons to create all the civilian products needed."

"A few years after construction has begun on Alpha 2, 4, and 7, Supply Core's industrial branch will have grown exponentially. It is then that Alpha 3 and 9 will begin to be transformed into military garrisons. Alpha 3's varying terrain and climates makes it a good place for a military academy. In addition to training cadets, the planet will also be home to our starfighter construction facilities. They will be placed on a southern continent with the academy and its training grounds residing on the other three continents. Alpha 9 will be home to our weapon fabrication facilities on the surface and our shipyard in orbit. The components of new warships will be created both on the surface and in orbit, with the surface components being flown up to the orbital shipyard. Hand held weapons will also be made in surface factories. Our RnD compound will be on the surface with a counterpart RnD station in orbit. Other miscellaneous military supplies such as uniforms, pilot helmets, datapads, etc. will also be fabricated in surface factories."

"These five planets will be the basis for our small empire. Alpha Prime will eventually be abandoned then reconstructed to specs as we spread outward to the remaining Alpha planets and the secondary Betas as well. With the Supply Core at full strength, the military will have all the material it needs. The other side of the coin, personnel, will be provided by our 300 million plus population through the academy which will train both warriors and technical and support staff. If all goes as planned, the military's two basic needs will be met in abundance, assuming our population continues to grow. Then we can focus on building a large, well trained, well armed military that can return to the Human Sphere and put things right."

"Will our society function as it does here or do you have something special in mind?"

"The civilian society will operate much as it does here with one major exception. All people will be given quarters, food and clothing. Civilians will work for a credit currency that will be used for amenities, though the currency itself will have to be created anew. I would guess many people will bring along Kataran credits and we'll exchange them for the new ones once the first CB is completed."

"Will we still have private industry?"

"Yes, but on a much smaller scale. Most civilian jobs will come from government run businesses. Oh, by the way. Our new governmental system is relatively simple. I rule, period."

Malcolm laughed out loud. "I bet the people are to going to be happy about that," he said sarcastically.

"I'm sure they will be, which is why I'm not going to tell them until we arrive at Alpha Prime and neither are you."

"My lips are sealed."

"Good. Now is there anything else you wanted to know?"

Before Malcolm could answer Legan's office door opened and in walked a young Lieutenant with a datapad clutched in his left hand.

"Sorry to interrupt you sir but this communiqué just came in on nova com. I thought you would like to see it as soon as possible."

"You thought right," Legan said excusing his interruptive behavior as the Lieutenant handed him the datapad then disappeared out the door he had just entered.

"What is it," Malcolm asked as Legan removed a datacard from a desk drawer and inserted the decryption key into the datapad.

"Well well, this is interesting. It seems someone in the Levonian Confederation doesn't care for the new area of peace."

"What do you mean?"

"I have a report from some people in low places that three warships were spotted in Levonian space," Legan said referring to the Midnight Star communiqué that he held in his hand.

Nova com was a unique ISC, interstellar communication frequency, that Midnight Star used to transmit information of great importance to Admiral Legan. Any curious persons would be inclined to believe the communiqué came from Kataran intelligence units off planet, not an unknown, independent intelligence operation less than 100 km away.

"I don't see what is so interesting about that. The Levonian Confederation has a small navy and keeps their ships on constant patrol in order to give the appearance of a larger force."

"What's interesting is that the three ships weren't Levonian. They were unidentified warships all spotted at different places at different times. What makes it even more interesting is the fact that there have been 17 other sightings in the Levonian Confederation of unidentified ships in the past three months. This is the first time warships have been spotted."

"That does seem a bit odd, but what does it have to do with the peace process?"

"Probably nothing, but looking at the situation from a purely hypothetical standpoint, if you didn't care for peace and wanted to seize power in the Kataran Republic what would you do?"

Malcolm thought about that for a moment then caught on. "I'd build up a military force outside the Republic's borders and wait for disarmament. Once the military is scrapped I would bring in my forces and seize control of the government."

"My thoughts exactly."

"Should we be leaving then?"

"We have no choice. If there is a rogue force out there they won't come out of hiding until the military is gone."

"Then we can leave, hide out in the new territories until they make their move, then come back and crush them."

"And continue on with disarmament shortly thereafter."

"You don't think an invasion would wake people up to the dangers of pacifism and that your triumphant return would swing their support behind you?"

"Is that before or after I'm court-martialed for treason, theft, and shoving the peace plan down the politicians throats."

"They wouldn't dare touch you, the people would eat them alive."

"Perhaps, but we'd be once again under political control and sooner or later the politicians would come up with another way to screw us up."

"You wouldn't have to return to government control, with the support of the people you could seize control of the government yourself."

"I could do that now but the problem is that administering worlds would keep us stuck in neutral. We wouldn't be able to retool the military to the extent we need to. Sooner of later the nonhumans are going to return and stomp us flat. The only way we're going to survive is if we make some drastic changes. If they came back now, we might as well be throwing spitwads. Our equipment is outdated compared to what we had when the nonhumans invaded before. The continuous civil wars we've fought have put us so far behind where we once were that it'll take decades to recover what we've lost. And I don't believe for a moment that the nonhumans have wasted the past 175 years. Their equipment is now probably eons ahead or ours. They would have little trouble smashing us to rubble if they returned while we're in this condition."

"I've never really considered the nonhumans to be a present threat. They haven't been heard of for so long that I'd pretty much forgot they existed."

"So did and does the senate, along with most of the populace."

"Is that the real reason you're taking us out of the Human Sphere?"

"It's the long term reason, yes. The short term reason is the peace proposal and the imminent disarmament. My men and I are the only people who have the skills necessary to prepare the Sphere for a resumed invasion. If I let us be destroyed, either through peace or continued civil wars, then all hope for the future would be lost."

"I see. Before now I though this was just a battle over pacifism and it was a battle I was willing to fight to the end. But it really isn't about that at all. Pacifism is irrelevant. You're fighting for the future, aren't you?"

"Very perceptive senator. Yes, I am fighting for the future. But in order to win that battle we need new weapons, faster ships, quick minds, and a combined will. The only way we can achieve that is to leave the stagnant Human Sphere and focus of our energies on a selftransformation. It won't be easy or quick, but it is needed if the Sphere is to survive. I'm not trying to change the whole Sphere, just a small piece. That piece will hopefully grow into its own nation. A nation that can look after the Human Sphere like a big brother."

"We'll be strong enough then to defend ourselves from any nonhuman invasion," Malcolm said as he nodded to himself. "We can then, after learning and rebuilding all we need, rejoin whatever is left of our people and rebuild the Human Sphere."

"When we return," he corrected Malcolm, "we will try to save the Human Sphere, but they will no longer be our people, or rather, we will no longer be their people."

Chapter Seventeen

S itting in a cushioned chair with his feet up on his desk, Jace Starfield, Director of Morning Dawn, the larger, older sister agency of Midnight Star, stared at the tiny swarms of red-gold tropical fish as they swam about their spherical tank. *What are you up to Treys?* he thought to himself.

Morning Dawn operatives had watched with interest as several notable corporations had went out of business without liquidating. His analysts had reviewed all correspondence, ISC transmissions, and appointments of the corporation heads and their immediate staff. The one common factor among them all was a senator by the name of Thomas Malcolm, a man who just yesterday paid a visit to High Admiral Treys Legan.

That prompted him to assign one of his analysts to investigate Legan's recent activities. After reading the analysts report, Starfield immediately gave the investigation top priority and turned his full staff loose on it. What they found was most disturbing, mainly because he couldn't figure out what was happening.

So it was to his great surprise when his office door opened and in stepped Legan. "Hello cousin."

"Hello indeed. Mind telling me how you got in, or more importantly how you found our facility?"

"Gramps left me a key. You're guards were somewhat surprised when I came in. I think they were a bit disappointed when I gave the recognition code and they found out they weren't going to be able to shoot me. Probably your influence on them."

"We're not accustomed to having guests, so the guards are naturally suspicious. You're lucky I didn't reprogram the computer. If I had you'd be wearing a body bag by now."

"If you'd tried to reprogram the computer you'd be the one wearing a body bag. Gramps installed a specialized circuit board into Morning Dawns central computer. It contains my code recognition package and will self-destruct the computer core if tampered with, but apparently you haven't tried since you're still in the land of the living."

"No I haven't, but rest assured, now that I know it's in there I'll find a way to take it out, so don't plan on coming back any time soon."

"For your own sake don't bother, I'm not going to be around much in the near future."

"Ah, something to do with you conspiracy then?"

"And what conspiracy might that be, oh wise one?"

"My Morning Dawn agents have uncovered quite a bit of information on your recent activities. From what I can tell you've gathered quite a large fleet of civilian ships. You also seem to have quite a few civilian and political connections and frequently contact them, either directly or through Senator Malcolm, finalizing what arrangements I don't know. I've also traced enough foodstuff shipments to feed an army for more than a year. Not to mention megatons of equipment from recently out of business corporations. So what are you up to and why the unexpected visit?"

"You tell me."

"Ok, it looks like you're putting together a supply fleet for your navy, which would suggest some unauthorized military action on a large scale. All indicators are you're not going to allow disarmament, instead you're going to seize control of the government for yourself. The supply fleet keeps your forces alive while you get regular means of supply under your direct control. The equipment you've been gathering should give you the means to create an industrial package that, with enough captured planets and a large enough conscripted workforce, would eventually give you the means to construct shipyards, just in case you failed to capture the existing shipyards intact. Everything seems to point to your turning tyrant."

Starfield smiled secretively. "That's what my analysts suggest, with good reason, but that doesn't sound like you. You've got something else planned."

"Smart boy. It seems I don't have all the family brains after all."

"So why *are* you here. Come to ask for my help?" he mocked.

"Actually, I have."

Isen Tyrel stood in the center of Morning Dawn's circular firing range perfectly still.

A tone sounded.

Then a second.

On the third...he moved.

Diving to his right behind a barrier he avoided two low powered laser blasts that intersected where his neck had just been. Rolling out of his dive and onto his haunches, he pulled up and fired two quick pistol shots at a floating drone.

On instinct he jumped backwards through a low back flip, landed on his knees and poured fire into a second drone while it was still orienting on his former position.

The drone dropped to the ground after six lightning fast shots.

Before the first drone could get off a shot, Isen jumped behind a crate to his right. The drone began to approach and circle around behind the crate, but before it got all the way around he jumped into its path and rolled onto his back beneath it. Three point blank shots later the drone dropped to the floor where Isen had just been.

Rolling off to the side he brought his legs up beneath him and visually scanned the large cluttered room. *Two down, ten to go.*

An almost inaudible whoosh of air was his only warning as another drone floated behind him and fired a ruby bolt into the floor. Half a meter to the right, Isen lay on his back pumping his pistol's trigger as fast as he could. The drone began to readjust its sights to the right as four perfectly placed shots deactivated it just as it began to fire.

Glints of metal in the shadows off to his right caused Isen to quickly side roll to his feet and dash behind a low wall. A power pack fell to the ground as Isen reloaded in the few seconds he had to spare.

He grabbed the deactivated drone he'd first shot down and threw it through the air past and behind the two drones. Their motion detection sensors followed it to the floor before their infrared sensors confirmed that is wasn't their target.

Isen sprayed red bolts into the back of the nearest spherical drone and got two shots of at the second before ducking behind the wall again. He popped up over the wall for a split second and got another shot off before nearly getting hit by the drone's return fire. Diving onto his side, Isen cleared the wall and peppered the target with shots until it fell to the floor next to its former companion.

Sweat beginning to drop from his forehead was cleared with a single swipe from his free hand as he saw a drone clear the corner of a crate and track towards him.

Isen pulled his hips forward and let himself fall on his back as he brought his gun hand up and fired. His shots hit true while the drone's single shot missed three centimeters above his head to burn slightly into the wall.

He picked up his feet and moved to new cover, stepping over the newly downed drone. Isen pulled himself behind a stack of crates head high and looked for the remaining four drones.

A faint hiss made him drop to a crouch and aim directly above his head where he downed another drone with five rapid shots. Catching the drone as it fell, Isen turned and hurled the deactivated sphere into the shadows, drawing two wide spaced shots from his left.

Dropping to one knee, he hinge swung himself around the corner and took a quick shot that missed wide left before swinging back behind cover. He swung out again and scored three clean hits on the nearest drone before again pulling back behind the crates.

Directly across from him was a shoulder high barrier five meters away. Throwing himself through the air, he ran/dove at the barrier, scoring another hit and two more misses on the nearest drone as it sprayed energy darts in his wake. Isen hit the ground hard on his right shoulder and let himself slide past the barrier on his side. He downed the farther drone in five snapshots before sending a final lance of energy into the nearer drone, sending it to the ground.

He picked himself up and pulled back behind the barrier looking the opposite direction of the two drones he'd just downed. *Come on, where are you?*

The last drone pulled directly in front of Isen. Jumping into a run, he sidestepped the first two of the drone's shots returning fire of his own. Dropping to his knees he let the drone's next shot pass over his recently lowered head and gave it a return salvo that dropped it dead as a rock.

The exercise end tone sounded and Isen got to his feet as the room's primary lights snapped on.

"32 seconds, not bad," the training instructor congratulated him. "Only a second off you record."

"Thanks. What's next on our agenda?"

"We're done for now. Take a shower and relax for a while. You did well for the day."

Before Isen could object, a female attendant walked into the training range. "I'm sorry to interrupt. Director Starfield asks that Agent Tyrel report to his office when he completes his training exercises."

"I'm finished now, but I have to catch a shower first. Will you tell the Director that I'll see him in approximately 20 minutes?"

She nodded. "I will."

Isen waved to the training instructor on his way out the door. "See you tomorrow if I can."

"Tomorrow then."

Isen gave him a final nod before disappearing down the hall.

After showering and dressing in the traditional black jumpsuits embroidered with the golden rising sun crest wore by Morning Dawn agents, Isen made his way to Director Starfield's office door in just under his promised 20 minutes. He knocked twice before entering to find the Director talking to a tall man with a thick build that suggested considerable power beneath his white naval uniform.

"I'm sorry sir. I didn't realize you had company."

"It's alright Agent Tyrel. He's the reason I called you in. Seems he has a mission for you that his Midnight Star agents can't handle."

Isen looked to the unidentified man. "High Admiral Legan I presume."

"Very good, though it would be difficult for someone to not recognize me, given the mass of negative news coverage that I've been getting lately."

"I try to keep my agents up to date. Mr. Tyrel if you'll please take a seat, Admiral Legan will humbly explain why Midnight Star needs the help of Morning Dawn's best agent."

The Director glanced at Legan and the Admiral began to explain once Isen had straddled a nearby reversed chair.

"Agent Tyrel, have you ever heard of the Legend of Crestanya?"

He thought for a moment. "No, I don't believe I have."

"It is told," Legan said, beginning to retell the legend, "that during the height of the Anteron Federation the Anteronian navy spread across this part of the galaxy like wildfire, conquering planets with ease and leaving behind their highly skilled armies to pacify the subjugated planets. They brought nearly a quarter of the galaxy under their control, ruling over not only human worlds but a host of nonhuman civilizations as well. Eventually they halted their massive annexation when their realm became too expansive to keep under a tight rule. For the next 12 years the Anteronian military strengthened its new border worlds and fully integrated the new territories into the Anteron Federation. The next four decades knew relative peace with a few futile insurrections on formerly independent worlds that were of no consequence to the increasingly political government. The era of peace left the military with a large number of crack units with no purpose. Peace keeping on conquered wolds was no challenge for the Anteron reserve units, let alone the line troops who were becoming increasingly restless. The supreme warlord and the other warlords that commanded the military decided to disband approximately 80 % of their military forces. The troops were said to have reluctantly returned to civilian life while their weaponry was stored in a newly constructed armory along with important equipment and carefully guarded databases. The warlords' intention was to create a doomsday depot. Should disaster or invasion ever befall the Federation, the warlords, as a last resort, could return to Crestanya, the armory world, and reactivate the decommissioned warships and ground assault vehicles plus whatever other armament or equipment was stowed on the planet and hopefully save the Anteron Federation from complete destruction."

"After the armory was completed and filled, the warlords devised and ingenious key which they used to seal the armory against anyone who might want to steal the treasures within. They kept the key in a hidden place during the years of peace. Over time, the peaceful era lead to political infighting among the populace and the Ruling Houses themselves. The situation became so intense that the warlords were forced to take control of the government and forcibly stop the infighting as it became violent. The warlords began to administer federation worlds themselves and found the distances between border worlds and capitol too great for them to maintain firm control on all of their planets. So they decided to divide the Anteron Federation into fifths, with each one of the warlords taking personal command of one of the regions. The armory key which had been well hidden and almost forgotten was retrieved and reengineered into five components that would combine to make the key complete. The warlords each took one of the five parts and had little trouble maintaining peace within their smaller kingdoms. After many years of peace, the death of the last of the five warlords sparked a massive civil war between the five Great Houses now that there was no one to hold them in check. They each seized as many of the military units left leaderless when the warlords died as they could. The nonhuman populations rebelled and regained their independence as the Great Houses battled each other over the human worlds that now make up the human sphere. Their infighting was the beginning of the long chain of wars that have plagued the Human Sphere and lost us most of the Anteron technology that we once had. Strangely enough the five keys disappeared and were never seen again. If you didn't already know, one of my hobbies is archeology, and in reviewing records from the post warlord era I got the impression that the Legend of Crestanya was just the wishful imagination of the Great Houses as they searched for means to annihilate each other, which did eventually happen. I thought the legend was just that, a legend, until I found this."

Director Starfield activated his deskbound holoprojector which already contained the datacard Legan had brought with him. An image of a fist sized hunk of black rock floated before Isen. On closer examination he could see that it was in fact synthetic material, not rock, and contained a number of embedded gems in a pattern that he couldn't identify.

"I stumbled across this while on a dig in the Drakoris system. I searched the Kataran databases but came up dry. No matches. Nothing even resembling it."

"It's one of the five keys isn't it?"

"Yes it is. If you look close you can see connection points on some of the faces. I can't prove it's one of the keys, but I have no doubts myself."

"Interesting, but I don't see how this involves me."

"Midnight Star has been fortunate enough to crack some of Peace Core intelligence's codes. As you probably know, they change codes at random intervals so the codes we have are no longer valid. But the communiqués we intercepted and decoded while the code was germane contained several references to Anteron artifacts and one reference included a report about acquiring the fourth of five artifacts, which were given a code name that we can't identify. This leads me to believe that Peace Core intelligence has found the other four keys. I want those artifacts so, along with the one I have in my office, I'll have a chance of locating the armory and acquiring whatever weapons or data it may contain. The one problem is that none of my agents are skilled enough to penetrate the Peace Core's headquarters. That's why I have come here. I want you to get these artifacts for me."

"If I may ask, what good would the armory do even if you did find it. Pacifism is the current fad and you'll be disarming soon. Finding the armory may be a significant archeological find, but it doesn't seem worth the risk."

"Admiral Legan is finished taking orders from politicians and has plans of his own which I'll fill you in on later. The question is do you think you can pull it off and, more importantly, do you want to try? I'm making this assignment optional, but you're the only agent he's offering it to. It's an even more difficult assignment because neither I nor Admiral Legan knows where the artifacts are located inside the compound. We know that the artifacts, if they are what we think they are, were transported to the compound and as far as we can tell never left it. You'll have to locate and acquire the artifacts in a facility that neither Morning Dawn or Midnight Star agents have ever penetrated. We don't even know how large the compound is. Also, Peace Core's security at the compound is the tightest in the Human Sphere. This mission would be suicide for any other agent, Midnight Star and Morning Dawn alike. You're the only person that has a chance of penetrating their security. Finding the artifacts and getting out alive will be all but impossible. So, what do you think?"

Isen's face lit up in a sly smile. "When do I leave?"

Alpha Prime

Chapter Eighteen

There they sat in all their arrogant splendor, proud to be at the top of their insular world. Legan stood before the High Council on their summons to discuss how to best to proceed with disarmament. He had dutifully reported, hoping to buy as much time as he could before the politicians forced his hand. He had only a handful of scheduling details left to finish before the fleet would be ready to travel. The time was nearly at hand. This was his last political appearance, the last time he would have to wear his political mask. After this there would be no more hiding.

"Admiral Legan, thank you for taking the time out of your busy schedule to speak with us. We all know the preparations for disarmament are taking a considerable amount of that time as well as your search for a way to save the military," Senator Carson said.

"I am no longer looking for a way around disarmament," he said truthfully. "I know there is none. If there was I would have found it long ago. Now my priority is to see that my men are treated fairly, not just tossed aside after all the sacrifices they've made."

"It is for that very reason we have summoned you. Some senators propose an immediate recall of all military forces so that they may be decommissioned at once."

"I would highly advise against that and even go as far as to say I will obey no such order. My men need time to find civilian employment while they're still on the military's payroll. I won't allow them to be thrown to the corporate wolves."

"We have no intention of forgetting your men Admiral," Malcolm said playing along. "As you are the Supreme Commander I trust that you know best how to facilitate the military personnel's transfer to civilian life. Please tell us how would you handle the situation."

Legan nodded to Malcolm slightly in thanks for the opening. "My suggestion to you is to do nothing for the moment as far as military deployments are concerned. I would advocate a search for possible job openings that my men and women may be interested in. A wise idea would be to offer permanent tax reprieve to any corporation who hires former military personnel, for the duration of their employment. In this way a great many career opportunities will be available to military personnel and only military personnel, that way they won't have to compete against civilians for jobs. I suggest a two year time span be given for disarmament. In the first year the military would function normally as the corporate sector is informed and prepares for the tax relief opportunity, which will be proportionate to the number of military personnel in their employment. The second year would consist of the military being reduced part by part over the year with the soon to be civilians released in waves as opposed to all at once. By years end there would be no active military personnel save for me. Then mothballing or scraping of our weaponry can take place."

"Why would you remain active instead of joining your fellow officers as civilians?" Senator Morrison asked.

"That is my one personal request of you. I ask to remain an active military officer for the remainder of my life. I would have no official duties nor receive any pay. I have been involved in the military since the day I was born and will be an officer the day I die. I could never be a civilian. I will always be a military officer at heart. You can't take that away from me and the one favor ask is that you don't take away my official status. I think I deserve that small amount of respect for the life I dedicated to defending my nation. Let me finish that life with the knowledge that I stood ready, till the day I died, to defend my nation even if the Republic never again needs defending."

The senators exchanged a few muted words before settling down and allowing Senator Morrison to reveal their consensus. "This council is of a mind to grant you your favor. The peace proposal calls for disarmament, not retirement. Though you will have no warships to command you will retain the active rank of High Admiral and the title of Supreme

Commander for the rest of your life." Morrison looked briefly at the other senators. "I think my colleagues and I agree with your recommendations for disarmament. I personally believe your plan will provide the most painless transition possible. There are, I believe, a few details that we need you to clarify though."

"Certainly."

After only a half hour of further discussion, the unusually congenial High Council dismissed Legan, having other business on their day's agenda. He returned to the hoverlimo that had brought him to the Senate building where Admiral Termel waited.

"How did it go?" He hesitated and added a moment later. "Sir."

Legan smiled at his confusion about how informal he should be with the High Admiral. "Better than expected," he said as the hoverlimo began to move with its escorts flying two each fore and aft. "They agree to the two year plan. We don't have to demobilize until the second year though we will be long gone before that and you'll have carved yourself a small empire by then."

"Yes, about that. Approximately 16% of my men wish to go with you to the new region."

"I know. I've already arranged to switch them with some of my men that wish to stay behind. You'll even end up with a small surplus of personnel."

"That's a relief. I think I'll need every man I can get."

"I'm sure you will. Have you chosen a planet for your base of operations yet?"

"Yes, it's designated Sierra 77 on our star charts. It's an uninhabited system with two habitable planets located in the Gelatin cluster of the Cathor Republic. It's within spitting distance of one of my family's businesses on Cathor itself."

"That should make your colonization of the system much easier. How soon will you be able to move? I don't want to leave before you're ready."

"I've got good employees and a trusting family. We're going to transfer all of our holdings to friends who will oversee our businesses. I don't want our enemies to close off our supply lines, so my entire family is moving to Sierra 77 with me."

"A wise move."

"To answer your question, I think we'll be able to go within a month." He looked to Legan questioningly. "Can you wait that long?"

"I was planning to. I have a few loose ends to tie up anyway." He looked at Termel, concerned. "You think you're ready for this? I've had seven years to prepare to go rogue, you've had less then two weeks."

When Termel cringed and didn't respond Legan immediately started to worry. "Something wrong?"

"No, no." He hesitated. "Would you object to a short story?"

"No. Please go ahead."

Termel's face seemed to gaze off into nothingness as he started to recall his past. "When I was twelve years old I was in the young rangers, a wilderness survival skills organization. Our troop of about 20 Ranger Scouts, the second highest rank we could receive, was taken on a seven day cross country hike. We camped in small two man tents which one of us would carry on a shoulder strap and the other scout would carry our food and other supplies. On the trip I was a supply carrier and the 3rd highest ranking scout on the trip, not counting our pair of guides. The first three days went by without a hitch. While strict in a disciplinary sense, our troop still managed to have a blast climbing the rocky terrain and navigating the thickly forested mountain ranges. We made good time hiking each day. From and hour after sunrise to an hour before sunset we traveled single file fighting off small vornacks, knee high predators on my home planet, with our three round laser pistols. Only Scouts and Rangers where allowed to carry firearms and the three round power clip made us conserve our fire and impressed upon us the necessity of making every shot count. We carried our TC3's in small hip holsters which allowed for quick draws that saved us a great deal of vornack scratches and bites. On the fourth day we came to a fairly wide river with an old pedestrian footbridge spanning the swift currents. We crossed in single file, one guide leading, one following. I was seventh in line and the only Scout unfortunate enough to break through a rusted metal plate and fall into the river. I was carried downstream for kilometers before pulling myself ashore at a calm section of river. My pack was lost, as was my pistol. I had no clue where I was or how far I had traveled. I decided to follow the river upstream until I found the bridge that had broken underneath my booted feet. I traveled three days, sleeping only a few hours each night, and I still hadn't found the bridge. The weather had become extremely hot and I became dehydrated no matter how much river water I drank. In addition to dehydration I was also dying of hunger. With sweat pouring down my face and running off my already sweat soaked clothes I trudged through kilometers of forest with no success. On the fifth day I dropped to the ground and couldn't get back up. I nearly lost conscience, but more importantly I had lost my will to fight. I lay in a heap on damp soil and fallen leaves, ready to die. But before that happened I had a vision. I half saw, half felt myself sometime in the future being called upon by millions and millions of stricken people to help them. I remember myself asking what good can I do, and one old, wrinkled man answered, "Only you can help us, no one else can. If you don't we're all lost." Then I saw my father who had died a year before look down upon me and say, "Son, this is a task that you and you alone can complete. People are counting on you for their very lives and the lives of their children, and their children's children, and all generations to come there after." I then saw a vision of myself, dressed in the tattered rags I now wore, paler than I knew I was straddled over my prone body shouting, "You can't let these people down. They are counting on *you* and only *you* can help them. You can't help them if you're dead. You can't die. Now get up!" I tried to get up only to fall down again. I yelled at myself to get up and finally did on the third try. I staggered a few meters before the dizziness cleared from my head. I slowly made my way up stream and a half kilometer later I found the bridge and got the attention of one of our guides that was left behind in case I returned before I finally blacked out. I woke up the next day at the local hospital with an IV in my arm and a host of doctors hovering near my bed in the gaps left by my family and some of my fellow Scouts. One of the doctors told me that at the level of dehydration I was at I should have been dead and he had no explanation why I had survived. Afterwards when I thought about what had happened I decided I had been hallucinating from my lack of fluids and foods plus the heatstroke I had suffered. It wasn't until the council of war that the vision replayed, word for word before my eyes almost as if the past 37 years hadn't happened. Then I knew that what had happened that day was more than a hallucination. It was a vision of the future. My future. I knew then what I had to do. You're Leaving, so I'm all that stands between these people and their annihilation. I won't fail them. So in a way I've been ready to become a rogue for 30 years longer than you have. And you know what, I think I'm going to thoroughly enjoy it."

"Well, you'll get to have fun snubbing Senator Mian. I wish I could see how she reacts when we all up and disappear right under their noses."

"Don't worry, I'll fill you in when you get back."

"I hope so. In all reality, my people probably won't be back until long after we're both dead. I'm afraid you're truly going to be on your own. The Human Sphere will be all yours. When my people come back they won't be returning home, they'll be returning to aid a brother. We're leaving for good. Our home will be in the new territories and that's where we'll stay. After we help your people clean up the Human Sphere, if both of us live long enough, we'll fight off any nonhuman invasion together. If no invasion occurs we'll go exploring and see what's out there."

"If you can live that long, so can I."

"It's a deal than. We'll both live to see the day when my forces return to the Human Sphere and show the politicians how true warriors fight. That is if you don't take care of things yourself before we get back."

"I only hope that's so, but I get the feeling that we're going to be out numbered, out gunned, and fighting for our lives each and ever day. Then again, if it wasn't a challenge it wouldn't be any fun."

"No, I suppose it wouldn't be. We do seem to seek out the most difficult way to get things done."

"Sometimes things can only be done the hard way, so it's better if we prepare ourselves before hand," Termel advised.

"Speaking of the hard way, is that what I think it is."

Termel turned in his seat to look out the forward viewport. "Looks like a mob surrounding the entrance to that housing complex."

"That complex is where my quarters are."

"Oh really," Termel said thoughtfully. "Perhaps we are seeing some of Senator Mian's handiwork. Look closely at the left flank and you'll see a man with a hover scroll sign proclaiming peace forever and calling for immediate disarmament."

"You've got good eyes. So what do you think. Should we try a back door or do you want to hear what they have to say?"

"Oh I think we have to see this."

"Me too."

Legan and Termel's hoverlimo pulled up and over to land on the floating plaza at the front entrance of the East Ridge housing complex, a 47 story building that housed some of the most luxurious quarters on the planet. Only because of his status as Supreme Commander did the East Ridge administrator offer him free quarters in an attempt to go one up on his competition and attract the extremely wealthy clientele. If not for the administrator's generous offer he never would have been able to afford a weeks rent, even if he had saved his pay since the day he started military service.

Legan and Termel exited the hoverlimo and were immediately surrounded by the mob who all at once began beating on the two officers. Legan blocked most of the haphazard blows until he saw Admiral Termel fall to the ground, blood streaming from a gash on the back of his head. It was then that Treys snapped into combat mode, moving to defend Termel.

One man who had begun to kick the Admiral while he lay unconscious on the stone-like plaza was thrown bodily back through the air by a right uppercut that broke a number of the man's ribs. Bringing his left foot up and around in a roundhouse kick, Legan dislocated the jaw of a woman who was clawing at his now bloody back.

Out of the corner of his eye he saw a figure dive towards Termel's prone figure. The man approaching from his right never made it as Legan brought his left knee around and planted it in the man's sternum, stopping him cold.

By now his police escorts had shoved their way through the now stunned crowd and formed a protective ring around the downed officer. "Admiral Legan, are you ok?" one of his escorts asked. "I'm sorry we didn't intervene sooner but we had no idea the crowd was going to turn violent."

"He'll be alright," Admiral Termel groggily interrupted. "He likes doing things the hard way."

"I though you were unconscious?"

"Nope, just got the wind knocked out of me." Termel winced as he felt the back of his bloody head. "And a piece of my head too."

"Sir, we have medics on the way."

"Thank you Lieutenant. Please take these three persons into custody," Legan said indicating the three civilians lying on the ground, two motionless and the third crying out in pain. "And see that they receive medical attention."

"Yes sir."

"You don't look so good yourself," Termel said.

"I'll live. My wounds are superficial, but your head gash isn't," Legan said removing his tattered uniform and tearing off a sleeve which he began to wrap around Termel's head. "Now hold still, you've lost a lot of blood."

"What happened to those three?" Termel asked, pointing to the newly restrained 'pacifists.'

"They received a lesson in reality. The hard way."

Termel laughed as much as his bruised ribs would allow. "Good thing I had an ex commando to protect me."

"There's no 'ex' about it. I'm still listed as an active commando."

"You don't believe in retiring do you?"

"No."

"Lucky me I guess," Termel said trying to get to his feet. He made it to his knees before the pain became too great and he had to sit again. "Remind me later that I owe Mian one, a very big one."

"You still think this was Mian's handiwork?" Legan asked as the medics arrived.

"Who else. If she wasn't directly responsible then she had a hand in the process somewhere. She is, after all, the one who started the pacifist movement."

Legan waved his left hand at the onlooking crowd while a medic bandaged his right. "They didn't look to pacifistic to me."

"No, I guess not, Termel said., suddenly out of breath.

"Take it easy my friend," Legan said putting his left hand on Termel's right shoulder. "You need to rest and let yourself recover. There will be plenty of opportunities in the future to settle your score with Mian, and when you do," Legan said in a low growl, "give her one for me too."

"Believe me, I will."

Chapter Nineteen

S uspended in midair 1.2 meters above the smooth granite floor of a 2 km long cavern, the 90 cm wide circular target board shattered as a low powered rifle blast connected with the third of four rings on the 1200 meter distant hologram.

"Three points," the computer informed Cara Venture who adjusted the sights of her tripod mounted sniper rifle while laying flat on her stomach on the cool stone floor. She tightened her finger on the rifle's hair trigger sending out a fiery red dart that shattered the renewed target.

"Seven points."

Gritting her teeth slightly she aimed just below the center and a hair to the left then fired. Again the target shattered and the computer spoke.

"Bulls eye."

"Computer, set for lateral movement and offset regeneration," Cara instructed.

A moment later the target began moving right and left at predictable intervals. She lead the target, letting it move into her line of fire, then twitched her finger. The target disintegrated while another instantaneously appeared five meters to the left.

"Five points."

She missed it high, gathered herself, then quickly dispatched her target with a second bolt.

"Seven points."

She continued to down targets with only three misses out of 52 shots. Deciding she'd had enough, Cara picked herself up off the floor, replaced the sniper rifle to its appropriate rack, and headed for the gym. After three hours of martial arts practice and showing up her instructor in a sparing match, she headed for the showers, exhausted.

Whenever Cara was given an assignment, she would spend the few days she had before the mission in intense training. Cara never slacked off between assignments, she was always working to improve her training marks, most of which were Midnight Star records, but her training always intensified when she focused on a mission.

Walking down the corridor that lead to the showers, Cara's right leg momentarily gave way and she had to catch herself on the wall with a sweat soaked forearm. She steadied herself then continued on down the empty hall.

Eventually reaching her destination, Cara slapped her palm against the activation pad and walked into the shower room as the 2 meter wide door slid up into the ceiling. She dragged herself down the wide center isle under a U-shaped, crystalline canopy, intricately designed to mimic a surface spa even though the entire Midnight Star complex was 500 meters under the surface of Katara Prime.

The shower room was as lavishly designed as the canopy, with almost microscopic scrollwork on the pristine white ceramic walls. The floor was a collection of lumination tiles that, with the canopy lighting, eliminated any chance of shadows ever forming.

Cara made it to her personal compartment, closed and locked the door behind her, then collapsed in a heap on the well padded dressing bench. She rested there for nearly ten minutes before finding the strength to stand and strip off her sweat soaked training garb which she placed in a small, wall mounted compartment that automatically took her clothes to the laundry.

Cara stepped across the small room and into the tubular shower which was partially embedded into the far corner of the rectangular room. With the touch of an interior keypad, she turned on the shower and roughly sat on the floor, bringing her knees up to her chin and wrapping her arms around her slender legs as the water flowed warmly over clammy flesh.

Stupid. I over did it again. The last thing I need on this mission is fatigue. Then again, if I don't train hard I won't keep improving. I need to be at my best for this mission. It's going to be the most lethal challenge I've faced yet and if I'm not sharp I might not get out alive. All I need is a good night's sleep then I'll be ready to go in the morning.

She sighed as warm water droplets ran down her long black hair then onto bare skin that had begun to return to its normal light tan. The obstacle course run she had taken before practicing at the firing range and the subsequent gym time had reeked havoc on her body and only now did the aches and pains begin to register.

Cara stretched out her legs and leaned her back against the curved wall, letting the porous ceiling massage her tight muscles with streams of water. She closed her eyes and nearly fell asleep, thinking back over her past 10 years with Midnight Star.

When she was 12 years old, both of her parents were killed during the Braxen Empire's invasion of Lorellia, her home planet. The building that she had lived in ever since she was born was destroyed when the ground battle moved into her city. Ground assault vehicles fought each other in the streets for 14 straight hours before the Braxen forces were finally driven off. During the battle a rogue missile hit one of the lower floors of her building, collapsing the entire structure.

By some quirk of fate she ended up inches below a structural support, unhurt aside from a host of cuts and bruises while her parents, only a few meters away, lie crushed beneath the mounds of rubble. It had taken two days before rescuers had pulled her out of the rubble, the sole survivor of the people who had been in the building when the missile detonated.

Her parents were all that she had had. No other relatives existed to claim her so she was herded into a camp of unidentified survivors where she met a woman that she talked to for hours, crying most of the time. Eventually the woman took Cara to her private ship, away from the chaos that had consumed the planet, and to the Midnight Star facility.

Over the next year she underwent extensive training that changed her life forever. The little girl she once was had died along with her parents. The empty shell of a person that survived was the raw materiel her instructor used to create a new person with a new life.

The first year was extremely difficult, but she emerged a brilliant agent. She began to excel beyond her classmates, receiving top marks in nearly every field, working harder and longer than any other trainee.

Her instructor began devising advanced training exercises for her specifically. During the next five years the tests and trials she endured changed her into the woman she is today. She became an active agent and after her first year in the field had risen to the top of the agent list.

But she had not been content. Cara continued to push her limits. She had her long time instructor create more difficult training scenarios for her to tackle, which she did with surprising ease. It took quite a while to develop challenges for her youthful skills, but when they did finally succeed in testing her limits, she just worked harder and longer than ever before. Cara would keep at it until she beat the scenarios, then she would ask for harder ones.

I don't ever quit, do I? Cara pulled herself up off the ground and leaned against the shower wall. *Not that I'd ever want to.*

She reached for the keypad and fell to the floor as her legs gave way. *Come on, pull it together. I've got work to do.*

Concentrating this time, she got to her feet and touched the keypad again turning off the water and activating the drying mode. Warm dry air flowed across her body from wall mounted vents. The fast moving air currents tossed her hair up above her head, nearly touching the intake vents around the edge of the circular ceiling. After only a few minutes she was dry head to toe. She deactivated the air bathe and stepped out of the now dry shower. She stretched sore muscles for a moment before dressing in a clean jumpsuit that was deposited in her small closet earlier that morning.

Gathering her composure, she left her little cubical and the shower room behind, and headed for the weapons lab two floors up. Even as tired as she was, Cara chose the stairs over the elevator, as she always did. After climbing the two flights of stairs she navigated her way through a maze of corridors, most of which were empty, until she came to the two double containment doors that lead into the lab.

She opened the doors and discovered why the halls were sparsely populated. Techs and analysts scurried about the hangar-like chamber, dismantling, sorting, and packing everything in sight into mismarked crates that would be transported with the regular supplies in the main convoy to Alpha Prime.

"Agent Venture," a tech dressed in an ankle length lab coat called out as he waved her forward.

She walked toward the weapons master, dodging crates and dashing personnel. "Have I come at a bad time?"

"Yes, but I'm afraid there isn't going to be a good time until we reach Alpha Prime, and that will be too late."

He motioned for Cara to follow him as he headed for a nearby door that lead to a small lab that had yet to be raided by the packing crews. Once they were both inside he closed the door and looked to Cara expectantly.

"Well, what do you need?"

"Level 5 insertion kit, delta grade security countermeasures, and a pair of your specialty specs, green tint if you can. Any of that going to be a problem Zephrim?"

"No, shouldn't be. That is quite a bit of heavy duty equipment. Guess the Admiral was right when he said you had a tough mission this time around."

"When don't I. This is a bit different though. I'll be entering a very hostile area and things could get very lethal if I slip up. This is going to be the biggest challenge I've ever had. I need all the help I can get."

"In that case I might have some items you'd be interested in. Wait here a moment."

Cara watched as Zephrim went out the door to fetch whatever gadgets he'd come up with this time. A few moments later he came back with a stack of small boxes.

"I've been working on a few new things that might come in handy." He reached inside a small box and pulled out an innocent looking datapad. "The Admiral told me you'd need to download files from a highly secured area so I put together a little kit of all the latest hacking techniques and equipment into this look a like datapad. As you can see it unfolds into a display screen, basic keypad, and seven different computer jacks that should allow you to access any mainframe. Just connect the datapad and select 'begin search.' It's set up to break any passwords and download everything it can find. The downside is it may take a while to break through the security measures. The actual download will depend on how much data there is to be had. The hacking programs *should* get you in without setting off any alarms, but stay on your toes just in case."

"Got it. What else do you got?"

He smiled. I've created marble size timed explosives and an alternative version for smokescreens. You activate them with a double click of the arming button. Deactivate with another click. The timers can be selected from 2 seconds to 30 minutes."

"And last but not least, you're new starmaster."

"Don't tell me you have it in one of those boxes too."

"Funny," Zephrim said sarcastically. "You'll have to go to the hangar to get it. It has a new and improved IS drive as well as our new stealth armor. Cut the engines and enemy sensors won't detect you unless they get within a kilometer. Even then they might miss you, depending on how their sensors are set up. But for the most part you'll be invisible with your engines off line and hard to track with your engines engaged. The shields and weapons, along with the sensors, have been considerably upgraded and a more powerful power core installed. Your starmaster should be able to outrun and outgun any other starfighter in the Sphere. You'll find your ship labeled a mark VII and is parked in slot A3. Now, if you don't have any questions, I'll get the rest of the equipment you need."

"I'm good to go."

"Ok, but don't get your hopes up."

Cara frowned, not understanding what he meant.

"We might be out of green."

After having her equipment stored in her new starfighter, Cara Venture returned to her assigned billet and rolled onto her bed, falling fast asleep the moment her head hit the pillow.

Cara woke the next morning fully refreshed after sleeping a full 16 hours. She showered a bit more quickly than yesterday, dressed in the specialized combat jumpsuit that was waiting for her, and headed for the hangar.

She walked at a crisp gate down polished corridors that would have echoed with her heal strikes had she been wearing civilian boots, but the Midnight Star standard issue combat footwear was specially designed for stealth and made virtually no sound at all. Her jumpsuit clung to her skin in a comfortable fit with slightly thicker armored patches covering her everywhere there wasn't a joint so she could maintain maximum mobility. Covering her knees and elbows where flexible pads that allowed Cara to tumble to her heart's content without her limbs going numb. The black fabric of her jumpsuit wouldn't reflect light under any circumstances and helped to reduce her infrared signature. She also wore black gloves that stopped just above the knuckles and left the ends of her fingers bare. Her dark hair was pulled back into a tight braid that trailed halfway down her back.

She entered the packed hangar and made her way to parking slot A3 where a sleek starfighter painted the same color as her jumpsuit waited with an alert pair of technicians standing ready to assist her.

"Agent Venture?"

Cara smiled. "That's me."

"Your transport ship is prepped and ready to go on tunnel 3. You're cleared for departure at your convenience."

She tilted her head towards her starmaster. "Any special instructions?"

"Not really. The fighter's controls are more or less the same as the original and the special adaptations are obvious enough. Your default ID codes have been loaded into the security system. You can enter new codes while you're enroute if you want. You ready to go?"

Cara nodded and one of the techs swung a ladder up next to the craft and steadied it as his counterpart mounted the ladder, climbed onto the cockpit roof, and opened the top hatch. She climbed to the top of the starmaster and dropped into the cockpit. Closing the hatch behind her, Cara watched out her side viewport as the tech retreated down the ladder and pulled it clear of her starfighter.

When Cara entered her ID code the ship's console lit up with red lights that quickly turned green. Flicking a switch, she brought up an enhanced tactical overlay which immediately tagged every ship in the hanger with a blue Midnight Star crest, signifying them as allies. Next Cara initiated engine startup and was pleasantly surprised when the ship's four Trencor II thrust engines thrummed to ten seconds quicker than the norm. After looking over the weapons diagnostic panel she was thoroughly impressed.

"You've been busy Zephrim."

Gripping the control stick, Cara gently raised her mark VII starmaster off the deck and slowly headed across the hangar above the myriad of ships that would soon be heading for Alpha Prime. She dropped the ship to a meter off the deck as she entered the mouth of tunnel 3, then increased speed.

Cara cruised down the long, straight tunnel with evenly spaced guide lights whipping past. Eventually the tunnel lights turned from white to yellow, then to red, signaling the end of the tunnel. Gradually slowing her fighter to a stop, Cara nestled her ship into a lift shaft compartment that, after a moment's wait, began to move upward.

After a minute long ascension the lift brought Cara's starmaster up into the belly of a cargo transport whose bay doors closed beneath her ship, sealing her in. She waited patiently in the pitch black hangar until feeling the transports engines come on line and the subsequent lift off.

The transport carrying Cara's fighter lifted off from East Republic spaceport and slowly climbed towards orbit where it made a routine jump to IS space heading for the Darra system. After only a few minutes out from Katara the transport reverted to realspace and released Cara's fighter from its belly hold. It then jumped back into IS space on its original heading to Darra, where after dropping off some insignificant cargo it would return to Katara and its specialized docking bay.

Left floating in space far beyond Katara's sensor range, Cara warmed up her IS drive and located the end point of the first leg of her trip, which stored in the ship's computer, and fed the planet's coordinates into the navigation terminal.

One of her secondary monitors counted down the seconds until her drive core was fully charged as she brought her ship around to the appropriate heading. She silently counted down the seconds in her head along with the ship's chronometer. When Cara and the chronometer reached zero the jump light turned green and she pulled back on a small lever to her immediate left.

The stars flared into a swirl of color as Cara made the transition from realspace to IS space. After checking to make sure she was on the right heading and finding that she was indeed on route to the first target system, Cara let out a sigh and relaxed, slumping slightly in her seat. *I've got a seven hour leg to endure so I might as well make myself as comfortable as possible.*

To that end she took out from under her seat a datapad that contained a number of technical manuals that Zephrim had given her.

Cara had discovered over the past few years that the best way to pass time on these extended trips was to sleep or work, and she didn't feel like sleeping anymore.

Selecting the data on the new technology she was bringing with her, Cara began to acquaint herself with every facet of the equipment's use. On this mission she was going to need every edge she could get.

Chapter Twenty

"Gentlemen please," a frustrated Senator Malcolm said. "I'll repeat this one last time so do listen carefully. Sometime in the near future High Admiral Legan will give the standby order which you all will pass on to your constituents. They will then make ready to leave, but still go about their daily routines. We don't want to prematurely alert anyone to our mass departure so all of our people must continue working their jobs, attending their local academies, and whatever else they normally do. The only thing they can and must do is pack their few belongings into the cubicles that we've given them and finalize any arrangements concerning the property they leave behind. Also, you must impress on them the need for secrecy. If they leak word of our plans the civilian extraction could be compromised. If that happens we might have a fight on our hands in one form or another, and that could cause people to be left behind or worse yet people could loose their lives. Make sure they understand that."

"Soon after the standby order is given, High Admiral Legan will then give the go ahead. Time of pickup and landing zone coordinates will be given with the order. When that time comes our people must drop whatever they are doing and get to the landing zones with their cubicles and family members as soon as possible. All of our people must be wearing their ID wristbands or they won't be allowed onboard the transports. We can't have unidentified people running around our ships, only the people on our lists will be admitted into the landing zones and only if they are wearing their IDs. In addition all family members must wear individual IDs, including infants. We can't take extra people with us that aren't on the list, we just don't have the extra room onboard our transports. I wish we could take everyone with us that wanted to go, but the reality is we have limited resources and that means we have to limit the number of people we take. Military personnel will be present at the landing zones to make sure the pickup goes smoothly and provide escort all the way to Alpha Prime. If anyone tries to interfere with our extraction, either mobs of civilians or armed opposition, High Admiral Legan's men will run interference for us as we board the transports. But the sooner we can get everyone onboard the easier their job will be, so encourage your people to arrive an hour or two ahead of the given time slot. The sooner everyone is aboard the sooner we can leave."

"After the pickups are made our people will have to endure approximately a month of space travel before we reach Alpha Prime. On arrival our new populace will move from the transports onto the surface and into temporary shelters as permanent facilities are being built. Now, those are the basics of what Admiral Legan has planned, but he has instructed me to tell all of you that certain aspects of this operation are classified and that you will just have to trust him. He has everything under control and all will go according to plan as long as we follow his instructions to the letter. We're working on a tight time table and can't allow any slip-ups. Does anyone have additional questions?"

Governor Mesbith of Alara spoke first. "Will our people be left behind if they arrive late at the pickup points?"

"The landing zone coordinators are instructed to wait for the duration of the allotted time frame or until everyone is aboard. After that, the transports leave or wait at the discretion of thecooridinator. It is vitally important that all of our people arrive at the landing zones on time or preferably early. Tell them to do whatever it takes to get to the pickup points on time or they may be left behind. The transports may wait for a time but they won't wait forever. See to it that your people arrive at the given time with their cubicles."

"Senator," Governor Beas of Hollander asked. "Some of my people are concerned about being separated from their family members. Are there any special procedures in place to prevent that from occurring and what will be done if it does occur?"

"A valid question Governor. All immediate family members have been assigned to the same transports. They will be kept together onboard as well as possible. If family members do get separated we can check their ID wristbands and reunite them in short order. If they're not wearing their ID wristbands things could get very complicated and people could be separated permanently. That's another reason why everyone, even us, must wear their ID wristbands throughout the duration of the trip to Alpha Prime and then for a short period on planet as well."

Governor Florel of Terona was next to speak. "Senator, it has come to my attention that certain persons are being assigned berths on luxury liners while the rest of us will be traveling on cargo transports. I have also discovered that the better supplies are being shipped on these liners so its passengers can be wined and dined during the trip to Alpha Prime while the rest of the civilians get to live off of survival rations for a month," she said with disgust.

Malcolm stared directly at Florel, anger rising within him before he forced himself to be calm. "Governor Florel," he said icily. "This entire operation is Admiral Legan's pet project and he will hand out ship assignments as he sees fit. If he chooses to give privileges to certain persons then so be it, but he will not disregard a single person. Everyone coming with us will be well taken care of, I have Admiral Legan's personal word on that. And I can assure you that no one will be wined and dined on this trip, but if Admiral Legan wishes it then so be it. But I know he won't waste cargo space on luxuries. The luxury liners themselves have been stripped down and turned into personnel and cargo transports. Nothing is being wasted or misused. Berth assignments will vary but everyone will have adequate supplies and living quarters so I don't want to hear any further whining about fair play. Admiral Legan is as fair as a person can be and we need to trust his judgement. Anyone else?"

"Just how large are the average living quarters on the transports?" Jonathan Periss, mayor of Katara Prime asked.

"Most of the personnel transports have been refitted with additional living quarters in the cargo bays. These improvised quarters are the smallest in the exodus fleet measuring 3 meters by 5 meters with a bunk built into the wall. The restrooms are communal plus there are large recreation areas within the transports to alleviate the claustrophobic nature of the living quarters. As I said before, we have limited resources and we need to make use of every square meter that we can. These quarters will be cramped but livable. They're meant for single occupants while larger quarters elsewhere on the vessel will be assigned to families."

"A month long trip for 300 million people is going to require a great deal of supplies," Kieti Oseru, chief executive of Fulnor Enterprises stated. "Even more supplies will be needed once we settle in on Alpha Prime. Do we have enough resources to support ourselves on the trip and how will we acquire additional supplies once we arrive, being so far away from the Human Sphere?"

"Yes, we do have enough resources to sustain us during our journey to Alpha Prime and then some. We also have adequate supplies for the immediate year after our arrival. We will not, however, return to the Human Sphere for additional supplies. Coming with us in the fleet is enough equipment to initiate industrial and agricultural programs that will supply all the resources we will need for an indefinite period. Even as we speak, an advance convoy is already at Alpha Prime setting up the beginnings of what will be our Supply Core. When the fleet arrives, immediate implementation of the equipment that we will be carrying will accelerate the growth of the Supply Core to the point of self sufficiency in approximately six months. After that point we should have enough of a surplus to allow our production facilities to diversify along the lines of current production in the Republic. Admiral Legan has made sure that we will be able to support ourselves once we reach Alpha Prime and has done so with exacting detail. So yes, we will have adequate supplies for the interim period and a surplus of supplies within a year after our arrival."

"I know this may sound trivial," Governor Xerus of Norelle said sheepishly, "but I was wondering if there is any way we could bring our pets along with us?"

"I'm afraid not. People aren't allowed to bring anything besides their cubicle and most pets can't live inside a meter wide box for a month. However, if you personally have any pets you wish to bring along I'm sure it can be arranged, but the masses won't be able to bring along pets."

"On behalf of my Teraxian hawkbats I thank you."

"Senator, a great number of people are wondering what they should bring with them and what they should leave behind," Terry Ramnes, CEO of Borconsia Corp. stated. "Principally they are asking if they should bring along their credits. Will we be using Kataran credits on Alpha Prime or will we be using a new currency?"

"Tell them not to waste their cubicle space on credits. When we arrive on Alpha Prime everyone will continue to be supported until the majority of our construction if finished. After that Admiral Legan will decide what will happen but I can assure you that Kataran credits will be will not be the currency where we're going."

"So you know what kind of economy we will have?"

"Those decisions will be made by the High Admiral after our new colony is self sufficient. Until then we all have to work together in order to survive. If anyone has aspirations of wealth bury those thoughts deep in the back of your mind. For the first few years on Alpha Prime we will all be one large family. All resources will be under Admiral Legan's control until our situation is stabilized. Even then I hope that we work for the common good more than our current society does. We're going to make our new home in an isolated area and because of that isolation we will have to count on one another in addition to Admiral Legan's leadership. I cannot be for certain, but I would expect capitalism will have less impact on Alpha Prime than it does on Katara."

"Senator Malcolm," addressed Senator Eckly, "do you know what form of government our new colony will operate under?"

"In the long run no, I don't know. But in the near future any governmental structure will be set aside until our colony is stabilized." Muffled gasps accompanied his revelation but quickly subsided. "Again, I can't emphasize enough how vulnerable we will be in the new territories. If we fail there will be no one to run to for help. We are going to be on our own. Time is not on our side so lengthy debates are out of the question. Admiral Legan knows the most about this new region and is the most experienced in autonomous command, which we will have to operate under until our colony becomes self-sufficient. The system of government that we will live under will be chosen by Admiral Legan when he feels the time is right. Until then we are in his capable hands and I have no doubt he will take us in the direction we need to go. If not for him, we would soon be living in a pacifistic state and be completely vulnerable to invasion. He is the one who has spent years planning this operation. He saw the current crisis coming years before the senate foolishly passed the peace proposal. We owe him everything and I do not believe any form of government could be more fair and efficient in our first few years on Alpha Prime than his personal command."

"I agree," Senator Jaxsen proclaimed. "Admiral Legan is the most capable leader the Human Sphere has known throughout my lifetime. Putting someone in a position of authority over his own is foolhardy. He's not bringing us out of the Human Sphere to repeat the same mistakes. Senator, I do have a question of a different nature. Concerning the standby and go ahead orders, how much time will we have to prepare and actually get to the pickup points?"

"After the standby order goes out I would expect anywhere from 1 to 5 days but the decision comes from Admiral Legan alone. There will be at least 24 hours between the go ahead order and the beginning of the pickup time slots, though word may not reach everyone at once. It's up to all of you to make sure the people in your regions are notified of both the standby and go ahead orders as soon as possible."

"When do we receive our ship assignments?" Jaxsen asked.

"Right now." Malcolm opened a small box on the table top in front of him and passed out a datacard to each of the 37 regional directors.

"On this datacard are the ship and quartering assignments for all of the 300 million traveling to Alpha Prime. Pass on the assignments to the individuals in your regions as soon as you can. The standby order could be given any day now."

"I was also wondering where all of the transports were gong to consolidate at," Jaxson said. "That's assuming we're traveling in one large convoy to Alpha Prime and not piecemeal."

"No, we're traveling in one major convoy that will gather at a point on the edge of the Human Sphere. But before that all ships will meet at various points throughout the Republic and eventually form into seven different convoys that will eventually combine into one at the primary rendezvous point then continue as a whole to Alpha Prime. Each of the seven convoys will be escorted by a number of warships that will leave after the transports to discourage any possible pursuit. Because of the warships' greater speed, they will be able to catch the transports even with their head start and will probably be waiting for us at Alpha Prime when we arrive."

"Senator," Governor Taren of Doralis III spoke up. "Will there be additional convoys coming to Alpha Prime after we get firmly established there?"

"No, not as far as I am aware. From what Admiral Legan has told me he wants the location of Alpha Prime kept a secret from the Human Sphere so we can build our new colony without their destructive influence. He doesn't want the senate to have the opportunity to try to regain control over us. Admiral Legan hopes that the Human Sphere will let us go peaceably but he doesn't intend to give them a choice either. As far as they'll be concerned, one day 300 million people from a scattering of planets will board a mixed fleet of civilian and military ships and disappear into the stars."

"So, how long do we stay out in these new territories? Do we wait until the senate asks us back?"

"I don't believe you understand what is going to take place Governor Taren. Once we leave it's for good. We're not playing some political game for control of the Human Sphere, we're leaving it behind. The new territories will become our *permanent* home and a nation independent of the Human Sphere."

"But why would Admiral Legan want to do that?" she asked aghast.

"From what the Admiral has told me, he wants to take this small populous and let it develop without the political infighting that has plagued the Human Sphere for decades. He wants the harsh reality of life in an untamed region of space to burn away the complacency and stagnation that pervades the

Human Sphere and force us to recognize skill and initiative rather than political savvy."

"So let me get this straight," Taren said. "Admiral Legan is rescuing us from the senate's foolishness by taking us out into the middle of nowhere and hopes to create a society, independent of the Human Sphere, which is based on efficiency, skill, and merit that will avoid the pitfalls of a political state?"

"Basically yes. I don't know exactly what Admiral Legan has planned but it would be something along those lines. I would also assume that our new nation will maintain a well trained and well funded military far superior to any military force the Human Sphere could ever field as a whole."

"That's ludicrous," Taren exclaimed.

"No, it's brilliant," Jaxsen said calmly. "For years Admiral Legan has pushed to build a bigger and better military but only got bits and pieces, never the whole package. He always knew that the Republic was shortchanging itself but never had the autonomy necessary to see his plans to fruition. Now he has *complete* autonomy and soon will have the necessary resources to build his personal military the way he wishes with no restrictions what so ever. In my opinion, Admiral Legan tearing off his political leash is the best thing that could happen for the Human Sphere."

"How can it be best for the Human Sphere if we're leaving it?" Taren asked sarcastically.

"He has to disassociate his men from all outside influences in order for them to reach their full potential. Senator Malcolm is right in saying that Alpha Prime will be our new home, but there will be billions of people crying out for help when the inevitable civil wars begin after the pacifism movement falls on its face. I don't think Admiral Legan will turn a deaf ear on the Human Sphere, not once he has created a military force according to his specifications. He won't act before he's ready, but when he is watch out. Sooner or later High Admiral Legan will return to the Human Sphere to save his people."

Chapter Twenty-One

Not sharing their respective awe, Isen Tryel sat at the head of a large conference table and listened to the Morning Dawn analysts as they explained to him the impenetrable security of the Peace Core facility that he was soon attempt to infiltrate.

"The surface structure consists of a 17 meter high hexagonal wall surrounding an internal compound also appearing hexagonal in shape in our orbital surveillance recordings." As the analyst spoke, another of his colleagues cued up the holoprojector to show a diagram of each component of the compound as it was described.

"At each of the six points on the wall are large, well armed lookout towers which are powerful enough to strike down vessels in low orbit. The towers cover both the immediate surrounding area and the inner courtyard where the compound's six landing pads are spaced at regular intervals. There are also six main entrances to the inner compound, each one facing its corresponding landing pad. It's also possible that there are secondary access points within the towers or the walls themselves, which are a good seven meters thick, but we think this unlikely. The basic layout of the compound suggests that the obvious entry points are the sole entry points, but we can't be for sure because the immediate area around the compound is seismic shielded, so we don't know what lies beneath the surface. To make matters worse, there is no way to approach the compound without being seen. The forest surrounding the compound has been cut back a full kilometer from the wall to provide maximum visibility for the guard towers. Also, there isn't any repetitive traffic into or out of the compound, only a few transports and shuttles making random arrivals."

The analyst looked to his nearby staff. "In our opinion there is no possible way to penetrate the facility's security. You can't sneak or con your way in. We'd send in remote drones if we could, but the entrances appear to be equipped with electronic countermeasures, according to a long range surface recon from one of our agents with a surveillance scope on a nearby mountain ridge."

"No facility is impenetrable," Isen said.

"You know a way in then?"

"No, but I'm sure I'll come up with something. Do you have anything else to tell me?"

"Just that there have been unconfirmed reports of the guard towers shooting any civilian hover cars or ships that get too close."

"I'll keep that in mind, though I don't intend on being that obvious. Now, if you'll excuse me, I have an appointment with Dr. Gerrikson."

Isen received understanding nods and began to leave the room.

"Good luck Agent Tyrel," one of the analysts all but shouted out.

He responded with a curt nod then stepped from the room. After leaving the briefing room Isen wound his way through a maze of irregularly shaped hallways, designed to confuse any possible intruders, until he reached the medbay.

Passing through the sterilization field spanning the doorway, his attention was caught by a waving female technician off to his left.

"Dr. Gerrikson and Weapons Master Chekei are expecting you Agent Tyrel", she said then pointed to her right down a hall leading away from the cavernous sickbay towards the specialized research laboratories. "This way please."

Isen let the young medical assistant guide him down the hall and to a nearby room which she indicated with her left hand. "Here you are Agent Tyrel. Good luck on your mission."

"Thanks Mandy," Isen said before she retraced her steps back to the medbay.

The metallic doors parted automatically as he entered the laboratory, passing through another sterilization field before the two senior technicians, one Medical, one Technical, noticed his arrival.

"Agent Tryel," Dr. Gerrikson warmly greeted Isen, "I'm glad you've finally arrived. Dr Chekei and I have some new gadgets for your upcoming mission."

"Good, I always have liked new toys. So what have you been up to this time?"

Chekei raised a palm sized tube of black looking goo up to eye level. "This is your new combat suit."

"Oh really. You must have had an awful time cramming it into that small container. It looks like you compacted the material under enough stress to liquefy it. Amazing," Isen said sarcastically.

Chekei smiled. "This is no ordinary suit. It's part mechanical and part biological. The black liquid in this tube is the biotech suit itself in its dormant state. Here, hold out your hand."

When Isen did as he was asked, Dr. Chekei opened the tube. "Try to hold still. This is going to feel strange at first."

Abruptly he dumped the liquid onto Isen's outstretched hand. Instinctively flinching at first, Isen managed to keep himself from swiping at the liquid as it quickly expanded up his arm then over the rest of his body from the neck down. In a fraction of a second the liquid solidified into a thin silky material that clung to his skin right through his clothes. In fact, he couldn't feel anything but the biotech suit.

"How does it feel?" Dr. Gerrikson asked.

"Strange. I can't feel my clothes underneath it. Almost as if they weren't there."

"That's because they're not. They've been absorbed into the suit itself, molecularly dissolved and their patterns stored in the suit's cellular memory so they can be reassembled when you remove the suit."

"Also note that I no longer have the tube that contained the liquid." Chekei said. "It's actually part of the suit itself and is molecularly stored within it. Just press the first button on your right collar to deactivate the suit."

Isen ran a finger lightly behind his collar and found several small bumps. He pushed the first one on his right but nothing happened.

"You have to press the inside and the outside. It's a safe guard against the buttons pressing up against your neck."

Isen did as instructed and abruptly the biotech suit slithered off his body and into a newly formed capsule lying in the palm of his right hand. His clothes were back to normal and a sly smile spread across his face. "You've been busy. What all can this suit do anyway?"

"We've constructed the suit to be modular so it can accommodate a variety of weapons and specialized equipment. Because the suit is part biological, it can use light or heat to recharge its internal power cells in addition to the conventional power outlet. It has enough juice to power directly or recharge any of your non particle weapons plus has ISC data dump capacity from onsite locations no matter how far the distance. The collar controls also allow you to utilize a self contained life support system that can actually operate in the vacuum of space for a short period of time. However, it was mainly designed as a countermeasure for gas based security systems and underwater travel. The suit dons a hood that covers all but the eyes which are insulated by a pair of nearly skintight force fields that can double as display screens. Imbedded sensors can, on command, display their data opaquely, translucently, or a real time tactical overlay. The biotech suit also contains an integrated database of useful information that can be accessed by means of the display screens and the scrolling buttons on your collar. You can reconfigure most of the integrated systems to your personal configurations fairly easily and store them in the suit's memory so they will be set up the same way each time you put on the suit. Also, the biotech security system allows only one wearer per suit. This particular model was fashioned to your DNA and will only mold to your body's contact, but even that can be overridden if you want. All you have to do is reconfigure the security setup through the interface screens. There are a multitude of options that you can utilize through the visual interface mode that you'll have to discover on your own. We built so many intricacies into the suit that we can't even remember them all."

Isen opened the flask and let the suit remold to his features. He experimented with the collar buttons as the two technicians watched silently. After finding the activation button for the hood and visual interface system he returned the suit to its hoodless state. "You said something about modular equipment?"

"Yes, we have begun to fashion a number of items unique to the biotech suit."

"Show me."

Dr. Chekei guided Isen to a nearby lab table where he picked up a standard issue blastech pistol with the only difference being that it seemed to be made of a hardened form of his suit's material. On the Dr.'s prodding he picked up the pistol and looked it over.

"Seems pretty straightforward. What's so special?"

"Press the secondary function button right above the trigger twice."

On the second press of the button the pistol melted in his hand and reformed into a different weapon attached to his wrist. "I must say you two have really out done yourselves this time. How many different weapons have you modified to fit this suit?"

"We've modified 18 different hand held weapons and are working on converting the remainder of conventional weapons so they will be adaptable to your suit as well as devising new, specialized armament unique to the biotech."

"Do you have any surveillance countermeasures modified like this?"

"Yes, but only the most widely used variants. You'll probably have to take conventional equipment on your mission."

"By the way," Isen said addressing the Weapons Master, "I've been told that the Peace Core headquarters are scan shielded below ground level, even on seismonics. Do you have anything that will get me a picture of what structures they have buried under the surface?"

"I've read the brief and I think I might have something that will come in handy," Chekei said pulling a small scanner out of a box full of other technical equipment. "This is an energy sensor recalibrated for subterranean use. It won't show you what's buried beneath the surface but it will tell you where the juice flowing, even glowpanels should give off enough energy to show up on the scanner."

"Chekei, you're a lifesaver. This is just what I need to get past their security, plus a few other odds and ends."

"How long do you have before you leave?"

"A little over 4 hours."

"We'd better get you the rest of your equipment then. I'll have everything on the list sent down here assembled in a package, but I assume you'll want to add a few things."

"Definitely. But before we start with that, I was wondering if this suit came in any other colors besides black."

"Like what?"

"Invisible."

"Third button on your left."

Isen smiled broadly. "You know, I think I'm starting to like this suit already."

After Dr. Chekei gathered all the needed equipment, Isen carefully packed it into a snug, body conforming back pack. After thanking both Dr. Chekei and Dr. Gerrikson, he went to the mission prep room where he donned civilian clothing and appropriated a standard issue blastech pistol just incase the new weapon systems didn't work as planned. He gathered enough power packs for a prolonged engagement, hoping he'd still be carrying them when he left the peace core facility.

He gathered up a few other trinkets before leaving the prep room and heading for the hangar, but when the door to the hall opened, Isen found Director Starfield waiting for him. "Agent Tyrel. Do you have a minute? I'd like to speak with you."

"Sure. Do you mind if we walk?"

"No, not at all," Starfield said as they began down the hall. "I know your departure window is near and I don't want to delay you. I do however want to make sure you understand what kind of trouble you're getting yourself into. You're going to try to infiltrate the most heavily guarded compound in the Human Sphere. You have no possible entry points besides the six main entrances, which are overlooked by the guard towers, so you can't get in that way. And even if you do miraculously manage to get past the security, you have no idea what the internal layout of the compound is. Plus, your objective is to acquire four artifacts that may or may not exist, and if they do exist are stored who knows where."

"I understand. So what's the trouble part?"

Starfield scowled then burst out laughing. "With that kind of attitude you might just pull this off."

"I intend to. Not quite sure *how* I'll do it, but I *will* succeed. There isn't a secure enough facility in the Sphere to keep me out." Isen sobered. "Seriously though, I know this is going to be a tough mission, probably the toughest yet. I don't know if the artifacts Legan wants will be where he expects them to be, but if they are I'll find them and get out in one piece."

The pair stopped at a small lift shaft at the end of a particular hallway and Isen stepped in while Starfield remained in the hallway. "I know you will Isen. I've got money riding on it. Good luck."

"Thanks," he said pushing the sole button in the meter wide lift. The curved door slid shut and Isen felt a small jolt as the lift started to rise. Small vertical glass slits flickered as level-marking lights flashed by as the lift traveled toward Katara's surface at a dizzying speed. After a long 20 seconds the lights slowed and the lift eventually stopped.

The door slid aside and Isen walked out into a surface hangar whose egress/ingress hatch dome was sealed tight.

"Agent Tyrel?" a Morning Dawn mechanic dressed in nondescript clothing asked.

"That's me," Isen answered stepping toward the bearded man.

"Your ship is prepped for launch," he said, then pointed to a triple hauled craft resting on a nearby pad. "She's the red Sunray on pad 3. When you're ready we'll open the dome. Just make sure to keep your engines in standby until you're clear of the building. We don't want any of the other ships getting knocked around."

"Will do. Are the coordinates preset?"

He nodded. "Did it myself 15 minutes ago."

"Well then I guess it's time for me to get going. Have your people clear the area. I'll send a confirmation signal when I'm clear of the dome."

The mechanic acknowledged him with a curt nod then began clearing the deck. Isen continued on towards his oversized starfighter and climbed aboard through the starboard hatch. After closing the hatch behind him he removed his pack and placed it gently on the floor. He walked forward along the spacious interior and seated himself in the lone pilot's chair in the cockpit.

He strapped himself in using a two piece harness that buckled over his chest and allowed his arms to remain untethered. Isen then brought up a diagnostic of his sunray that showed all systems operational and in good repair. Bringing his engines online but still in standby, he looked out the cinematic viewport at the now clear hangar deck.

All of the techs had retreated behind a protective barrier while the mechanic he'd spoken with stationed himself at the communications console built into a wall niche. With a flick of a switch, Isen started his ships IS drive core charging so he would be able to make the jump to his target system as soon as he reached an upper orbit. Before powering up the repulsor lift coils Isen activated his tactical overlay and brought his weapons and shields online, also on standby.

Gripping the control stick lightly but firmly, Isen stabilized his ship as he fed power to the lift coils and brought his red sunray up slightly to hover a meter and a half off the ground. Reaching to the control console, Isen pressed a specialized button directly below the shield controls. When he did, the shield indicator changed from green to gray but no other noticeable changes occurred that Isen could see.

However, from the techs' point of view the hovering sunray suddenly disappeared from sight a moment after Isen activated it's cloaking device.

Isen waited patiently as the mechanic then slowly opened the hemispherical dome covering the hangar. When the dome had completely retracted into the building, Isen fed power to the lift coils and floated out the top of the dome. Once clear of the building and after making sure there was no nearby traffic that might accidentally collide with his ship, Isen sent a short pulse on a rarely used comm frequency and received an almost immediate reply form the hangar, signaling that they knew he was clear.

Isen then turned his attention to navigating his way through the heavy traffic common to a capitol system both on the surface and in orbit. He weaved his way between vessels that were oblivious to his presence and eventually reached orbit.

After meandering his way out of the space lanes he checked his console and found the IS drive fully charged. He then called up the coordinates for the planet that housed Peace Core's headquarters. After aligning his ship with the glowing indicator on his viewport, Isen took a moment to check his scope, making sure the area was clear of other ships, then engaged the IS drive which jumped his sunray into IS space.

Once he confirmed that he was on the right heading, Isen unstrapped himself and walked to the back of the ship where he had dropped his pack. Taking out the clear, palm sized tube, he dumped the biotech liquid onto his left hand and watched as the tube dissolved and the black goo spread over his body, then transformed into a flexible, but well armored combat jumpsuit.

With a touch of his collar, goo rose up and covered his head save for his eyes. Isen then activated the built in view screens and began to familiarize himself with the suit's systems.

He had a long trip ahead of him and when he arrived at Peace Core headquarters he intended to know the biotech system inside and out.

Chapter Twenty-Two

S tanding at the control console in Alpha Prime's ground based command station, General Legan shook his head in disgust. "What is it now Senj?"

"Apparently some of the shipping crates were mislabeled and the equipment got mixed up. Administrators Arus and Sico are arguing over who owns what and have stalled their units' operations until the disagreement is resolved."

"Would you please tell the fish and game wardens," Alec said angrily, "that Administrators are supposed to operate in conjunction with one another, not be at each other's throats. Then instruct them to assemble the mislabeled equipment in," he glanced over his shoulder at the holographic map on his right, "sector 47 by tomorrow morning and I'll be there to sort things out. However, we can't afford to have the agricultural and aquacultural units shut down. Tell them to restart their operations immediately and make sure they understand that's an order, not a suggestion."

"Yes sir," Senj replied before moving to the communication console.

"One more thing Senj. I have to fly up to the command station and report in to Admiral Plescal. You're in charge until I get back."

"Understood."

Alec left the mobile command station's bridge bulge and made his way to his day quarters on a lower deck of the ship. "Lights," he called out into the darkened room.

The lights snapped on and Alec walked across the small living area and into his bathroom. He shaved the unusual amount of stubble that had somehow found its way to his face without him noticing, then took a quick shower before changing into a fresh uniform. Once he had secured the clasps on his polished, knee high boots securely around his calves, Alec grabbed his datapad and rushed out the door.

After a minute's walk through the bowels of the ship he reached the external ramp and strode down to his starmaster, which was nestled in beside the mammoth command ship. Alec pulled the cockpit hatch open, picked up his helmet from the seat, and plopped down into the well cushioned command couch.

He placed the helmet on the cockpit floor between his legs. He wasn't wearing a flight suit and didn't really need the helmet unless he got jarred around enough to bang his head against the wall, which didn't have a very good chance of happening on a quick flight up to the mid orbit command platform where Admiral Plescal was waiting for him.

Alec ran through the startup procedures in short order, then lifted his ship steadily off the ground until he was well above the command ship. Then he kicked in his three Trencor II thrust engines and rocketed up towards orbit at a high rate of ascent, far faster than he needed to, but it felt good to feel the acceleration push him back into his seat after a long morning playing bureaucrat. The IDF then automatically kicked in and the inertial pressure dissipated.

Activating his sensors, Alec located the command platform and readjusted his trajectory to intercept it. Soon he received contact from the space traffic controller over the conventional comm frequencies instructing him to approach from the station's lower hemisphere and land in bay 7.

Alec acknowledged the controller then cut communications with a touch of a button. He cut his speed back as he approached the station and dialed down the control stick's sensitivity. He extended his landing gear and retracted the wings before coming to an almost complete stop just outside his assigned hangar bay.

With a gentle yet firm grip on the controls, Alec glided the starfighter through the open hangar doors, let himself be directed to an open slot by means of automated guide lights, then touched down on the deck. The fighter bounced slightly as its landing gear compressed to counter the increased weight before settling to a complete stop.

Alec powered down the engines and the rest of the ship's functions before popping the top hatch and pulling himself on top of his ship. He was about to slide down the fighter's curved side and drop to the ground, but stopped short as a tech quickly rushed a wheeled ladder over to his fighter.

Alec stepped down two rungs, placed his heels on the outside struts, and let himself slide the rest of the way to the floor. His boots clicked on the hangar deck when he landed but the sound was drowned out by the perpetual commotion of techs and mechanics pulling apart, retooling, and putting back together various ships and offloaded equipment in preparation of the main fleet's arrival.

As Alec headed toward the hangar exit he navigated around a welder, hoping his uniform wouldn't catch any stray sparks. After successfully avoiding burning any holes in his gray uniform he stepped into the adjacent hallway, letting the doors slide shut behind him and muffle the maintenance racket.

Leaving the noise behind entirely, Alec walked down the hall to his right until he found a lift shaft which he took to the upper command level. After finding the Admiral's office empty, he traveled to the center of the command level and climbed a short flight of stairs as he mounted the upraised central command center, a larger version of Alec's ground based command center. Sitting in the central command chair, Admiral Plescal waved him forward.

"Come in General."

"I thought we would be meeting in your office."

"Sorry about that. We've been busy up here lately."

Alec waved away his apology. "It's the same way on the surface. Unfortunately there's no easy way to rush development, so we're stuck overseeing all the details at light speed."

"I'm afraid I must agree with you. Our orbital operations have kept me and my staff working in shifts around the clock trying to orchestrate this mess. We're making unbelievable progress but I think our nerves are wearing thin."

"In that case," Alec said, pulling the datapad out of his pocket and removing the datacard, which he handed to Plescal, "I'll not waste anymore of your time. This is the progress report you asked for. As far as surface operations are concerned Phase 3 is complete, all Supply Core units are now at minimal production capacity and the refugee cities are 73 % complete."

"Excellent General. Our orbital facilities are still in Phase 2, but we have managed to get the mining station operational. Administrator Nartalo has asked for permission to start mining the first of three asteroid fields in this system and I've decided to let him loose. There's no point in holding up his operations until the other units catch up. I instructed him to wait until you could arrange an escort for his ships, not that I think they're in danger, but it would help if someone's out there to play traffic cop. I also imagine a number of your squadrons could use some additional flight hours."

"Yes they could, especially Sentinel squadron. I've had them dirt bound sorting through cargoes for the past few days. How soon does Nartalo want to move?"

"He's ready now. I gave him orders to wait for your fighters to load onto his ships before he microjumps to the asteroid field. In addition to getting some extra flight hours I want you and whoever you take with you to make sure he gets his equipment deployed safely. You might have to shoot down some stray asteroids until he activates his debris screens."

"I don't think any of my pilots will object to a little target practice. Firing off a few rounds ought to do them some good." He considered. "How many ships is Nartalo taking?"

"18 I believe."

"In that case I'll take Talon squadron along too. That'll give each of Nartalo's ships at least one escort."

"Talon squadron is based on this station correct?"

"Yes they are. I'll have to call up the Sentinels from the ground though. If you don't mind Admiral, I'll start bringing up my people right away."

"Please do General. How long should I tell the Administrator he'll have to wait?"

"I can have my people on his ships in less than an hour."

"I'll pass that message on then. Happy flying."

42 minutes later Alec's ships were aboard three of Nartalo's Delta class transports, each half the size of the

Perseverance, when they made a microjump further out into the system which lasted less than a second.

Now dressed in a gray flight suit that matched the helmet that he now wore, Alec pulled his fighter out of the *Ralrook*'s cargo bay and took up position above the ship and waited for Sentinel squadron to form up on him as Talon squadron began to assemble to port. He could barely see the asteroid field ahead of him in the distance without the aid of his tactical overlay, which highlighted the nearest asteroids a pale blue. Below him the transports formed themselves into a single file line then began to move forward.

Alec matched their speed and course as a secondary monitor flashed to life with a diagram of the asteroid field and a highlighted region straddling the edge of the asteroid field. Nartalo's voice crackled over the newly active comm channel.

"General Legan, this region is where we're going to establish our outpost, if you would, please clear the are of debris."

"Administrator, are you sure you want to be that close to the heart of the asteroid field?"

"We have to be if we want to get at the largest asteroids. Once we get our defense screens up and running the smaller asteroids won't give us any problems. But we do need the immediate area clear of debris before and during setup."

"Understood Administrator. Keep your ships at least five klicks from the edge of the field until we're done with our sweep."

"Will do General. *Ralrook* out."

Alec punched a few commands into the starboard command console before activating his comm unit. "Ok Sentinels, Talons, I just sent you the dimensions and coordinates of the area that needs cleared of annoying rocks, so power up your weapons and let's move in."

Complying with his own orders, Alec punched his throttle up and jetted toward the field.

"Talons, take the port half. Sentinels, we have the starboard. Split up by pairs and let's reek some havoc on some rocks."

"Affirmative General," Talon Lead confirmed.

Alec switched to the personal comm channel he shared with his wingman. "Senj, you have lead. I'll pick up whatever pieces you drop."

"Copy Lead," Senj said as he pulled past him.

Alec dropped his fighter in on his tail and followed him into the sparse region of the asteroid field. His wingman's accurate blasts left little for Alec to pick up, but he did get to fire a few shots off. The first live shots he'd fired since his last trip to the Norkel firing range seven months earlier. All training exercises after that had been in simulators. He hadn't even fought in a powered down space brawl. The frustration of the past few weeks of ground work on Alpha Prime disintegrated much like the jagged hunks of rock that passed through his sights.

The more imagined than felt vibrations reverberating through his control stick were a welcome change to his keypad weary fingers as he triggered blast after blast of laser fire at asteroids Senj passed up as they entered a more dense region of the field. His wingman slowed and drifted to port, allowing Alec to take lead, which he did with more than just a touch of eagerness.

With Senj dropping in on his tail, Alec let loose with his triplet of laser cannons sprouting blue laser fire, connecting with nearly all of the ever growing asteroids he targeted. The couplet continued to switch off throughout the 22 minutes it took to clear the desired region of foreign objects.

After Alec ordered in the transports and assigned each of them an escort to pick off any asteroids they might have missed his content smile faded as he looked at his scope. "Senj, take a look at your sensors. Do you see what I see?"

"Fraid so boss. What do you want to do?"

"We have to move everybody out." Alec toggled a switch on his comm unit. "Administrator, I'm going to need you to pull your people back out of the area. We have a dense cloud of asteroids traveling on a vector that will bring them right through the space you're occupying."

"We've already deployed some of our equipment."

"Then undeploy it."

"We can't. The systems are on automatic deployment and it's a one time shot. Once it's deployed the only way to move it is to dismantle it."

Alec thought for a moment. "Senj, do you have a full complement of torpedoes on board?"

"You're not serious?"

"Dead serious."

A long pause followed and at last Senj answered. "Oh, why not. You only live once. Yeah, I'm full. We going in alone?"

"That field doesn't exactly invite a crowd."

"Administrator, get you equipment on line and your defense screens up as soon as possible. Move all other ships out of the asteroids' path. We'll keep them off you as long as possible."

"General, we'll never be operational in time. Our sensors are just starting to show the field and it's just moving too quickly."

"Just do it. Every second you waste could cost you your life. Legan out," Alec finished as he swung his starmaster around and headed toward the asteroid field with Senj following in his wake. "Sentinels, Talons, Senj and I are going to try to divert this swarm, and if we can we'll kick up some other rocks in your direction. Knock as many of them down as you can."

Alec turned his fighter slightly to the left, heading directly for the moving swath as they neared the first of the asteroids. "Ok Senj, you ready?"

"Now or never Alec. Let's go. You've got lead."

"Pull power from your aft shields and channel it into your forward shield," Alec ordered, toggling with the shield controls. "Pull power from your engines too, we can't maneuver in that field at full speed anyway."

"Copy Lead."

Alec began to weave between asteroids as he entered the uncleared area with his tactical overlay now highlighting the quartet of monster sized rocks that were pulling the swarm along.

"Senj, we're going to have to split up. I'll take starboard, you go to port. Make sure you clear your line of fire before popping the asteroids."

"What asteroids? All I see are small moons."

Alec had to smile at that, even given the dire situation. "Before you pop the moons then. We'll need to fire in tandem in order to catch most of the...ankle bitters," Alec said as he let himself get a little too close to a particular chunk of rock before evading.

"30 seconds to range," Senj informed.

Alec now had to focus entirely on his flying to avoid running head on into one of the numerous rotating boulders in front of him. His shields would protect him from a minor collision but even the slightest bump could send him off course and end up getting him sideswiped by one or more of the pitted rocks.

The 30 seconds seemed to take 30 minutes to pass before the particular quartet of asteroids were within his firing range. Immediately Alec let loose with numerous splinters of blue energy that vaporized all but the largest of the objects in his path. His shields sparked as pieces of disintegrated rock poured over his ship like a fountain of sand.

Soon his lasers began to chew into the nearest of the large asteroids, barely touching its surface at this distance. He continued firing to make sure his line of fire was clear of obstacles. Out of the corner of his eye he saw a sprinkling of blue fire and small explosions.

"Senj, you ready," Alec said still spraying laser fire ahead.

"I'm ready."

"Fire all eight torps on my mark, then turn tail and head back to the squadron or any where else you can get out of this field."

"Understood Lead. Standing by."

"Fire," Alec said as he lifted his finger from the laser trigger and pressed his thumb down on the torpedo trigger eight quick times then weaved his fighter through a 180 degree turn and headed out of the asteroid field with Senj's ship mirroring his own.

Alec's torpedoes impacted one by one onto the surface of the first asteroid, blowing chunks off but failing to destroy it. Likewise seven of Senj's torpedoes impact on his target asteroid. The 8th prematurely detonated when it got clipped by another, smaller asteroid, spraying the nearby rocks in all directions.

While knowing the torpedoes probably wouldn't destroy the asteroids, Alec had hoped to divert them away from the convoy. When the torpedoes impacted, they sent both asteroids backward into their companions. The four asteroids and their companion swarm rammed into each other, slowing their momentum and redirecting their course. Alec's asteroid actually fused with its counterpart and began a slow spin, picking up numerous craters from smaller asteroid collisions.

While the larger asteroids were no longer an immediate threat, the torpedoes had sent debris in all directions from their impact point, including back at the convoy. Alec and Senj successfully escaped the asteroid field with only a minor loss of shield power on both vessels. They passed by the two squadrons arrayed to pick apart the incoming swath of rocks and circled back around to join them.

"Lead, next time you come up with a plan like that find yourself a new wingman."

"If I ever think of doing something like that again, just shoot me on site."

"Don't think I won't."

"Alright, we've swallowed the mouthful. Now let's pick up the crumbs."

When the debris cloud entered firing range, 72 laser cannons rained blue fire on the approaching rocks and vaping them on the spot. After a few minutes of mop up work the threat was neutralized.

"Good work Sentinels, Talons. I guess we got some action out here after all."

"General Legan, our defense screen is now active. We should be able to handle what little of the debris field you left intact. Also, our sensors show that one fragment of the larger asteroids will pass in our direction, but now that our systems are up and running we should be able to deal with anything the field can throw at us."

"Good to know Administrator. We're going to hang around until you complete your setup operations but when you're finished we'll need a lift back to the command station."

"Our pleasure General. And thanks."

"You're welcome. Legan out."

Alec then sunk down into his seat letting out a long sigh. *That was too close. This field should have been thoroughly scouted before we moved in. Somebody's oversight nearly got Nartalo and his men killed. Not too mention Senj and me.*

Alec forced himself to laugh as his hands began to shake. *I guess I'll keep this day as a reminder why we need to stay sharp at all times. Thanks for the endless training sessions Pop. I owe you big time.*

Chapter Twenty-Three

T he swirling vortex of color visible through the forward viewport dissipated into a starlit background as Cara Venture's starmaster dropped out of IS space into the Hedron system, home to the Kataran Republic archives which she would soon be attempting to infiltrate.

But before Cara could do that she had to land on Hedron III undetected. That would be some feat considering the intricate traffic control system in place to handle the vast number of ships flocking to the near utopia conditions on the library world. The only planet in the Human Sphere that had been immune to the previous civil wars, Hedron III was unofficially off limits to militaristic campaigns lest they destroy the centuries old records contained, not only in the archives, but throughout various academic installations spread throughout the planet.

The hands off policy, plus the tropical climate and crystal clear oceans, also made Hedron III into quite the tourist magnet, so it was no surprise to Cara that well over 2000 vessels now orbited the planet. She herself had come out of IS space beyond the orbit of Hedron III's solitary moon, well beyond the sensor range of the traffic control satellites in low orbit.

Activating her quartet of Trencor II thrust engines, Cara throttled up to 10 % and headed for the nearest of the satellites at something akin to a slow crawl for spacecraft. Her starmaster's stealth armor would shield her from the satellite's sensors, but the armor wouldn't do a bit of good if her ship's ion trail was picked up.

Keeping her fighter pointed directly at the satellite to cover as much of her low power ion trail as she could, Cara flicked on overhead switch that brought some of Zephrim's special equipment online. Nearing the satellite, Cara cut her engines and let her ship continue to drift forward. When her range finder dipped under five klicks Cara hit the recently installed activation button and waited.

A few moments later a soft green light on the console blinked on, informing Cara that Zephrim's virus had been inserted into the traffic control net and as far as it was concerned her ship didn't now, nor ever would exist.

Throttling up to 80% power Cara began her descent to the planet, following the prescribed space lanes so that if any human eyes spotted her drive glow they shouldn't be able to single her out from the other ships heading to the surface. She followed the line of tourist traffic down into the atmosphere before veering off toward an uninhabited section of jungle.

There she found a small lake and took the opportunity to fly beneath the dense, dark green canopy. Cara maneuvered underneath the tree cover and landed her ship a good half kilometer from the edge of the lake. Taking a quick glance at her infrared sensors she noted the presence of some not so small wildlife outside the fighter. For the moment they appeared to be keeping their distance, but she knew that wouldn't last long. *Looks like I'm going to have some target practice.*

After shutting down the fighter's systems Cara opened the hatch and pulled herself out onto the cockpit roof. She then poked her upper body back into the cockpit and folded the back of her seat forward and down to expose the small equipment trunk that held her gear. After appropriating her stash, Cara pulled herself out of the cockpit and sealed the hatch.

Lowering herself to a seated position, Cara placed a hip against the top of the curved section of the hull, pushed off, slid down the side of the starmaster, and dropped to the ground in a crouch while managing to keep her delicate equipment from hitting the soggy ground. She visually scanned the immediate area to make sure none of the critters were too close, which they weren't, yet.

Gently laying her pack on the ground, Cara pulled out a gun belt, which she fastened around her narrow waist, followed by a pair of blastech pistols that rested comfortably on either hip. Fitting the ergonomically designed pack across her shoulders she started her seven kilometer trek towards the nearest settlement.

Traveling directly opposite the lake, Cara trudged her way through the vegetation darkened undergrowth which was surprisingly sparse due to the oppressively thick canopy. On what seemed like clockwork timing Cara annoyingly dispensed with small predators by means of a number of ruby red bolts from her blastechs. She shot down most of the predators fairly easily but one in particular made it within a meter of her before she drilled what passed as a forehead on the clawed, 80cm high biped. That close encounter left Cara in a nervous sweat throughout the rest of her cross country trip that seemed to her to take days, not just a few hours.

When she emerged from the tree line at the edge of a small river that separated wilderness from civilization, Cara caught a cool breeze coming off the water. She touched her exposed fingertips into the tranquil water and flinched. *It's ice cold. Just my luck, this stream must flow out of an underground aquifer. I'm going to freeze my tail off.*

She pulled her pack off her back, closed the watertight seal, and held it above her head as she stepped into the semiclear water. Gritting her teeth against the cold so they wouldn't chatter, Cara wadded a third of the way across the river before stepping off into nothingness.

Her head dipped under the water but she held onto her pack and kicked her way to the surface. She coughed and sputtered until all of the freezing water was out of her mouth as she swam in place. *Stupid Cara, stupid.*

After swimming across the deep section of the river she fought against the numbing cold pervading her muscles. Before hypothermia could get a grip on her, she touched the bottom of the riverbed and waded up onto the shore where she crouched and managed to keep from collapsing. *Alright, my jumpsuit will dry itself out but I have to keep moving for sake of body heat, this sun won't last long. Now, where am I?*

Cara scanned the legion of buildings in front of her, the nearest being some 500 meters distant across a reed like grass field that appeared to end at a low permacrete wall. Off to her right was an extremely large complex that overlooked all but two of the buildings in sight, and those two resembled vertical needles, nothing compared to what Cara immediately identified as the Kataran Republic's archive facility.

Not wasting any time, Cara settled her wet pack back on equally wet shoulders and began to drag herself though the waist high reed grass toward the section of wall nearest the archive building, which now eclipsed Hedron III's setting sun. She moved slowly, conserving what little energy the river hadn't drained from her body. The sharp reed grass tried to slice into her legs but her jumpsuit's specially designed fabric was impervious to their sharp edges. *At least this grass will keep those critters off me. And that's if they can swim.*

She failed to suppress a shudder that was half physical and half mental. *I'm not looking forward to the return trip through that jungle.* Cara forced a smile through teeth that were all but chattering. *I'll bet the tourist information center left those things off the holographic brochure.*

After wading through the grassy field for a good 15 minutes, Cara reached the low wall just as the sun dipped below the horizon. Removing her pack and crouching behind the wall, she pulled out and unfolded an arms length, thick scoped rifle, which she pointed into the wall and fired.

A 12 cm long needle hook embedded itself half way into the permacrete leaving the ringed portion of the hook exposed. Cara pulled a clip from her pack and slapped the high tensile wire package into the underside of the rifle. She pulled a circular connector from the bottom of the newly inserted clip and latched it to the hook in the wall.

Taking another of the needle hooks out of her pack she reloaded with the wire package automatically attaching itself to the now chambered hook. Cara unfolded the short tripod from the underside of the rifle and rested it on top of the chest high wall before scoping out the archive facility.

From what Cara could tell the facility had two different roof levels. Cara counted 32 stories to the main rectangular roof that had smaller blocky extensions sprouting off each end which gave the building a stubby H shape. From the center of the H extended a three story high windowless cube. On the roof of the cube rested a mass of communications towers that all had blinking red lights.

Cara scoped out a particular spot on that cubical structure about three meters above the main roof as her target, but held her fire. She waited until the last traces of sunlight disappeared and the stars began to shine then placed her eye back to the stationary rifle resting on top of the low wall when the first of the night's chilly breezes hit her. Though most of her jumpsuit had dried quickly enough, moisture remained to make her shudder from head to toe.

She steadied herself as much as she could then pulled the hair trigger, spitting the needle hook up towards the not so near building where it, like its counterpart on the wall, embedded itself into the permacrete. The rifle pulled the wire tight then spit out the cartridge which hung near the base of the wire, connecting the two sections.

Cara dismantled both the tripod and the rifle back into their convenient carrying size and placed them into her pack. She then removed a gripbar which sported a small mechanical pulley that she attached to the wire.

Pulling on her pack again, Cara climbed over the wall then grabbed the gripbar with both hands. On the touch of a button she slowly began to rise along the wire.

Only minutes before, the setting sun would have given her a rather obvious silhouette, but now she rose to the roof in darkness with the city lights below her and the dim starlight above as the only illumination. A quarter of the way up her hands began to go numb. A spark of fear flashed in her eyes before she could force it down.

Redoubling her effort, Cara closed her eyes and focused on nothing but holding on to the grip bar. The higher she went the more the cold wind cut through the wet spots on her jumpsuit, but she barely noticed it. All her attention was on her grip.

As she neared the rooftop, faint red highlights washed across her face and hair from the now very large warning lights on the communication towers. Soon she felt a jolt and released the assent button while holding in on the break, stopping her as she brushed up against the wall. Cara opened her eyes and looked down, making sure she was over the roof before dropping from the gripbar to the rooftop's metal plates.

For a moment she rubbed her hands together to bring back enough feeling to open her pack. Cara then took out a small case that contained her green sunglasses. Normally sunglasses aren't very effective when there's no sunlight, but these specs served a different purpose.

Cara put on the sunglasses with the wrap around side clips pressing snuggly against her head, just above the ears. *Now, if the blueprints are accurate there should be a shallow air duct in*, she pointed to her immediate right, *that direction*.

Bringing her slightly less numb hand up to the side of her head, Cara tapped an almost invisible button activating the sunglasses' X-ray mode. Not finding anything at first glance, Cara began walking across the rooftop with the wind biting at her now completely dry jumpsuit. Carrying her pack in a one handed grip she searched the immediate area and found nothing.

Starting to become concerned, Cara continued forward hoping she hadn't made a mistake. The air duct was her best option for entering the facility undetected, and she didn't feel like having to come up with another plan on the spot.

After a few more steps the air duct suddenly came into view, approximately two meters beneath the rooftop. Cara followed the duct, dodging between all kinds of equipment protruding out of the roof, most of which were no more than a meter or two tall. After following the duct through the miniature rooftop cityscape Cara finally reached her entry point: A meter high air vent covered by a thick grate.

Cara tapped the button on her glasses, disengaging the X-ray scan and activating an electrical current locator overlay. In front of her on the vent appeared thin lines overlapping the grate with one line leading down into the building itself. Cara smiled. *Sometimes the obvious is the best way to go.*

Circling around to the side opposite the thin tendril leading into the building, Cara switched her glasses back to normal vision but in doing so passed through the infrared setting and caught a glimpse of a large heat bloom. She extended her hand over the grate and felt a good amount of heat.

Cara mentally shrugged. *At least I won't be cold any more.*

She lowered herself to her knees and pulled out a handheld plasma torch from her pack. Instinctively she glanced to either side. *I hope nobody see this. At this height I'm out of most of the buildings' line of sight, save for those two towers.* Cara set herself. *I guess there's only one way to find out.*

Flicking on the torch, Cara began to cut into the 3 cm thick side panel of the vent, bypassing the security alarms altogether. Even with the top of the line torch it took Cara a little more than seven minutes to cut a hole big enough for her to climb through. Pulling the freshly cut section of panel out onto the rooftop, trying to make as little noise as possible, Cara felt a wave of heat flow over her body, chasing away some of the lingering numbness in her limbs.

Grabbing her pack, she entered the air vent and smoothly dropped to the horizontal duct two meters below. She touched her glasses again and activated the night vision mode. The duct was, like the vent, a square tube one meter wide and high and forced Cara to crawl on her hands and knees, pushing her pack along in front of her.

After only a couple of minutes in the duct she was sweating profusely. Swiping a sleeve across her forehead, Cara continued to crawl through the duct before she came to a T-junction.

Stopping at the T, Cara pulled a datapad from her pack and called up a schematic of the air conduit system. She found her position shortly and mentally recorded the next few turns so she wouldn't have to pause as often. While Cara hoped her torchlight had gone unnoticed, she wasn't willing to risk her life on that assumption. The faster she moved the more distance she could put between her and the cut air vent, as well as anyone who might discover it.

Making a right turn she headed toward the center of the building beneath the upraised block structure on the building's roof. Cara encountered two more intersections, making another right, then left, before arriving at a vertical shaft. She looped a safety strap from her pack around her wrist then pulled out four magnetic couplers, two for the wrists and two for the knees.

After securely fastening them in place Cara turned about in the cramped tunnel and slowly started feet first down the shaft. Letting her pack hang from her right wrist, she climbed down the shaft wall, first only moving a few centimeters at a time but as she became more accustomed to the motion she began to develop a rhythm that brought her to the next horizontal shaft fairly quickly.

Carefully climbing into the new shaft, Cara cringed when she caught a glance of how deep the shaft went. After she was safely in the new air duct she swiped more sweat from her face then started crawling again.

Still wearing the magnetic couplers, Cara crawled through an ever increasing number of intersections as she moved throughout the 31st floor. Eventually she came to another vertical shaft but paused a moment to catch her breath. Sweat soaked from head to toe, Cara sat with her back against the too warm wall and tried to breath evenly in the extremely humid air.

Pull it together Cara, we've still got a long way to go, she told herself. Pulling out her datapad, she rechecked her position. *Ok, two more floors. That's not so bad.* She laughed in spite of herself. "Problem is it gets worse from there."

Dragging herself to her knees she once again turned around and headed feet first into the vertical air duct. This time however, she didn't stop off on the next floor. Instead, she passed by the ducts above the 30th floor and got off on the 29th floor's ducts. Resting a moment before crawling again, Cara reactivated the X-ray mode on her sunglasses and got an entirely new perspective of her surroundings.

Above and below her she saw rows of offices and the hallways connecting them. A few faint images moved about in precise patterns through the hallways which she assumed were security guards given that is was night and most, if not all employees would be at home by now. She followed the blurry images down the hall until they became too faint, then she reluctantly started crawling again. Two turns later she finally spotted her target: a lift shaft running perpendicular to her air duct.

Cara crawled in front of the section of wall adjacent to the lift shaft and studied her X-ray scan closely. As far as she could tell there was about a 15 cm space separating the air duct and the lift shaft.

Switching over to electrical scanning she noted that there was a power line to her near left that she would have to avoid but it didn't look like it would be much of a problem. Cycling through the various modes on her glasses to give her a more complete picture of the wall she was now facing, Cara mentally planned out where she would cut then returned to the night vision mode and dug into her bag once again.

Pulling out the hand held torch, she adjusted the controls to produce a very fine plasma flame. Before turning it on Cara moved her pack out of the way and repositioned herself as far away from the wall as she could. *It's hot enough in here already and the plasma torch is just going to make it worse. Oh well. The sooner I get through this wall the sooner I get out of this heat.*

Taking a deep breath of the hot, humid air, Cara closed her eyes for a moment. She exhaled slowly, clearing and focusing her mind. Cara then lit the torch and began cutting.

Chapter Twenty-Four

C utting through the thin metal of the duct wall didn't take Cara too long, but pulling out the wall's innards without cutting through any wires and setting off an alarm took time. After she'd cleared a hole large enough to crawl through Cara began cutting the lift wall and in a few minutes had the freshly cut panel pulled back into the air duct.

Getting her first taste of cool air in more than an hour, Cara carefully climbed into the hole and looked down the shaft. A slight breeze from above prompted Cara to jerk her head back into the hole a split second before a lift car from above came rushing down the shaft.

After catching the breath that she'd suddenly lost, Cara gingerly poked her head back out the hole, just far enough to see the miniscule dot below her that was the vanishing lift car.

Finding the portion of the lift shaft above her clear, she pulled herself out the hole and clung to the side of the wall with the help of the magnetic couplers as she reached back into the hole and pulled out her pack which she awkwardly slung across her shoulders. She maneuvered herself into a depression in the shaft wall that the lift cars shouldn't be able to touch and started her slow descent.

Taking care to make sure she didn't slip up and fall down the dark abyss, Cara passed floor after floor, having to scrunch up against the wall on several occasions to make sure a passing lift car didn't catch her pack and pull her of the wall. *Don't the people here ever sleep? Most ordinary civilians would*

*be at home in bed by now. This place is awfully busy for such a
late hour.*

She continued down the shaft until eventually reaching
level 13, where she carefully pulled off her pack and let it hang
by the safety strap still connected to her wrist. Then she took her
left arm off the wall, reached into her pack, and again brought
out her plasma torch. Once in hand, she continued down a few
meters until she passed over a panel that extended a few
centimeters out into the shaft.

Cara had passed many such panels on her descent but
this one was the one that she wanted. Hoping she had the right
panel, Cara aligned her torch with the maintenance tunnel access
hatch. Sealed years ago when the building had been renovated,
the maintenance tunnel led to a ladder that had traveled the
length of the lift shaft in the depression that Cara had climbed
down in. Now that the ladder was removed there was no need for
the maintenance hatches and therefore they had been sealed off
to prevent anyone from falling down the shaft.

Just as Cara was about to ignite the torch a thought
flashed through her mind. Switching modes on her sunglasses,
Cara scanned the hatch. Immediately glad she'd not cut the
hatch, Cara let out a sigh of relief. *If they've got security systems
on sealed hatches in ladderless lift shafts, then these people are
either paranoid or they've got something to hide. I'm guessing
the latter.*

Cara reached into her dangling pack and switched the
torch for a small, flat metallic strip, 3 cm in diameter and 10
centimeters long. She placed it on the center of the hatch where it
held fast. Hitting the first of three flat buttons, Cara activated the
alarm neutralizing device and waited for the indicator light to
cycle from red through orange and yellow to finally green.

Cara then took out her plasma torch and began cutting
free the sealed hatch. The sealant they'd used was a bit tougher
than she expected but the torch still melted it away from the
hatch after she chose the correct flame intensity. A few minutes
later Cara replaced the plasma torch into her pack and pulled free
the hatch with a hefty tug on the finger holds.

She climbed into the maintenance tunnel then puled
another countermeasure device from her pack and placed it on
the inside of the hatch. She waited for its indicator light to show

green before she reached out into the lift shaft and around to the hatch exterior where she touched the second button.

The device fell neatly into her hand and after pulling herself back into the maintenance tunnel, Cara closed the hatch. She pulled free the second device and placed both of them back into her pack, then headed off down the maintenance tunnel.

Unlike the air vent and lift shaft, the maintenance tunnel was well lighted, so Cara switched her sunglasses back to normal vision. Forced to crawl on her knees once again, Cara pulled herself down the ovoid tunnel. The thick knee and elbow pads saved her joints a great deal of wear and tear plus allowed her to slide a bit down the smooth, narrow floor.

Cara maneuvered through seemingly endless lengths of tunnel and a number of intersections before arriving at the end of one particular tunnel. After confirming her location with a quick glance at the facility's blueprints, Cara adjusted her sunglasses but found no security systems on the hatch. Switching to X-ray mode, she scanned the room on the other side of the hatch and found it clear of all personnel. That was good. Cara didn't like the idea of staying in the cramped tunnels any longer than she had to. Even though she was no longer drenched in sweat, the temperature change had started to cause her to cramp up.

After switching her sunglasses back to normal vision, Cara slowly turned the short handle that released the hatch. She heard a soft click as the latch pulled free of its housing, then pushed open the hatch and climbed out into a maintenance room.

Resembling a fat L, the high ceilinged room was filled with rows upon rows of shelves that contained enough spare parts to keep a warship in good repair for more than a decade. On about half of the shelves sported transparent crates that contained everything from nuts and bolts to meter long sections of pipe. On the other half of the shelves rested pieces of equipment too large for crates.

Cara saw a number of power generators, fluid pumps, large spools of thick wiring, and even an olive green whirlpool. She didn't have a clue what a whirlpool was doing in an administrative building, yet there it was.

After a cursory examination of the room's contents, Cara worked her way along the isles toward the end of the L opposite the hatch that she'd entered through. At the end of the room she found the windowless door that led into the lowest public level of the building.

The first 12 levels of the building housed the archives themselves and were off limits to the general populous. Levels 13 through 32 contained general research facilities and hard copies of all the unrestricted files the archives contained. Also, the upper floors had access to the archives computerized database but the interface terminals were configured so that the public could access *only* the unrestricted records. Cara would have to find a terminal on one of the first 12 floors in order to download the classified files. The problem with that was the first 12 levels were crawling with guards. The lifts in the building had been redesigned to go no lower than the 12th level where they opened into a small foyer that contained two large metallic security doors and a least six armed sentries. Those two doors were the only way in and out of the restricted levels and required a passcard, retina scan, and personal password from the small number of select people with access to the files. Admiral Legan himself didn't have access, thus resulting in Agent Venture's mission to acquire the files before the fleet left the Human Sphere.

I know these records are important, but what could be so vital that Kataran Intelligence wouldn't let the Supreme Commander in on? she thought to herself as she scanned beyond the maintenance room door. *This is going to be tricky. If any of these techs spot me, or let alone one of the guards, I'll be lucky to get out of here alive.* She forced herself to focus on the task at hand and as she did so she let out a long sigh, relaxing her tired muscles.

Ok, Cara. You've gotta be sharp. Time for a game of cat and mouse. You've been through worse in training before, so just stay cool and you'll get through this.

She pulled out her datapad and checked the route she had developed from the surveillance reports of the few Midnight Star agents that Admiral Legan had recon the civilian levels while on 'official business' as the Admiral's personal staff. Their reports laid out the patrol patterns for the scattering of guards on the upper levels and which rooms were normally locked and unlocked. It had taken well over a year to compile that data and Cara intended to put it to good use. The route she had devised was complicated and time critical, but she knew she would be able to pull it off if there weren't too many techs on the level. The guards' movements were predetermined but the techs came and went as they pleased.

As Cara spotted two fuzzy images walking side by side down the near hall, she pulled on her pack and put her hand on the door handle.

Alright, this is it.

Cara waited until the pair rounded a corner before she opened the door, closed it behind her, and ran down the hall in the opposite direction of the guards. 50 meters down the hall she stopped at the corner of a T-junction and extended a straw sized probe emanating from her wrist around the edge of the wall.

An image of the adjacent hallway appeared on her right lens and showed another pair of guards striding away from her down the hallway and beyond the range of her X-ray scans. When they turned into a side hall she took off down the hallway. Her sunglasses showed no people in the nearby offices and she took that as a good sign. 12 seconds down the hallway she found her next stopping point: a small janitor's closet which was locked, as expected.

Cara pulled out a specially designed electronic skeleton key from a wrist pocket and inserted it into the lock. Two seconds later the indicator light went green accompanied by a muffled click. Cara pulled open the door and all but threw herself into the small room. When she shut the door it automatically locked again as another pair of guards stepped into the hallway she had just left.

Mind racing and heart pounding, she waited to the count of 37 before opening the door to find an empty hallway. After quickly closing the door, Cara rounded a nearby corner on down the hall and took off at full sprint. Peripherally she spotted a tech down one of the side hallways and hoped he'd not spotted her. Either way, she was flying down the dark red carpeted floor and all that he would have seen was a black blur. If he chose to take a closer look it would do him no good. She took a left at the next corner, nearly slamming into the far wall as she hardly slowed for the turn. Now that she was in a different hallway the tech would be unable to locate her even if he did catch sight of her the first time.

Cara made two more turns, first a right, then a left, before stopping at another corner and again extending her wrist probe. Seeing that the guards' backs were to her she silently stepped across the intersection and then returned to her fluid gate. At the end of the hall she took a right at the T-intersection and ducked into the 3rd office down the hall on the left, which was unlocked just as the other Midnight agents had reported.

The office was deserted, thankfully. Cara watched through the wall as another pair of guards strode by on their monotonous patrol, though their crisp step suggested that they were still highly alert, even if they were bored out of their minds. She waited till their images vanished from her lenses as the guards walked beyond her scanning range. Silently counting to 20, Cara waited at the door to give the guards enough time to make their turn.

18, 19, now!

Springing out the door, she backtracked a few strides then headed down the opposite hall of the T-intersection. As she ran the 30 meter length of hall, Cara's muscles began to fatigue but she ignored the burning in her legs and rounded the next corner, keeping her speed as constant as she could. After three more hasty turns she slid into another unlocked office and closed the door a split second before two rifle bearing guards turned into her hall.

Breathing quite heavily, Cara leaned her back against the office wall and rested for a moment. *Ok, now for the hard part. I have to time this just right or the whole mission is blown.* Cara watched intently as the guard pair passed by her door without hesitation. *I'll have to remember to thank Zephrim for these specs. I'd be lost without them.*

She braced herself as the moment approached. *This is it.*

The moment the guards rounded the next corner she jumped out the door and ran as fast as her tired legs would carry her down an extremely long hall. When she came to one particular intersection she rounded the corner to the right, stopped, and extended her probe around the corner to look on down the hall. Half a second later a pair of guards appeared in the next intersection on down and immediately disappeared, continuing down the hallway perpendicular to the hall Cara started running down again.

She slowly and quietly stepped across the next intersection, oblivious to the guards, and sped back up. She stopped short two intersection on down and waited for the hallway to her right to clear before continuing on.

Cara ducted left into a T-junction outshoot of her hallway a moment before two pairs of guards passed each other in precise timing at the next intersection on up. Again she took off down the main hallway and this time slipped into the guards' hallway as silently as she could, impatiently scoping out the hallway behind her. It seemed like forever until the pair of guards appearing behind where she had just been running turned off into the T-junction offshoot, leaving her hallway clear again. When it was she gladly continued down the hall, leaving behind the two pairs of guards that failed to detect her though she was only meters behind their backs.

Swerving around another corner farther down the hall, Cara took out her skeleton key on the run. Stopping at the last office before the next intersection, she inserted the key and quickly sealed herself in.

Through the wall she could see another pair of guards coming down the side hallway. She breathed a sigh of relief as they continued past the intersection. *Almost there. This is really getting tiring.* She let out a silent laugh. *No pain, no gain. And in this case no gain means I'm dead in a hurry. I have to hold together for a few more hall lengths, then I can rest a bit.* Cara shook her head to clear it. *I can think things through later, right now I have to concentrate.*

She pulled her wrist probe out, opened the door a crack, and extended it into the hallway and to the left where she saw another pair of guards walking her way. She waited till they rounded a corner before pulling in her probe, fully opening the door, and sprinting down the hallway that the guards had just vacated.

One intersection past theirs she turned to the left then made a right 22 meters on down the hall. She had one 150 meter section of hallway left to run before another left turn would bring her to the final office on her route. Fighting past her ever growing fatigue, Cara pushed herself down the hallway with as much speed as she could manage.

Once again she was drenched in sweat, this time from her own body heat. As she ran little droplets sprayed off her elbows and onto the walls. She felt as if her heart was going to break out of her chest the last 50 meters. Symmetric veins pulsed at the sides of her forehead in rhythm with her quick strides.

Finally she rounded the corner and found the particular office, opening the lock and entering just before two more guards came around the corner on down the hall. The door locked when she shut it behind her as she all but threw herself into the office.

Seeing through the wall that the guards hadn't spotted her, Cara removed her pack and lay it on the floor. She took a knee beside it and began to retrieve her datapad when her breath caught in her throat, stopping her. *That was too close. Good thing I'm in shape or I'd have never made it. Some of the things I do are just plain crazy, but thankfully the crazy things are what people least expect. I guess that's why I'm still alive.* She smiled cockily. *That and the fact that I'm just plain good at this.*

Now that her breathing was under control, Cara took out her datapad and began looking over the building's blueprints once she switched her sunglasses back to normal vision.

Being that the only way into the restricted area was through the well guarded lift foyer, Cara had elected to find another way in. Having to blast her way through armed guards would alert the entire building to her presence and that wouldn't bode well in her attempt to download the files that Admiral Legan wanted so badly. So she had to find an inconspicuous means of entering the lower levels, which brought her to the office she was now kneeling in. *Hard to believe this inconsequential office is my ticket to the lower floors.*

Cara took her first real look at the octagonal room. The farthest side from the door sported a large bookshelf in front of which sat a thick, wide desk, clear of any of the typical office debris. Bracketing the desk and imbedded into the nearest two walls were circular aquariums full of tiny little fish that seemed to glow in the aquarium's light, the only illumination in the room besides Cara's datapad.

The two walls perpendicular to the door were left bare, save for some large potted plants whose greenery seemed to enshroud the room even in the dim light. Directly right of the door sat a large and very expensive holoprojector. It was a floor-based model that would vertically display 2 to 3 meter long images when activated, but for now it was powered down.

The last section of wall contained a shoulder high, antiquated vase decorated in red and gold hieroglyphics depicting the anointment of some mythical king of an equally mythical land. The floor was covered in a very thick and soft, grayish carpet as far as Cara could tell in the dim light. The ceiling was covered in a pattern of ridges, depressions, and bumps that she couldn't identify.

Nice place, but a bit too cozy. Whoever's office this is probably doesn't get much work done. Though I must admit that I'm tempted to lie down and take a short nap, but I know I can't spare the time. The longer I'm here the more the chance there is of my being discovered. I have to move quickly if I'm going to have a chance of completing this mission and getting out of here alive. She started to get to her feet but stopped halfway as her muscles momentarily cramped up. *Then again, if I rush things I'll end up just as dead, only sooner. I have to take this in strides while I recover.*

Cara pulled herself the rest of the way to her feet, stretching out as she did so. She looked again at her datapad and the building blueprints that it displayed. Then she zoomed in on the office that she was currently standing in and took a closer look at the immediate structure. Cara then began digging into her pack for the equipment that she would need.

I guess I better get started.

Chapter Twenty-Five

On approach to the Kataran Republic's mothball shipyard in orbit around Dendo, High Admiral Legan's shuttle thrusted through space by means of a quartet of cylindrical engines that appeared to be strapped to the aft end of the shuttle's boxy hull.

The forward end of the shuttle balled out to form a spherical cockpit while the underside of the sphere sported a pair of starfighter grade laser cannons mounted on a small hemispherical bubble that allowed them to move within a 170 degree firing arc. Though not very useful in battle, the guns seemed to give shuttle pilots some piece of mind in the fact that they weren't flying an unarmed craft and could defend themselves if necessary.

But today the weapons would not be needed. The trip over to the shipyard from the *Republic*-class warship *Rogue*, which Legan used as his flagship, was a routine maneuver in friendly territory, far from the political hotbed of Katara.

Watching out the forward viewport, Legan sat in the third cockpit seat behind the pilot and copilot and marveled at the sight of the shipyard. Never having visited the station himself, Legan discovered that the rumors he'd heard of its size and craftsmanship didn't scarcely do it justice.

Long ago the Republic had created the station, designated Gamma 7, as the sole resting place for all of the Republic's retired warships. Designed as a large, flat oval with both vertical and dorsal bulges at the midpoint, the structure mimicked the dimensions of the galaxy. Gamma 7's entire hull was sculpted into curves, with not one jagged corner on the metallic monstrosity. Well over 40 kilometers in length, the entire mothball fleet was stored *internally*.

All that was visible from the exterior was a wide expansion of bluish gray hull plates punctuated by thin lines of light that would, on closer inspection, reveal themselves to be widely spaced viewports. The bulk of the illuminated viewports concentrated at the rounded peak of the dorsal bulge. The central control center was in itself a small city of techs, mechanics, and historians that diligently restored, then maintained the vessels in the condition that they had seen while in active service.

Fortunately, Aeron Piate and his staff had excelled at their job in the past five years since Legan had appointed Piate, not by accident, to the Gamma 7 administratorial position. They had not allowed a single vessel to deteriorate under their watchful eyes and had replaced and repaired to specs the vessels their predecessors had neglected. Over the past three years Piate and his techs had also done some extra work on a few of the ships at Legan's request, which was the reason the High Admiral was paying a visit.

"Shuttle 375B requesting landing instructions," the copilot called into the comm. "Gamma 7 please respond."

After a moment's hesitation the comm crackled to life. "Shuttle 375B, state your business."

"Gamma 7, this is High Admiral Legan's personal shuttlecraft. The Supreme Commander is here to inspect your facilities."

After another longer pause the flight controller's voice came back a bit more relaxed. "Shuttle, you have landing clearance for hangar bay 76 on the upper hull."

"Bay 76, acknowledged. Shuttle 375B out," the copilot said, flicking off the comm.

The pilot punched a few commands into the navigation console and a vector box appeared on the tactical overlay. Steering the shuttle to port using one of the two control sticks in the cockpit, the pilot centered the vector box on the shuttle's line of sight and began a long approach to the exterior hangar bay assigned by the flight controller.

Maintaining a constant velocity, the shuttle appeared to make little headway toward the station for several minutes until the enclosed shipyard suddenly began to expand and fill the screen. Only when the shuttle's tactical overlay painted a red dot in the center of the vector box did Legan truly comprehend the dimensions of the immense station. His shuttle pilots apparently saw through the optical illusion the same time as he did.

"Wo. Look at that thing," the copilot said.

"I see it Krett. Good thing we have a navigational tie in to the station's flight control system or we'd never find the right hangar," the pilot replied.

Gradually the dot on the viewport grew into a 200 meter wide VIP shuttle bay set on the upper incline of Gamma 7's hull. Just as Legan began to worry, the hangar bay's double doors split on a horizontal bias and retracted into the station's frame, locking into place a few seconds before the shuttle entered the hangar and touched down gently on the polished deck.

After the pilot shut down the shuttle's systems the copilot lowered the starboard ramp. Legan left his seat and began to walk out the back of the cockpit and to the main hold where the ramp exit was when he noticed that the pilots had remained in their seats.

"Go ahead and lock down the shuttle, then find the station's rec room. Consider yourself at liberty for the time being. We're going to be here for a while."

"Yessir," the pilot said gratefully as Legan walked out the back of the cockpit, then down the extended ramp.

When he had walked halfway across the empty hangar the inner door slid aside to reveal a small delegation of the station's personnel. Legan continued walking forward until he met the 5-person group and Piate extended a hand to him. He took it and smiled warmly.

"I was wondering when you would be dropping by," Piate said. "I think you'll be satisfied with our work."

"I'm sure I will be. I must admit, this station is larger than I'd imagined."

"Yes, Gamma 7 does seem to surprise the few visitors we get here with its sheer size, but that's nothing compared to the view of the interior. I'll take you on a short tour in a minute, but first let me introduce you to my senior staff," Piate said, motioning to his four companions.

"On my right is Dr. Cherol, our chief analyst."

Legan took her hand briefly. "Doctor."

"And Torrey Mickain, our resident historian."

Legan settled for a nod to the man standing out of arms reach who returned the gesture.

"On my left is Race Jeritt, our head computer tech, and Gury Fulmor, our chief mechanic."

Legan also extended nods to the two men.

"Now that you've met the people largely responsible for the refits you ordered, we can head on inward to the shipyard. That is, unless you're pressed for time."

"Not at all. I'll be remaining here until the fleet is ready to leave."

"Good, then we'll have plenty of time to talk." Piate waved a hand toward the door leading into the station proper. "This way."

After Piate had taken Legan on a short tour through the city and then the command center, where Piate's companions returned to their posts, the Gamma 7 administrator led Legan to a lower observation deck. When Piate negated the viewports' polarizers the sight before him took Legan's breath away.

Looking out and down into a vast chamber, he saw row upon row of outdated warships stretching for kilometers to both his left and right. Glistening white and gray hulls shone brightly in the light of more than 500 trillion glow panels spaced throughout the artificial cavern. On some of the nearer ships Legan could make out identification numbers that, if he remembered correctly, marked some of the vessels as more than 200 years old.

"Amazing, isn't it?" Piate finally spoke into the silence. "All these warships, gathered together from many a decade, silently waiting for the day when they will once again be called forth into the wilds of space." He looked down at the floor for a moment. "It's sad that they've been consigned to death because people fear their own inhibitions."

"If I wasn't already convinced of what has to be done, this sight would have eradicated any doubt. I've never seen such a concentration of military might before. Even if these ships are antiquated, they could overpower any of the other nation-states' navies. I'm glad this station is so remote, or the senate would have already picked it dry in the name of peace."

"Well, as far they're concerned the ships are all disarmed and have had their primary power cores removed. It's only because they're not aware of our refits that they've let them alone."

"Speaking of which, how many ships do you have space worthy?"

Piate smiled with pride. "All of them."

Legan's eyes went wide for a moment. "All of them?" he repeated. "How did you manage that?"

"I'll admit, it wasn't easy. But I couldn't leave any of these ships behind. I had to call in every favor owed to me, send identical requisitions to different supply depots, squeeze every last credit out of every historical organization in the Republic and some outside as well, and organize a number of equipment misplacements at several of the Republic's storage facilities in order to get everything I needed to bring these warships back to life. I did not compromise on quality though. Every piece of equipment that I begged for, cheated out of, or just plain thieved was top of the line and authentic to each of the ships, save the ones that you wanted upgraded."

"Are you finished with the upgrades too?"

He nodded. "We have some touchup work to do on a dozen or so ships, but it will be completed in the next two or three days."

Legan slowly shook his head. "You've really outdone yourself this time Aeron. I was hoping, but not expecting, that you'd have managed to get half of the ships ready. How you pulled this off I don't have a clue, but I'm glad you did. By the way, did you include all of the ships in the list you sent to Senator Malcolm?"

"No, just the ones we've reconfigured into personnel and cargo transports. The pure warships were left off the list because at the time we hadn't finished refitting them and weren't sure how many we would be able to get ready, so we left them all off. If you're running short on space, there's ample quarters and cargo room in the ships, but you'll have to transfer some extra supplies. We've only got enough onboard for about a 12 man crew."

"It's a tight fit right now but we can make do with the ships on the list. I will have to reassign some of my offices to fly the extra ships though."

"I'm sorry about that. I should have informed you sooner."

"Don't worry about it. I'll gladly trade some paperwork for a few hundred more warships." Legan frowned slightly. "Exactly how well armed are they?"

"We've restored all of the ships, including the ones we've converted into transports, back to their original condition. We did however tinker around with the existing systems and were able to increase their shields and weapon power on an average of 5%. Though we didn't try to restore the ships you specified for overhaul to their original specs. Instead, we took the basic designs and added to them as we saw fit. Those ships are now up to today's standards and then some. We did add extra shield generators to the now transports, even if they didn't fit with the original design. We though it a reasonable upgrade considering the personnel and cargo they will be carrying are going to be essential for your soon to be empire."

"Good idea. I don't plan on fighting any battles on the way out, but if someone does try to stop us having extra protection for our transports makes sense." Legan smiled again. "Well, you seem to be the man with all the good news. Anything else you want to tell me?"

"Actually there is. The *Tenacity* is also finished."

Legan's face blanked for a moment. "I'd almost forgotten. Where is she?" he asked, turning back to the window.

"1st quadrant, row 4, slot 7," Piate said, pointing off to his right.

Legan counted the various slots until his eyes fell on the only colored ship in the entire facility. Painted blood red, his grandfather's former flagship rested motionless up against a horizontal docking pylon that ran half the length of the ship's starboard hull. The triple engine design was unique to the ship and requested specifically by his grandfather when he had decided to build the one of a kind warship during his tenure as Supreme Commander.

"Aeron, that one ship is responsible for saving the Republic in three separate civil wars. It's the antithesis of the twisted pacifist philosophies that have plagued our people the past few years. When my grandfather commanded her, the *Tenacity* was the warship of all warships. She stood for truth and justice. Her mission was to destroy the forces of evil and protect the Republic from ruin. When he died, along with the rest of my family in the avalanche that consumed the ski resort that we had chosen for a family reunion, the *Tenacity* had died with him. Long past her prime, she was decommissioned, discarded like an empty power pack. They shoved her off into some administatorial closet where she was left to waste away. I haven't set foot on her since. I didn't want to see her in such a decrepit condition. I should have died in that avalanche with the rest of my family, but I didn't. Seeing her now, back the way she used to be, makes me think she held onto life all those years because I had lived, and through me my grandfather. And now, by some quirk of fate, the *Tenacity* will once again fly under the command of a Legan."

Aeron stepped beside Legan and put a hand on his shoulder. "I know how much this ship meant to your grandfather and how much it must mean for you. That's why I personally oversaw the refit and upgrades. But unlike the other ships, I went all out on the *Tenacity*. She's the same ship with the same attitude, but ten times as lethal as before. When she was your grandfather's flagship there was no other ship her equal and I've seen to it that it's the same way for his grandson."

Legan looked at him questioningly.

"I spent a tenth of my resources on her alone. My entire staff worked on the redesign and I think you'll like the changes we've made. Pound for pound, she's the strongest and fastest in the Human Sphere. Only the *Goliath* outguns her, and that's because of its sheer size. The *Tenacity* has stronger shields and more potent omnilaser batteries than the *Goliath*, but I also included a revolutionary type of hull armor. I know you had land based, assault vehicle grade armor placed on the *Goliath* and that it was the first major warship to carry such expensive defenses, but the armor I've placed on the *Tenacity* is a different matter altogether. It has the same strength and approximate thickness as the *Goliath*'s, but the kicker is when it's powered up its strength increases exponentially."

"Powered armor? I've never heard of it."

"It's my own design. I worked in the Kataran RnD department for five years. We had experimented with the idea but didn't get very far with it. After I left the department I continued to think on the idea off and on for a number of years until something clicked in my mind. A little oversight we'd made had suddenly become apparent and after I corrected the formula things developed fairly quickly. I didn't have the facilities to actually create the armor until I took over operations here. Then, with the help of my staff, we developed the prototype system a little over two years ago and have been improving it ever since. With the new armor and the other modifications we've made, the *Tenacity* should be able to fight the *Goliath* to a standstill. The *Goliath*'s strengths are its number of guns and thick hull armor, plus it out masses the *Tenacity* three to one. The *Tenacity* has fewer guns, but the guns she does have are more accurate and pack a stronger punch. Her shields and armor are also stronger, plus she's a great deal more agile than the *Goliath*. Though I don't expect it to happen, it would be interesting to see what would happen if the two ships ever went head to head."

"You've really improved her that much?"

He nodded. "I thought that if she was going to sail once again she should sail as the master of the stars like she did in her legendary past."

Legan stared out the viewport at the distant *Tenacity*, his eyes watery. "I owe you a great deal Aeron. I never thought she'd truly be herself again. When I was a year out of the academy I flew starfighters out of her hold. Whenever in her shadow I felt an intimidation that was comforting to her pilots and must have struck fear into our enemies. That intimidation came from the fact that she was the most powerful warship in existence. That was her identity. Without that dominance it would be like trying to fight with your hands tied behind your back."

He looked Aeron straight in the eye. "Thank you for untying her hands. And in some ways mine as well."

"You're welcome, but you don't owe me any debt. When I was a young boy my home planet of Xyrel was invaded by the Levonian Confederation. Our small navy held off the Levonians for a while, but they received reinforcements and began to systematically tear our ships apart one by one. At the time I was on an orbital agrostation on an academy field trip. I watched the nearby battle out a viewport while my classmates hurried to the center of the station, prompted by our teachers, but I snuck away from the group and stayed behind. I figured that if the agrostation came under attack there wouldn't be any safe place to hide, so I might as well watch what was happening."

"I took pride in our military forces as they held off the invaders, but my heart sank when the enemy's reinforcements arrived and our ships began breaking apart or sometimes blowing up in brilliant explosions that rocked the agrostation and knocked me to the ground more than once. The enemy kept getting closer to the agrostation and I knew then and there that I was going to die. One of the enemy cruisers destroyed another agrostation next to ours then reoriented itself on us. Froze with fear, I watched as the cruiser swung its bow around and seemed to point it straight at me. I waited for the explosion, but to my dismay it was the cruiser that exploded. I saw a heavy rain of laser blasts fall upon the cruiser's hull and vaporize hull plates when the blasts shot right through its shields. A wave of torpedoes fell upon the bridge, then the whole ship exploded."

"Still froze from shock, I saw a hunk of the dead cruiser floating towards me, but before my mind caught up with what had just happened a huge red bulk interposed itself between the agrostation and the debris, which bounced off its shields and floated clear of the agrostation. I watched in amazement as the red warship destroyed ship after ship of the enemy's invasion fleet before Kataran reinforcements arrived, which prompted the Levonians to retreat."

"So you see, I owed a debt to the *Tenacity,* which I was glad to repay. You don't owe me anything. I'm just glad you gave me the chance to repay the warship that saved my life." Aeron took on a look of expectation. "So, do you want to go aboard?"

Legan just smiled.

Chapter Twenty-Six

D ropping out of IS space into orbit round Eclicion, Isen activated a small holographic map of the planet which appeared to his immediate left. On the sphere a small dot in the northern hemisphere began to pulse red, indicating the location of the Peace Core Headquarters. With his ship's cloaking field still active, Isen had to get a position fix on the facility using his passive sensors. The scattered settlements across Eclicion had enough of a power output to register on his ship's sensors and allowed his navigation computer to recognize the pattern and overlay it on the holographic map.

Isen punched a few commands into the display console and a small dot appeared at the upper right corner of his viewport, thanks to the tactical overlay. Isen readjusted his heading and brought the dot within a small circle that represented the ship's line of flight. If he stayed on this vector the computer would guide him toward the power signature that it had tagged as Livel, the third largest city on Eclicion.

Once the principle spaceport in the Urius district, Livel was home to many small time traders who used the number of well defined space lanes that intersected at Eclicion to turn a small but adequate profit making cargo runs to a multitude of nearby systems. Several major corporation headquarters had been established in Livel due to the influx of traffic that used the spaceport as a way station between Katara and the coreward districts. At its peak, Livel sported a population of well over 50 million, but recent wars had caused trade routes to shift away from Eclicion. Livel all but dried up as a spaceport for a few decades before the traders had slowly begun to return to the original trade routes, bringing life back to Livel. Though it wasn't the interstellar nexus it had once been, Eclicion had risen from the ashes and become a mediocre, but stable, trade planet. Because Eclicion was somewhat centrally located with short, safe routes to nearby major systems, Livel was the ideal spot for Peace Core to establish its headquarters.

Situated outside the city itself, the headquarters compound was located just north of the city but still within Livel's traffic control airspace. The light but constant traffic in and out of the spaceport that had grown into a city allowed for Peace Core vessels to arrive and depart the compound without drawing too much attention to themselves.

After a bumpy transition into Eclicion's thick atmosphere, Isen maneuvered his ship down and into a shallow canyon southeast of the city. Still cloaked, he set the sunray onto the gravel covered canyon floor and began to power down the ship.

Picking up his equipment bundle, Isen hit the hatch release and was momentarily blinded as the hatch swung open and let the morning sunlight into the dimly lit ship interior. He blinked his eyes several times until they became adjusted to the light, then stepped through the hatch and onto a dry riverbed.

Turning around, he dug into his nondescript bundle and brought out a small transmitter. Isen pressed one of the buttons on the palm sized device and the rectangular side hatch that appeared to be floating in mid air swung shut and closed the open doorway, then disappeared into nothingness as the cloak reabsorbed the hatch. Aside from a slight wavelike disruption where the quartet of landing pads had sunk into the soft ground, there was no indication that there was anything before him but a dry creek bed, let alone a 22 meter long starfighter.

Pulling his bundle over his left shoulder, Isen started walking toward Livel.

Now walking through Livel's streets, Isen's clothing and even his bundle blended in perfectly with the apparel of the average trader/smuggler that the streets were full of. Isen slowly traveled a meandering path through the city as he made his way north toward the Peace Core compound. Walking along reasonably crowded streets, Isen passed underneath the ever constant shadows of Livel's towering buildings that the city's hover traffic wrapped around in an ever flowing grid like pattern.

After a few hours of navigating Livel's permacrete jungle, Isen emerged from Livel's northern border and inconspicuously drifted away from the perimeter buildings and into the nearby underbrush. He walked a kilometer or so north before he came to the edge of the manmade clearing that surrounded the Peace Core headquarters. Keeping his distance from the edge of the clearing, Isen let his bundle slide off his shoulder and gently fall to the ground. He crouched down and pulled out the specialized scanner that Weapons Master Chekei had made for him. He unfolded the scanner's upper sensor array and laid the device on the ground.

With a touch of a button he activated the automated scanning sequence. Isen had prepared to sneak over the compound wall and hope to find another way into the underground facility besides the main entrances. If he couldn't, he'd decided to wait for one of the Peace Core personnel to open the doors and sneak in then. The problem with that plan was that it could be days before a Peace Core vessel arrived or departed. Isen was pretty sure that if he got over the wall he'd be able to gain access to the interior of the compound one way or another, even if it did take him a few days to do so. However, when he'd gone over the scenario in his mind he had discovered another possibility that he'd been reluctant to reveal. The odds of him being correct were slim but, then again, the odds were *always* against him and he'd come out on top before. Besides that, he just had a feeling about the place. It wasn't the kind of feeling you tell others about, but one that prompted you to find out for yourself.

After a few minutes the scanner signaled that its sensor sweep was complete and after checking that he was out of sight, Isen activated the holographic display. He almost laughed out loud as a thin tendril extended from the Peace Core compound toward the city about 50 meters below the surface.

He'd been right. While identifiable Peace Core craft transferred personnel and equipment through the six surface entrances, the nondescript transports that Peace Core used had to move their highly secretive cargoes into the compound by another means. Isen assumed that the line of electrical current that his scanner projected before him came from an underground tunnel that connected the compound to a number of 'civilian' hangars.

With his relief at finding an alternative entry point to the compound, he almost overlooked the massive underground facility that the scanner had discovered.

"There's a lot more compound than our analysts anticipated." He smiled. "It should be interesting to see what they've gone to so much trouble to hide."

Pulling another scanner out of his bundle, Isen scanned the area with conventional sensors then overlaid the results onto the holographic display. The underground portion of the compound disappeared as did the tunnel in the new sensor readings, but they did show the majority of the city's structures. He reconfigured the display to eliminate the electronic signature of the structures he'd scanned with the conventional sensors.

The result was a continuation of the tunnel into the city where it branched off several times to dead end at 17 different positions in the city that glowed before him in white blue lines. Isen pulled out of his bundle a datacard onto which he stored the locations of the 17 docking bays.

Packing up the two scanners, he slid the datacard into a pocket that contained a compatible datapad. Taking one last look back at the Peace Core compound, he started to walk back to the city. When he reached Livel's border, Isen smoothly reintegrated himself into the flow of pedestrian traffic. Traveling in what seemed like a random path, Isen gradually made his way to the portion of the city where the nearest of the 17 docking bays was located.

Pulling the datapad from his pocket, Isen installed the datacard and began a position check as he read a local news story he'd downloaded on his first trip through the city. Even though Isen was still moving, the datapad was able to get a position fix within the city by tapping into the traffic control system's navigational beacons. It then overlaid the map on the datacard and gave a small beep when it had finished its calculations.

Tapping a button on the datapad Isen removed the news story from the display and studied his current position on the map as he carefully wove himself in and out of pedestrian traffic.

256 meters east, 27 meters south, he repeated mentally as he read the range finder.

He looked in that general direction and quickly found his target: a large circular docking bay with a domed roof. A fairly common design.

13 minutes later he ducted off into a side alley and disappeared into the shadows. He found a back door to the docking bay with a keypad lock on it. After taking a small, flat metallic device out of his bundle, Isen pressed and held a particular seam on his bundle, which transformed from a long tubular dingy brown duffel into a smaller black, body hugging backpack. He then pulled from a pocket a small transparent tube of black goo which he poured out onto his right hand. The biotech suit quickly formed to Isen's features and absorbed the backpack straps into itself giving him full range of arm movement.

He brought up his headpiece with a touch of his collar and activated the suit's X-ray scanner. Finding no one on the other side of the door, Isen held the flat code breaker up against the side of the keypad. After a few seconds it displayed the entry code which he promptly punched into the keypad.

The door indicator went from red to green along with a small click. Isen opened and stepped through the door into one of the support facility rooms around the perimeter of the docking bay as he reached back over his shoulder and put the code breaker back into his pack. Quietly closing the door behind him, Isen took a quick glance at the room he was standing in.

Roughly a curved rectangle, the musty room contained shelves full of grimy, low quality space parts arrayed in something like organized chaos. The parts appeared to be grouped together by type, but were so scattered around the room in little piles here and there Isen couldn't tell if they were placed in those positions by design or if that's where the mechanic had just decided to drop them. The room itself was lit by a single functioning glow panel that continuously flickered on and off.

The remainder of the glow panels were either shattered, cracked, or scavenged for parts. Shadows were everywhere in the claustrophobic storage room but were easily dispersed by the biotech's automatic night vision that activated once Isen deactivated the X-ray scanner.

Suddenly the building began to vibrate and Isen knew this was his chance. His left hand shot up to his collar and activated the suit's personal cloaking field which covered both him and his pack. He exited through the room's second door which unlocked when he opened it and relocked when he shut it as Isen began to walk down a ring like hall that covered the inner circumference of the docking bay.

Isen circled the main chamber until he found an access door a quarter of the way around from the storage room. It was closed but not locked. After checking his X-ray scanner and finding a number of people across the bay but none directly in front of his door, he slowly turned the handle and as silently as possible pulled the door open enough for him to slide through.

He finished closing the door behind him as the two dome halves finished retracting with a large jolt that put an end to the vibrations. Isen looked at the hangar personnel but none seemed to have noticed him. The rumble of the retracting dome must have swallowed up the sound of him opening and closing the door.

A few moments after the dome halves secured, a beat up, 20 year old freighter appeared above the now open dome and began a not so steady landing approach. When it finally did settle to the deck with a not so gentle bounce on legarthic hydraulic landing struts, three of the dozen or so mechanics moved to each of the hangar's three doors. One passed directly by Isen, and took up position outside, Isen found out with a quick X-ray scan.

When the three men had secured the exits, the dome began to close again with the same rickety vibrations that it produced on opening. After it was sealed the transport lowered a portside ramp which the remaining men strode over to and climbed up, save for one left behind to watch the hangar.

Approximately 30 seconds later they came back out of the transport pushing large crates on hover carts, which they placed off to Isen's left. They continued to off load crates for a good 15 to 20 minutes, during which time Isen took an X-ray look at the innards of the transport. What he found he didn't expect, but it didn't surprise him either.

Though the readings he was getting were imprecise, he could identify a new Acelon II power core, Brandii class sublight engines, and a number of retractable weapon's pods, all of which were not included in this type of freighter's design schematics.

He couldn't tell for sure, but he also bet that the ship's frame and everything else aside from the hull plates were either new or well maintained. All of which was in stark contrast to the ship's exterior.

From his scans Isen also identified six of the transport's crew that remained in the cockpit and another two who assisted the docking bay personnel in the transport's hold but did not step foot outside the ship. He could also tell from the sound of the transport's engines, now that it was inside the docking bay, that there was an exhaust redistributor installed on the transport. Reshaping the ship's thrust cone and slowing the velocity of the ionized gasses, the redistibutor would effectively hide the true power of the ship's engines as well as change their pitch in a subtle, but very artificial way that someone with a trained ear could detect. Also, the ship's engines hadn't been completely powered down. As far as Isen could tell, the transport wasn't planning on staying long.

When the mechanics finally emerged from the transport empty handed, apparently they had returned the hover carts to the two men in the cargo hold, four of them walked to different wall segments and opened disguised panels. One of the men shouted out a countdown which the other three repeated with him.

"Five, four, three, two, one, mark."

All at once they tapped solitary green buttons on the hidden wall panels. Immediately nothing happened, which confused Isen a bit until a large groan echoed throughout the docking bay. As the groan subsided, a 10 meter wide cubical section of floor near the piles of crates rose up to reveal a hidden lift pad.

When the floor section had risen to its full height and locked into place the mechanics started moving crates onto the lift pad, which was now level with the docking bay's deck. Using new hover carts that had come up with the lift, the mechanics stacked the crates close together on the pad, which Isen now began moving toward slowly.

Careful not to reveal his presence, Isen stepped softly on the docking bay deck in order to minimize the rippling effect his footfalls created in the biotech's skintight cloaking field.

Designed to run on relatively low power, the biotech's cloaking system was easily disrupted by motion. Running under cloak would create distortion ripples in the cloaking field that could be detected by the human eye. A physical impact could even cause the cloak to momentarily fail. But if motion is restricted, then only minor distortion occurs at physical contact points. As it was now, the only distortion Isen's suit was experiencing was a negligible shimmering where his booted foot contacted the bay floor.

He walked with steady strides until he reached a position near, but out of the way of, the mechanics where he stood and waited for them to finish loading the crates onto the lift. After another 15 minutes or so they placed the last of the crates on the lift then placed their hover carts, folded up, on top of the crates.

Then one of the mechanics nonchalantly touched an unseen button on one of the supports holding up the section of bay floor.

The lift and section of floor began, to Isen's surprise, to lower into the deck. Leaving caution behind, Isen ran across the few meters of deck separating him from the lift, dropped as softly as he could to the deck and rolled on his side into the lift as the top of the front crates evened up with the floor, leaving about a meter and a half of visibility for the mechanics to see him.

As soon as he was on top of the crates he stopped his roll and held dead still. He waited for one of the mechanics to shout out that they saw him when he turned shimmery as he rolled on the floor. The upraised section of the docking bay floor groaned and sealed back into place without so much as a word of alarm.

Isen let out a sigh of relief then realized that the lift was still going down. He held up a hand in front of his face and saw the red coloring that the biotech suit painted onto its built in tactical overlay where his hand should have appeared, letting him know that the cloaking field was still operational.

Better slow my breathing before it gives me away.

Calming himself and getting his breath under control, Isen collected his thoughts. *As far as I can tell I haven't been discovered yet. My cloak is still operational and I've found my way into the Peace Core compound. I hope. So far everything has gone well even if it was impromptu.*

Isen sat up on top of one of the crates and let his feet dangle over the edge.

Now, where exactly am I? he thought to himself as the lift cleared the short vertical shaft and emerged into a large circular room with a number of mobile cargo palettes ready to haul off the incoming crates. The room exited into a large open tunnel that extended forever as far as Isen could see. The tunnel was well lit and wide enough for the cargo palettes to travel three abreast. A number of men dressed in Peace Core uniforms started to move toward the lift as the lift locked into place.

Isen quickly stepped down from the crates and moved off to the right as the Peace Core officers began moving the crates onto one of the nearby palettes.

Isen, even though he was invisible, ducted behind one of the farther cargo palettes and watched the Peace Core men load the cargo palettes as he thought about what to do next.

Alpha Prime

Chapter Twenty-Seven

Walking out of one of Midnight Star's training rooms, a sweat soaked Gradir Cerus had a man coming down from the observation gallery loop an arm around his shoulders then put him in a not so gentle head lock.

"Hey Grady, nice quals run, 5732. If my memory hasn't failed me, that's a new high score for you. Congratulations, you've now convincingly pulled away from me to claim top *male* agent status."

"Thanks for pointing that out Sil," he said sarcastically, extricating himself from the headlock. "I really appreciate it."

"Hey buddy, don't look so glum. You're only, let's see. Uh, 1417 points behind Cara now."

"Oh, that makes me feel a lot better."

"You *are* gaining on her Grady."

"Yeah, until her next quals run." He shook his head. "I don't understand how she does it. I work my tail off, but she still blows my scores away."

"Ah, Grady, it's not what she does different than us. She's just better than us. And you're probably right, she'll push her score up even higher when she gets back."

"If she gets back. Cara couldn't tell me where she was going."

"Duh."

Gradir glared at him but continued. "*But* she did say it was going to be the toughest assignment she's had yet."

"You have any idea what the Admiral wanted her to do?"

"None. I had wondered why she wasn't going to help us with the *Goliath* mission, but apparently Legan had something more important for her to do."

"If she was assigned to our mission, *we*'d be helping *her*, not the other way around. But wherever Cara is I hope she makes it out in one piece. It would be a shame if that perfect body of hers comes to any harm."

"You're all heart Sil."

"I don't have to be, that's you're department. So, gotten anywhere with her lately or is she still shooting you down?"

"Vaped is a more appropriate term. I don't know what's with her, I've tried just about every approach I know and I get the cold shoulder each and every time."

"Maybe she just doesn't like you."

"Nobody else has had any luck either, including you."

"Hey pal, I'm just playing it smart. I'll let you guys wear her down, then when she opens up in a millenium or so, I'll step in and steal her away. Patience is a virtue you know."

"Keep on dreaming pal, with the energy she's got nobody will ever come close to wearing her down."

He smiled. "Hope springs eternal."

"Yeah well, pass me some, I'm out of ideas. She's a permacrete wall as far as my efforts are concerned."

"Yes, but a very well endowed permacrete wall. That woman has better curves than I thought could ever exist."

"Sil, you can stop drooling now."

"Come on, admit it. You agree with me, don't you?"

"Yes, she is rather attractive, but I don't fantasize about her every time my head hits the pillow."

"Then what's the point of sleeping?"

"Getting your rest so you can smoke your fellow agents in the next days drills. Something you could work a little harder on."

Silas waved him off. "You can have your drills. I'll keep Cara."

"Only in your mind."

"Yeah, but in my dreams she's real enough."

"Fine, you can dream all you want. I'll be working toward the real McCoy."

"Good luck. You can keep trying for the impossible all you want, but me, at least I'll have her in my mind. You won't have anything but her cold stare."

"Hey, if the impossible is what it takes, then the impossible is what I'll do."

"Yeah, I'd like to see that."

"You might just get to. When she gets back it'll be my turn to be her sparring partner," he said with a broad smile. "Who knows, maybe her throwing me around the mat will draw out a spark of compassion."

"All you'll get from her is a headache. And how exactly did you manage to become sparing partners with her? I've been trying for the past two years."

"One of her regulars cracked a few ribs and, until he gets healed up, I'll be replacing him."

"Did you strain any muscles when you jumped to volunteer?"

"Actually, I was asked as a favor to fill in. Being the team player that I am, I graciously granted his request. I get to spar with Cara and he owes me a favor. Sounds like a pretty good deal doesn't it?"

"I take it back."

"What back?"

"Wishing you good luck. You've already had better luck than any man's entitled to."

"You think getting my butt kicked is lucky?"

"Wanna trade partners?"

"No thanks."

"Didn't think so."

"It's not that I'm going to like getting beat into a pulp," he said sarcastically, "I just can't stand your partner."

Sil laughed. "Yeah, Jeniel is after you like you're after Cara. Why don't you just give in? As far as looks go, Cara doesn't have her beat by much, and you won't have to spend your entire life chasing after her."

"True, but you have to agree there's some kind of overpowering allure that unattainable women have."

"What happens when you finally catch them?"

"I'll let you know when I find out."

"Yeah, do try to remember to let me know what Jeniel says it feels like."

Gradir laughed. "Why don't you leave Cara to me and *you* take Jeniel?"

"Believe it or not I tried."

"She turned you down?"

"Shot dead on the spot."

"Better stick with dreams. You don't have any luck, do you?"

"Afraid not my friend. Any advice you could spare would be appreciated."

"With you, I wouldn't know where to start."

"Yeah, probably isn't a good idea to ask advice from a single guy who's stupid enough to pass up a beautiful woman who wants him for the million to one chance of getting the woman who doesn't."

"Hey, I live for challenges. Besides, the Admiral is always telling us to strive for excellence. So then why would I settle for anything less than the best?"

"I don't think that's quite what he had in mind."

"Who really knows what a High Admiral has in mind?"

"We could always ask him."

"Why don't we. I think he'd appreciate better interagent relations."

"All the more reason to hook up with Jeniel."

"True, but if we all took the easy way out we'd loose our well honed skills and combat edge. We have to have the mentality to tackle the tough assignments and I wouldn't want to ruin that common spirit by setting a bad example."

"Yeah, gotta love that take one for the team mentality. I'll bet Cara feels the same way. That's probably why she's so resistant to my charms."

"That, or she has decent taste."

"You're in the same boat I am. Single, lovesick, and about to go on one of the Admiral's pet operations. Speaking of which, it occurred to me that with Midnight Star pulling out the same time we hit the shipyard our only way of rejoining them is to travel to the rendezvous point on the *Goliath*. If we fail to capture it or delay too long we'll be left behind."

"Yeah, that tidbit hit me after we left the Admiral's office. I was also wondering if Cara was in a similar position."

"Could be. Save for the *Goliath* operation and whatever mission Cara is on, all other operations have been canceled and their field agents recalled. Lately there have been more agents in the compound than I knew we had, all of whom were packing up their personal effects."

"Yeah, the techs have started pulling permanent equipment out of the walls and packing it up into mislabeled crates. Looks like everybody will be leaving soon and Legan doesn't want anyone to find out."

"I don't understand why he wants our existence to be kept secret from his own officers. You'd think everyone he's taking to Alpha Prime would be trustworthy. At least the military anyway."

"True, but why take the chance. It doesn't hurt anything to keep Midnight Star a secret."

"No, I suppose not. It just seems a little strange."

"Don't worry about it. The Admiral knows what he's doing. Besides, we've got more important things to worry about in the near future."

"Yeah, taking control of the largest warship in the Human Sphere, even if it is in a shipyard, with five agents isn't exactly going to be easy."

"No, but then again it wouldn't be much fun if it was easy."

"You think this is going to be fun?"

"Of course. We love challenges. The bigger the better, right?"

"You might feel that way, but me, I'm a survivor. The easier the challenge, the longer I live."

"Sil, don't tell me you're scared of some dock workers?"

"If we only have dock workers opposing us then what's the challenge?"

"The challenge is in the timing and stealing the ship out from under their noses."

"Sure that'll satisfy you challenge hunger, or have you just flipped out?"

"Maybe you're right. Maybe I shouldn't be craving challenges and just be a survivor like you. I was just trying to think of how Cara would approach the situation."

"Then again what's the point in surviving if you don't have any fun."

"Are we having a change of heart?"

"You'd have to ask Cara because she has it. But as far as challenges are concerned, bring 'em on."

"That's the spirit. Glad you're back to your senses."

"Yeah, well I wouldn't want the love of my life to disapprove of my attitude."

"You mean aside from disapproving of you altogether?"

"Well, general disapproval isn't as bad as specific disapproval. And general disapproval can easily become general approval with the help of some specific approvals."

"Are you referring to, the real Cara or the Dream Cara?"

"Whichever on it works on."

He laughed. "Getting back to the *Goliath* assignment, we have our mission briefing in less than an hour and you need a shower."

"Me? You're the one drenched in sweat."

"True, but Cara likes the sweat soaked look. You're not soaked, you just stink."

"Well, Cara isn't here to see you in all your sweaty glory and the only reason I stink is because your sweat rubbed off on me."

"It wouldn't have if you hadn't put me in that head lock."

"That's a sacrifice I'm willing to make to congratulate a fellow agent, being the selfless person that I am."

"So choking me was your way of congratulating me?"

"I figured you'd want a congratulation that was challenging."

"Yeah, challenging me to breathe."

"Can you think of a better way of saying a job well done?"

"Oh, if I strained my mind I could probably come up with something."

"I'm sure you could but I wouldn't want you to hurt yourself."

"Thanks for caring."

"Well, I suppose I'll have to take care of you until Jeniel relieves me of the job."

"Don't hold your breath."

"I might as well, sooner or later you're going to come to your senses and stop breaking that poor woman's heart and leave Cara all to me."

"That poor woman has a quals score only 72 points behind yours. I think she can take care of herself. And as far as Cara is concerned, we've got more competition than each other."

"True, but one agent less means more hope for me."

"Ah, in case you hadn't realized, Cara isn't a prize that the winner of some competition gets automatically. She doesn't have to take any of us and appears to like it that way."

"That's your opinion. Personally I think Cara's madly in love with me and is just being a good sport to give everyone else a chance at her before she reveals her true feelings."

"Whatever," he said as they walked into the shower facility. Gradir pushed Silas toward his shower compartment as he opened the door to his own. "Take a shower. And you might want to try banging your head against a hard wall. It might get rid of your delusions."

Seated at a long, elliptical table, Gradir Cerus, Silas Trazel, Bryen Quesel, Ketch Adell, and Mejal Croneis listened as the Midnight Star analysts detailed the shipyard's defensive emplacements which the five agents were already well acquainted with after hours of mission prep they themselves had done.

"On the rectangular frame of the shipyard are a number of omnilaser batteries, pulse cannons, and a few torpedo launchers that will hamper your extraction of *Goliath* and therefore must be neutralized."

Ketch raised a hand.

"Agent Adell."

"When you say neutralized do you mean destroyed?"

"How you deal with the weapons emplacements is up to you but our suggestion is that you take out the power nexuses. As you can see, the weapons emplacements are grouped together at the four corners of the command station. Each cluster is fully automated, with a central power nexus feeding all the weapons including the missile launchers. If you take out the four nexuses, the shipyard's weaponry will no longer function. The shipyard's tractor beams are another story. Placed at seemingly random intervals around the shipyard's frame, they will each have to be taken out individually. To answer your question Agent Adell, destroying the nexuses and the tractor beam power lines will neutralize the shipyard's ability to detain or destroy *Goliath*, but it may not be necessary. It's possible to disconnect the power lines without setting off any explosions, and may I remind you that every problem you encounter does not need to be blown up to be solved."

"Hey, I'm a pyrotechnic specialist, I like blowing things up."

"Given the seriousness of this mission, I suggest you refrain your desire to demolish, but the final decision is up to your squad when you're on location so I won't lecture you again."

"Thanks and by the way, 'desire to demolish' is a catchy phrase. Do you think you could have some T-shirts made up with that phrase in red on top of a debris cloud?"

"I don't think that would be a good idea. You're impulsive enough as it is."

"Just a thought."

"Well, getting back to the mission. As I was saying, the shipyard's weaponry and tractor beams must be deactivated by some means, but you also have to deal with the mooring beams and the docking clamps holding the *Goliath* in place before you'll be able to move the ship. Again, you can take out the port and starboard power nexuses on the docking slip in order to deactivate the mooring beams. The docking clamps are another story. The clamps physically attach to the ship and circle the docking port which should be open at all times allowing yard workers access to the ship without having to use shuttlecraft. You'll have to manually retract the clamps, blowing up the controls won't remove the clamps from the ship's hull."

"Once you remove the clamps and deactivate the mooring beams you can retract the gangway and leave the yard. But before you do any of that, you have to evacuate the *entire* ship. We can't have anyone left on board because when you leave the yard you'll be traveling directly to the rendezvous point. Use *Goliath*'s internal sensors to make sure the ship is clear of any personnel besides the five of you, then get out of there as soon as possible. This mission is time critical so you'll have to secure the ship in short order and travel at flank speed in order to meet up with the fleet before it leaves for Alpha Prime. For security reasons, no one but Admiral Legan knows the coordinates of Alpha Prime, so you'll have to meet up with him to get the flight data for the trip to the new territories."

Gradir raised a hand and the analyst gave him a slight nod prompting him to proceed. "If for some reason we fail to accomplish the mission, will we be left behind or will there be a way for us to catch the convoys?"

"If you fail and still have time to reach the rendezvous point before the fleet leaves it won't matter. *Goliath* is your only way to Alpha Prime. The transport that you will take to the system will not be waiting for you. It will drop you off at the shipyard then head directly for the rendezvous point in order for it to catch the convoys before they leave for Alpha Prime. Only the *Goliath* has enough speed for you to arrive in time to meet up with Admiral Legan and the convoys."

"How exactly do you suggest we evacuate the ship, besides getting on the intercom and asking them nicely to leave the ship so we can steal it?" Bryen interjected.

"Our suggestion is that you activate the automatic abandon ship protocol. Loosing some escape pods isn't critical, but if you can find a way to evacuate the ship without sounding an abandon ship-wide alarm, be my guest. I don't care how you get the personnel off the ship, just do it."

"Exactly how many people do you expect will be on *Goliath* and in the shipyard command station?" Gradir asked.

"*Goliath*, as far as our intel shows, has approximately 400 workers on board her at any one time. The command structure holds another 1500 or so techs and mechanics, plus additional workers on the other vessels under construction."

"Exactly how complete is *Goliath*?" Mejal asked.

"Very. The *Goliath* is complete save for some internal finish work. All the critical systems are complete and operational. You shouldn't have any equipment related problems with the extraction. Our reports indicate that the *Goliath*'s craftsmanship is next to none. Not surprising considering the 475 billion credits or so the Republic forked over for her construction. When you reach the *Goliath*'s bridge, you'll have to enter a number of authorization codes, which we will supply, in order to power up the ship and activate the navigation system. You'll have to manually enter the coordinates for the rendezvous system and maneuver the ship out of the docking slip, but once you're clear of the shipyard the autopilot will handle the rest of the trip. It would be a good idea to raise the shields once you get free of the docking clamps considering that there will be armed patrol craft in the area. You'll also have to raise the shields manually, but once you do they should be able to easily absorb the patrol craft's fire, assuming they are brave enough to attack the strongest warship in the Sphere. Don't bother messing with the weapons systems, you won't need to return fire. Even if all the patrol craft they have in the system concentrated their fire on one section of your shields, 50% shield power would be sufficient to repel their fire."

"What about on board the shipyard command station. Will there be any armed guards?" Gradir asked.

"The yard has its own armed security force but they're not well trained and few in number. They shouldn't pose much of a problem."

"Will any of them be stationed on the *Goliath*," Ketch asked.

"Possibly a few at the docking port. Maybe some in the interior of the ship. You'll have to find out when you're there. When you infiltrate the yard you'll have to assess the situation for yourselves. Use whatever methods you feel necessary to neutralize the yard's defenses and free the ship, but remember that this is a time critical mission. You may encounter some resistance from the yard's personnel or security guards, but your chief opponent will be the clock. You must get the *Goliath* out of the shipyard and to the rendezvous system before the fleet leaves for Alpha Prime. If not…"

"we're screwed." Silas finished.

"Unfortunately Yes."

Chapter Twenty-Eight

"Here you are," Cara said, spotting a small gap between two support beams running vertically through the far wall.

Of all the support beams running through office walls, this pair was unique because of a design flaw. According to Cara's information, when Kataran Intelligence remodeled the building they completely redesigned the lower 13 levels, tearing out pieces of the building then replacing them with new materials. They had succeeded in not having the building fall down on top of them during construction, but the engineers who had reconstructed the lower levels had made a significant mistake.

They had slightly mismeasured the length of some of the support beams. So when they tried to connect the horizontal beams to one of the building's larger and stronger vertical beams they came up short by a few meters on this particular vertical row of connections, and *only* that row of vertical connections. Instead of tearing apart a good portion of their new structure, the engineers had decided to use existing material, rather than ordering specially cut beams which would have let everyone know of their mistake, to place a secondary vertical support pillar for the too short horizontal beams to attach to. In doing this they left a 52 centimeter gap between the two vertical pillars, which they had deemed inconsequential.

This meant that at this beam junction there was a small vertical shaft running the length of the lower 13 floors without horizontal cross beams in the way. The top portion of that shaft was in the far wall of the office Cara was standing in.

"Didn't think you'd be that hard to find," Cara said, pulling out a small laser cutter.

Rather than using her plasma torch which would have set the ceramic wall on fire, Cara aligned the cutter with the edge of the gap between the two support pillars, visible thanks to the X-ray mode on her sunglasses, and began to cut. A vivid blue beam barely a millimeter in diameter jumped the 2 cm gap, cutting through the 6 cm thick wall panel slowly but evenly.

Bracing her hand against the wall as she cut, Cara dragged the blue beam along the edge of the left support pillar, letting the beam cut almost all the way through the duraplast wall but keeping the beam from cutting into the wall on the other side of the gap.

After 10 minutes or so of cutting, Cara deactivated the laser cutter and put it back into her pack, leaving a rectangular section of wall panel hanging in place by less than half a centimeter of wall panel. Her hand came out of her pack cradling a flat surface gripping device which she attached to the still attached wall segment.

Grabbing the device's handles with both hands, she gave it a gentle tug but it wouldn't budge. She then gave it a not so gentle tug but it still refused to tear loose.

Growling quietly, Cara held onto the handles and pulled her feet up and placed them alongside her hands, but all off the wall segment.

"Should have cut a little further," she said.

Cara concentrated for a moment then gave the wall segment a wicked jerk.

Breaking off fairly easily, the wall segment pulled away from the wall intact as Cara flew a good two meters through the air before landing hard on her back with a loud thud.

"Ouch," she coughed after catching her momentarily lost breath, then falling silent as she realized she might have been heard.

Rolling to the left onto her knees she scanned the hallway for alerted guards. A few moments later two guards came into view and turned into the hallway, but to her relief passed by without the slightest hesitation.

Come on Cara, no more stupid mistakes. You were lucky this time.

Picking up the wall segment she had dropped, Cara released the gripping device which she gently dropped into her open pack. She took the meter high wall segment and stuffed it into the crack between the office's desk and the adjacent wall, out of sight. *Not like anyone is going to miss a hole in the wall,* Cara mentally commented. *But it's one less thing for me to trip over on my way out.*

Moving back to her newly cut entry point, Cara picked up her pack off the ground and moved to the hole in the wall. After reattaching her pack's safety line to her wrist, Cara wedged her way through the hole and into the vertical shaft.

While a good two and a half meters wide, the support pillars gave her plenty of lateral arm space but the half meter distance between the two pillars had her scrunched up as she clung to the left most pillar, courtesy of the magnetic couplers.

With her pack held wide of her body and tied to her right hand, Cara began to inch her way down the narrow shaft. Still fatigued from sprinting through the halls and her previous climb, Cara was at least grateful that she could lean her back against the other pillar and rest her tired muscles from time to time.

When she had sufficiently lowered herself down the dark shaft, Cara looked to the left through the wall and didn't like what she found.

"Oops," she said upon seeing two figures in the adjacent office, one through the exposed wall segment and the other, more blurry figure through the lift support beam standing at what Cara speculated as a wall mounted data terminal. She turned her head and looked to the right to find the other office accessible from the shaft occupied as well. *I had wanted to access one of the terminals on this level, but I guess I'll just have to go lower.*

Resetting herself, Cara began to lower herself down to the 11th level, ignoring the ever growing soreness in her lower back. Small metal clicks accompanied her descent as she attached and released the magnetic couplers, but fortunately the walls were thick enough that the sound didn't penetrate. When she reached the 11th level her annoyance began to grow as she found the next two offices also occupied.

Gritting her teeth Cara moved on to the next level, and the next, and the next, and the next until she finally found an unoccupied office on the 3rd level.

It's about time.

Carefully easing her way over to the wall on her right, she double, then triple checked to make sure the room was deserted. Once satisfied, she dug into her hanging pack and pulled out the laser cutter. With a great deal less precision, Cara cut out an ovalish section of wall, leaving a few strips still attached after burning shallow grooves in one of the office's paintings hanging on the wall across from the segment she had just cut through.

Taking her right knee off the pillar, she lifted her leg and kicked in the panel as quietly as she could. After repositioning herself in the shaft, Cara pushed her pack through the freshly cut hole then pulled herself into the opulent office. Getting to her feet, Cara stretched out her aching back muscles, suppressing a yelp when they screamed in protest.

Shaking off the soreness, Cara gave the large office a quick visual scan after she deactivated her sunglasses' X-ray mode. With an unusually high 15 meter tall ceiling, the office enclosed a rather complex water fountain in the center of the room. Comprised of numerous small jets of crystal clear water, the water formation emerging from a circular marble base resembling a large flowing 'M'. Sprouting from the floor, the two rows of tiny water jets were inclined slightly toward the center where they fell into an upraised pillar after curving over in mid air.

Though the room was fairly humid, the atmosphere didn't feel oppressive. In fact, the flowing water and the floor imbedded glow panels at the base of the room's five walls that gave off a muted pinkish light created a very soothing environment. *This isn't so much an office as it is a relaxation room. I must have come out into one of the archive administrator's personal meditation rooms*, Cara thought to herself as she slowly circled the room. *Or lair*, she added a moment later as she approached a very curvy desk that seemed to have grown out of the floor.

Cara walked around to the desk's large, self-conforming chair. She resisted the urge to appropriate the inviting chair and instead nudged it aside as she examined the extravagant desk. Designed to look like a wave flowing out of the floor, the desk rose highest at the midsection and tapered off down the sides until it smoothly reintegrated with the spongy floor. From above, the desk resembled a faint crescent with the tips pointing back toward the chair and the wall behind it.

On the front surface of the wave desk a solid wall of water flowed from a ridge on the top down into a thin crevice in the floor which further added to the slightly clean chlorine smell that was detectable in the office's atmosphere. Rising from the center of the wave desk, a computer terminal angled its way toward the user on a short, smooth neck that seemed to grow out of the wave with its counterpart keyboard forming a soft arc where the administrator or whoever else owned this office sat.

Cara turned on the viewscreen and was surprised when a schematic of the archives filing system appeared.

Forgot to log off the system I see. Bad for you, good for me.

Cara searched through the filing system enough to make sure that she really did have access to the archives files then looked for the dataport.

"Oh no," she said aloud as she looked around the office. *Just my luck, this office has 'view only' access. I'll have to try one of the other offices.*

As she moved toward the hallway door she reactivated her sunglasses' X-ray mode. Seeing that the hall was clear of guards she reached for the activation panel as she belatedly remembered seeing an object in her peripheral vision. Turning to the right she looked down the hall and caught sight of some bad new.

Great, they have wall mounted cameras. They sure don't want to make this easy do they?

Reaching into her pack, which was still hanging from her now sore wrist, Cara pulled out a thin flexible tube and a mechanical wristband. *Fortunately for me, these sort of security measures were anticipated.* Cara pulled out one of her metal plates and placed it on the door. She then toggled the controls on her wristband and the door opened a crack.

Stooping next to the door, Cara bent the tube at a right angle and slid it through the door crack and pointed the bent part at the camera that was a little more than 15 meters down the hall to her right. Cara aligned the tube with the camera's position using the small viewscreen on her wristband, then hit an activation button on the end of the tube still in the office, shooting out an almost invisible projectile that stuck to the wall about 10 cm to the left of the camera. Cara pulled the tube back inside the office and put it into her pack.

Now seeing the inside of her pack on her wristband, Cara switched the small viewscreen to receive telemetry from the small projectile. She was glad when a row of tiny bars, starting with red and rising up through orange and yellow to green, appeared on the side of the wristband's viewscreen, which meant that the projectile's signal was coming in strong. She hit a button on her wristband that sent a command to the projectile to jam the camera. When it received the signal, the projectile sent out a localized interference signal that caused the camera's recording mechanism to repeatedly record the same image over and over. When the tiny sensors in the projectile confirmed that the camera was jammed, it sent a signal to Cara's wristband, illuminating a small green light.

Cara then pulled her skeleton key out of her wrist pocket and stood ready at the door. Taking one last glance at the hallway and adjacent office to make sure no one was around, she took a deep breath, held it for a moment, and let it out slowly.

Then she moved.

Whipping open the door she dashed out of the office, making sure the door close behind her, and quickstepped down the hall to the next door. Finding the door locked, Cara quickly inserted her skeleton key, waited impatiently while it took a few moments to unlock the door, and quickly entered the office when the door unlocked with a click. Closing the door behind her, Cara turned around and looked through the walls to make sure no one was in sight, then fiddled with her wristband.

First she deactivated the projectile bug in case someone on the other end of the camera counted passing guards on patrol. Then she sent a signal back to the metal plate in the first office, having it close and lock the door. Cara then deactivated the X-ray mode on her sunglasses and found the office to be completely dark, so she turned on her night vision.

When she did, she found a considerably smaller office with a normal ceiling and no water fountain. Looking around the room she spotted a computer terminal on the far wall and crossed the room to check it out.

Apparently this office's owner wasn't as careless and didn't leave the terminal without logging off. Cara looked for the dataport but to her dismay couldn't find one. She quickly checked the desk and the rest of the room but came up empty.

I don't like the look of this. I guess I'll just have to try another office.

Moving back to the door where she'd dropped her pack, Cara reactivated her X-ray mode and found a quartet of guards striding through the hall. *I guess they like even numbers.*

After the guards had left the hallway Cara reactivated the projectile's jamming system, picked up her pack, and left the office. The door locked behind her as she crossed the hall to another nearby office, brandished her skeleton key, and let herself in. After readjusting her sunglasses to the darkness she checked another wall terminal and got the same results.

Starting to become very annoyed, Cara forced herself to focus. *Alright, I can't find dataports in these offices, but maybe if I move to a different section of the floor I'll have better luck.*

Cara moved back to the door and pulled out the flexible tube again before punching commands into her wristband. *Ok, I've got the projectile on the wall set to activate if I near its line of sight. That should make things easier, but I still have to avoid the guards.*

After taking a quick scan of the hall Cara left the office behind and moved to the end of the hallway where the jammed camera was mounted and stuck the projectile launching tube round the hallway corner. Looking at her wristband display, Cara spotted another camera a good 40 meters away and carefully aimed the small tube.

Touching the firing button with her thumb, Cara launched the projection at the camera and came within a meter of her target. The projectile signaled back that it had test jammed the camera and awaited her signal. *Guess a meter off was close enough.*

Checking through the wall to make sure no one was in the hallway Cara reloaded the projectile tube, then stepped around the corner. Before she stepped into the hallway the projectile at the far camera detected her near its line of sight and immediately jammed the camera. Likewise, when she cleared the other projectiles line of sight it disengaged its jamming, letting the camera record normally. Between Cara and the far camera was a cross hallway which she stopped at and fired another projectile at a 3rd camera off to her right.

Before she proceeded she got a small vibration from her wristband that prompted her to quickly duck into the hallway on her right. That allowed the 2nd projectile to disengage its jamming and let its camera record the image of the four security guards that would soon be rounding the 1st projectile's corner and into the line of sight of the 2nd camera.

When that happened, Cara felt a differently placed vibration on her wrist thanks to the projectiles' motion detectors. Cara then moved farther along the right hall until she encountered another intersection where she quickly placed another projectile on the camera covering that hallway. She then rounded the corner to her left and, by means of the skeleton key, entered the nearest unoccupied office.

When she closed the door behind her she felt a vibration on a 3rd section of her wrist. She waited what seemed a long while for the 4th but it never came. *They must have kept going straight towards my 2nd projectile instead of turning my direction*, she thought as she walked over to the wall mounted computer terminal.

Again she failed to find a dataport at the terminal or anywhere else in the office. *I guess I'll have to try farther away.*

Cara moved to the office door and did a quick check of the hall before she exited the office and moved further down the hallway. After placing a few more projectiles she entered another office with the same results.

Frustrated yet determined, she continued deeper into the level, dodging guards and jamming cameras as she checked another, and another, and another office before finally returning to the original office after a dozen or so tries.

Opening the door by remote, thanks to the metal plate that she had placed on the door earlier, Cara stepped into the luxuriant office a step ahead of another quartet of guards. After making sure they passed by Cara went over to the desktop computer terminal. *I guess I'll have to find the archive databanks and download the data directly. Hopefully I can find out exactly where the databanks are from this terminal.*

Dropping her hands to the keyboard, she looked at the viewscreen only to remember that she'd forgotten to switch her sunglasses back to normal vision. She lifted her right hand towards her sunglasses in order to correct that little oversight but it never made it to her glasses. Instead her hand froze by her ear as she noticed something out of the corner of her eye.

Cara dropped her hand and walked toward the fountain, her eyes on the floor. She dropped to a knee in front of the fountain and studied her sunglasses' readout carefully. After a few moments of contemplation she got to her feet and switched off her X-ray scan but didn't activate the night vision.

In fact, she took her sunglasses off entirely, putting them up on top of her head so she could see better in the dim light. Cara then took a step back and looked the fountain over. She stared at it for a few minutes then slowly walked around the fountain, coming to a stop at her original position and completing her circle.

She then stepped to the fountain and began to run her hands over the knobby central podium that collected the air born water into a pair of parallel trays that fed into a small reservoir that the fountain's spray jets pulled water from. When Cara moved to the side facing the wave desk, she felt a small nub move slightly. She ran her hand over the same area and located the particular nub, which she then depressed into the podium a full two centimeters.

Cara then jerked back as the podium and fountain as a whole split in two.

The two halves still sprayed water that was collected into each half of the podium, but the fountain had slid apart far enough over the floor to reveal a steep winding stairway. After recoiling from the sudden movement of the fountain, Cara stepped forward and stood over the stairway entrance, her frustration gone and fatigue forgotten.

"Well, well, well. What do we have here."

Chapter Twenty-Nine

P eering down into the passage opening, Cara smiled to herself. "I love secret passageways, they always lead to something that someone doesn't want you to find," Cara said as she pulled on her pack and started down the spiral stairway. "And something hidden inside a high security facility has to rate pretty high on someone's priority list."

Stepping below floor level, Cara moved clear of the fountain's proximity sensors and it resealed above her head. A previously unseen hand sized wall panel glowed green and caught Cara's attention.

Must be a release switch. I'll need to make use of that on the way out, she thought as she wound her way down the staircase to where the 2nd level would be. Finding no outlet, she continued her descent, passing the 1st level and ground level seeing nothing but more stairs.

I wonder how far down this goes, Cara thought, finding out some 12 levels later when the stairwell emerged onto a small platform extending into a large vertical cavern 40 meters wide and carved out of solid bedrock. Highlighted by evenly spaced spotlights imbedded in the roughly carved yellow-green rock, a 25 meter wide cylinder rose up from the cavern floor to what appeared to be near ground level as far as Cara could see, straining her neck to get a good look at the top of the cylinder.

Extending from the right side of the platform that Cara was standing on, a catwalk attached to the cavern wall spiraled up to a faintly visible platform that connected to the central cylinder. Off to her left the catwalk wound three quarters of the way around the datacore before leveling out onto the plated cavern floor.

"Looks like I found the datacore," Cara whispered to herself. "But it doesn't explain the secret passage. That other platform probably has a maintenance entrance from the 1st level, so why bother concealing a lower entrance. It doesn't make any sense," Cara said, then shook her head slightly as she refocused. "Doesn't matter why the stairway was built, I'm here to download the archive files."

Stepping forward Cara peered over the edge of the railing at the base of the datacore where she spied a bank of computer consoles encircling it.

"Looks like that's my best chance. Better get moving before someone decides to visit."

Stepping softly, Cara walked down the left portion of the catwalk trying to avoid making the highly audible clanking that boot heels commonly made on metal grating. Partially succeeding, Cara circled the datacore with muffled footsteps until she was far enough around to see a tunnel mouth directly below the platform that she'd been standing on. Stopping on the catwalk, she stared at the darker, rocky tunnel that appeared to have been cut out of the bedrock more recently than the cavern had, judging by the coloration of the rocky walls.

"Guess this is the reason for the stairwell. They probably have the upper access sealed off so nobody will find the new tunnel. That would explain why the core is completely deserted, but it would also mean that whatever the secret is, it's something the higher ups don't want their own people to know about. Looks like it deserves some investigation, but first I have to download the files."

After walking down the remainder of the catwalk, Cara crossed the smooth plated cavern floor to the circle of consoles ringing the gigantic datacore. After only a cursory examination Cara spied a dataport at the foot of one of the consoles.

"Finally," she said, digging into her bag and pulling out Zephrim's specialized downloader and data jacks. Cara connected one end of the two meter long cord into the downloader, which she gently placed on the floor. On the other end of the cord was the datajack which she plugged into the dataport. Crossing her fingers, Cara hit the activation button on the downloader, which began to hack into the archives system.

Slowly, Zephrim's programming wormed its way past intelligence's built in firewalls, its progress showing on a horizontal, color coded readout that blinked into existence, then went dark along the with rest of the bar. Simultaneously, a timer appeared and began to count down from 9 minutes and 37 seconds. *Good, it's penetrated the security.* Cara looked up and around the cavern but there was no one in sight.

Time for a little recon.

She glanced down at Zephrim's handiwork. "I'll be back for you in a little bit," she said almost inaudibly before she headed off down the tunnel.

Cara pulled her sunglasses down off her head and checked the X-ray mode, but found that it wouldn't penetrate the dense rock walls. *Looks like I'll have to do this the old fashioned way.* The tunnel was lit well enough by a string of widely spaced glow panels running down the center of the tunnel ceiling that Cara didn't need to use night vision, so she reset her sunglasses to normal vision. Hugging the right wall she made her way down the tunnel, soft footfalls patting on the uneven bare rock floor.

50 or so meters in from the cavern, the tunnel split into two diverging offshoots from the Y-shaped intersection. Sticking to the wall, Cara moved into the rightmost offshoot but found nothing but more tunnel ahead, curving off to the right.

Dropping into a half crouch, Cara slowly crept around the gentle curve of the tunnel until the far wall began to grow brighter. Slowing even more, Cara worked her way along the wall until she could see a sliver of the tunnel's exit. Dropping into a full crouch, she crawled along the wall using her right arm for balance so she could stay on her feet, until the whole of the tunnel opening came into view.

Pressing herself against the cold, knobby wall, Cara suppressed a shiver but couldn't keep her eyes from widening at the sight before her. Endless lines of tightly packed starfighters of a make she couldn't identify filled more than half of the low ceilinged hangar that seemed to extend forever from Cara's viewpoint. Also off to her left, Cara saw row upon row of mobile assault vehicles, all hovering silently, patiently waiting to be let loose.

Managing to tear her eyes away from the overwhelming sight, Cara backtracked a few steps around the gentle curve of the tunnel and pulled off her pack, out of sight of the hangar. Quickly digging through her pack, Cara pulled out a small camera and datacard. Cara extended the camera's rifle like scope and inserted the datacard into a side slot.

Leaving her pack behind, Cara inched her way along the wall until she could see the entire hangar opening, then she lifted her camera and steadied the 15 cm scope on a small niche in the wall. Centering her sights on the tunnel mouth, Cara touched a pair of buttons on the underside of the camera. The first button activated the auto record mode that would feed all visual, IR, and UV info through the side slot and into the datacard.

The second button Cara pressed and held with her right thumb, causing the camera's scope to zoom in on the nearest of the starfighters. After giving the fighter a good look over, Cara switched to the mobile assault vehicles, then zoomed in down the immediate row of starfighters.

Spotting a few techs working on some of the farther starfighters, Cara zoomed in and gave their uniforms a closer inspection. She found the same ringed 'M' symbol that was on the starfighters and mobile assault vehicles on an arm mounted patch and over the left breast of a particular tech's uniform. Cara didn't recognize the symbol, but was sure Midnight Star's analysts could identify it after she got them the datacard.

If I get them the datacard, she reminded herself. *I'm not out of this yet.*

Moving off the tech, she continued to zoom down the line of starfighters until her scope reached its limit. She held the image a moment to give the analysts more data to work with and managed to catch a glimpse of the hangar's far wall before bringing the camera's focus back to normal with a touch of a third button.

Shutting it off, Cara retreated back to where she had left her pack and put the camera away. *I wish I could get a closer look at the hangar, but I don't have the time. The downloader should be about finished by now and getting those files back to Admiral Legan takes priority. The visuals on this datacard will have to be enough.*

Slinging her pack on her shoulders again, Cara retraced her footsteps back to the datacore, giving the second tunnel a quick glance as she went by. Stopping just before she entered the cavern, Cara tentatively poked her head out the tunnel and looked up for a few moments before finding the catwalk clear.

She circled to the opposite side of the datacore to sure that nobody was hiding in its visual shadow but similarly found that portion of the cavern clear. She stepped over to the console where the downloader was attached and found that the downloader had already completed its work.

Pulling out five specialized datacards designed to hold the entire complement of restricted files, Cara carefully placed them into slots on her combat suit's belt. After making sure they were all secured enough that no amount of movement would dislodge them, Cara detached the downloader from the console. She put the downloader back into her pack then took two steps toward the catwalk before she stopped and looked back at the tunnel.

I have to get these files out of here but I need to check out that other tunnel first. Cara sucked in a deep breath then let it out in a quiet sigh. *I hope this doesn't blow up in my face.*

Turning away from the catwalk, Cara stepped to the tunnel and hugged the left wall. When she came to the Y, Cara turned left and followed the inside of the tunnel's curve, mirroring her route in the hangar's tunnel. Instead of opening into a chamber like its twin, this tunnel ended in a T-junction.

Cara cautiously checked left and right but saw nobody in the tunnel itself. Off to her right about 20 meters the tunnel opened into a large room with a great deal of electronic equipment. Off to her left the tunnel looked to dead-end about 50 meters on down so Cara decided to check out the chamber to her right.

Cara pulled her camera out of her pack then crouched along the right side of the wall and started to crawl forward. She stopped about two meters from the tunnel's outlet onto the main floor when a tech came into view.

She retreated enough to be out of his line of sight then looked the room over with her camera. In the section of the room visible to Cara, a 15 meter high viewscreen predominated the far wall, displaying a map of the Human Sphere. Though she was able to only see the right most three quarters, Cara was able to see a number of tagged dots that were spread along and beyond the Republic's coreward border. The majority of those dots inhabited the Lenonian Confederation, but Cara couldn't make out the electronic tags so she zoomed in on the dots on the border and found military unit ID's on each and every one of them.

Those aren't Admiral Legan's units or Levonian troops, the unit ID's aren't right. It looks to me like an independent military force is preparing to invade the Republic.

Cara then scoped out each and every one of the remaining dots and their ID tags. *This will give our analysts something to keep them busy, but I need to see the rest of the map.*

Dropping silently to her belly Cara crawled forward until the entire viewscreen was in view. Though she was in the tech's line of sight, he had his back to her, hard at work at the consoles in front of him.

Taking the opportunity while she had it, Cara scoped out the dots on the newly exposed portion of the viewscreen then zoomed out and did a slow sweep of the room. Off to her right was the beginning of a row of consoles that centered on the viewscreen and had an opposite number off to her left. Directly in front of the viewscreen was a 12 meter wide holoprojector plate. Though deactivated now, Cara guessed that the holoprojector could display a 20 meter wide image, equally high, and 10 meters thick in exacting detail based on the general make. Though she'd never seen this particular model, it looked like a larger version of the projector at Midnight Star's headquarters which was *supposed* to be the largest in the Human Sphere. Apparently it no longer was.

Behind the banks of consoles off to Cara's right was a stairway leading up to a platform that started from the top of the viewscreen wall and disappeared out of Cara's view. Cara assumed another platform extended from her left, based on the symmetrical nature of the room, but couldn't be sure because most of the left portion of the room was obscured by the tunnel wall. Being that the room was symmetrical, it seemed odd to Cara that the tunnel she was in opened out into the right side of the room instead of the center. She wondered if another tunnel exited the left side of the room, but it wasn't important enough to risk detection for.

Deciding that she had enough data to give the Midnight Star analysts a place to start, Cara did a final sweep of the room then pulled back out of the tech's line of sight. She then retracted the camera's scope and placed the camera back into her pack. She crawled backward on her haunches a few more meters then stood up, pulled her pack back onto her shoulders, and retreated back to the T-junction.

Before turning left to head back to the datacore chamber, Cara decided to check out the dead end tunnel on her way out. But when she walked toward the rock face at the end of the tunnel offshoot, Cara noticed a slight indentation on the left wall.

On closer inspection Cara found a two meter high, one meter wide opening carved into the rock wall that led to a small, circular room. In the center of the room stood a smaller version of the datacore back in the main cavern. Three meters high and two meters wide, the datacore in front of Cara looked to be of a newer construction than the main core. Also, the stone in this small dome like room appeared more freshly cut than that of any of the other chambers.

Cara then made a snap decision. She passed through the rock carved opening and moved to the bank of computer consoles encircling the smaller datacore. Cara slid her pack off her shoulders and let it drop softly to the floor. Then she took out the downloader and datajacks again, along with a fresh set of datacards.

Cara found the dataport quickly enough and attached the appropriate datajack to both the console and the downloader. She then hit the activation button and started the download.

Chapter Thirty

C rouched behind the far right cargo palette that was resting a few meters from the lift chamber's wall, Isen watched as the Peace Core officers transferred the unmarked metallic crates that the disguised transport had brought in from the lift floor to the first cargo palette. Apparently well trained, the men proceeded to efficiently unload the lift with not so much as a word between them.

There were no orders given. No vocal coordination of the cargo transfer. No conversation between the men. Not even a mumbled complaint about being given such a monotonous duty. Gone from their faces were the expressions of disinterest common to men working manual labor, who's only concern was passing by the hours until quitting time.

Instead, the expressions on these men's faces were ones of alertness. They were focused on the job at hand and did not allow their attention to flag. Their constant awareness of the situation, evident by rhythmic glances around the chamber at all but precise intervals, and the efficiency with which they handled their task told Isen one important thing: These men were professional soldiers, not simple cargo handlers, and they shouldn't be messed with. As far as Isen was concerned these men were positively lethal.

Yeah, well so am I. Good thing for them I'm cloaked or I'd have to give them an up close and personal view of my fist.

The Peace Core officers had finished loading the first cargo palete and started to load the second when one of them climbed into the exposed front cab of the first cargo palete and took off down the tunnel at a not so reasonable speed.

In a hurry are we? Well, that's fine with me. The sooner I'm out of here with those artifacts the better. I'd rather be on a mission where I got to blow something up instead of playing sneak thief, but duty does call. And since I don't feel like walking down that tunnel, I'd better catch a ride before they all leave.

Already the Peace Core officers had filled the second cargo palette's surface with tightly packed crates and had begun to stack the crates two high with the help of their cargo lifters.

Designed to move specialized crates, the cargo lifters had a magnetic, 4-pronged lift carriage that slid into shallow indentions on the undersides of the crates. Once the driver, who stood on a foot pad attached to the lifter and gripped a T-shaped control bar, maneuvered the four tines underneath a crate, he would thumb a switch on the control bar and activate the low power magnets in the tines that would help steady, but not hold tight, the silvery crates. Using the imbedded repulsor technology, the Peace Core men had no trouble lifting the remaining crates on top of their cousins a good two meters off the floor.

Not wasting any time, Isen stood up behind the third cargo palette then crossed the cold, gray tiled deck in a brisk walk, creating only a small distortion by his nearly silent footsteps that was unnoticeable except to someone who knew what to look for. And these men where not on the very short list of people who did.

Seeing that the double stack of crates was too high for him to easily climb on top of, Isen gently dropped to his knees and rolled underneath the hovering cargo palette. *I hope all this rolling hasn't damaged any of the equipment in my pack. The equipment was built durable enough but I gave it a good jostle when I rolled into the lift.*

Isen rolled onto his back with his pack between him and the deck and looked at the underside of the cargo palette, 25 cm above his nose.

Now, let's see if this works.

Steadying himself on top of his pack, Isen extended his hands and knees up until they contacted the smooth, gray ventral surface of the cargo palette that housed its repulsor coils.

"Stick," he mumbled softly to his suit.

The biotech's built in computer system recognized the command as Isen held his left thumb against his index finger and activated its built in touch pad, enabling the biotech's voice recognition system. When the suit responded to his command,

Isen felt the material on his wrists and kneepads momentarily liquefy as they changed composition. He flexed his wrists and ankles slightly, signaling the imbedded sensors to cause the newly reformed material to adhere to the underside of the cargo palette.

Isen pulled his weight off his pack then began to readjust his arms and legs, releasing each adhesion point individually and maneuvering himself until he hung in a spread eagle position with his pack raised 15 cm or so off the deck. Relaxing his muscles and letting his limbs' tension hold him up, he waited for the Peace Core officers to finish loading the second cargo palette, which he now hung from, and start loading the third.

Isen didn't have to wait long. Barely 20 seconds after he had secured himself to the cargo palette's underside, he felt a slight jolt as one of the Peace Core officers started the cargo palette down the large tunnel to the main compound. As the cargo palette accelerated down the tunnel, its motion caused the tunnel's contained atmosphere to whip under the cargo palette, creating a strong air current that seemed to want to tear Isen free of the speeding craft.

I hope the suit holds on. If not, I'm going to lose more than my cloak when I hit the floor. This guy has to be doing at least 120 kph. Isen focused his thoughts toward the cargo palette's open cab. *Hey buddy, I know you're in a hurry, but would it hurt you all that much to slow down enough so I won't get sucked off this thing. If you don't mind, I'd kinda like to live.*

As if in response to his plea, the cargo palette's engine increased its whine and the wind tugging at Isen's body strengthened as the driver accelerated again.

Thanks a lot pal. You're a big help, Isen thought toward the driver as he pulled himself as tightly as he could up against the cargo palette's smooth belly, trying to decrease his surface area and let the wind pass by as best he could. Keeping his wrists and ankles tightly flexed in order to make sure that one of his adhesion points didn't accidentally release, Isen clung to the cargo palette as his muscles began to object to his rigid position.

Come on. The compound can't be that far off. Isen closed his eyes as he focused on maintaining his hold. *Thanks to speedy up there we should reach the compound any moment now. Gotta hold on a little longer.*

A few seconds later, which felt like a few years to Isen's arms, the cargo palette's driver began decelerating as he approached the end of the tunnel. Gradually the wind that had threatened to tear Isen free of the cargo palette and splatter him on the tunnel floor decreased enough that Isen could relax his body and hang limp from the repulsor coils as his limbs began to slowly regain their strength.

No doubt about it now. I really like this suit. When I get back to Morning Dawn headquarters I'll have to have a talk with the two senior technicians about some personal customization, plus maybe something a little more inconspicuous than a tube to carry it around in. This suit definitely has possibilities. So far it's worked perfectly on its trial run, but I'm sure the techs will be able to find ways to improve it.

Eventually the cargo palette slowed to a crawl before it exited the tunnel into another large room. The driver of Isen's cargo palette maneuvered in beside the first cargo palette and parked about five meters away over bright yellow guide lines on the chamber's deck.

Once the cargo palette had come to a stop and the driver had dismounted the control chair, Isen released his right knee, then his left. Once he had both feet quietly on the floor he moved his hands closer together, a few centimeters at a time, until he felt his pack touch the floor. Isen then released his wrists and gently fell back onto his pack without hearing or feeling anything break.

He looked left toward the other cargo palette and saw the gap between the two transports was clear so he rolled out in that direction. When he was clear of the cargo palette, Isen gathered his legs beneath him and stood on one knee. "Unstick," he whispered. The biotech material on Isen's wrists and knees then returned to normal as he gave his muscles a little bit of rest, taking a moment to look around the chamber from his crouched position.

He couldn't see much with both cargo palettes blocking his peripheral view and his back away from the tunnel's mouth, but he did see more Peace Core officers finish unloading the first cargo palette and start on the second. Also, on both sides of the tunnel mouth, oblivious to the third cargo palette that was now approaching in the distance, was a pair of fully armored and armed Peace Core guards.

Isen gritted his teeth. He'd ran across their likes before on of his missions in the past eight months and had found them to be quite troublesome. They weren't the brightest stars in the galaxy, but they weren't stupid either. What they lacked in original thought they made up for in alertness and unit coordination. Their weaponry skills were about average, as Isen had found out when a squad of six raided one of Touromi's warehouses that Isen had been in at the time.

Touromi was one of the larger smugglers in the Human Sphere that dealt in illegal weaponry and was at the time supplying an unknown buyer with enough warship grade omnilaser batteries and pulse cannons to arm a good sized insurgent force. Isen had been dispatched to discover who the buyer was and uncover any threats to the Kataran Republic or any other nation-states.

He'd been successful in infiltrating Touromi's organization and was close to discovering the buyer's identity when Peace Core had raided the warehouse that he and 22 of Touromi's men were stationed at. In the first five seconds after the Peace Core troopers blew a hole through one of the warehouse's side walls, 7 of the 23 of them were killed by well placed blaster shots to the chest or head. Once Touromi's men had drawn their holstered weapons, they began to return fire into the still smoke covered wall where the shots that had killed their comrades had come from, as they backed toward whatever cover they could find.

Isen had ducked behind a nearby crate and drawn an old model Xarquillian plasma pistol, highly illegal. He had held his fire until one of the troopers cleared the smoke, then he dropped him to the ground with a not so small heavy pistol blast to the head that melted through his glossy black helmet.

As soon as Isen took down the trooper his buddies sprayed cover fire over Isen's crate, making him duck for cover. Not waiting for the troopers to give him a chance to return fire, Isen crawled/ran away from the troopers and swung around behind a row of crates that allowed him to stand up behind his cover instead of down on his knee at the other, shorter crate. Turning back around, he peaked a look around the side of the crate and spotted five troopers sighting in on a knot of the remainder of Touromi's men who had taken up a position behind a row of low crates.

One of the Peace Core troopers pulled out a grenade and brought his arm back to throw it at the four remaining men, but Isen's pulse shot to his chest stopped him dead in his tracks. The grenade exploded in the dead man's hand, sending two of his fellow troopers airborne into a stack of crates.

The smoke from the grenade's explosion blocked Isen's view, but he heard the remainder of Touromi's men surrender and the boot clicks of more troopers flowing in through the hole in the wall.

Isen had then retreated into the bowels of the warehouse and eventually escaped Peace Core custody.

They're good, but no match for a Morning Dawn agent. I'd even bet that Midnight Star's agents could take these guys out without too much trouble.

Isen slowly got to his feet and walked around the front of the cargo palette. *Wo. They're not taking any chances are they?*

Standing along the translucent partition that divided the chamber in half were 14 more Peace Core guards, four of which were flanking the only passage through the 20 cm thick partition that the cargo movers were taking the crates through one at a time.

Great. Checkpoint with full scanners and an abundance of guards. My cloak is designed to hide my visual and infrared signatures, not to defeat active sensors like the sunray's system. Isen looked around the room quickly as the third cargo palette arrived and parked in its appropriate position. *Looks like that's the only way in, but my cloak will set off the alarm, even if all the sensors get is a blurry image.*

Isen watched as the checkpoint guards held the cargo movers in a short line as the sensors made sure each and every crate was carrying what it was supposed to. Suddenly a thought occurred to Isen.

The sensors. They scan horizontally across the arch. I can see that by the markings on the sides of the archway, but there are none on the top. Isen spied one of the nearby crates on a cargo lifter waiting its turn to be scanned, second in line. Isen knew this was going to be his tricky, but it was the only chance he had of getting by the sensors and the guards.

Isen stepped quickly across the plated floor, his biotech boots making virtually no noise at all, and stopped a meter from the hovering crate. Isen pressed his left thumb to his fore finger.

"Stick," he whispered.

Again the material on his wrists and knees reformed into adhesive material. The first crate in line then moved to be scanned and Isen's target crate moved up a few meters to the first position in line.

Once the Peace Core cargo mover stopped the crate, Isen stepped to it and very carefully touched his right wrist below the top of the crate and flexed it. The adhesive immediately stuck and Isen began to transfer some of his weight to the cargo lifter, letting its repulsor coils slowly adjust to the increased weight without any wobbling that might alert the cargo mover. Isen then lifted his right knee to his chest and flexed his ankle, sticking his knee to the crate.

Slowly he let the cargo lifter take his full weight, then he pulled up his left leg and held it close to his chest with his left arm, which he also stuck to the crate at his wrist. He ducked his head below the top of the crate and mentally sighed in relief when the crate didn't tip over onto its side. *I'm glad this crate is heavy. Invisible or not, tipping over this crate would attract a lot of unwanted attention. Especially if it pinned me to the ground.*

The first crate scanned clean and a nearby guard directed the cargo mover to one of 12 lifts on the other side of the translucent divider after glancing at a nearby console.

"Take lift 7. That crate goes to storage bay 3, section 17."

The Peace Core officer confirmed his understanding with a curt nod then moved toward the number 7 lift.

Another guard waved Isen's crate through and Isen watched the floor pass by from his crouched hanging position. Isen saw the archway on his left pass by him then heard an alarm signal.

Isen unflexed his wrists and ankle, gently dropping to the floor beside the crate that the cargo mover had stopped at the sound of the siren and just past the archway and its sensors. Moving out of the way of the guards clustering around the crate, weapons drawn, Isen half ran to the number 7 lift, stepping into the lift right before the cargo mover quickly pushed a level button, closing the doors and getting away from a bad situation.

Isen climbed up the side wall and hung above the crate so the cargo mover wouldn't accidentally bump the crate up against him. *Well, it worked. They saw my image on the horizontal sensors and thought someone was hiding inside the crate. I don't know what they'll do when they open it up and find no one inside, but I'll be far enough away that it won't matter.*

Isen hung patiently to the lift car wall until the lift doors opened onto a lower level. The cargo mover exited the lift car with Isen silently dropping off the wall and following at his floating heels. The cargo mover turned right down the truncated triangular corridor that the lift opened onto.

Isen followed off to his left so he could see ahead of him, walking a meter or so away from one of the three rows of wide glow panels that had replaced the tips of the triangle in the hallway design.

Occasionally encountering another Peace Core officer or tech in the corridors, the cargo mover led Isen through a labyrinth of the triangular corridors, arranged in a never ending block pattern, until he stopped at an unremarkable door that slid apart on a diagonal slit when he touched a panel on the door jam. The cargo mover entered the room with his crate and unknown to him a Morning Dawn agent a few steps behind him.

Isen rocked back on his heels a bit when he got a good look at the storage room. A good 12 meter high ceiling was covered in a scattering of glowpanels that provided minimal lighting to the room. A number of dark shadows encircled clusters of crates stacked in a 3x3x3 fashion and spread out at seemingly random intervals throughout the storage room which was the size of a small hangar.

The cargo mover took his crate over to a uncompleted cluster and stacked the crate into a vacant spot. After he was satisfied that the crate was snug in its niche, he returned to the same door, hit an interior panel, and left the storage room on his cargo lifter when the doors slid apart. Isen stayed behind and watched as the metal door closed in the cargo mover's wake.

Well, looks like I'm on my own from here on out. Let's take a look at the other end of the room.

Isen walked toward the crate clusters and began to weave his way between the metallic mounds resting on a spotless white floor. At least he thought it was white, the dim lighting wasn't enough to be sure of the color, but he could feel the perfectly smooth surface as his flexible boots glided across the floor.

Halfway through the maze of completed and uncompleted crate clusters, Isen caught a faint glow out of the corner of his eye off to his left. Turning to face it directly, he saw blue highlights reflecting off the polished floor that were apparently coming from behind a full cluster of crates.

Isen stepped into the bluish glow, his cloaking field passing it on to the floor as he stepped around the corner of the stacked crates to find that the glow was coming from behind another stack of crates.

Looks like these crates are more reflective than they appear.

Isen traced the path of the glow back to its source on the storage room wall, then smiled.

Just what I was looking for.

Chapter Thirty-One

"**A**lright guys, listen up. This is how I want to do this," Gradir Cerus said to the other four members of his squad sitting with him at a small table in *Twinkle*'s mess hall. Currently enroute to the Xenarin system, the Midnight Star squad was circled around a small holographic projection of the Xenarin shipyards that was centered on the main construction facility that held the *Goliath*.

"Once the transport drops us off at the shipyards, we'll split up into three groups. Sil, I want you and Mej to take care of the weapons emplacements. Bryen, Ketch, you two will handle the mooring beams holding the *Goliath* in place. I'll take out the tractor beams then meet you four at the *Goliath*'s umbilical to the station. From there, Bryen, Ketch, and me will secure the bridge and evacuate the ship. Once everyone is off, Sil and Mej will retract the docking clamps and seal off the entry point. Once they do that, we'll detonate the explosives. If all goes well, the mooring beams should disengage and the weapon systems should go off line, but if for some reason they're not, we'll have to use the *Goliath*'s omnilasers to knock out the mooring beams and suffer whatever damage ensues as we break free."

Gradir looked each of the four men in the eye before speaking again. "We *are* going to get the *Goliath* out of the system one way or another. If we can do it quietly, then fine. But if we can't and have to blast our way out, then so be it. Our transport won't be back to pick us up, so the *Goliath* is our only ticket out of the system and we can't afford to mess up or we'll be left behind when Admiral Legan's fleet leaves the Sphere. Even if we get the *Goliath* to the rendezvous point, the fleet may have had to leave us behind if we get there late, so we have to make sure we get into and out of the system as quickly as possible. Understand this: Failure is not an option. If we mess up and miss our time window then we're stuck here."

"Enough with the preaching Grady, we already know the risks," Ketch said.

"Hey, I just don't want to get left behind because you guys didn't take the mission serious enough."

"We never take anything serious and we're the best there is."

Silas cleared his throat. "Don't you mean second best Ketch?"

"Females don't count."

"I'll be sure to tell Cara that when we see her again."

"Go ahead, I wouldn't going a few rounds with her."

"Enough about Cara," Mejal interjected, "get your minds back on the mission."

"Easy for you to say." Ketch said. "You're one of her permanent training partners. Us mere mortals can only fantasize about what it's like to get thrown around the gym by that knockout."

"Actually," Sil jumped in. "Grady's going to be her temporary training partner when our mission is over."

Ketch shook his head in amazement. "Some guys just have all the luck."

"Ok you guys," Gradir spoke up. "You think you can stop drooling for a little bit."

Ketch eyed him incredulously. "You're just as bad as us, if not worse. Don't pretend you're not crazy about Cara. We all know better."

"Of course I am," he admitted. "But I also know that the sooner we get the *Goliath* to the rendezvous point, the sooner I'll see Cara again. That's all the motivation I need to stay focused on the mission."

Ketch considered that for a moment. "Good point. Do you want me to run up to the cockpit and ask the pilot if he can speed us up a bit?"

"Thanks, but I don't think that will be necessary. Our arrival time is scheduled during the shipyard's lightest shift so we'll have less people to evacuate from the *Goliath*. Plus, we don't want to raise an alarm throughout the Republic that might hamper the civilian extraction. The Admiral planned our arrival time to coincide with the mass exodus of the military and the number of civilians he's taking along. Even though I'd like to see Cara again as soon as possible, I don't think we should mess with the Admiral's time table."

"You're probably right, he doesn't like people changing his plans without good reason. And I don't think he'd consider 'I wanted to see Cara' a good reason."

"Ah, if you guys hadn't noticed, we're on our own after the transport drops us off," Bryen said. "I don't think our arrival time is all that critical considering that the Admiral left the details of the mission up to us."

"It doesn't matter either way," Mejal said. "We're almost there and increasing or even decreasing our speed won't change our arrival time very much. So let's use the seven hours we have left doing something else besides bickering. Like checking our equipment out."

"Aren't you grouchy today," Silas said. "You get up on the wrong side of the bed this morning?"

"More like he fell off the top bunk," Ketch added.

"No, it's just the jumpsuits they sent with us," Mejal said pointing a thumb back over his shoulder to the cargo bay.

"What about 'em?" Gradir asked.

"They didn't send any red ones."

Pacing her office floor with her hands clenched behind her back, Lena Mian waited for General Dyson's shuttle to land. Dressed in a tight fitting red uniform, complete with glossy knee high black boots and elbow length golden tassels flowing from a narrow oval seam that looped around both shoulders, she looked every bit a military commander.

Trained from birth by her father until his death, Lena had devoted 16 years of her life to becoming a military officer herself. When Captain Mian died in the Sarcosan civil war, Lena had given up her future military career and instead took to her god parents profession: Politics.

After two years of study under Governor Barcash, her godfather, she was elected to represent her home district in the Valcarian Senate. Her election was due in great effort to Barcash's support, but once she took office Lena began to make a name for herself. She quickly rose to seniority in Valcary's senate, despite her youth and inexperience.

When Barcash stepped down from the governorship a few years later, Lena replace him, winning the governor's chair by a narrow margin. Eventually she rose to regional representative in the Durrel district assembly, then to Durrel's representative to the Republic senate. It wasn't until her second year in the Republic senate that she discovered her true heritage. When that happened Lena began to formulate her plans to resurrect the Anteron Federation and those plans involved recovering her military skills.

She continued her own training where her father had left off and at the same time began to politically support the pacifism philosophy. Though she needed to appear naïve and disavow violence in order to promote her peace plan, Lena never took to pacifism.

In my chest beats the heart of a warrior. The pacifistic philosophy that I claim to cherish makes me sick in the stomach. I let General Dyson lead my military forces because I'm tied up with politics, but when I seize power and toss aside my senatorial robes, I'll take direct command of my military again. Lena growled. *That is* if *I'm able to seize power.*

The comms button her desk blinked to life and Lena impatiently punched it. "Yes."

"General Dyson is on his way up Excellency."

"Bring him to the command center," Lena said, switching off the comm and heading for her office door before the Lieutenant could acknowledge her order. She walked down a short hall and out onto a raised semicircular platform that centered on a large viewscreen. Directly below the viewscreen was a deactivated holoprojector, the largest unit in the Human Sphere, that had two sections of control consoles radiating out from it.

Lena walked down a nearby stairway and took up a standing position of the command platform set opposite the viewscreen. After a few minutes General Dyson emerged from a tunnel on Lena's left and walked up next to her and saluted.

"You wanted to see me Empress."

"Yes. It has come to intelligence's attention that a number of civilians scattered throughout the Republic are making ready to evacuate their home worlds and move to an unknown location. A good number of the civilians spoke of unspecified pickup points on a number of different planets from which transports were supposed to take them to a new home. They said that in the near future they would be given the location of the pickup points and the time that the transports would arrive. Also, the name Legan kept popping up frequently in the reports that I've received from our field operatives, so I had some of our analysts do some checking on the military. Everything came up clean except for the fact that Legan hasn't made any move toward disarmament. The fleet is going about business as usual and that makes me think that Legan has no intention of disarming. I would have expected him to try to seize control of the government, but the number of civilians that he is apparently going to transplant suggests that he is going to retreat to the backwater of the Republic or into one of the other nation-states, taking the military and his supporters with him."

She looked General Dyson directly in the eye. "We cannot allow Legan to escape with the Republic's fleet. I want you to bring our forces to full alert and reposition them around the planets that intelligence has labeled as the civilian pickup points. When Legan's ships arrive I want your forces to follow them to wherever their destination is and either capture of destroy his fleet."

"Empress, I'm afraid our own fleet may be inadequate to accomplish the task," he said activating the holoprojector, utilizing the control board in front of him. He brought up a map of the Human Sphere that mirrored the display on the viewscreen before he changed the viewscreen over to a wall full of unit designations and their constituent warships. He then compacted the wall sized list into the left half of the viewscreen, and brought up the stats on the Republic's military that corresponded with a new swath of dots covering the Kataran Republic's portion of the holoprojection.

"As you can see our forces are equal to approximately two thirds of the Republic's military and are currently spread out across the Sphere. I can bring a good number of them together at whatever planets you wish, but I won't be able to move the majority of our units that our stationed outside Republic space into position for at least three weeks. And if the planets on your list are in the rimward section of the Republic that three weeks increases a great deal. But even if I could gather all of our forces together, Legan's fleet still out guns us."

"I'm aware of our situation General. I've already transferred enough Peace Core vessels to your command that you should be able to out gun whatever ships that Legan takes with him."

"Peace Core vessels are armed with non lethal weaponry only. If I use them against Legan's fleet they'll be torn to shreds."

"*Normal* peace core vessels would be, but the ships I'm sending you are fully armed warships."

"I wasn't aware that Peace Core had any true warships."

"I've made some major changes to the organization that the public and the senate are oblivious to. The Peace Core vessels that I'm transferring to your command are superior to most of Legan's warships and should strengthen our fleet enough that you'll be able to crush Legan's ships, both the military and the civilian vessels. When you find his base of operations I want everything and everyone destroyed or captured, no exceptions."

"I understand Empress. It will be done."

"I know it will. I've been building up my resources for a number of years and I am well prepared for any hasty arrangements Legan has made. I had hoped for the government to dismantle the fleet in the name of peace, but apparently Legan isn't going to let that happen. It doesn't really matter though. The Republic's military will still be destroyed, but this way our troops will get some valuable battle experience."

"Have you considered the possibility that Legan may have already discovered our forces?"

"It's crossed my mind in the past but I know better. I've taken great care to hide my organization from the senate and Legan in particular. That's why I had you station a good portion of our fleet outside the Republic. No, Legan doesn't know we exist and won't until it's too late."

Suddenly an alarm sounded.

"Lieutenant report," Mian shouted.

"Intruder alarm Excellency. We have an unauthorized data download in place. Location…" the lieutenant said trailing off.

"Well, where is it?" Dyson anxiously asked.

"Sir, my readouts show it to be in the coreroom itself."

"Which core room?" Mian asked.

"The auxiliary."

"Lieutenant," Dyson said, "order all guards in the immediate vicinity to converge on the intruder's position."

"And," Mian added, "bring down guards from the upper floors. We can't let whoever this is escape."

"Do you want the intruder taken alive?" the lieutenant asked.

"No," Mian answered icily. "Order the guards to shoot to kill."

Chapter Thirty-Two

After checking the immediate surroundings to be sure that the deserted storage room was indeed deserted, Isen reached a hand up to his collar and deactivated his cloak. He shimmered for a moment then became completely visible as he walked toward the wall mounted computer terminal.

With his hand still underneath his collar, Isen retracted his head covering and unmelded his pack, which he promptly dropped at the base of the computer terminal. Kneeling over it, Isen withdrew a hard, oblong lump of black biotech material. Turning the multifaceted object over in his hands several times, Isen finally found the activation button, which he pressed after placing the globule on his right forearm.

The material quickly liquefied and melded to his suit much like his pack had, forming a smooth gauntlet running from elbow to wrist, where it sprouted a short cord. Moving his newly equipped forearm toward the console's dataport, Isen whispered to the suit's built in computer as he plugged the datajack in.

"Ok Flare, I need you to find a schematic of the compound. Bring it up on the console's viewscreen."

"Acknowledged," the suit responded through a small speaker on his forearm, matching Isen's whisper in loudness.

Letting his hand hang at his side, Isen stood up beside his pack and watched multiple images on the viewscreen flash in and out too fast for his eye to track as his suit's computer, now enhanced by the forearm module, sorted through the Peace Core database. It wasn't long until a diagram of both the surface and underground sections of the Peace Core headquarters appeared on the viewscreen in front of him.

"Highlight this portion."

In response to his command, Flare, the name Isen had given to his suit's computer, painted a small green dot in quadrant two of level 17 on the slowly spinning wire frame diagram that appeared on the screen in front of him. Pyramidal in shape, the compound extended over 300 meters below Eclicion's surface. On the display numerous vertical lines representing lift shafts rose from the base of the structure until they contacted the roughly diagonal subterranean edges of the compound where they dead-ended. Only three shafts in the center of the structure extended to the above ground peak of the pyramid.

On closer inspection Isen spotted a number of horizontal lift shafts connected to the vertical shafts, forming an irregular grid system. Apparently the compound's engineers had patterned their lift shaft network on the ones used in large starships that allowed for multiple lift cars to be running at the same time in the same shafts. Like starships, the Peace Core compound likely had an internal traffic computer that controlled the routes that the lift cars took to their destinations, preventing in-shaft collisions and facilitating more effective internal transport.

In between the narrowly spaced lift shafts on the diagram were small segments of levels divided by fine lines that represented a vein like network of hallways intersecting each other at right angles. Though blocky in nature, the tiny rooms, divided by even finer lines, were irregularly shaped and spaced between hallways almost as if the engineers who had designed the levels were bored enough with a typical square grid that they drew lines between the hallways' outline at random.

Spaced almost as far apart as they could be at the bottom of the meter wide viewscreen, was a pair of large chambers that spanned the lower three levels. Isen assumed that at least one of the chambers held the compound's power core and after locating the almost invisible labels on the nearly full viewscreen he confirmed his supposition. The labels read 'Primary power core' and 'Secondary power core' though the chambers mirrored each other in size and shape with no reason that Isen could see for one to be superior to the other.

In fact, most of the compound was symmetrical in shape, bisecting itself along an east-west axis. Even the tunnel that Isen had entered the compound from had a counterpart running off to the north. *That's strange, the tunnel off to the south that I came in on leads to the city, but there aren't any cities to the north. I wonder what it leads to.*

"Flare, can you find a diagram of the north tunnel?"

"Searching…found. The tunnel leads to a small surface outlet 3.7km northeast of the compound."

As Flare was speaking the diagram of the underground pyramid shrunk down into the lower left hand corner of the display while the tunnel extended, tracing its underground course to where it surfaced in the thick of the forest.

"The data indicates that the surface outlet is a camouflaged hanger containing a number of land speeders."

Looks like the peace core officials built a bolt hole for themselves in case the compound ever came under attack. "Flare, zoom back in on the compound and search for the areas with the highest security."

"Acknowledged."

Isen watched the screen as the pyramidal structure reformed and the various levels were colored in one by one. The upper levels showed different shades of blue that faded into yellow as you followed the lift shafts down from the surface. Eventually the yellow became orange on the lower levels with one section of the 37th level glowing bright red.

"Bring up a diagram of the red section."

"Acknowledged."

"And you can cut out the verbal confirmation. From now on just give me a soft tone."

Flare answered him with a high pitched beep.

"That's better," Isen said as the new diagram appeared.

Spreading across nearly three quarters of the 37th level, the area labeled 'ultra secret' was divided into 47 different sections, all of which connected to a hallway system that had only one entrance. The sparse labels on the various sections only indicated that the restricted section consisted of a number of laboratories and sterile storage compartments.

"Flare, can you bring up the inventory lists for all items stored in the restricted section?"

In response to his question the diagram of the restricted area was overlaid with the beginning of the 1st section's inventory list arranged in alphabetical order.

"Search for Anteron archeological artifacts."

The entire listing ran over the viewscreen in a blur until a long list that extended off the viewscreen appeared.

"Ok, now search for any references to 'key' or 'armory.'"

The list was then shortened to 7 items.

"Call up any data you can find on these seven and give it to me one item at a time."

Isen sifted through the data on all seven items but not one of them was an armory key piece. Each of the seven were historical records that told of the armory and the segmented key and were probably what had prompted Peace Core to search for the little known artifacts, but they weren't what he was looking for. He thought for a moment, then something that Admiral Legan had said came to mind.

"Flare, search the previous list for any mention of '4 of 5' of something."

A quick beep proceeded the appearance of a 'No match found' prompt on the screen.

"Ok, try the original item list."

After a short delay Flare located a single item listed as pentagon and brought up the data. Isen looked the data over and confirmed that these were the artifacts. *Gotcha. They've got 'em listed under a code name so a general search wouldn't be able to locate them.* Isen frowned as a troubling thought occurred to him.

"Flare, did you trigger any system flags during your search?"

"Checking. Negative: All computer functions remain nominal."

"Good," Isen said letting out a sigh of relief. Stealth was the only means that would allow him to acquire the artifacts. If his presence was detected he'd be lucky to get off the planet alive, let alone with the artifacts.

"Flare, can you give me the location of Pentagon?"

One of the sections in the restricted area flashed green. "Level 37, lab 18."

"Great. Now download the compound's schematics to memory along with all information regarding Pentagon. Then lock the terminal back down. Give me a beep when you're finished."

13 seconds later his forearm beeped, then Isen removed the datajack from the console and retracted the cord by touching a button near its base on his wrist. After the cord and jack liquefied and were reabsorbed into the gauntlet Isen stooped down and picked up his pack.

After melding it to the back of his biotech suit Isen donned his head cover and reactivated his cloaking field. His suit's power level flashed on his tactical overlay for a second and Isen cringed. *13% power isn't enough for me to stay cloaked for the duration of the mission. It must be these energy efficient glow panels, they're not letting my suit recharge fast enough.* Isen thought for a moment.

"Flare, where's the nearest tech ready room?"

A diagram of the 19th level appeared on his tactical overlay and Flare highlighted a small room near one of the lift shafts in the 1st quadrant. *Better get moving before my cloak runs out.*

Moving back to the door, Isen activated the X-ray mode on his tactical overlay and scoped out the hallway.

Looks clear, he thought, switching back to normal vision. Isen hit the door's activation panel and stepped into the hallway. He began to retrace his steps back to the lift he'd come down on but stopped as he changed his mind.

"Flare, show me the way to the lift shaft on this level that passes closest to the ready room."

After hearing a small beep in his right ear, Isen saw a trail line materialize in front of him. Looking like a suspended pipe just below head height, the virtual trail line was superimposed over his normal sight by the tactical overlay and gave him a red guide wire to follow to the appropriate lift.

After following the trail through a series of left and right turns down both long and short hallways Isen reached the particular lift that the trail line ended at.

"Kill the trail Flare."

The trail line disappeared and left behind an empty hallway. Isen tapped the solitary button on the lift panel causing a miniscule distortion of the end of his index finger. After waiting a minute or so, the lift's doors opened to reveal an empty car. Isen stepped in and hit the 27th level button on a large key pad that had an ID card slot that the techs and guards would use to give the computer the exact location of their duty post. The computer would then reroute the lift car to the nearest lift exit on that level. Not having a lift card himself, Isen had to settle for the conventional system.

After reaching the 27th level Isen left the lift car unnoticed by a few passing techs and made his way to the ready room with the help of another virtual trail line. When he came to the appropriate door Isen used his X-ray mode and scoped out the interior. He spotted one individual sitting at what Isen guessed to be a table in the center of the room.

Guess I'll have to do this the hard way.

He hit the door panel and stepped into the room as the door halves swooshed apart. The tech looked at the newly opened door and appeared a bit confused when no one walked in.

Isen waited until the door closed again before he stepped behind the tech's chair as the man shrugged and returned his attention to the datapad lying on the table in front of him. Isen set himself.

Gotta make this quick.

Isen raised a stiffened hand up past his head and snapped it down on the back of the tech's neck. The man went limp and slid out of his chair and onto the floor, making no sound save for a muffled thud when he hit the carpet.

Isen's hand and most of his right arm became visible for a few seconds before the cloaking field reformed. Isen knelt beside the tech and deactivated his cloak. He retracted the hood then placed a pair of fingers on the man's throat.

When he got a steady pulse Isen removed his pack and pulled out a needleless hypodermic injector. He put the device to the man's neck and injected enough sedative to keep him out a good 12 hours. After putting the injector back in his pack, which he left on the floor, Isen hauled the tech next to a row of nearby lockers by the armpits, dragging him away from the table. Isen then walked over to the door and locked it with a touch of the door panel on which a red lock light illuminated.

Someone might wonder why it's locked, but that's better than having them walk in and find me here. He looked past the two rows of lockers lining the walls to the racks of Peace Core uniforms on the far wall.

Let's hope they have one that's my size, Isen thought as he walked to the far end of the room and began to sort through the clothing.

Alpha Prime

Chapter Thirty-Three

As Cara watched, the decryption indicator bar on the downloader rose into the first of the green segments, only three notches away from completion.

Almost there. Another minute and it'll be past the security. A few more minutes after that it will have finished the download and I'll be able to head back out. I might get out of here alive after all.

Then an alarm sounded.

The repetitive, ear piercing siren was accompanied by a number of slowly flashing red lights that suddenly appeared on the ceiling.

"Dammit," Cara yelled.

She yanked the datajack free of the console and stuffed the downloader into her pack. Half running to the chamber opening, Cara slid the pack onto her shoulders. She brandished her right pistol as she paused at the doorway, just enough to poke her head around the corner and find the tunnel clear. *It won't be clear for long*, Cara thought as she emerged from the coreroom and began running down the tunnel towards the T-junction.

When she was halfway there two figures appeared at the other end of the tunnel carrying weapons. Cara brought her pistol up and sprayed laser bolts at the pair as fast as she could pump the trigger. Running as she was, a good number of her shots went wide, but enough hit home to drop the guards to the floor without them getting a shot off.

She slowed as she came to the T-junction and drew her other pistol. Another guard then appeared above his fallen comrades and took aim at Cara. As he lined up his rifle on Cara's chest he took a laser blast in the head and was dead before he hit the ground.

Cara lowered her left pistol and sneaked a quick peek around the corner.

She spotted three guards running her direction a good ways down the tunnel. Two in front with the third trailing 10 or 15 meters behind them. *If I stay put I'm dead. Gotta keep moving.* Cara gritted her teeth. *Here it goes.*

Cara stepped around the corner into the larger tunnel and blasted away at the guards with both pistols. The rightmost guard went down quickly, but his counterpart ducked down next to the tunnel wall and fired back at Cara. The third guard took up a position of the opposite wall and began taking shots at Cara while her attention was on the first guard.

Cara weaved back and forth randomly as she made her way down the tunnel, pistols blazing. Instead of focusing her fire on just the first guard, Cara split her attention and took aim at both guards at the same time. It was a skill well developed through years of training and one that Cara had excelled at time and again. Keeping in motion so the guards would have a tougher shot to make, Cara gave each of the two guards one of her pistols to contend with. Green laser fire sprayed on either side of Cara as her right pistol took out the guard on her right, then swung in line with her left pistol just in time to fire off a shot that passed through the spot where the left guard's head had been as he fell to the ground with a charred hole in his chest.

With guns in hand, Cara dug a spare power pack out of a belt pouch and replaced the right pistol's power pack, which she let drop to the floor after pressing a side mounted release button. Before she could replace the other power pack, green laser shots streaked over her head from behind. As she ran, Cara half turned and fired haphazard shots back at the swarm of guards that were appearing at the T-junction.

Once Cara was far enough down the tunnel that its gradual bend covered her from their fire, she focused her full attention ahead and picked up her pace as much as she could. A few seconds later a single guard appeared in front of her which she gunned down at full sprint. Hurdling the fallen guard Cara continued on down the tunnel until the Y-intersection came into her view with two, three, then four guards rounding the V-shaped corner of the intersection.

Not slowing or weaving, Cara fired both weapons at the cluster of guards. Before they fully noticed her, Cara dropped one of the guards with a shot to the forehead that blew off a third of the man's head and momentarily blinded the guard behind him with a splattering of blood and brains. Shocked at the violent death of their comrade, the other two guards momentarily froze. That hesitation cost them their lives as she dropped one of the two clean guards spinning to the ground with a shot to his left shoulder. The other guard was knocked back against the wall with a blackened crater where his chest used to be.

The bloodstained guard cleared his eyes of blood just in time to see the deadly blue splinters coming from both of Cara's pistols slam into his chest. He stood motionless for a moment. His rifle fell to the ground from his limp hands as his vision blurred. Then everything went black.

Cara slowed at the intersection and spread her arms wide to cover both of the tunnel offshoots. She saw guards coming from her left and fired a few quick shots in their direction that made them stop their advance and duck down along the tunnel walls. She turned into the right tunnel that lead back to the datacore and sprinted for all she was worth.

Not wanting to find out how many guards were trailing her, Cara kept her attention on the tunnel ahead of her. She knew that trying to fight off the guards behind her was futile. There were just too many, plus the delay would let even more guards catch up to her. No, the only way she was going to survive was to run and gun it back to the fountain and head on back up to the roof.

Seeing that the stretch of tunnel ahead of her was clear, Cara pulled out another fresh power pack from her belt and fumbled it into the appropriate slot on her left pistol as the discarded power pack bounced noisily behind her.

When Cara neared the tunnel opening a few long distance blasts showered the tunnel walls in sparks as well as blowing out small pieces of the primary datacore ahead of her. One of the wild shots grazed her shoulder and almost sent her tumbling to the floor.

Cara fought for her balance as she tried to push aside the searing pain, only partially succeeding. She steadied herself and continued to run down the tunnel, managing to keep a grip on her pistol. Finally Cara exited the guard infested tunnels and headed for the catwalk ramp off to her right.

A pair of shots that hit the floor two meters in front of her made Cara jerk to the side and take cover along the wall. She looked up and quickly spotted a stream of guards flowing down the spiraling catwalk a number of levels above her. *If they make it to the stairway before I do then I'm dead for sure.*

Cara bit back a yelp as a shot blasted the wall to her left and sent sparks flying into her wounded shoulder. *It's now or never. Move it Cara.*

She took off running for the nearby ramp as fast as her legs, still a bit tired from the climbing earlier and now burning from the run through the tunnels, would allow. It didn't help any that she was carrying a not so light pack on her back, but she didn't have a choice. Cara needed her pack if she was to have any chance of getting out of the building alive.

When she hit the catwalk Cara didn't bother returning the ever increasing shots from above. She put all her energy into climbing the curved ramp and hoped one of the guards wouldn't hit her with a lucky shot.

After what seemed like an eternity Cara reached the stairway platform as the guards behind her swarmed out of the tunnel and began climbing the ramp. Cara didn't see them, but she could hear far too many bootstrikes on the metal grating of the catwalk, both above and below her. She ducked into the stairway alcove just as the first of the upper guards appeared from behind the datacore and took a quick shot at Cara that missed high.

She began climbing the numerous stairs as she reholstered her pistols and awkwardly pulled a handful of small spheres from a belt pouch. She separated a green sphere the size of a marble and depressed its single button. Cara let the sphere drop on the stairs and begin to roll down them as she continued upward.

Five seconds later, as it was rolling down the stairs, the green sphere exploded into a cloud of equally green gas in the face of the first guard climbing the stairway. A few seconds after sucking in a mouthful of the gas the guard dropped to the steps unconscious, then he began to roll back down the steps, tripping up the guards behind him.

Still climbing the stairs, Cara dropped two more green spheres behind her. Then when she was approximately half way up the stair case, Cara selected a red sphere and threw it down the stairway behind her.

Twelve steps later she heard and felt a large explosion below that knocked her into the stairway wall. She dropped to the ground as her left shoulder hit the wall and her vision blacked out for a moment. Trying to focus her mind amidst a maelstrom of pain, Cara weakly got to her feet then shook her head to clear it.

She only succeeded in making herself dizzier, but started up the stairs anyway. Cara staggered a bit until the pain subsided enough to let her start running up the stairs again. She then glanced down at the last of the spheres that she had somehow managed to hold on to and depressed its button. Cara let the blue sphere drop behind her as she continued upward, not wasting any effort to look behind her.

After bouncing around a bit, the blue sphere came to a precarious stop on the edge of a step where its tiny vents opened and poured out a rapidly expanding cloud of dark smoke. After a few seconds that section of the stairway was completely obscured by the smoke that, unlike the anesthetic gas, would not dissipate very quickly.

After even more of the endless stairs Cara finally reached the top of the stairwell and reached her right arm across her body and pressed the activation panel.

A small spike of fear shot through her gut when nothing immediately happened, but after a brief hesitation the fountain slowly began to separate. Cara squeezed herself through the still opening gap as soon as she could and emerged into the luxurious office with the wave desk and a significant hole in the wall.

Cara reached into another belt pouch and withdrew more of the small spheres. She replaced the red ones to her pouch, but the rest she activated and tossed down the stairwell as the fountain began to reseal. Not wasting any time, Cara took off her pack and withdrew the magnetic couplers that she quickly fastened to her wrists and knees. Cara then took her datapad out of her pack and clutched it in her left hand. Grabbed her pack with her right hand, Cara crossed to the hole in the wall and tossed it down the dark shaft.

Activating her nightvision, Cara stepped through the hole in the wall and carefully attached the magnetic coupler on her right wrist to the right support beam, then the couplers on her knees.

Trying to avoid using her left hand for anything besides holding onto the datapad, Cara clung to the wall with only three grip points instead of four. Three were sufficient, but not being able to use her left arm would slow her climb. Cara didn't know how much time she had before the guards emerged from the hidden stairway and she didn't feel like sticking around to find out.

Cradling her left arm and datapad against her side, Cara began to climb.

Chapter Thirty-Four

S tanding in the center of one of the *Tenacity*'s gymnasiums, Treys watched the three commandos that were circling him like vultures closely. With his attention more on his peripheral vision than straight ahead, he tried to keep aware of all of their positions at the same time. Not an easy task.

The commando behind him and to his left rushed Treys and prepared to deliver a blow to his head that would have worked his jawbone over *really* good. Treys faked a block with his left arm then dropped down into a roundhouse kick that knocked the commando's legs out from under him and dumped him to the ground.

Coming to his feet, Treys sidestepped away from one of the other two commandos who were now moving in at him. Retreating a few steps, he put all three of the commandos in front of him so he wouldn't have to defend his back for the moment.

The downed commando got to his feet, but held back as his comrades approached Treys side by side. When they were just beyond arms length they split. One engaged Treys while the other circled around behind him.

Treys countered each of the commando's blows, redirecting them away from his body with a series of forearm blocks. As Treys let one of his opponent's blows push him backward, he twisted his hips and kicked out to the side of his body with his right leg, nailing the commando behind him in the gut.

Turning back to the first commando, Treys ducked under a right hook then exploded upward. He kicked out with his left foot and caught the commando under the chin. The man fell backwards as Treys completed his backflip and landed next to where the other commando was holding his gut.

Treys fell to the floor, his legs suddenly collapsing underneath him, as the third commando nailed him in the back of the knees with a low sweeping kick. Landing flat on his back, Treys rolled away from the commando and got to his feet.

He quickly blocked a punch from his right as the commando that he'd kicked in the gut rejoined the fight. As he engaged him in a rapid battle of fists, the second, then the third commando angled in on Treys and helped their friend maneuver him back against the wall.

Alternating between the three commandos, Treys skillfully blocked their combined attack, but he was losing ground fast. He let himself be pushed back until he was two meters away from the gymnasium wall, then he went on the offensive.

Blocking his opponent's arms wide, Treys delivered a hammering blow to the far left commando's chest. Had he wanted to, Treys could have broken ribs with that blow, but instead he gave the man a jolt that sent him flying backwards, stunned but mostly unharmed. As he did so, the middle commando came at him on his right.

Treys twisted his upper body away from the commando's direction of movement but left his right leg in place. The commando tried to jump over his outstretched leg, but Treys's right hand caught his foot in mid air. He let the commando's momentum topple him over, then he released him to fall hard on his stomach.

Treys was then propelled forward onto the floor when the third commando nailed them in the back with a very firm kick. He ducked and rolled through a somersault willing away the ache in his lower back.

The commando came after him again and Treys let fly a sweeping kick trying to take out the commando's legs but only succeeding in making contact with the recycled air. When the commando landed on his feet after jumping over Treys's kick, he half dropped to the floor and kicked straight out at Treys's once again exposed back. Only this time his kick didn't land on target.

Treys let his failed sweep kick rotate him back around on his left knee so that he faced the commando as he kicked out. Treys jerked to the right and caught the man's leg under his left armpit, pinning it there with his arm. Quickly getting to his feet,

Treys lifted the commando's leg up enough to off balance him, then he pushed his leg forward.

The commando fell onto the tumble mats with a loud thud as Treys moved around him and back to the center of the gymnasium. From there he watched as the three men got to their feet and slowly approached him.

Afraid of the old guy now aren't you? So much the better. Treys set himself as the one he'd nailed in the chest approached him while the other two stayed out of his way. *So you guys are switching to one on one. Looks like you're starting to learn after all.*

The commando moved within three meters of Treys then stopped and set himself. *I guess you want me to make the first move. Well, if that's the way you want it, then I'll be happy to oblige.*

Treys stepped forward and struck fast with a straight right followed by a similar left. The commando blocked both wide of his body then slid in a right punch that Treys ducked left to avoid.

Treys then side kicked into the commando's left gut, but the man flexed enough to absorb most of the kick's strength. Treys pulled his leg back quickly, then sidestepped the commando's return kick meant for his gut.

The commando aborted his kick when he saw that is was going to miss and instead reset himself for Treys's attack. It came in the form of a reverse left kick that drove the commando back a couple of steps but failed to knock him to the ground. He then came back at Treys with a right, left, right combination.

Treys blocked the first two punches wide but pulled the third across his body. He took a step forward and landed his right knee into the commando's gut, dropping him to the floor and out of the fight for the time being.

The other two commandos exchanged glances, determining who would fight Treys first. The commando on the left lost and moved forward to engage Treys. Unlike his fallen comrade, this commando didn't wait for Treys to make the first move.

He moved in fast, faked a head height punch, and kicked out straight at Treys's midsection. Treys started to block the punch but noticed his error early enough to twist his body and partially deflect the kick.

He stumbled backwards to his left with the commando giving him no time to recover. Treys took a blow on his left shoulder that spun him around enough to present the commando with the right side of his face. Taking advantage of the opening, the commando delivered a left hook to Treys's jawbone that dropped him face down on the floor.

When Treys didn't move from his kneeling position, the commando relaxed, thinking he'd won. Suddenly the commando found himself falling to the floor as Treys back kicked the commando's left leg out from under him then swept away his right as he quickly switched his kick's direction.

Letting his sweep kick move his right leg wide of his left, Treys switched his weight from his left side to his right and side rolled away from the commando and onto his feet. When the commando finally realized what had happened and began to get to his feet, Treys sprinted the few meters separating them and jump kicked into the commandos gut, catching him off guard and knocking him back three or four meters, where he fell to the ground clutching his stomach.

After seeing what happened to his comrades, the third commando approached Treys carefully and delivered quick, light punches that Treys easily blocked. The commando threw in a few sidekicks, getting a feel for Treys's fighting style before he turned it on heavy.

Then Treys found himself slightly off balance and retreated a few steps until he got his fighting rhythm back. The commando and Treys exchanged a number of blows, all of which were blocked or ducked. The commando alternated between aggressive offense to protective defense while Treys let him control the flow of the fight.

He was good all right. Never giving Treys an opening to exploit, yet keeping on the offensive enough that Treys couldn't relax. They continued to defend against each other's attacks for a full two minutes before Treys decided to turn it up a notch. He shortened his blows and decreased their strength, letting the commando slowly move him backward.

When the commando had adjusted to his forward moving attack, Treys increased the ferocity of his attack beyond the level he'd been fighting at before and stopped the commando dead in his tracks. Treys drove him back, not letting him regain his composure. Slowly the commando's blocks became less and less effective against Treys's hammering blows. The commando was now fighting completely defensive minded, and quickly losing his edge. Treys switched his aim from the commando's body to his arms, knocking them away from his chest centimeter by centimeter.

Once Treys had his chest exposed, he drove a stiffened palm into the commando's sternum, knocking out his breath and landing him back first onto the floor. He rolled backward, not by choice, but from the force of Treys's blow and collapsed into a heap on the floor.

Before the other two commandos could rejoin the fight, a man standing at the gymnasium's exit clapped loudly. "Very good Legan. Your skills are quite impressive, as is your stamina."

"Thank you General," Treys said breathing heavily. "Am I to take that to mean I passed?"

"You're still standing aren't you."

"More or less. Your men are well trained, save for attack coordination."

"How so?"

"When they fought me three on one they had a significant advantage which they failed to use properly. They got in each others way, making them hesitate enough for me to take the upper hand." Treys let out one last heave as he got his breathing under control. "It's a tough skill to master for a pair, even harder for three. But it can be done with enough time and training."

"Something we'll work on on the way to Alpha Prime."

Treys looked to the three commando's behind him getting to their feet. "You guys alright?"

They nodded but didn't speak.

"Well Admiral, you're now a level seven commando, but I was wondering why you waited so long for the combat analysis. You completed your skills tests over eight months ago."

"I've been busy with fleet matters. You wouldn't believe the amount of paperwork that's passed over my desk in the last year and a half."

"I can imagine. I don't suppose you'll have any extra time when we reach Alpha Prime either."

"No, probably not."

"Too bad, I think you could make level nine with a little more training. You skills are superior to most of my men, except that you're a bit out of practice. It looked to me like you haven't fought at this speed for some time."

"I haven't. But I don't intend to let my skills deteriorate. I've been training enough to stay combat ready, but eventually I'm going to return to line troop readiness level, when I have the time."

Before the General could respond the gymnasium door opened and a Kataran Captain stepped through. "Admiral, I hope I'm not interrupting."

"No, we just finished. Is there a problem Captain?"

"No problem. I just wanted to let you know that the last of the crew came aboard a little over an hour ago."

"Are we spaceworthy yet Captain Yader?"

"Completely."

Treys nodded to General Cardon. "If you'll excuse me General, I need to report to the bridge."

"Of course Admiral."

Treys nodded to the three commandos now standing in a cluster off to Cardon's left. "Thanks for the workout," he said as he followed Captain Yader out of the gymnasium.

The pair hopped into a nearby lift car that took them directly to the bridge. Still dressed in his sweat soaked combat fatigues, Admiral Legan strode onto the bridge and took up position behind his command chair. "Lieutenant."

"Sir."

"Send to all vessels. Code Yellow."

Chapter Thirty-Five

"**O**K guys. Time to suit up," Gradir told his squad as he tossed a pile of clothing on the mess hall rec table. "What's this?" Silas asked.

"Those are replicas of Xenarin uniforms."

"And what exactly do you want us to do with them?"

"Put them on over your jumpsuits."

"But they're...ugly," Silas said, pointing at the mound of bright yellow cloth with equally bright green trim running across the shoulders and down the lengths of the arms and pant legs.

"Ugly or not, we're wearing them. I'd rather not have to fight our way around the station if we can pass off as shipyard workers."

"You don't think our assault rifles will give us away?"

"Not if we're carrying them and our other gear in standard issue tote bags," Gradir said, waving vaguely off to his left at the door that led into the cargo hold. "Now, if you'll quit whining, put these on. And make sure that your cuffs and collar cover your jumpsuits."

"Ok," Bryen said. "But you first."

Gradir shook his head. "Children," he muttered.

Picking up the top uniform and pulling off his name tag, Gradir unzipped the front zipper down to where his navel would be and stepped into the one piece suit. His right boot caught in the pant leg, making Gradir loose his balance. He made a vain grab at the wall which was too far away and fell to the floor. The other four agents burst out laughing. He ignored them and pulled his boot through the tangle while he was still on the floor. Then he stood up and pulled his arms through the sleeves and zipped up the front all the way up to his adams apple, eclipsing the last bit of his black jumpsuit. Gradir eyed his squad.

"Your turn."

Their smiles faded and after a moment's hesitation they reluctantly began putting on the uniforms. Soon the five of them stood in the mess hall resplendent in their garish uniforms and looked each other over.

"Whoever designed these things should've been vaped on the spot," Ketch said pulling at a sleeve.

"Yeah, I think I'm allergic to the color," Silas commented.

"I know they're bad, but I'd rather humiliate myself than get shot at."

"Speak for yourself Grady," Mejal said. "I'd rather *be* shot then wear this...this whatever."

Before Gradir could respond, the pilot's voice came over the mess hall's speakers. "Fifteen minutes to reversion. If you're not already at the airlock then get there."

"Alright guys, let's get into our space suits." Gradir extended his hand toward the cargo bay. "Whiners first."

They glared at him but said nothing as Silas opened the door and led Gradir and the others across the cargo bay to a pair of glossy black crates. Silas punched a short code into a built in keypad and popped open the lid. Mejal did likewise on the other crate and began pulling out the zero gee suits along with the rest of their gear and some carrying bags of a familiar color.

"They had to go and make their gear satchels the same color as the uniforms," Mejal said in disbelief. "I wouldn't be surprised if everyone on the station was blind. These colors are already starting to hurt my eyes."

"Then get unto the space suits and shove the satchels into their storage packs."

"Good idea," Silas said. "Much more of this and I'll go color blind."

The five Midnight Star agents pulled on the armor like, non glossy, black space suits after each of them loaded a portion of the squad's gear into the hard shelled, rectangular pack attached to the back of the space suits. As they were putting on their hard carapaces, the ship's comm crackled to life again.

"We've just dropped out of IS space. Drop off point ETA is seven minutes. Check in when you're set to go."

Ketch finished suiting up first and waited on his companions before heading to the nearby airlock that was alongside the cargo bay's closed loading ramp. Ketch pulled on his helmet and secured it in place before opening the airlock's interior doors. The others followed suit and joined Ketch inside the airlock. Gradir squeezed into the airlock last and sealed the door behind him. Touching a panel on his left wrist, he keyed open his squad's comm channel.

"Everybody set? Mej?"

"Check."

"Ketch?"

"Ready."

"Bryen?"

"Good to go."

"Sil?"

"I'm good."

Gradir switched frequencies. "*Twinkle*, my squad's in the airlock and set to go. What's the count?"

"Two minutes, four seconds. A pair of Xenarin patrol ships are heading our way to escort us out of a restricted zone, as I'm told by the yard's traffic controller. We'll beat them to the drop off point by about 30 seconds. I'll give you the count at 10 seconds to go, then you're on your own. Good Luck."

"Thanks *Twinkle*, Cerus out." Gradir switched back to his squad's frequency. "Which of you guys are closest to the control panel?"

"I am," Mejal said.

"Go ahead and depressurize the airlock, then get ready to open the outer hatch. We've got less than two minutes to drop off and a couple of Xenarin patrol ships in the area. I know the exhaust from these suits is supposed to be invisible, but use the thrusters sparingly just in case. Switch to the transport's frequency for the count down then switch back to this frequency once we're outside the ship."

Gradir heard a jumble of acknowledgements then four clicks as the others switched frequencies. He did the same and waited for the pilot's countdown. An eerie whistle echoed through the airlock as its atmosphere was pumped out, then quickly enough complete silence. After a short wait Gradir jumped slightly as the pilot's voice blared in his helmet.

"Ten, nine, eight, seven, six, five, four, three, two, one, mark."

Mejal then hit the hatch release, opening the airlock to space. Ketch was the first out, then Bryen. Silas followed Mejal on the heels of the first pair and Gradir pulled himself out last. He pushed off the ship's hull following the direction of the rest of his squad as they slowly moved away from the ship at a slight angle from its line of flight. Drifting towards his comrades, Gradir put distance between himself and the *Twinkle*.

"We're clear," he said into the vast emptiness above, below, and all around him. In response, the *Twinkle* slowed its fly by approach at the shipyards and let the Xenarin patrol ships herd it away from the shipyards. Gradir switched his comm back to his squad's frequency.

"Ketch, you there?"

"Yeah."

"Take point. Everybody else form up on him."

Silence was the only reply he got, but Ketch did move forward with the help of a thruster blast. Mejal pulled up behind his right with Bryen taking up a similar position on his left. Silas similarly staggered himself behind Bryen and Gradir moved into the remaining position behind Mejal. Using the transports momentum, the Midnight Star squad flew towards the shipyards in a V-formation, keeping their spacing at approximately two meters. They let themselves drift for a few minutes with Ketch having to make only a few minor course changes before Gradir finally broke the silence.

"Ok guys. Spread out and hit the retros."

Complying with his orders, Silas and Bryen swung wide with the help of a thruster burst then hit their retro thrusters and shot back behind Ketch. At the same time Mejal and Gradir moved to Ketch's right and waited until he shot back behind them before they hit their retros. With Gradir now in front, the five agents fired their thrusters for a good 30 seconds before coming to a stop two kilometers from the outer edge of the shipyard. It took a few moments for them to recoalesce into the V-formation again, but once they did, with Gradir now at point, Mejal spoke up.

"I think the *Goliath*'s on the other side of the station. Grady, do you want to circle around or find an airlock on this side?"

"We'll go this side."

He studied the massive station closely. The main body of the station consisted of a pair of elongated pyramids, one dorsal, one ventral, rising from a flat, rectangular midsection that radiated construction pylons that outlined the yard's shipways. Gradir spotted an empty slip and pointed a hand toward it.

"Let's try that vacant dock. There shouldn't be any personnel in the area to spot us."

"Lead on," Silas said.

Gradir thrusted forward, angling towards the slip with his comrades following close behind him. As the station eclipsed the stars from his view through the space suit's face plate, Gradir could just begin to make out individual lines of lighted windows on the nearest pylon. It took four and a half more minutes of drifting until Silas located an airlock.

"Grady. Lower right, five rows up from the bottom."

He looked at the section of work platform that Silas had indicated and after a few seconds of searching found it as well. "Got it. Follow me."

Gradir thrusted again and vectored in at the spec of an airlock. Slowly it grew larger and larger until Gradir could make out the glowing lights on the exterior control panel. Gradir drifted towards the pylon's hull and gave a short burst of retros to slow him enough that he could catch himself on the airlock door. The other agents stayed out of his way as Gradir micro thrusted his way over to the control panel. The green lit pressurization button told Gradir that the airlock was pressurized and turned to yellow, then red when he pushed it and activated the depressurization cycle. Hitting the only other button on the panel, Gradir opened the airlock's outer hatch, turning the also green lit button red. Gradir maneuvered himself into the open airlock and dropped to the deck as the artificial gravity took hold of him. He moved on into the large airlock with the others soon following.

Once all five of them were inside, Ketch sealed the hatch and repressurized the airlock. When the control panel indicated that the air pressure had been equalized with that of the station's interior, Ketch opened the interior hatch and Gradir led the squad out into a large ready room, filled with bright yellow space suits.

"Oh great," Silas said as he removed his helmet. "More monuments to bad taste."

"At least they didn't paint the entire station the same color," Bryen said, starting to strip off his space suit.

"Let's get these suits off before someone walks in on us," Gradir said. "Then find an empty locker and shove 'em in."

The others did as ordered, pulling their suits off and transferring their gear into three of the ugly satchels before literally jamming the suits into the lockers lining the ready room's walls. They managed to fit the suits into the lockers with Silas having to kick the door shut on his locker to get it to close all the way.

Silas picked up one of the satchels, Ketch another. Gradir picked up the last satchel and swung it over his shoulder. He reached down and touched the pant leg on his right thigh, feeling the palm sized blaster pistol that he had stowed in a hidden pocket on the yellow and green uniform.

"You guys ready?"

He received four nods then turned away from the airlock and walked down the length of the ready room to the far door.

"Remember, we're supposed to be Xenarin dock workers, so try to relax and blend in. There shouldn't be a lot of personnel in this section of the station but we might encounter a few. Don't jump if someone suddenly appears around a corner. As far as they're concerned we're supposed to be here, so try to act as casual as possible." He smiled. "Sil, all you have to do is start day dreaming about Cara and follow us. We'll get your attention if we need you."

"Funny Grady, real funny. Can we get going now, these uniforms are starting to burn out my retina."

"Once we get aboard the *Goliath* you can take it off," he said turning back to the door. "Heads up guys. Here we go."

Chapter Thirty-Six

G radir opened the ready room door and glanced down the hallway.

"It's clear," he said stepping out the door.

His comrades followed him out and down the hallway to the left. Silas took up position off Gradir's left with Mejal, then Ketch and Bryen following. They walked down the hallway until they came to a cross corridor where they turned right, heading towards the main body of the station. After passing 27 intersections they came to the end of the hallway and a lift shaft.

Gradir pushed the call button and waited. It wasn't too long before the lift shaft doors opened to reveal a circular lift car occupied by a pair of yard workers dressed in the same uniforms that Gradir and his squad were wearing. The two men stepped aside further into the lift car to make room for the *Goliath* squad.

Gradir offered a quick nod then entered the lift car, standing beside the control panel. As Silas and the others walked into the large lift car, Gradir glanced at the controls. Arrayed in a pair of vertical columns, the level select buttons ranged from U21 at the top of the left column through M at the top of the right column to S21 at the bottom of the right column. The level indicator showed them on S17 with U6 highlighted.

When Ketch entered the lift and the doors closed behind him, Gradir punched the M button and waited patiently as the lift rose. The yard workers didn't care to make casual conversation and Gradir was thankful.

When the lift stopped and opened onto the main level the Midnight Star agents got off and let the pair of yard workers continue upward. When the doors closed behind them and left them alone in the empty hallway, Silas let out a sigh of relief.

"That was too close." He looked to Gradir. "Why did you choose this level?"

"I wanted to get off before those two did," he pointed a thumb back over his shoulder as they walked down the hall, "Plus this is the main level of the construction pylon. It should have an entrance to the station proper."

"I think that's it up ahead," Mejal said looking down the hall at a wide archway.

"Looks like it," Bryen commented. Gradir dug into a pocket and pulled out a small datapad.

He punched in the position coordinates inscribed on a panel atop the archway as they stepped into a large hallway nexus. A number of yard personnel were visible in the three connecting hallways, lazily going about their business. Gradir moved toward a wall and out of view as he studied the datapad readout.

"Ok guys, time to split up. Sil and Mej, take the right tunnel and take care of the weapons emplacements, start with the ones on this side first. Ketch and Bryen, go through the center of the station to get to the *Goliath*'s slip. I'll take the left hall and work my way up into to the tractor beam emplacements."

Gradir eyed the other agents and hefted his datapad. Taking his cue, each of them pulled out similar datapads from individually tailored hidden pockets.

"Mark our position now as Main body, level 127, sector 15, nexus 53."

"Got it," Silas said, returning his datapad back to his pocket. "We meet up at the *Goliath*'s docking umbilical?"

"Right. Plant your explosives then wait up for everyone else near the umbilical without drawing attention to yourselves. Once we're all there we'll board the *Goliath* together."

Gradir looked at the others for more questions but they had none.

"Alright, let's get moving. Good luck."

"Mej, how close are we?" Silas asked as they walked down the outermost corridor of the station.

Mejal took a quick glance at the datapad he had concealed up his sleeve. "Two more intersections ahead, then three left."

"Good, I'm starting to get tired of all this walking around."

"It won't take us very long to rig this nexus, now that we know what we're doing," Mejal said. "Then we can head back to the umbilical."

They didn't say anything else until they came to an unremarkable door that led to an interior room. Using a skeleton key, Silas opened the door and stepped inside with Mejal on his heels. Silas locked the door behind them while Mejal started to pry open a maintenance hatch on the back wall. After releasing the side mounted latches, Mejal pulled the metallic covering off the wall and gently placed it on the floor.

"After you," he said, motioning to Silas.

"Thanks."

Pushing his near empty satchel into the maintenance shaft ahead of him, Silas crawled into the cramped tunnel.

"You think they could've made these a little wider," he said as Mejal crawled into the shaft behind him.

"You gotta give them credit though. This is a good way to keep their maintenance personnel in shape. I don't think any of the pot bellied mechanics at Eastport cold fit into these tunnels."

"Point."

Silas crawled down the length of the tunnel until it opened out into a small cylindrical chamber about the size of a lift car. He pushed the satchel out first, dropping it softly to the floor, then pulled himself out. He picked up the satchel and moved out of Mejal's way as he crawled out behind him. Mejal stood up after dropping to the floor in a crouch then looked at Silas.

"Three down, one to go."

"Yeah, let's make it quick," Silas said pointing to a floor level access panel. "Your turn."

Mejal pulled out a small tool kit from another of his hidden pockets and quickly removed the access panel. Dropping to his belly, Mejal pulled his upper body through the hatch and began fumbling his way through a mess of wires. He managed to pull the mass of wires apart enough that he could see the top portion of a large power conduit.

Moving his hands along the conduit, he pushed tubes of optical cable aside until he felt the conduit dead end at the power nexus that fed the nearby weapons emplacements. Mejal reached his right hand back at Silas. Soon he felt a weight in his hand and pulled it in with him. Maneuvering the explosive around the bundles of wires, he brought it in front of his face and rotated it around in his hand under the faint illumination of several rows of small indicator lights.

Repositioning it to his liking in his hand, Mejal placed it on the power conduit up against the power nexus. He reached his hand back two more times and placed the remaining explosives above the first and on the power nexus itself, sealing them all in place with a tube of putty like adhesive that he pulled from his left sleeve. After making sure the explosives were secured in place, Mejal pulled the wiring back into place and extricated himself from the claustrophobic compartment.

"That's it," he said as he stood up. "Time to get to the docking umbilical."

"Good," Silas said. "It's about time we got out of these uniforms."

Pulling themselves up a vertical shaft by means of a narrow ladder, Ketch and Bryen maneuvered themselves through the innards of the *Goliath*'s port docking pylon.

"Hand me the tool kit," Ketch called down to Bryen.

"Here," Bryen said, reaching up with the palm sized black, book like case.

Ketch took it in his right hand and brought it up to rest against the shaft wall and one of the ladder rungs.

"Thanks," he said, opening the case and pulling out a small lever. He closed the case and handed it back down to Bryen. Getting a good grip on the ladder with his left hand, he began to pry open an unremarkable panel on the lift wall.

"Heads up," he said before giving it one final jerk and tugging it free. The panel fell down the shaft, ricocheting off the walls until it hit the shaft floor 37 decks below. Ketch maneuvered himself into the opening and wedged himself between an overhead bulkhead and a 50 cm wide power conduit at the base of the opening. Bryen climbed up the ladder to the opening and reached under his armpit and into the satchel he carried on his back. He pulled out another of the triangular shaped explosives they'd planted in the starboard construction pylon and reached it into the opening.

"Here," he said.

"Got it," Ketch said, taking it from Bryen as he laid horizontally along the length of the conduit.

He placed it as far ahead of him as he could reach and secured it in place with a tube of sealant putty. Ketch took another explosive from Bryen and placed it next to the first explosive but on the side of the conduit instead of on the top.

"All set," he called out. Bryen backed down the ladder and let Ketch crawl out of the opening onto the ladder. They climbed down 15 levels before veering off on a horizontal maintenance tunnel that opened out into a corridor on the M level. They swiftly made their way off the pylon and along the outer corridor of the main section of the station until they reached a hallway nexus that contained the *Goliath*'s umbilical entrance.

"I don't see any of the others," Bryen said.

"No, I don't either. We'll just have to hang around here until they arrive."

Holding one of the triangular explosives in his teeth, Gradir lowered himself into a maintenance pit in one of the internal crawlspaces on level 67. He pried himself into the space between two small pipes and pulled apart the wiring beneath them to reveal the power conduit that fed the number 3 tractor beam projector.

As he'd one four times before, Gradir sealed the explosive onto the conduit and carefully pulled himself out of the maintenance pit. He reached into his gear satchel lying on top of the grate plate that he removed earlier and pulled out his last explosive. Gradir pulled himself back into the pit and sealed the explosive in place. After moving the wiring back in place, he pulled himself out of the pit with a sigh of relief.

"Finally, I'm done. Time to get out of here."

Gradir pushed aside his satchel and pulled the grating panel back into place. Dragging the satchel in front of him, he backed down the crawlway and eventually stepped out into a small maintenance room. He replaced the crawlway hatch then swung the satchel over his shoulder.

Gradir opened the door and locked it behind him before striding down the corridor to a nearby lift shaft. After entering the lift along with a female technician, Gradir waited patiently through a series of stops to pick up and drop off personnel before he got off on the 127th level. It took him a good 15 minutes to navigate the labyrinth of corridors between the lift shaft and the outer corridor that ringed the station proper. Then he walked through the corridor, passing pylon after pylon, until he reached the corridor nexus that contained the *Goliath*'s umbilical.

When he entered the high ceilinged room he found his fellow agents carrying on a conversation about the latest version of the cloud reaper racing hovercraft and other trivial matters. Gradir walked toward the cluster of lazy yard workers who immediately dropped their act when they caught sight of him.

"What took you so long?" Silas asked.

"I had five targets to deal with, you two only had four." He glanced quickly at each of the agents. "I assume you all completed your assignments."

"We did," Mejal answered.

"Well then," Gradir said tilting his head at the short, extendable tunnel that connected the station to the *Goliath*, "let's go."

Chapter Thirty-Seven

After finding a Peace Core technician's uniform and labcoat that suited him, Isen pulled them free of their respective hooks on the wall and laid them out on the ready room table.

Putting his hand to his collar, Isen deactivated the biotech suit. It crawled off his body, reconstituting his civilian clothing and pulling itself into its clear tube that formed in his right palm. Isen placed the tube on the table directly under one of the overhead glowpanels, letting it soak up the light and start replenishing the energy that the cloak had drained. He then picked up the technician's uniform and began pulling the one piece suit over his existing clothes.

"Come on, work with me," pleaded Isen when his left boot got stuck in the pant leg. He gave it two more tries before the pant leg untwisted enough for his boot to slide through. "There."

Isen pulled his arms through the sleeves and zipped up the back of the uniform, completely obscuring his civilian clothing. He pulled on the labcoat then walked over to the unconscious Peace Core tech that was dressed similarly to Isen.

After frisking the unconscious man, Isen pulled from his pockets four datacards, an ID chip, an electronic pen, and a small chronometer. Isen laid all the items on the table, including the datapad that the man had dropped when Isen knocked him out. He searched through the datacards using the datapad, finding nothing but technical jargon.

"These don't help me any, but our analysts might find them interesting," he said, pocketing the five datacards into one of his labcoat's pockets.

Disregarding the pen and chronometer, Isen picked up the ID chip and looked it over. The thumb length rectangular chip appeared to be compatible with the slot in the lift car, which gave Isen an idea.

He reached across the table and retrieved the biotech cylinder. Opening the lid and pouring its contents into his palm, Isen resuited.

"Flare, can you scan this chip?" he said after the computer upgrade reformed along with the suit.

Holding the chip above his right forearm, he waited for Flare to reply.

"Insert into slot."

Isen wondered for a moment what Flare meant until a portion of his forearm attachment liquefied and created a small opening. He put the ship into the slot then the attachment molded to it. After a few seconds Flare responded.

"Yes."

"Does this chip have enough clearance to let me into the restricted section?" Isen asked.

"No..."

"Great. I'll have to find another way in or jump someone else."

"But it could," Flare finished.

Isen looked a bit confused. "Explain."

"The data I downloaded on Pentagon contains the clearance codes necessary to access the project. It also includes the codes required to gain access to the restricted area. My upgrade attachment has the capability to rewrite the ID chip with the proper codes. Do you wish me to rewrite it?" Flare asked.

"Please. Include all the codes you have available."

Flare responded with a beep and went to work. Two minutes and 17 seconds later the rewrite was complete.

"Codes installed."

"Release the chip."

Flare complied and the material around the slot liquefied and pulled back enough for Isen to snatch the revamped ID chip away. He held it up to the light and looked it over.

"Good work. I owe you one."

"Clarify."

He smiled. "Never mind."

Isen reached up to his collar and deactivated the suit again. But this time he placed the biotech tube into his labcoat's pocket instead of on the table. He walked over to where his pack was lying on the ground and pulled out his blastech pistol. He slid it into an interior pocket of the labcoat and stood up, making sure that it wasn't visible through the fabric.

"Good. At least I'll be able to carry this. I just hope I don't have to walk through any scanners."

Isen then closed and picked up his pack, putting it in one of the nearby lockers. He looked over at the unconscious technician lying prone of the floor. "What am I going to do with you buddy?"

Isen looked around the room for a place to stash him, but there wasn't anything in the room besides the racks of clothing, the table and chairs, and the lockers. *The lockers*.

Isen walked to the end of the left row to where the largest of the lockers were. He opened one of the shoulder high compartments and looked inside. The locker was considerably deeper than it was wide and looked to Isen that his unconscious friend might just fit in.

He walked over to the nearby tech and hauled him to his feet. Isen ducked under his left shoulder and pulled the man's arm across his back. He dragged him over to the locker and pushed him in back first. The Peace Core technician slumped down to the locker floor, leaning against the right wall. Pushing his legs up against his chest, Isen managed to close the locker door on the compacted man.

"Sorry about this pal, but I can't let someone find you lying on the floor. You'll probably be all cramped up when you wake up, but you'll live." Isen turned back towards the door and fingered the ID chip in his pocket. "Time to get going. I hope this works," he said, then walked to the door.

Tagging the wall, he unlocked and opened the ready room door, then stepped into the hallway. Recalling from memory, Isen started off to his left and began weaving his way in and out of a number of corridors as he headed for the lift shaft that would take him to the unrestricted section of the level 37. All the lift shafts that passed through the restricted section didn't have outlets on that level so Isen had to find one of the lift shafts on the other side of the compound that would let him get off on the correct level.

After about 20 minutes of traversing endless corridors, Isen finally found the lift he wanted. *About time. At least nobody saw through my disguise. Yet.*

Isen called for a lift and waited patiently until the lift doors opened to reveal an empty lift car. *Good. I don't particularly feel like chatting with any Peace Core personnel right now.* Isen stepped into the lift car and punched the 37th level button. As the lift doors began to close Isen heard some quick footsteps outside, then a hand darted through the doors, stopping them from closing. *Great.* Isen reached out and helped pull open the lift doors for a short, red haired woman about 25 years old.

"Thanks," she said.

"No problem," assured Isen as the lift doors finally closed.

The woman dug out her ID chip and swiped it through the wall slot. She looked at the illuminated '37' button and turned to Isen questioningly.

"You forget your chip?" she asked.

"No," Isen said holding it up for her inspection. "Sometimes I just like to do things the hard way. Too much amenity let's the mind begin to stagnate," he said, tapping his temple with his right index finger.

"I know what you mean. After dissecting prepared corpses for two years I got out of the habit of dissecting live specimens and I lost valuable data because my skills had atrophied. I learned from my mistake and now periodically request live specimens just so I keep in practice."

"Good for you," praised Isen, even though his stomach had become considerably less stable.

Come on lift, hurry up.

"I'm sorry, I've been impolite." She extended her hand. "I'm Dr. Quetrel."

Isen took her hand and gripped it firmly. "Dr. Corellen. Nice to meet you," Isen said, picking a name from a memorized list designed for such purposes.

"Are you in medicine a well doctor?"

"No, my specialty is archeology."

"How interesting," she said as the lift came to a stop on the 37th level. "What research project are you assigned to?"

The lift doors swooshed open and Isen stepped partway out into the hall then turned back to face Dr. Quetrel.

"I'm afraid that's classified, but thanks for taking interest," Isen said as he threw the woman a quick wink.

She smiled bashfully as Isen stepped clear of the lift and let the doors close in front of him. Isen began walking down the corridor to his left even though he felt like slumping against the wall in relief. *That definitely wasn't any fun, but at least I didn't reveal myself. At least not until she checks the personnel files for a Dr. Corellen so she can ask him out on a date. I just had to throw her that wink didn't I.* He considered his actions for a moment. *I guess I made the right call. It distracted her from questioning my identity. And if she checks on Dr. Corellen, I'll be out of here before she can cause me any trouble.*

Isen made his way down the short hallway and took a left at a T-intersection and found himself at the double metallic doors that lead to the restricted section. *Looks like this is it. I hope Flare's handiwork passes their security.*

Isen fished his ID chip out of his pocket and inserted it into the receiver panel built into the wall. At first nothing happened, and Isen started to worry about setting off an alarm, but after a few seconds' delay the red indicator light above the chip slot cut out and a green indicator light adjacent to it illuminated. Isen then hit the door activation switch and pulled out his ID chip.

The metal containment doors broke their seal with a hiss and slid apart all but silent. *So far so good. Let's just hope my luck continues.*

Isen stepped through the doors and let them reseal behind him. *Now, where's lab 18?*

Chapter Thirty-Eight

Standing on the *Tenacity*'s bridge, High Admiral Legan stared out the forward viewport at the rows of starships moored at the Republic's mothball facility. Some were warships, most were transports, but all were starships that deserved to be let loose into the vastness of space where they belonged. If Legan had not intervened, the host of starships in front of him would still be stripped down and stowed away like useless machinery, destined to never again see the stars, only to waste away as historical monuments and remembrances of the past.

No my friends, your time of stagnation is at an end. You served us many years ago, then were thrown aside as outdated machinery. Now as fate would have it, you are once again called into service, but not as relics of a bygone era. I've made sure of that. Both you and I are of a different era. I may have just been a boy when my grandfather commanded the fleet, but the style of warfare which he imparted to me in those few years has never left me. I'm a part of a past which I did not live and the sole retainer of my grandfather's military philosophy. Legan focused his attention on one of the nearby warships. *I think it's about time we show these pompous pacifists what old school is all about.*

"Admiral," Yader called coming to a stop a few meters behind Legan on the upraised bridge platform.

"Yes Captain, what is it?"

"Sorry to disturb you sir, but you said that you wanted to be notified when it was 1900 hours."

"I did indeed. What's the fleet's status?"

"Both the vessels here at the station and the ones abroad have signaled their readiness and are awaiting the final order."

"Very well. Give the order Captain. Code green. 18 hours."

"Yes sir."

Yader turned to the starboard crew pit. "Comm. Orders to the fleet. Code green. Implementation time is 18 hours from now."

"Aye sir."

Still focusing on the viewport Admiral Legan raised his voice enough for the Lieutenant at the communications station to hear. "Then contact the station's command center and ask them to open the main doors so the fleet can leave."

"Yes sir."

"Captain?" Legan said, his voice back to its normal low, powerful tone.

"Yes."

"You have the bridge. I'm returning to my quarters. Make sure that all the appropriate ships safely clear the station. Then see to it that the remaining warships begin powering up. That goes for the *Tenacity* as well. It won't be too long before we leave as well."

"Yes sir."

Legan then left the bridge and took the nearest lift car through the bowels of the *Tenacity* to the lift exit nearest his quarters. He hit the door activation panel with his left palm and quickly stepped into his quarters. He locked the door behind him and crossed to his personal communications terminal and swung into its soft chair.

Legan switched on the terminal and punched in a lengthy command code that would guarantee a secure line and prevent any record of the transmission from being made. After a few more keystrokes a 30 cm high holographic projection of a man from the shoulders up materialized before him.

"Good afternoon admiral. What can I do for you?"

"Has all of our equipment been loaded?"

The hologram nodded. "All equipment and personnel are currently on their assigned ships."

"Then I assume the dismantling is complete."

"Yes, the Midnight Star headquarters are no more. Everything down to the computer mainframe was carted off and the exits were sealed. It's an empty complex now."

"Good. Where are you presently?"

"I'm on the *Orion*, which is currently in the *Audacity*'s hangar bay along with a number of other smaller transports. I'm using the *Orion* as our operational headquarters and so far no one's bothered us. The ships in this hangar bay are pretty tightly packed, so I don't think we'll have any problems staying hidden. But just incase someone does come snooping around the ship, I've got everything set up inside to correspond with our cover story."

"Good job. Did any of our people have trouble infiltrating the crew?"

"Only a few, but the problems themselves were trivial and solved quickly enough."

"Have you any reports from Agent Venture or the *Goliath* team?"

"No I don't. But if they're following mission protocols they won't be checking in until they meet us at the rendezvous point."

"I know. I just wanted to make sure that they didn't have to abort the mission. What about our Morning Dawn loner?"

"The same."

"Do you have anything special to report?"

"No, except that the *Audacity* just jumped to IS space. Am I correct in assuming that the civilian pickup is underway?"

Legan nodded. "I just gave the word a few minutes ago. All the civilian ships and their escorts should be heading to their pickup points. I'll be heading to the rendezvous point with the rest of the warships a bit later, but the majority of our fleet is now mobile. If there's nothing else, I'll let you get back to work. If something comes up you can reach me on the *Tenacity*. Go ahead and send any message through normal channels, just include the epsilon encrypt code. That'll reroute it directly to me without anyone else seeing it."

"Will do Admiral. Command out."

Legan switched off the terminal and moved into one of the self conforming chairs in his quarters that was facing the viewport. Looking out over the docking pylon, Legan watched as the majority of the ships at the mothball station slowly maneuvered out of their docking slips and into a long line leading to the open main doors.

Well, you're free at last. This may be just be a transportation convoy, but you'll never again be stuffed up inside a station.

An odd sensation began creeping up his spine and Legan tried to identify it. He was sure it had something to do with his last thought. Legan got up out of his chair and walked to the viewport as he tried to lock down on the unsettling feeling.

All at once the answer formed in his mind. *It's the convoy. This mission isn't just going to be a cargo run, it's going to be more dangerous than that.*

Legan looked out at the patch of space visible through the open main doors. *This is too easy. We're not just going to walk away from the Human Sphere unhindered. There's something or someone that will stand in our way. I can feel it. We're not out of the woods yet. This could just be my imagination, but I don't think so. I've had this feeling before battles in the past, all of which were particularly nasty.*

Legan continued to watch the never ending stream of starships flowing out of the mothball station and heading to their designated planets to pick up the civilian population. *Right now everything seems all right, but I've got a feeling this is just the calm before the storm. But regardless of whether I'm right or wrong, there's nothing I can do right now but stay alert.*

Legan placed a hand above the viewport and against one of the *Tenacity*'s bulkheads. *And besides, if something does try to stop us, they'll get to see why you're the toughest warship in the Sphere. The hard way.*

Chapter Thirty-Nine

C limbing as fast as she could one handed, Cara scurried up the vertical beam and didn't waste time looking back down the dark, narrow shaft. She knew that if the guards discovered the hole she'd cut in the wall before she reached her exit point, all they would have to do is fire up the shaft and then she'd be done for. With that thought as ample motivation, Cara pushed away the stinging pain in her left shoulder and focused all of her energies on climbing.

After what seemed like a few centuries, Cara pulled herself through the hole on level 13 and into the well carpeted office that she'd been tempted to take a nap in. That temptation was long gone with her shoulder screaming out in pain and adrenaline running thick in her veins. She knew it was only a matter of time before Intelligence pulled out the building's blueprints and traced the route of the shaft. When that happened, guards on every level would be flocking to the shaft's location and it would only be a matter of time before they discovered and killed her.

I have to keep moving, if I don't get out of this building now then I won't be leaving at all, save for in a body bag.

Cara pulled herself up off the thick carpet and walked over to the office's desk. She took the datapad out of her left hand and laid it on the desk, where she brought up the floor's blueprints using her right hand only on the datapad's controls.

"Now, how do I get back to the maintenance room?"

Studying the floor layout, Cara began to mentally plan out her route. "My evasive route doesn't work in reverse, plus the guards patrol patterns have probably been altered due to the alarm. So if I'm going to have to fight my way across the floor, I might as well take a more direct route."

She looked over the blueprints one last time, then content with her understanding of the floor plan, she forced herself to pick up the datapad with her left hand then rotated her arm around to see how much range of motion she had. Cara forced down a scream and continued to rotate her arm until she started to get light headed.

"Great. It's going to be a lot of fun running with this shoulder." She winced as she lifted the datapad to her chest. "Gotta do it though. If not then I won't get out of here alive." Cara reached down and pulled a spare power pack from her belt. "I still might not get out of here if I can't get past the guards on this level."

She pulled her right pistol out of its holster with her fingertips and braced it against the door. Cara hit the release switch, dropping the old power pack to the floor. She turned to pistol upside down and lightly pressed her left forearm against it, pinning it to the wall as she inserted the fresh power pack. Cara repeated the process with her left pistol then activated her sunglasses' X-ray mode.

"Hall looks clear. Let's hope it stays that way." She switched back to normal vision and brandished her right pistol. "At least I don't have to carry the pack anymore."

Cara brought her wrist up over the door's activation panel and hesitated for a moment as she gathered her thoughts.

"Go!"

She opened the door and took off to her right down the hallway. Cara passed the first intersection, then the second, and turned the corner at the third, right behind a pair of guards. Not giving them time to turn around, Cara gave each of them a blaster bolt in the back of the head, then jumped over their falling bodies as she continued down the hallway.

Her shoulder was already screaming by the time she jumped, but the landing jarred her shoulder enough that she momentarily lost her grip on her datapad. She did manage to snatch it back out of the air, but at the cost of more shoulder movement. *Gotta stay focused.*

Cara ran past another intersection at a swift jog, then rounded the next corner to her left and into the hallway that would take her back to the maintenance room's hallway.

Bringing her pistol up as she rounded the corner, Cara prepared herself for a running light fight.

To her surprise the long hallway ahead of her was completely empty. Not waiting for an explanation, Cara took off at full sprint down the hallway as a red blaster bolt flew past her head and exploded a glow panel 12 meters ahead of her. *Great. I've got guards behind me. Can't fight them. Just weave and hope you don't get hit.*

Cara began drifting from wall to wall as the blaster fire increased. *Come on. Run!*

Cara squeezed every bit of energy out of her body as she flew down the hall, leaving the guards behind.

Leaving the *guards* behind yes, but she couldn't out run their blaster shots. They continued to fire mercilessly at her down the hall with more of their shots impacting the hallway's walls and ceiling as each second went by. One of the fiery red darts skimmed centimeters over Cara's wounded shoulder and nailed one of the two guards appearing at the next hallway intersection.

Cara let loose with a number of blue bolts as she quickly closed on the remaining guard. Still froze from his partner's unexpected death, the guard didn't have time to draw his blaster rifle on Cara before her hurried shots impacted his thick torso and slammed him back against the crossing hallway's wall. Cara ran on past the intersection without slowing and killed her weave as the trailing guards ceased their fire after accidentally killing one of their comrades.

With the trailing threat temporarily neutralized, Cara focused her full attention forward and was ready when a lone guard appeared at the next intersection and brought his rifle to bear on Cara.

She drilled the man in the forehead with one quick shot that dropped him to the ground after Cara was already two steps past him. *Almost there.*

Breathless more from her injury than the actual running, Cara made it down the remaining stretch of hallway without running into any more guards ahead of her. When she reached room 314 she took the next left and ran down about 20 meters of hallway until she reached the maintenance room.

Cara all but tore the skeleton key from the left wrist, sending a fresh spike of pain across her left shoulder and up her neck. Knowing that the trailing guards would catch up to her shortly, Cara inserted the skeleton key into the slot on the door and waited impatiently the two seconds it took to unlock it.

Hurriedly opening the door, Cara stepped into the maintenance room and locked it behind her. Wasting no time, she crossed the L-shaped room and knelt down in front of the maintenance tunnel hatch.

Swinging it open, Cara painfully climbed in headfirst and twisted her body around enough to close the hatch behind her. Crawling as fast as her injured shoulder would allow, Cara navigated the light confines of the maintenance tunnel until she reached the now unsealed lift shaft hatch. With her left arm almost completely numb, Cara forced open the stubborn tunnel hatch, ignoring the security system that she could do nothing about without the security countermeasures that were in her pack. And her pack was at the bottom of the bulkhead shaft.

She didn't have much choice in abandoning the pack. With her shoulder injured, it would have slowed her down more than it was worth. Besides, stealth wasn't an issue anymore. They already knew she was here, and it wouldn't help them much more to know that she was in the lift shaft. As long as she stayed in the ladder depression the lift cars couldn't touch her. And this time she wouldn't have to worry about the lift cars snagging her pack and knocking her off the shaft wall.

Before she pulled herself out of the maintenance tunnel hatch, Cara unzipped the front of her jumpsuit and slid the datapad underneath it. Rezipping her jumpsuit was a bit troublesome and the datapad itself was uncomfortable to say the least, but at least she would have her left hand free.

For all the good that would do. Her hand and arm were already numb but climbing a wall one handed wasn't very easy and Cara didn't like the idea of free falling down the lift shaft. Keeping her attention focused on her left arm, Cara climbed out of the hatch onto the shaft wall and began to climb.

It was awkward at first, not being able to feel her magnetic coupler or the wall when she released her right hand, but Cara kept her balance as close to the wall as possible. That way she wouldn't have to pull as much with her left arm and she would have a better chance of catching herself if she did loose her grip. Cara climbed slowly at first, but as she became more accustomed to the right biased climbing she was able to increase her rate of assent.

A breeze of air on the back of her neck was her only warning as a lift car flew past Cara from below. The sudden appearance of the lift car blowing by her caused Cara to almost loose her grip. With the combination of her injury and the high level of adrenaline in her system, the unexpected appearance of the lift car shook Cara up thoroughly.

She made sure that she had a good grip on the wall then tried to calm herself. *Come on Cara, snap out of it. You're past the worst of it. Only climbing and crawling left, assuming Intelligence doesn't send any guards up onto the roof.*

That idea cleared her mind in a flash. *Ok, climb now, worry about the rest later.* When her arms refused to move a spike of fear drove itself into her mind.

"Move!" she yelled to herself.

Reluctantly it seemed, her arms slowly moved up the wall. She got moving again and made it a point to herself not to stop again until she reached the top.

She caught a glimpse this time and was ready when another lift car came up from below and passed her by. Still climbing, a bit of her fiery attitude started to come back.

"Trying to knock me off the walls are they? Well, let them try. It'll take more than a couple of lift cars to get the best of me."

A bit more determined than before, Cara began to climb faster and more forcefully than before. Soon she reached the top of her climb and the hole that she'd cut into the wall of the heating duct.

Time for another sweat bath. Not exactly the most comfortable experience but at least it will be a step closer to getting out of here.

Cara looked for approaching lift cars from above and below but found the shaft clear, for the moment. Using her magnetic couplers carefully to extricate herself from the wall's depression, Cara climbed into the wall opening.

A blast of heat hit her when she ducked her head into the hole and only got worse as she pulled herself completely into the shaft. She crawled down the heating duct away from the hole a few meters then sat down and leaned her back against the uncomfortably warm metal of the duct wall.

Cara unzipped her jumpsuit and pulled out the datapad, but left her jumpsuit unzipped down to her waist for ventilation as sweat began to form on her forehead. She new that she had to keep moving, but Cara allowed herself this short rest while she studied the blueprints of the duct system.

"Alright, if I can make it through these ducts then I'm out of the building and home free."

Cara let the datapad rest on her upraised knees and dropped her right hand to her belt. She ran her fingertips over the small pouches that held the datacards from the downloader. "I hope you guys are worth all the trouble."

Chapter Forty

After letting the containment doors close behind him, Isen began to casually walk down the triangular corridor ahead of him. *Now, if I remember correctly, lab 18 should be four intersections this way, and two to the right*, he thought to himself as he strode down the empty corridor.

When he reached the first intersection, Isen glanced down the cross corridor both ways but didn't see any Peace Core personnel. He continued on to the second cross corridor and found it similarly deserted. *I wonder where everyone is at. Could be I caught them on a down shift.*

Isen passed by the third empty cross corridor then turned right at the fourth. Finally he spotted a technician walking the same direction that he was a block section ahead of Isen. Walking silently, Isen shadowed the tech until he passed the second cross corridor. Isen followed him until he reached the containment door emblazoned with a large black '18'.

Letting the tech continue on his way, Isen whipped out his ID chip and inserted it into the appropriate slot on the door's activation panel that was located on the door jam. The panel's indicator light changed from red to green, then Isen removed his ID chip and touched the appropriate button on the activation panel. With a quiet whish of atmospheric equalization, the containment doors split on a diagonal bias and retracted into the walls, revealing a large, dimly lit rectangular laboratory.

Isen quickly stepped through the archway and resealed the doors behind him He visually scanned the room and found it as lifeless as the majority of the corridors had been. *Well. Better start looking.*

Isen started his search along the right side of the room between the wall and the large, primary worktable in the center of the room. Weaving his way around smaller worktables scattered around the room, Isen examined the storage compartments built into the walls and started to get a bad feeling. *These compartments are full of scientific equipment, not artifacts. Unless there are different storage compartments elsewhere in the room, I'm in trouble.*

Isen continued searching the right wall, finding various sized beakers, laser scalpels, test tubes, and a variety of other tools and instruments, but no artifacts. After about 40 meters Isen came to the end of the long wall and started to search the shorter wall opposite that of the containment doors through which he entered. Becoming more discouraged by the second, Isen completed his survey of that wall then moved on to the long left wall.

Finding more of the same, Isen began to wonder what he was going to do now. *Flare had said that pentagon was stored in lab 18, but this* is *lab 18 and the artifacts are no where to be seen. If Flare's information was incorrect and the artifacts aren't here, then I'm lost. I can't blindly search the entire restricted area, let alone the whole compound.* Isen's face turned grim. *If I can't find the artifacts in here, I may have to jump one of the techs and get the information from him. I can't leave here empty handed.*

Isen continued down the left wall, still coming up empty until a recessed meter wide door materialized out of the shadows. Isen let out a sigh of relief. *Good. I was starting to worry.*

Isen examined the access panel on the right door jam. Finding no chip slot, he lightly tapped the activation button. The previously unseen door pulled up into the ceiling and revealed a slightly brighter room illuminated by rows of lighted display cases.

Isen stepped into the room, then after making sure the room was empty he turned around and lowered the door with a touch to the interior access panel. The pressure sealed door hissed shut and left Isen standing in the middle of along, narrow room that ran parallel to the work section of the lab that he'd just been in. Both of the low ceilinged room's walls contained shallow storage compartments with see through coverings and interior glow panels. *Looks like the lab's storage compartment. Maybe Flare's information wasn't wrong after all.*

Isen began searching both walls as he walked down the room to his right. Resembled a wide corridor, the storage room had more the appearance of a trophy room than sterile storage chamber. Each of the numerous archeological artifacts that the room contained were mounted on two or three centimeter high pedestals within their storage compartments. *Looks like Admiral Legan was right. Peace Core has been collecting a lot of artifacts, but I don't see anything like the Admiral's piece. The hologram he gave Morning Dawn depicted a hand sized lump of black synthetic material, but these artifacts aren't black or that size*, he thought to himself as he reached the end of the room. *Hopefully it's on the other end.*

Isen walked back to the side door and began searching the others compartments. He got nearly three quarters of the way down that half of the room before he came across a three meter wide section of the wall opposite the door that didn't contain any artifacts or storage compartments. *The rest of the room is filled floor to ceiling with display cases, so why leave this segment blank?*

Isen stepped back as far as he could, brushing his back up against the other wall, and studied the odd wall segment. It had numerous bulges and impressions that ran all over the wall in thick and thin lines that Isen couldn't identify the reason for. There were also a number of solitary, squarish bulges that appeared at random between the paths of the intersecting trough and mound lines.

Isen studied the design layout for a few minutes then walked up to the wall segment and pressed a thumb against one of the squarish nubs that was all but imperceptibly discolored, probably from repeated use. The nub depressed beneath his thumb's pressure until it clicked into place.

Isen withdrew his hand as the wall segment itself depressed a few centimeters. It then rose up into the ceiling, leaving behind a display window and narrow door. Isen froze for a moment when he saw the objects in the small room behind the viewpanel.

Sitting atop waist high pedestals were four fist sized lumps of almost metallic material, all of which were space black. Isen smiled broadly.

"Gotcha," he whispered.

He noticed a fifth pedestal in the back that completed the pentagonal configuration, but it was empty. *Sorry boys, Legan has that one. And soon he'll have these four too. Just as soon as I find a way to get them out of here.*

Isen looked the door over and found a small slot on the door itself, but there wasn't an activation panel. *It's worth a shot.*

Isen pulled out his ID chip and inserted it into the door. To his surprise the lock clicked and the door opened inward.

"Looks like my lucky day."

Isen stepped through the doorway, pulling out his ID chip from the door slot and replacing it in his pocket. As he did so he noticed a small panel on the inside of the door jam. *Interior but no exterior access panel. Peace Core must want these things awfully bad if they're going to hide a room like this in their own compound.* Isen smiled again. *Glad to be able to take them off your hands fellas.*

Isen stepped to the edge of the five pedestals and looked them over carefully.

"Better be sure about this," he said as he pulled out the biotech vile. After a few seconds the suit formed on his body then Isen activated the hood.

"Flare, you there?"

A soft beep answered him.

Smart computer. "Give me a security scan on the pedestals in front of me."

Another beep proceeded the appearance of a sensor enhanced image of the pedestals on his tactical overlay. Isen studied it closely but couldn't find any trace of security measures.

"Flare, do you detect any alarm systems on the pedestals?"

"Negative."

"Didn't think so." Isen reached up to deactivate the suit but hesitated a moment. "Flare, what's the battery condition on the cloak?"

"23 percent."

"Ok, kill the sensors."

Isen's tactical overlay disengaged, returning him to normal vision as he deactivated the suit.

Stepping into the center of the pentagon, Isen picked up each of the artifacts one by one and placed them into the deep pockets of his labcoat. He looked down at the slight bulges where the artifacts were and frowned.

"I guess it'll have to do."

Isen then stepped out of the room and closed the door behind him. Just as he was wondering how he was going to lower the display cover, it began lowering on its own. *Must be connected to the door.* Isen shrugged slightly. *Makes it all the easier for me.*

Isen turned away from the hidden room and started to walk back to the lab when something that he'd seen in his peripheral vision belatedly caused him to stop in his tracks. He turned back around and looked down the opposite end of the hallway to where a soft blue glow illuminated a small section of floor surrounded by shadows and the dim light from the display cases' glow panels. In fact, all the glow panels in the room were white.

I've got a little time, Isen thought to himself as he began to walk towards the blue glow, intent on investigating its source.

Chapter Forty-One

Isen moved toward the blue glow and discovered a narrow, open doorway set into the wall between display cases. One step into the doorway he froze in his tracks as the source of the blue glow came into view.

Situated at the far end of a not so small, elongated room was a clear vertical tube filled with back lighted fluid. Floating inside the tube was a shadowy figure with its arms and legs suspended at odd angles due to the fluid's neutral buoyancy. All around the vertical column's wall alcove were rings of diagnostic equipment with the numerous pinpricks of indicator lights flashing off and on in a highly distractive and randomized pattern. The rest of the room was more or less bare, save for a number of shoulder high cabinets set into the walls that contained a number of viles, syringes, and other medical equipment.

Isen stepped into the room and walked up to the vertical tube. As he got closer to the tube, the image of the floating figure began to materialize until Isen stood directly before the tube and could see the interior plainly. Floating lifeless in the bluish liquid was a woman, completely naked, with a breath mask over her face and four different IV's inserted into her right arm. Isen looked closely at her bluish skin and green, shoulder length hair that was suspended around her head with a few tendrils floating before her closed eyes. He took a closer look at her frame and came to a chilling revelation.

"You're not human," Isen whispered. *I though her skin and hair color were affected by the blue light at first, but she* does *have blue skin and green hair. She looks human enough, but her figure is slightly different from that of a human. Sleeker I think.*

Isen looked her over from head to toe in one quick glance, shaking his head slightly. She was in pretty bad shape. Bruises blossomed around the IV points on her forearm and the flesh on her wrists and ankles was rubbed raw. She also had a patchwork of scars on her midsection that sent a chill through Isen. If it wasn't for her injuries and her obvious state of malnutrition, she'd have been strikingly beautiful, instead of looking half dead.

"You're really beat up aren't you?"

Isen took a glance at the surrounding diagnostic panels and got a quick appraisal of her situation. *It looks like they've got you in stasis...and on essential nutrients only*, he added after a closer examination of the panels. *How kind of them.*

Isen turned to look back at the doorway as conflicting emotions fought a brief battle in his mind. He turned back to look at the humanoid woman and made a snap decision. *Now that I've got the artifacts that I came her to retrieve I should head out of here as quickly as possible, but I can't leave you here.*

Isen began going over the control panels, looking for a way to bring her out of stasis.

"Hold on Blue, I'm going to get you out of there."

After a few minutes of further study, Isen had a reasonable idea of how the equipment worked and lifted a hand to the control panel.

"I hope this works." Isen depressed a wide button that glowed green as he crossed his fingers on his other hand. After a few seconds the diagnostic monitors began to show change. Slowly, the woman's vital signs increased from barely existent up to nominal, as far as the equipment was concerned.

The fluid's temperature gage also began to rise, bringing up the woman's internal temperature close to room temperature from well below freezing. The diagnostics also showed her breath rate increasing as the breath mask started pumping more oxygen. The few sporadic bubbles that had been emerging from the breath mask had increased to a constant steady flow that rose to the top of the tube and disappeared.

When all of the woman's vital signs had reached normal levels one large square button began flashing green on a panel off to Isen's right. After a brief hesitation Isen pressed the button, then jumped back as the tube and the diagnostic readouts began to pull out from the wall.

The section of wall continued to move forward until the top of the tube was fully exposed. On the side of the wall segment was a built in ladder that led up to a fairly large platform with the top of the tube open in the center.

Isen quickly climbed the ladder, dropped to his belly, and leaned over the top of the tube. Looking in, his face took on blue highlights from the glowpanel that comprised the base of the tube and spread it's diffuse glow up through the liquid and out passed Isen's face to illuminate a section of the ceiling above his head.

After rolling up his sleeves Isen reached down into the chilly liquid and gently raised the woman's arm up. He slowly removed the IV needles and let them drift on the stasis fluid.

Bending down as far as he could, Isen dipped his arms in up to his shoulders and, as gently as he could, took hold of the woman under the armpits and pulled her to the surface. The neutral buoyancy of the liquid made the task relatively easy until her upper body broke the surface. Isen then slipped his left arm through her left armpit, across the top of her chest, and back through her right armpit, pinning her against the side of the tube. Then with his right hand he removed her breath mask and dropped it back into the stasis fluid where it floated alongside the detached IV's.

Returning to a two handed grip, Isen pulled the woman completely out of the tube and laid her down on the platform beside the tube opening. He knelt over her and felt for a pulse. *Weak but steady.*

Isen relaxed shoulders that he hadn't realized were tense as he let out a sigh. She was still alive.

"Let's get you down from here."

Isen pulled the unconscious woman to her feet and dipped a shoulder under her waist, lifting her into a rescue carry. Slowly, he backed toward the side ladder and dropped to a knee at the top. Isen stepped onto the ladder with the woman over his shoulder and grabbed the top rung with his free hand as he began down.

When he had descended as far as his arm would reach, he gingerly flexed his other wrist out and grabbed hold of the nearest rung while still holding onto the woman. Repositioning his now free hand, Isen lowered himself down the remaining rungs and stepped hesitantly to the floor.

He walked a few strides from the tank and laid the woman as softly as he could on the cold floor. Kneeling over her, he thought quickly. *She's going to need some clothes*. He fingered his lab coat and uniform. *I guess these will have to do. I'll have to move the artifacts to Flare's...*

Suddenly a hand jabbed out and nailed Isen in the chest, half throwing him off the now conscious woman. She kneed him off to her side then started to scramble to her feet and head for the door when Isen caught hold of here ankle.

Her momentum dropped her hard to the floor, stunning her long enough for Isen to roll her over and pin her to the floor face up. She struggled far more than Isen would have expected from someone in her condition, but he managed to hold her fast.

"I know you probably can't understand a word I'm saying," he grunted out, "but I'm here to help you."

The woman still continued to struggle, not that Isen though he could simply speak to her. He grabbed both of her hands and brought them together above her forehead. He held them in place with his left hand as he bodily pinned the slippery woman to the floor. Isen brought a finger to his lips and made a shushing sound.

"Can you understand quiet?"

"I can understand you just fine," she said in near perfect basic.

Isen was shocked at her being able to speak their language and involuntarily relaxed his guard enough that the woman got her hands free and shoved him off her. Isen's quick reflexes overrode his shock and brought him to his feet in a flash. He caught the woman before she reached the doorway, wrapping both arms around her waist and holding her tight. She continued to struggle, but Isen's grasp held firm.

"Would you please stop struggling. I'm not your enemy. I'm here to get you out."

At that last statement she stopped trying to shake free but still resisted his grip.

"You're not Cres. Who sent you?" she asked.

"I work for Morning Dawn. I was sent here to retrieve a number of special artifacts from Peace Core custody. I infiltrated the compound and located the artifacts. I was ready to leave when I spotted this room and found you here. I didn't want to leave you in Peace Core's hands so I removed you from the stasis tank and was about to give you some clothes when you hit me."

"You're not one of them?"

"No, I'm not."

"Then why are you wearing their uniform?"

"I stole it in order to sneak in here."

She frowned. "They don't know you're here?" she asked.

"No, and I'd like to keep it that way if you'll keep quiet."

"Let me go," she demanded.

"Only if you promise not to run. If you do, I'll just catch you again anyway."

"Alright."

Isen slowly slackened his grip and when she quit resisting him he let her go.

"You said something about clothes?" she said wrapping her arms across her chest.

"Yeah, hold on a minute."

Isen pulled out the three artifacts from his labcoat's pockets and placed them next to the one that had fell out onto the floor. He then emptied the rest of the objects in his pockets and placed them with the artifacts, forming a small pile on the floor. Isen slipped off the labcoat and tossed it to the woman.

"Put that on for now."

She caught it out of the air and quickly pulled it over her now quaking form. Isen began to pull of his boots and technician's uniform as he looked at the woman.

"What's your name?"

She stared at him for a moment, then seemingly reluctant, she answered him. "Mysonanda."

"My name is Isen Tyrel," he said, handing her the tech's uniform and the boots. "Here, put these on under the labcoat."

Mysonanda took the uniform, but hesitated on the boots. "Don't you need those?"

"Nope, I've got another pair."

She didn't entirely believe him with no other boots in sight, but she took them anyway. He watched her as she dressed and as she pulled on the first boot she noticed his attention.

"Something wrong?" she asked sarcastically.

"You're shaking."

She glanced down at her arms then looked back at Isen.

"I'll live." She pulled on the other boot then donished the labcoat. "What now?"

Isen didn't say anything but reached down and picked up the biotech vile. Standing in his combat jumpsuit and socks, Isen opened the vile and poured it into his palm. Mysonanda's eyes went wide as the biotech material spread over Isen's body, forming his suit and it's corresponding pair of boots. When his suit solidified, Isen smiled at Mysonanda.

"Told you I had another pair of boots."

"What is that?"

"Our way out." Isen hefted his forearm out of habit. "Flare, give me the spare pack."

His forearm attachment beeped once, then an identical version of the pack that he'd left in the ready room formed on his back. Isen touched the appropriate collar button and unsealed the pack from his back and pulled it off his shoulders. He knelt beside his pile of items on the floor and began putting them into the auxiliary pack.

He hesitated when he picked up his blastech. *Wish I could carry you, but you don't cloak. My other weapons are in the other pack.* Isen put the pistol into the pack and mentally scolded himself. *Stupid. I should have absorbed all of the biotech items, not just the computer enhancement.*

Isen put the ID chip into the pack then closed it. As he pulled it on his back and resealed it to his suit, Mysonanda interrupted his thoughts.

"What's Morning Dawn?"

"What…oh. Morning Dawn is an elite agency unknown to most humans that serves as a watchdog for the region. We gather information and take covert action against any threats that rear their ugly heads."

"Which part do those artifacts fall under," she said, pointing to his pack.

"Neither really. I was asked to acquire these artifacts for Admiral Legan as a favor."

"Who's Admiral Legan?"

"He's the commander of the Kataran military, the largest and strongest war machine in what we call the Human Sphere."

"Then it was his warship that captured our vessel," she said vehemently

"No, it must have been a Peace Core vessel. Admiral Legan doesn't have anything to do with Peace Core. What happened?"

She pitted Isen with a harsh stare. "We were on deep space patrol when one of our engines exploded, taking the back quarter of our ship with it. We managed to seal off the rest of the ship then sent out a distress signal. Then the warship arrived and docked with us. They boarded our ship and slaughtered our crew, save for me. During the firefight a bulkhead fell on top of me when a blaster bolt blew it out of the ceiling. I was knocked unconscious and woke up tied down to a to table with my clothes removed. Next thing I know, I got a needle jabbed into my arm and I passed out." She shivered more from memory than the hypothermia. "I wake up again in a cell to find out that they had done some exploratory surgery," she recalled as she rubbed her hand over her stomach.

"They observed me for a few hours then dunked me in that tank. They brought me out whenever they wanted to run tests or cut me up some more. Luckily, I was unconscious when they did most of the tests, but the ones I was awake for weren't pleasant in the least."

"How did you learn basic?"

"I didn't. I woke up from one of their experiments knowing the language." She looked down at the floor for a moment. "Thanks for pulling me out of there. And I'm sorry about fighting you before. I thought you were one of them."

"Don't worry about it."

"So, what next?"

"We get out of here." Isen turned his attention to his suit. "Flare, bring up the compound's schematics."

Chapter Forty-Two

C ara put her datapad back underneath her jumpsuit and pulled the zipper up far enough to hold it in place. *Ok, move it Cara.*

Reluctantly, her muscles and pain ridden shoulder complied, rolling her sideways and back onto her hands and knees. Cara's left arm gave way when she put pressure on it, collapsing her to the duct floor. *Come on, fight it.*

Putting her weight on her right arm, Cara got back up onto her hands and knees then tested her left arm. Streams of pain flowed across her shoulder, but she held firm. Slowly, she began to crawl down the duct, trying to work through the pain and barely succeeding. After about 30 seconds, she'd regained a semblance of rhythm and started to make relatively good time down the duct.

Cara soon came to an intersection and made a sharp left, being very careful not to brush her shoulder up against the corner of the duct. On down the new duct, Cara made a right turn and crawled down a longer duct that ended at the vertical shaft that Cara had climbed down on her way in.

Come on shoulder, hang in there a little longer. Cara reversed her position in the cramped duct, then backed out into the vertical shaft. Using her magnetic couplers, Cara climbed up the vertical shaft two floors before she crawled into the duct on the opposite wall. Once she was all the way inside the duct, Cara dropped onto her face as the pain momentarily overwhelmed her.

Sweating profusely, Cara laid there a moment until she got herself back under control. Then, very slowly, she pulled herself up into a siting position and leaned back on the duct wall. She pulled out her datapad again and focused enough to memorize the next eight turns.

"Right, left, left, right, left, right, right, left," she whispered as she put the turns to memory.

Cara repeated the order two more times then tucked her datapad back underneath her jumpsuit and started crawling. She remembered each of the turns correctly and after Cara made the last turn in the air duct maze she crawled down a short duct that opened out into another vertical shaft. *Last one. I'm almost there.*

Cara swapped back for front again and crawled out legs first into the vertical shaft. She climbed up a single floor to the top of the shaft and climbed into the air duct system that led to the roof vent. Cara pulled out her datapad once again and memorized the last bit of her escape route. She then typed in a short password, verified it, then erased the datapad's memory.

Cara took one last look at the datapad then tossed it down the vertical shaft. She zipped up her jumpsuit to her throat and felt its appropriate fit against her sweaty skin. *That feels better. Lighter too.*

Now a bit more comfortable, Cara started to crawl down the last section of the building's air ventilation system that she would ever see.

Still pain racked, Cara crawled through the duct until she came to an intersection where she turned right. *Almost there. Come on Cara, hang on.* A left turn at another intersection eventually brought Cara to a T-junction with a duct running off to her left. She turned into that offshoot and crawled down the duct until she reached the overhead air vent that she'd cut through the side of in order to gain access to the building's ventilation system.

Cara used her magnetic couplers to climb the two meters up to the vent itself. Painfully, she pulled herself out of the vent and into the cold night air. Immediately a chill ran down her spine as her sweat soaked jumpsuit began to cool.

"Finally," she whispered, short of breath.

Wasting no time, Cara weaved her way through the cityscape of rooftop protrusions back to the block like structure rising from the center of the building and hopefully her cable line. It wasn't until Cara was ten meters from the communication block itself that she spotted her gripbar hanging near the wall a few meters off the ground.

Greatly relieved that her guide wire was still in place, Cara climbed up the side of the communications block using her magnetic couplers until she hung next to the gripbar. Reaching out with her right hand, Cara grabbed the rightmost handle and depressed the brake button. Holding the gripbar in place, Cara released her left wrist from the wall and grabbed hold of the gripbar.

"Don't give out on me now," Cara said, clutching the gripbar and mentally reminding herself not to let her hands slip free, no matter how badly her shoulder hurt.

The sky was cloudless and there wasn't the least bit of a breeze, but Cara's muscles and joints were already beginning to cramp up from the cold. *I hope my hands don't get numb enough that I can't hold on.*

Cara released her knee couplers and swayed gently as she hung by both hands from the gripbar. Her shoulder screamed in protest, but Cara held on never the less. *Better get moving before I freeze up.*

Using her thumb, Cara set the gripbar to slide on its own accord, then released the breaking button. She started to slide down the guide wire and quickly gained speed. Cara let herself fall as fast as possible, with her descent creating a wind that blew her hair up over her head and cut through her jumpsuit, chilling her to the bone. She managed to keep her grip even though she was in all but free fall.

When she had descended along three quarters of the wire's length, Cara began pumping the break. Her descent speed slowly decreased until the she pressed and held the break button when the ground started to grow dangerously large.

The gripbar groaned loudly and started to drastically slow her descent. When she reached the end of the line she was still moving fairly good, so Cara let go of the gripbar and dropped the last two and a half meters to the ground.

She absorbed most of the drop with her legs and rolled out forward to deal with the extra momentum. Cara nearly blacked out as she rolled over her injured shoulder and ended up lying face up on the ground. The gripbar hit the low wall that the guide wire was attached to and chipped off a section of permacrete before it rebounded back up the wire a meter or so.

Cara laid dazed on the ground for a few moments before she rolled over on her right shoulder and got to her feet. She looked back at the gigantic building to see if Intelligence had people waiting for her on the outside. *Good. The perimeter is quiet, for now. Let's get out of here before that changes.*

Cara pulled herself over the low wall and into the razor grass field, lit only by the moonlight and diffuse city lights. Cara waded her way through the sharp grasses with her jumpsuit brushing aside their potentially lethal caresses. It took her a long time before she finally emerged from the razor grass field onto the shore of the ice cold river.

Cara hesitated when she remembered her last trip across the river. *Don't have any choice. I have to get back to my ship soon or I won't live through the night.*

Flinching as she did so, Cara lowered herself into the river and began to wade across. When the water reached waist high Cara began to swim, remembering the drop off that had caught her off guard before.

When her shoulder went under water, Cara let out a scream that she couldn't hold back. A mouthful of ice cold water brought her focus back to the task at hand as Cara struggled against the extreme stinging pain in her shoulder and kept swimming.

By the time she reached the opposite shore her shoulder was already numbing up and that made Cara both thankful and fearful. *I'm glad the pain is subsiding but that means I'm going into hypothermia. I have to get out of here now.*

Cara began walking in the direction of her ship. Remembering the predators that she had to fight off on her first trip through the woods, Cara dropped her right hand to her gun belt but didn't draw her pistol. Instead she began to run. *If any of those predators find me I'm not going to be able to fight them off in my condition, and I'm not going to make it back to the ship in time before I freeze to death if I walk. Running's the only choice I have, besides, the extra body heat should help slow down the hypothermia.*

Cara ran through the seven kilometers of forest without stopping, fearing that she might not get going again. At long last she found her ship with the help of her sunglasses amidst the predators' howls and their ever constant footfalls trailing behind her. Far beyond exhaustion, Cara reached the ship and immediately started climbing the built in steps until she got on top of the starmaster and out of reach of the predators now encircling the ship.

With her body completely numb, Cara fumbled around with the top hatch until she managed to unseal it and open it up to a vertical position. Dropping roughly onto the seat with her booted feet, Cara pulled the hatch closed and resealed it from the inside.

She then all but collapsed into her seat, now that she was safely inside her ship. Pulling herself away from the unconsciousness that seemed to be cloying to her mind, Cara focused enough to engage the automatic start up procedures and was unbelievably relieved when she felt a tickle of warm air as the ship's life support systems reengaged.

Cara kept herself awake throughout the start up procedure and began rubbing her cold, numb fingers trying to get the circulation going again. When the ship's systems came alive, Cara fumbled around with the controls and slowly brought the engines up to power. Then with her right hand on the control stick and her left hand on her right wrist to steady her shivering arm, Cara lifted her starfighter up off the ground and out over the lake, taking off a good number of tree limbs as she did.

Pulling back on the stick, Cara angled her ship towards orbit then turned her attention to the IS drive. She started powering up the IS core and called up the destination coordinates that Admiral Legan had programmed into her ship himself. With that task finished, Cara focused her attention on making orbit.

When she finally did escape Hedron III's atmosphere, the IS core was fully charged. Cara maneuvered her ship onto the appropriate heading, then engaged the IS drive. A moment later Cara was enmeshed in a swirling vortex of color and finally surrendered to unconsciousness.

"Lieutenant, have the mooring beams and docking clamps been deactivated?" Admiral Legan asked the officer at the ops station on the *Tenacity*'s bridge.

"Yes sir. The stations automated systems disengaged them less than a minute ago and are now opening the main door."

"Excellent. Captain Yader?"

"Sir."

"Are all of our passengers aboard?"

Yader nodded. "The last few techs came onboard 15 minutes ago. The other ships also report that all personnel are aboard."

"Very well then. Comm, signal the remaining vessels to depart the station ahead of us."

"Yes Admiral."

Legan turned to the forward viewport and watched over the next few minutes as the other 17 warships not assigned to convoy escort duty moved from their docking slips and out the station's large main doors. *Free at last.* "Captain?"

"Admiral," Yader said, stepping beside his superior officer.

"Take us out."

"Aye sir," he said turning towards the starboard crew pit. "Retract the docking umbilical and close hangar bay doors."

"Yes Captain."

A few moments later the ops officer spoke up again. "Hanger bay doors closed Captain."

"Umbilical retracted," another Lieutenant sang out.

"Helm, take us out of the station, thrusters only."

Captain Yader then joined Admiral Legan at the forward viewport and watched as the helmsman professionally maneuvered the warship out of its slip and along the station's interior.

"It appears we have a well trained crew," Captain Yader said softly enough that only Admiral Legan could hear.

"They're capable, but they also have a great deal to learn before they become seasoned naval officers."

Yader nodded his agreement but didn't reply as his attention was taken away by the view of the cavernous doors directly off the *Tenacity*'s bow.

"Quite a sight isn't it?" Legan said into the silence.

"Yes, too bad we have to leave this station behind. It's definitely one of a kind."

"When we get to Alpha Prime we'll build structures that will dwarf this station," Legan said to Yader's astonishment. "We're not going to play by the Sphere's rules anymore Captain. No more limitations. From now on this military will grow and change according to my designs, not the politicians." Admiral Legan turned his head to the helm station. "Is the IS core charged?"

"Yes," the Lieutenant answered as the *Tenacity* pulled clear of the station.

"Bring us about on the heading for the rendezvous point and engage the drive."

Legan turned back to the viewport and watched as the helmsman swung the ship's bow to the starboard and back around over the top of the station. The *Tenacity* steadied on a single vector then jumped to IS space, leaving the Human Sphere behind.

Chapter Forty-Three

"**R**ight behind you boss," Silas told Gradir as the five Midnight Star agents stepped through the umbilical archway.

They walked through the seven meter long tube before finally setting foot on the *Goliath*'s deck. Just inside the ship, the five agents moved off to the right in the large, empty corridor alcove that they found themselves in. They stopped in the alcove and took out of their nearly empty satchels, five communication earpieces, which they quickly donned.

"Call us when you're ready," Mejal said. "

Will do. Until then stay out of sight," Gradir said as he led Ketch and Bryen away from the alcove, leaving Silas and Mejal behind.

The three made their way down the corridor to the right until they came to the nearest lift shaft. Gradir punched the call button and waited patiently in the deserted corridor with Ketch and Bryen behind him. Eventually the lift doors opened and the three agents stepped into the lift car. Gradir went to the back while Ketch moved to the control panel. He keyed in the destination coordinates and soon the lift car was on its way to the bridge. Now that the lift doors were closed, Gradir reached into his satchel and pulled out an assault rifle.

"Finally," Ketch said aloud as he reached into his satchel. He pulled out two assault rifles, tossing the left one to Bryen, who snatched it from the air.

"Leave the satchels," Gradir said as he pulled out a datacard then dropped the empty bag on the floor. "And the uniforms," he added. "Ketch."

Taking the cue, Ketch reached over to the control panel and hit the stop button. The lift's motion ceased and the three agents proceeded to remove their bright yellow uniforms. Once they were dressed in the standard Midnight Star combat jumpsuits again, Ketch let the lift continue on its route to the bridge.

After a few minutes the lift car came to a stop and the doors opened onto the bridge. The trio fanned out across the bridge and brought their weapons to bear on the two technicians that turned to face them.

"Hands up," Gradir said, hefting his rifle for emphasis.

"What do you want," one of the techs asked as he brought his hands up over his head.

"I want the two of you to take a trip with my friend here," he said, motioning to Ketch with his free hand. "Take them back down to the umbilical, but wait in the lift shaft until I give you the signal."

"Gotcha," Ketch said, turning toward the techs and motioning to the lift. "This way gentlemen."

Gradir and Bryen helped cover the techs as Ketch herded them into the lift car. Once Ketch and his reluctant companions were eclipsed by the lift doors, Gradir and Bryen turned back to the control consoles.

"Take the helm," Gradir told Bryen.

He nodded and moved to a particular set of controls and appropriated their floor mounted chair. Gradir moved to the operations station and inserted his datacard. He punched a few commands into the computer then let the pass codes on the datacard do their work.

20 seconds later all of the bridge safety lockouts were disengaged and Gradir pulled up the emergency protocols. After he typed in a few special commands that Admiral Legan had supplied him with, a siren blared out over the ship's intercom system. Gradir turned on the comm unit and spoke into the air.

"Abandon ship. All hands, abandon ship. This is not a drill. Repeat. This is not a drill. The life support systems are failing. Depressurization is eminent. Repeat. Depressurization is eminent. This is not a drill. All hands, abandon ship."

When he finished, he flipped off the intercom. Bryen clapped his hands slowly, with the sound echoing loudly throughout the empty bridge.

"Stunning performance Grady, I almost believed it myself."

"Thanks," Gradir said as he reached a hand up to his ear. "Silas, evacuation is under way and Ketch is on his way down with a couple of guests. See to it that they make it off the ship."

"Got it Grady. Let us know when everybody is off."

Gradir heard a click as Silas switched off his comm, then turned his attention back to his console. He called up a sensor scan of the interior of the ship and keyed for life forms. A large and extremely complex diagram splattered with a number of spots appeared on his display screen. He waited until all of the dots, save for seven, disappeared as the techs working on the ship's systems fled the ship through the docking umbilical and ejected in the ship's escape pods before he activated his ear mounted communicator.

"Ketch, get your two friends off the ship, then help Sil and Mej with the docking clamps."

"On my way now."

Gradir switched frequencies on his earpiece. "Sil, once Ketch get the techs off the ship, disengage the docking clamps."

"Alright, I'll signal when we're ready," Silas said, then shut off his communications device. "Time to go Mej. Ketch is on his way down with a couple techs. Once they're off we leave," Silas said as the two agents walked out of a small med station, leaving their uniforms and satchel on the room's floor as they walked the 23 meters back to the docking umbilical, assault rifles in hand.

"Good, I'm ready to get out of here.

As the pair reached the umbilical alcove they spotted Ketch and his two prisoners striding down the corridor at a swift gate.

"Nice of you to show up," Mejal said.

"I would have been here earlier, but we had to wait until the ship was evacuated. Walking through the ship with an assault rifle is a little conspicuous," Ketch said as he pointed the two techs toward the umbilical.

They complied and walked through the umbilical with Ketch and Silas trailing. When they reached the umbilical archway Ketch gave the two techs a shove across their backs with his assault rifle.

"Make yourselves scarce."

They hesitated for a moment, then scurried away down the station's corridors.

"Let's get these docking clamps released," Silas said as he stooped down and opened an access panel on the station's archway.

Ketch mirrored his action while Mejal walked into the umbilical and covered them as they worked. In tandem, Silas and Ketch pulled the manual release levers for the docking clamps a full 180 degrees. The clamps retracted with a large groaning sound followed by an indicator light on a small panel above each lever.

"I'm good," Ketch said, closing the access panel and standing up.

"Same here," Silas said, joining him as they stepped into the umbilical.

Ketch reached back into the archway and touched a panel that closed the airlock as he jerked his hand back into the umbilical. He then retreated back into the ship with Silas and Mejal, sealing the *Goliath*'s airlock as well. Silas touched his earpiece as the trio headed down the corridor to the nearest lift shaft.

"Grady, docking clamps are released. You can retract the umbilical now."

"Good, now get up to the bridge," Gradir replied, moving to another console.

After a moment of searching he found the docking controls and retracted the umbilical. The ship mounted viewcam showed that the umbilical was fully retracted, so Gradir returned to the ops console. He then secured all external hatches and docking ports, then waited for his fellow agents to arrive.

He didn't have to wait long. A few seconds after he completed his task Gradir heard the lift doors swish open and turned around to see his comrades walk onto the bridge.

"Time to get out of here," Gradir said. "Ketch."

Smiling, Ketch pulled a small remote from his belt and flipped on the arming switch. "Boom," he said, pressing the detonation button.

The explosions within the station rocked the *Goliath* slightly, but weren't visible through the forward viewport. Gradir did see the green mooring beams on the bow disengage as Mejal moved to the sensor station.

"All mooring beams are disengaged," he reported. "The sensors also show that the station's weapon emplacements and tractor beams are off line."

"Good. Bryen, how are the engines coming?"

"We're at 93% power now and the IS core is charging as we speak."

"Ok, activate the autopilot and feed it the rendezvous coordinates."

Bryen pulled a small datacard out of his pocket and inserted it into a slot on the helm console. He typed a few commands into the console and started the ship in motion.

"Mej, raise shields."

Mejal nodded and moved to the tactical station. A momentary shimmering covered the bridge viewport as the ship's shields were activated, then disappeared as quickly as it began. When the *Goliath* was free of the yard's construction slip, the autopilot maneuvered the ship away from the station and onto their destination heading.

"Looks like we're going to have company after all," Silas said as a number of Xenarin patrol craft began to close in on the *Goliath*.

"Yeah, the comm light's been blinking ever since we evacuated the ship. I don't think the yard administrator is too happy that we just made off with his prize possession," Gradir said as the patrol ships began to fire on the *Goliath*, whose shields easily absorbed their weak fire.

"20 seconds to jump," Bryen called out.

"Looks like we're going to make the rendezvous point on time after all," Ketch said.

"Apparently so," Gradir said, watching the indicator on Bryen's console count down their remaining seconds in the Xenarian system.

When the counter reached zero, the *Goliath*'s autopilot jumped the ship into IS space, leaving the helpless patrol craft in its wake.

Chapter Forty-Four

D epressing the appropriate button on his collar, Isen activated the biotech suit's hood and looked over the building's blueprints.

"Flare, highlight the level where the northern tunnel enters the building."

A soft beep in his earpiece proceeded an enlargement of the Peace Core compound's second level.

"Now scroll down to the entry point."

The image on his tactical overlay expanded beyond his vision until one particular segment of wall was all that Isen could see.

"Pull back out a bit. There. Trace that interior tunnel."

On his tactical overlay Isen watched as Flare followed the path of the smaller tunnel until it stopped at an interior office on the fourth level.

"Mark that spot Flare, and plot the quickest route there from the last place that I deactivated the cloak. Then give me a trail line on that route and from here to its starting point."

A few seconds later a red tubular line appeared in front of Isen's face and led out the door. Isen deactivated his hood, which slithered back down his neck, reintegrating itself into his suit, then he turned to Mysonanda.

"Who were you talking to?" she asked.

"My onboard computer. It's mapped out an escape route for us. It's not the same one that I'd planned on using, but you're being here changes things."

"Sorry."

"Don't worry about it. We'll get out alright, it'll just be more difficult. Ok, here's the deal. This suit has a cloaking device…"

"You're kidding," Mysonanda interjected.

"No joke. I had to use it to get inside the compound, so it's a little low on power now. Never the less, I'm going to escort you to a room where I had to stash my gear. You're dressed as a tech so try to act like one. Don't react if you see people in the hallways. There weren't many techs out and about on my way in here, but the corridors aren't completely empty. Just walk as if you're bored out of your mind and let me guide you to where I want you to go. You won't be able to see me, but I'll nudge you in the right direction."

"Ah, if you hadn't noticed, I don't exactly look human. Don't you think the blue skin will give me away?"

"It might, but if anyone starts to give off an alarm I'll deal with them."

"I hope you know what you're doing."

"Me too," Isen said, reactivating his hood. He waved a hand toward the door and the trail line that only he could see. "This way."

When Mysonanda started for the door Isen went with her and led her out into the elongated storage/display room. Not stopping there, the pair continued out the room's wider door and into the main lab room. Out of the corner of his eye, Isen saw Mysonanda flinch when she recognized the room.

"Don't worry," he comforted, "you'll never have to see this place again."

She didn't respond but followed Isen as he weaved his way around the various lab tables and chairs. When they reached the door Isen hesitated before opening it and turned back to look at Mysonanda.

"This is where I disappear. Start walking to the right and I'll handle everything else."

He then reached up to his collar and pressed the cloaking button. After a moment of shimmering he disappeared from view, then just as suddenly the door opened.

"Nice trick," Mysonanda said as she walked out of that dreadful laboratory and down the hall to the right.

She walked straight on until a pair of invisible hands gripped her firmly on the shoulders and steered her to the left when she reached the third intersection. Mysonanda flinched when she entered the new corridor and spotted a tech on down the hall.

"Keep walking," Isen's voice said from nowhere.

Gritting her teeth firmly, Mysonanda fought her natural impulse to run and kept on walking. When the tech came close enough to her to realize that she wasn't human, his face lit up in surprise and just as quickly went blank with him falling to the ground as a forearm appeared behind his head momentarily.

Mysonanda kept walking as the unconscious man was pulled to his feet by an invisible force and tossed into a nearby room whose door opened before and closed behind him on its own accord. *He's good*, she thought as an imperceptible smile formed on her tight lips. *Of course the cloaking device doesn't hurt either.*

She continued on down the corridor to a pair of metallic doors that opened up before her. Mysonanda walked on through the doors, which soon closed behind her, and continued to walk through the corridors as the invisible hands guided her through a number of turns. Finally she reached a lift shaft without being spotted by any other techs and watched as the lift call button depressed into the wall. The lift doors quickly opened to reveal an empty lift car which Mysonanda anxiously boarded. The doors closed and the lift started to move as Mysonanda closed her eyes.

"Don't worry, we'll make it," Isen's voice said reassuringly as she felt a hand on her shoulder.

She opened her eyes and involuntarily jumped back when she saw Isen standing beside her.

"Don't do that," Mysonanda gasped, trying to catch her breath.

"Sorry. I need to conserve as much energy as I can. This suit recharges itself, but the cloak pulls an awful lot of power. The cloak's power reserve is down to 19%. Hopefully that's enough to get us out of here. It wouldn't have been on the old route, but the new route shouldn't require as much cloaking," he said as the lift began to slow. "Ok, the room with my gear should be a short walk from this lift shaft. You alright?"

"I'll make it."

"Good, then take this," Isen said, pulling a small object off his sleeve.

Mysonanda took the weird black device. "What is it?"

"It's my suit's skeleton key. I can't use it while cloaked."

"What do I need it for?"

"I locked the room where I left my gear."

"Oh," she said as Isen nodded to her then disappeared from sight. A few seconds later the lift doors opened and Mysonanda was gently pushed out of the lift car and to the right. The new set of corridors that Isen guided her through were empty, save for a tech at the far end of one of the halls that was too far away to really notice her. The invisible hands then stopped her in front of an unremarkable door.

"This it?" she asked.

"Yes," the invisible man answered.

Mysonanda then opened the door, utilizing the skeleton key without needing any instruction, then walked into the ready room. She gasped as she found two men sitting at a table in the center of the room. They turned towards the door and then jumped to their feet when they saw her.

"What the hell are you?" one of them said as the door closed behind Mysonanda.

She felt a soft squeeze on her shoulder and decided to stand her ground.

"None of your business," she said defiantly.

"Oh, yeah, well you..." the other man said, stopping in mid sentence and dropping to the floor.

"What the..." was all the first man could utter before he too fell to the ground.

Isen then rematerialized, standing over the two men.

"Watch them," he said, moving towards one of the lockers.

He opened one and pulled out a pack similar to the one he was carrying on his back. Isen then unsealed and removed the spare pack and emptied its contents into the primary pack before reabsorbing it into his suit. Isen then pulled on and absorbed the straps of his primary pack.

"Keep the key," he told Mysonanda. "You might need it later." Isen then walked across to the other row of lockers. "You still in there pal," he said opening one of them.

He proceeded to pull out another unconscious tech with Mysonanda watching curiously.

"Old friend," Isen told her as he laid the man next to his fellow techs. Isen then walked up to Mysonanda and looked her in the eye. "Let's get out of here."

"Please," she said playfully.

After recloaking, Isen led Mysonanda out of the ready room and to another lift shaft that took them up to the fourth level. The made it to the room where Flare's guide line ended, with Isen only having to take down two more techs and a security guard along the way.

"Here?" Mysonanda asked when she was abruptly stopped.

"Yes," Isen's voice answered.

Mysonanda then pulled out the skeleton key from one of her labcoat's pockets and opened the door. She stepped into the large office, dimly lit by a thin line of diffuse glow panels ringing the irregularly shaped ceiling. Isen followed her in and closed the door behind them.

"Good. There's the lift shaft," Isen said as he circled around in front of Mysonanda, then decloaked.

"Where?" she asked.

"Over there," he said pointing to the wall, "behind that bookshelf. I can see it on my X-ray sensors."

"Is there anything that suit can't do?"

"Yeah, recharge faster. I'm down to 6% power. If I hit zero the suit will automatically shut off the cloak instead of draining power from other systems," he said, moving to the bookcase.

He reached a hand onto one of the shelves and slid his fingertips across the tops of the books until he located the book that covered the release switch that he could see thanks to his sensors. Isen pulled the book out and pressed the button behind it on the shelf wall. As he replaced the book into its slot, the adjacent section of the wall-spanning bookshelves silently slid out on a hidden hinge to reveal a pair of lift doors.

Isen quickly found the call button on the door jam and pressed it. The lift doors opened immediately, shedding bright light into the seemingly dark room. Isen then looked back at Mysonanda.

"After you," she said, beating him to the phrase.

Isen simply smiled and led the way into the lift car. When Mysonanda followed him in she hit the only button in the lift car, shutting the doors and speeding them on their way. They stared at each other silently for the 47 seconds that it took for the lift car to travel to the northern tunnel entrance.

When the lift car began to slow, visible by the decreasing rate of lights passing by the narrow, waist high strip of viewport encirling the lift car, Isen recloaked and waited for the lift doors to open.

When they did, he followed Mysonanda out into a small hangar occupied only by a pair of hovering, open topped hovercars. Isen quickly decloaked when he saw that the hangar was devoid of personnel, and moved toward the rightmost hovercar with Mysonanda following close behind. They both climbed aboard the four seated craft with Isen taking the driver's on the front bench seat.

"Keys in the ignition. How convenient."

"What is this place?" Mysonanda asked.

"My best guess is the compound administrator's bolt hole," he said as the hovercar's engine hummed to life. "The blueprints show the tunnel ending at a small camouflaged exit in the forest north of the city."

"What happens then?" she asked as they took off down the tunnel.

"We get back to my ship and off the planet. We'll have a long talk after that and decide what to do with you."

When she looked a bit fearful he smiled softly.

"Guess I should have put that another way. We'll decide what to do in the time being, but eventually we'll get you back to your people. You're *not* going to be turned into a guinea pig again. Our people don't do those sort of things."

Her expression softened a bit then she lowered her head slightly. "Sorry. I didn't really think you'd do something like that. I'm just..." she trailed off.

Isen slipped an arm across her shoulders and pulled her close. She didn't resist him, instead she slid closer to him on the bench seat and melted against his side, finally letting her weakened state show. Isen held her for the few minutes it took them to travel the length of the tunnel, then nudged her to get her attention as the tunnel's end came into view. Mysonanda pulled away from him and focused her attention on the tunnel opening ahead.

Isen parked the hovercar in the middle of a hanger smaller than the one at the other end of the tunnel. He and Mysonanda got out of the hovercar and left it behind as they walked toward the far wall and a row of seven speeder bikes. Isen climbed onto the nearest one and pulled Mysonanda on behind him. He then powered up the bike and slowly steered it over to an open lift that approximated the bike's shape.

Isen slid the bike's aft end around and let the speeder bike drift into the lift sideways. After steadying the bike with a hand against the wall, Isen fiddled around with the nearby lift controls and started the lift up. They rode the lift up for about 20 meters before it stopped inside a pitch black room. But before either of them could utter a word of concern, a large hatch pulled open in front of them, letting in rays of sunlight and revealing a forest landscape beyond.

Isen twisted the speeder bike's right handle and shot them out of the camouflaged exit. Mysonanda looped her arms around Isen's waist and pulled herself tight against his pack as they sped off through the woods.

"Flare, locate the ship and guide me to it, but avoid the city."

Flare beeped its conformation and a moment later gave Isen an arrow pointing off to his right. Weaving in and out of trees and shrubs, Isen maneuvered to his right until a dot appeared on the right of his tactical overlay. He centered the dot in the small sphere that Flare provided and raced on through the forest.

When they had cleared the city the dot moved to the right and Isen followed it, turning south back towards his ship. Isen flew through the forest meters above the ground with Mysonanda leaning heavily on him and resting her head on his pack. Isen remained silent until they reached the small valley that held his sunray.

"Mysonanda, we're here," he called back over his shoulder as he slowed the speeder bike to a stop and deactivated his hood.

"Where's your ship?" she asked.

"Over there," he said pointing off to his right.

"I don't see it."

"You shouldn't. It's cloaked."

"Oh."

After a nudge from Isen, Mysonanda pulled herself off the speeder bike. Isen followed suit then unsealed his pack and slid it off his shoulders. He opened it and pulled out a small remote.

"Come on," he told Mysonanda, motioning to her with a tilt of his head, "This way."

Isen led her a hundred or so meters away from the speeder bike then abruptly stopped, with Mysonanda bumping into his shoulder.

"Sorry."

Isen hefted the remote, pressing a small blue button. Suddenly, a door appeared out of thin air, hovering half a meter off the ground. With a soft hiss of repressurization, the door swing open revealing the inside of Isen's ship.

"Impressive. Very impressive," Mysonanda said, turning to face Isen. "I guess I'm lucky it was you who stopped by to rescue me. Thanks by the way."

"Your welcome. Now if you don't object, I'd like to get off this planet now rather than later."

She laughed quickly. "No objections here."

"Well then," Isen said, motioning to the door with his left hand, "after you."

Chapter Forty-Five

"Twenty seconds to reversion," the Lieutenant at the *Tenacity*'s helm station sang out as the ship barreled through IS space.

Standing a few meters from the forward viewport, High Admiral Legan waited patiently as the Lieutenant continued the countdown until the color vortex that engulfed the ship snapped out of existence, revealing a dimly lit star field with the sun of system F-147 the only interruption in the vast emptiness. Calmly, Legan turned to the portside crew pit. "Sensors, give me a sweep of the system."

"Aye sir," the Lieutenant at the corresponding station replied.

Legan turned back to face the viewport again and waited, gazing out at the space beyond the Human Sphere.

"Admiral, sensors report three clusters of vessels scattered around the system. The first group consists of seven warships lead by Admiral Senxir's *Boldheart*."

As the Lieutenant spoke, he activated the bridge holoprojector and a spherical diagram of the system appeared on the central walkway two steps aft of where Legan was standing. As common, the *Tenacity*'s position was marked with a small green dot. Three blue dots appeared at various points in the same hemisphere of the system that the *Tenacity* was now holding position in. Each of the four dots sported a small identification tag that allowed Admiral Legan to follow the Lieutenant's recitation.

"The second group is convoy number two, complete with its escort. The last is the group of warships that left the Gamma 7 station with us."

The Lieutenant at the comms station interrupted. "Admiral, we're receiving a transmission from an unknown source."

"What sort of transmission?" Legan asked, though he already had a good idea where it was coming from.

"Someone identifying themself as Nova 4 is asking permission to board the *Tenacity*."

"Permission granted. Reply on the same frequency."

"Sir," the Lieutenant at the sensor station called out, "the *Tenacity*'s sensors don't show any other vessels in the system."

"It's there Lieutenant," Legan assured. "Captain Yader?"

"Yes sir."

"A small fighter with a friend of mine will be landing in the starboard hangar bay. I want you to escort her to my ready room, then return to the bridge. Also, order the techs to leave her fighter alone until I order otherwise."

"Aye sir," Yader said, then turned on his heels and headed for the bridge lift.

Legan turned to face the starboard crew pit, catching the eye of a particular Ensign. "Open starboard hangar bay doors and inform the deck officer to expect company."

Instead of finding his 'friend' in his ready room, Admiral Legan was informed that she'd been taken to the infirmary and wasn't in very good condition. When Legan arrived in the *Tenacity*'s infirmary he found her sitting up on a med table with the left sleeve of her jumpsuit cut free and an active heeling wrap around her shoulder and upper arm. Captain Yader was hovering nearby, looking concerned.

"How is she," Legan asked the attending doctor after giving Yader a quick nod.

"Not good," a female physician replied. "She has a blaster wound on her left shoulder that I've taken care of. She's also suffering from severe dehydration, exhaustion, and a touch of hypothermia, but she won't let me treat her for them."

Legan looked at the woman as she rolled her eyes and shrugged her shoulders impatiently. "Clear the room doctor, I'll take it from here."

When she started to object he added, "That's an order."

The doctor sighed then moved toward the nearest door, signaling a handful of other infirmary personnel to follow her out. Captain Yader also left with them after a slight head signal from Legan. When the infirmary door closed behind the last of the medical personnel, Legan calmly, but quickly turned back to the injured woman.

"What happened Cara?"

She smiled slyly before answering. "I had a disagreement with some of the security guards. I won, but not before they got a piece of me."

When Legan didn't speak Cara continued. "I infiltrated Intelligence's headquarters and gained access to the restricted levels but couldn't find a dataport. After searching through a number of rooms I returned to my entry point and stumbled across a back door stairway to the main datacore itself. I downloaded the files from there but discovered newly cut tunnels in the bedrock surrounding the core. I investigated and found a huge underground hangar full of fighters and ground assault vehicles along with a command center of some sort."

She winced as she readjusted herself into a more comfortable position sitting position. "I took pictures but had to ditch my pack on the way out. Sorry."

"Don't worry about it. You're more important than any intelligence. How did you get that," he asked, motioning to her shoulder.

"On my back out I discovered another room carved into the bedrock that contained an auxiliary datacore. I tried to access it but triggered an alarm halfway through the hacking sequence. When that happened the facility started to swarm with guards, so I had to fight my way out."

She glanced to her shoulder. "I didn't get away as cleanly as I hoped."

"Do you still have the chips?"

Cara smiled as she dug into her belt pockets with her right hand. She pulled out the 5 datacards that held the Republic's sealed files and handed them to the Admiral.

"Everything should be there if Zephrim's device worked like it should have."

Legan clutched the extremely important datacards in his right palm. "These should be helpful." He turned his attention away from the datacards and back to Cara. "Are you going to be alright?"

"I'm a bit wrung out, but besides the shoulder I should be fully recovered after two or three days of rest."

"You'll have plenty of time to recover during the trip to Alpha Prime. It'll take the *Tenacity* a good 17 days to get there."

"I'll be sure to use the time wisely Admiral."

"I'm sure you will Agent Venture. Are you well enough to walk?"

Cara eyed him incredulously. "If I wasn't then I wouldn't be here."

"True. If you don't object to a short walk then I'll show you the way to my quarters. You can get cleaned up and wait there until we find you some permanent quarters. Feel free to help yourself to my wardrobe. When you're assigned quarters I'll have some of our nondescript clothing brought up from storage, but until then you'll have to make do."

"Sounds good to me," Cara said as she slid off the med table. "I could really use a shower."

Legan showed her to his quarters, walking slow enough for Cara to keep up with him in her weakened state. When the pair reached their destination Legan opened the door to his quarters and let Cara in, but stayed outside himself.

"I'm needed on the bridge, but feel free to make yourself at home while I'm gone. If you need anything the comms panel is next to the door lock, plus there's another one on the low table next to the couch. I'll be on the bridge for another seven hours, so until then it's all yours."

Admiral Legan returned to the bridge and his Admiral's chair and issued orders to the other vessels in the system to gather near the *Tenacity*'s position and organize themselves in an orderly pattern. After giving those initial orders, Legan watched over the bridge officers as they went about their routine duties for another three hours before the Lieutenant at the sensor station broke the silence.

"Admiral. New contact has dropped out of IS space, ID transponder marks it as the *Goliath*."

"They're hailing us," the comms Lieutenant reported.

"Open a channel."

Legan waited until the Lieutenant signaled that the channel was indeed open, then he spoke into the air. "This is High Admiral Legan onboard the *Tenacity*. Report your status."

Immediately Agent Cerus's voice came back over the *Tenacity*'s comm speakers.

"The *Goliath* is fully operational, but is running on automated systems only. The sooner we get a full crew aboard the better. But for now things are under control."

"We'll be sending the *Goliath*'s crew over once they arrive with the remaining convoys. Until then, move into a flanking position off the *Tenacity*'s port side and wait for further instructions."

"Acknowledged *Tenacity*. We'll be at your position in a little over three minutes. Request that all other vessels give us a wide berth. The *Goliath*'s helm is a bit sluggish."

"We'll make room. Legan out." After the comm officer closed the channel Legan glanced in his direction. "Lieutenant."

"Yes sir," he said, turning to his console and beginning to send messages to the other ships to clear the way for the *Goliath*.

After a few minutes a large black bulk appeared off the *Tenacity*'s port bow, gradually slowing to a stop when its midsection paralleled the entire length of the *Tenacity*.

"Admiral. The *Goliath* reports that it's in position and powering down most of its systems until the crew arrives."

"Acknowledge that and tell them to sit tight. It may be a while before the rest of the convoys arrive."

"Aye sir."

Chapter Forty-Six

"So, where exactly are you from?" Isen asked Mysonanda as they hurled through IS space.

"A good ways rimward from here. Our patrol route took us far beyond Cres territory in toward the core. We were nearing the apogee of our patrol loop when our ship broke down and the…you called them Peace Core…jumped us." Mysonanda paused as she sipped some more of the dark, warm beverage that Isen had given her earlier in an elongated mug.

Isen took the opportunity before him and asked a question that had been floating around in the back of his mind. "You said 'Cres' territory and back in the compound you said that I wasn't 'Cres'. Is that the name of your people?"

She eyed him for a moment then resolved herself to answering his questions. "Yes," she said, nodding her head. "We're called Cres."

When Isen remained silent she continued. "I'm a Secora in the Cres Empire's Tenisha. We're the first line of defense for the Empire and also its main offensive weapon. The Empire has a great number of neighboring enemies that have repeatedly invaded our territory, but in each instance the attackers have been repelled. Because of the hostile nature of the region, we try to keep surveillance at a maximum, hence my patrol. The Empire keeps the borders and the surrounding regions under close observation. My patrol assignment was the latter. Our patrol route took us through the majority of the Dhorena, translated dead zone. We call it dead because no one will colonize the region. It's an unspoken rule that the region remain neutral and the hostile forces around us and the Empire keep each other out by threat of force. The Brahracs tried once to expand their territories into the Dhorena, starting a war that widdled their territory down to less than a third of its original size. Our enemies keep constant patrols throughout the region, spying on each others vessels, as do our ships."

Mysonanda looked down for a moment. "Our territory is the most expansive in the charted regions, but there are rumored larger threats beyond its boundaries. As it is now, the Cres Empire is having a rough time dealing with the endless attrition resulting from the near constant attacks on our border worlds. We're holding our own, but only because the forces opposing us are fighting with each other. If they ever had it in their minds to band together, the Empire would be destroyed."

She sighed. "Now I find another threat in this Peace Core of yours. Distant as it may be, we don't need any more enemies."

"I wouldn't worry too much about Peace Core. They, along with the rest of the Human Sphere, tend to be insular, though your capture could attest otherwise. If they ever are to be a threat to the Cres Empire, it will be after they accomplish whatever plans they have for the Sphere."

"That's something then." A stray though suddenly crossed her mind. "By the way, where are we heading anyway?"

"We're traveling to a rendezvous point outside the Sphere to meet with Admiral Legan and deliver the artifacts that I took from Peace Core to him. It'll take us another 20 plus hours and a course change before we get there. In fact, our reversion point should only be a few minutes away," he said, standing up from his chair at the small wall mounted table at the back of the sunray.

Isen made his way forward to the cockpit with Mysonanda trailing a few steps behind him. He plopped down in the pilot's seat and took a quick glance at the status board. The readouts showed that all of the ship's systems were operating nominally and the countdown clock at the base of the forward viewport read less than three minutes.

"Good. Timed that about right."

Isen let the clock count down to zero with Mysonanda hovering silently off his left shoulder, then disengaged the IS drive before the automatic cutoff could take effect. The ship snapped back into realspace amidst the doldrums of emptiness that existed between systems. *Sensors show this place dead as can be. Time to report in then.* Isen got up out of his seat and moved back into the ship's midsection.

"What are you doing?" Mysonanda asked.

"I'm going to report in to my superior. Stay out of sight until I say otherwise," Isen said as he stepped in front of a wall mounted communications panel. He keyed in the proper codes and quickly made contact with Morning Dawn's headquarters. Jace Starfield's face and shoulders appeared on the viewscreen before him as Isen gave the man a curt nod. "Mission complete Director."

"You have the artifacts then?"

"All four."

"Any trouble?"

Isen hesitated before answering. "Trouble no. Complications yes." Isen started to say something but stopped short.

"What is it?" Starfield asked.

"You'd better see for yourself," Isen said as the he motioned his shipmate to his side.

Starfield's breath momentarily caught in his throat, but it wasn't discernable on the viewscreen.

"Hi," Mysonanda said.

"Hello indeed. May I ask who you are, you don't look like you're from around here," Starfield said almost sarcastically.

"My name is Mysonanda."

"Well then Mysonanda, would one of you please tell me what's gong on."

Isen put a hand on Mysonanda's shoulder to stop her from speaking. "I found her in a stasis tube near where the artifacts where being held. From what she tells me, a Peace Core vessel boarded her patrol craft, killed the crew, and took her back to their headquarters to experiment on. I managed to remove her from stasis and get her out of the compound without too much trouble, but Peace Core should know by now that she's missing."

Starfield rubbed his thin goatee for a moment as he considered the unexpected news. "Agent Tyrel, I have a favor to ask of you."

"Go ahead."

"I'm not making this an order, but I would like you to go with Admiral Legan and help him in whatever way you can."

"You want me to work with Midnight Star?"

"If that's what Legan wants, I'm assigning you to him personally, if you agree to go."

Isen considered. "If that's where you want me sir, then that's where I'll go."

"I thought you'd say something like that. I *am* surprised though at your companion. You'd better take her with you to Legan. He's in a better position than I am to deal with the situation."

"Understood."

"But first, if I may, I'd like to ask the lady a few questions."

Mysonanda smiled sardonically. "Certainly."

"Admiral. Convoy number six has just dropped out of IS space."

"That's Senator Malcolm's convoy," Captain Yader commented.

"Indeed." Legan tilted his head to the side. "Comm, inquire the newly arrived convoy on their status."

"Aye, sir...Admiral, message from the starboard hangar bay. An unidentified vessel is currently in one of the hangar's parking slips."

Captain Yader took a step toward the Lieutenant. "How did the ship get into hangar bay?"

The comms officer relayed the question to the hangar bay and shortly received a panicked answer. "Sir, the deck officer reports that the ship appeared out of thin air on the parking slip."

Yader turned to Legan and raised an eyebrow. "Thin air?"

"I think we'd better have a look for ourselves," Legan said as he moved toward the bridge lift. "Inform the deck officer not to take any action until I arrive."

"Yes sir," the comms officer replied as Admiral Legan and Captain Yader stepped into the lift car.

Three and a half minutes later, the pair of commanding officers stepped through the hangar doors and onto the polished deck and strode across the hangar deck to the knot of maintenance personnel scattered around a ship that was vaguely familiar to Legan. As the pair reached the assembled onlookers, Captain Yader raised his voice. "Which of you is the deck officer?"

"I am," a tall, lean man dressed in a dull orange mechanics suit called out as he raised a hand high enough to be seen over the 30 or so techs gathered around him.

"Report," Legan ordered as the group of techs parted to let him and Captain Yader through.

"Sir. This ship appeared here out of thin air."

"So I've heard."

"I was in the control room when I heard someone shout. I looked up and saw this…" he pointed to the ship three meters behind him, "…thing sitting on the deck. We tried to contact whoever's in there over the comm, but we didn't get any response."

"I assume no one has left the vessel?"

"No sir."

Legan nodded to the man then stepped around to the front of the ship. He faced the tinted forward viewport and was about to speak when the ship's side hatch hissed open. A young man dressed in a black jumpsuit stepped out of the ship onto the hangar deck, turning to face Legan.

"Did you forget our appointment?"

"Of course not. But I didn't expect you to show up in this fashion."

"Well, I though it would be better if only this ship's crew knew that I was here instead of your whole fleet."

"A wise precaution, but unnecessary. Everyone here is moving to Alpha Prime, so word of your existence won't be getting back to the Sphere."

"Call me cautious then."

"Since you're here, I assume your mission was a success?"

"It was, but there have been some slight changes since the last time we spoke." Isen waved a hand back towards the open hatch. "If you have the time, I'd be happy to fill you in."

"I think my ready room would be a more appropriate place for our conversation."

"If you'll join me inside my ship you'll see why that's not a very good idea."

"As you wish." He raised his voice so all around him could hear. "Clear the area. This ship is off limits to all maintenance personnel." Legan looked specifically to the deck officer. "Understood?"

"Yes sir," he said, then focused his attention on the techs. "You heard the Admiral. Clear the area."

Legan faced Captain Yader as the group of techs began to disperse. "Captain, you can return to the bridge. I'm going to have a discussion with our friend here."

"Yes Admiral," Yader acknowledged. He then headed back to the bridge as Legan moved toward the ship's hatch with Isen stepping back into the ship ahead of him. Legan followed him into the ship wondering what 'changes' Agent Tyrel had been referring to.

Chapter Forty-Seven

Watching out the forward bridge viewport as a number of small white flashes appeared in the distance, Admiral Legan pondered Isen Tyrel's unexpected companion.

Mysonanda's appearance is going to force me to change my plans considerably. I had hoped that this operation would be allowed to grow in isolation, but that's no longer an option. When we send Mysonanda back home the Cres Empire will know we're out here. I had hoped to avoid that eventuality long enough for us to get a solid grip on our new territory, but that woman deserves to be returned home after all she's been through. I could arrange it so she doesn't know Alpha Prime's exact location, but the Cres would still know that we exist.

Legan's train of thought was interrupted by a voice coming from the portside crew pit. "Admiral, convoy number 5 has dropped out of IS space on the edge of the system."

"Thank you Lieutenant. Comm, signal the *Diligence* and request their current status and ship count."

The Lieutenant at the communications station nodded his acknowledgement then went about contacting the convoy's flagship.

"That's the last of the convoys Admiral," Captain Yader commented as he stepped to Legan's side on the command walkway. "How long do you expect it will take before the fleet is ready to travel?"

"I would guess another hour or two. We have to make sure all of our ships are accounted for before we leave. We can't afford to leave anyone behind."

"No we can't," Yader agreed as his attention was drawn to the viewport by a large number of pinprick flashes illuminating a portion of the star field off the ship's port bow. "I thought convoy number 5 was the last group of ships that we were waiting for."

"They were," Legan said in a growl as he also noticed another group of vessels dropping out of IS space directly behind convoy number 5. He turned toward the portside crew pit, suddenly alert.

"Sensors, identify those ships."

"Checking now," the Lieutenant answered, picking up on the Admiral's tone. "A third of the vessels are carrying Peace Core insignia, the other two thirds' ID transponders are either deactivated or non-existent."

Legan turned back towards the viewport for a moment.

"Battle stations," he ordered calmly.

His order was followed by a siren that blared three times then fell silent as the bridge lighting took on a reddish tone. "Order all transports to cluster around convoy number 3 in a spherical defense pattern. Then have all warships, save for the *Goliath*, move between the transports and the incoming ships. Have the *Goliath* take up a defensive position with the transports and have all other warships form up on the *Tenacity*. Helm, take us to point."

Legan then returned to his Admiral's chair as the *Tenacity* veered off towards the incoming ships. Captain Yader also returned to his appropriate chair and activated the display screens on his ring-like consoles in tandem with Legan.

"Why did you order the *Goliath* back?" Captain Yader inquired as the *Tenacity* outstripped the rest of the fleet as it drove toward the incoming ships. "If there's to be a battle we could certainly use her firepower."

"The *Goliath*'s crew has only had five hours aboard ship, and that's not enough time for them to get her battle ready."

Yader nodded his understanding as he turned back to his consoles as Legan turned to the starboard crew pit.

"Helm, hold here. Comm, signal the fleet to form up on the *Tenacity* and screen for the convoy."

The *Tenacity* slowed to a stop and let the other warships catch up to her position. The fleet then spread out in a blockade formation centered on the *Tenacity*.

"Shields up," Captain Yader ordered. "Activate all weapons systems and power up the armor."

"Signal the convoy to move past us and take up position behind the transport cluster," Legan ordered.

"Should we launch fighters?" Yader asked.

"Not yet. Have all ships to hold back their fighters until I order otherwise."

"Aye sir."

"Guns, target the lead vessels but hold your fire until I give the command."

Legan and Yader then waited patiently for the minute and a half that it took for convoy number 5's ships to reach the fleet's formation. The convoy's ships weaved through the waiting warships then headed off towards the transports that were now arrayed in a spherical formation. The convoy's escort warships followed their transports through the mass of waiting warships then swung back around and joined the battle formation.

"45 seconds to firing range," one of the bridge officers called out.

"Admiral, have you taken a look at the enemy fleet's composition?" Yader asked.

Legan nodded. "Numerically we've got a slight edge on them and our ships are more powerful than theirs. We should be able to drive them off, but it's going to get bloody."

"By now they should know that as well as we do, but they're still coming," Yader said.

"Indeed, they are. Either they're extremely foolish or they have something up their sleeve." He craned his neck to the right. "Order all ships to launch fighters, but have them take up position behind our formation until we engage the enemy fleet."

"Admiral, enemy ships are launching fighters. Now ten seconds to firing range," the Lieutenant at the sensor station reported.

"Guns stand by." Legan watched the enemy vessels on his personal tactical display as they neared the red shaded area that defined the *Tenacity*'s weapon's range.

"Fire."

The *Tenacity*'s gunners let loose with a firestorm of red omnilaser blasts that lanced out at the approaching ships. The rest of the fleet followed suit, firing a mass of blue omnilaser blasts at the enemy ships and their fighter screens.

The majority of the long-range blasts passed harmlessly by the approaching vessels but enough hit home on the smaller enemy warships to produce an impressive show of fireworks. A number of the enemy's starfighters that were proceeding the capital ships were destroyed in the initial barrage before the enemy fleet returned fire.

The Peace Core vessels responded with a barrage of blue omnilaser blasts and waves of missiles and torpedoes while the rest of the enemy fleet shot fiery red laser blasts at Legan's ships.

"Those Peace Core vessels have standard weaponry on them," Yader observed. "I thought they were only supposed to carry non lethal weaponry."

"Apparently some modifications have been made," Legan said as the *Tenacity* shook slightly from multiple missile impacts. "Ops, have the fighters loop around our formation and attack the enemy ships on their flanks."

The swarm of starmasters waiting behind the fleet's formation dispersed to the fringes of the formation and fell on the outermost enemy capital ships and starfighters with a vengeance as the two enemy fleets closed to point blank range on the *Tenacity* and the rest of Admiral Legan's fleet.

"Guns, target the two cruisers off to starboard and fire torpedoes at the battleship to port."

In accordance with the Admiral's orders bright red darts blossomed from the *Tenacity*'s forward guns and peppered the two cruisers' hulls, blasting through their shields as if they weren't even there.

At the same time the forward torpedo launchers let fly in pairs 22 bright white projectiles toward the Peace Core battleship that was chewing away at the *Tenacity*'s forward shields. The first eight torpedoes detonated against the battleship's forward shields, stressing them to their limit. The next pair took the shields down and kissed the hull with a large golden brown fireball. The remaining 12 torpedoes detonated on the battleship's hull, blasting apart the bow and turning the surviving section of the ship into a lifeless corpse as its engines died and the ship's interior lighting went out.

The two cruisers fared no better as the *Tenacity*'s omnilaser blasts tore into their hulls until the cruisers' weaker return fire slowly faded as their gun batteries were either destroyed or had their power conduits severed.

"Helm, quarter turn to starboard. Guns, concentrate fire on the *Delta*-class dreadnought and it's frigate escort," Legan ordered.

The *Tenacity* pivoted to her right and brought both her starboard and port guns in line with the quartet of enemy warships that had engaged the *Brilliance*. A river of red splinters erupted from the *Tenacity*'s hull and crossed the 2.3km gap to where they impacted on the *Devastator's* shields.

Occupied with her attack on the *Brilliance*, the *Devastator* was unaware of the *Tenacity*'s presence until she took the brunt of the omnilaser onslaught. The Devastator's port shields held up under the barrage for a handful of seconds then collapsed as the combined firepower of the *Tenacity* and the *Brilliance* was too much for the dreadnought to handle. The Kataran warships bored through her portside and bow hull plates with relative ease now that the shields were down, but the carnage didn't stop there.

The *Brilliance*'s gunners continued to gouge out the interior of the *Devastator* as the *Tenacity* switched the her attack to the three frigates that had stopped their assault on the *Brilliance* and were now pounding on the *Tenacity*'s shields.

"Guns, focus 50% of the batteries on the lead frigate and split the remainder on the trailers," Legan ordered as the *Tenacity*'s deck shook from a rather violent barrage of missiles from a Peace Core *Freedom*-class cruiser that decided to join the fight. "Comm, have the *Courage* and *Intrepid* fall back into flanking positions off our aft quarter."

"Aye Admiral."

"Captain Yader, cover their retreat with a torpedo salvo."

"Yes sir," he said turning to carry out his orders as a large fireball off the starboard bow covered the *Tenacity*'s bridge in a golden glow for a few seconds before it dissipated and left the *Devastator*'s debris to drift throughout the battlefield.

"Comm, order the *Brilliance* to take up our position and have the *Courage* and the *Intrepid* form up on her instead. Helm, ahead one quarter."

As the *Tenacity* launched a wave of torpedoes in the wake of the pair of retreating warships, she continued to pour omnilaser fire into the three frigates harassing her bow shields, which were now down to 67%. The *Tenacity* then began to move forward towards the frigate formation as the *Brilliance* moved to support the *Courage* and *Intrepid*.

The frigate closest to the *Tenacity* then exploded, splitting the ship in half when the omnilasers punctured her power core. With one less target to worry about the *Tenacity*'s gunners brought more fire on the remaining two frigates as the Peace Core cruiser continued to strip away power from the port shields.

The frigates didn't last long under the increased fire. The port frigate suffered an internal explosion in its engine compartment that sent it drifting away unpowered and losing atmosphere. The starboard frigate continued its attack on the *Tenacity* despite the loss of its sister ships, but it fared no better. The *Tenacity*'s guns finished off what little defenses it had left and quickly turned it into a lifeless hulk.

"Guns, hit the cruiser," Legan ordered.

Now that the frigates had been dealt with, the *Tenacity* was free to deal with the Peace Core vessel that had tore away more than half of the power on the port shields. Still continuing forward past the dead frigates' remains the *Tenacity* pulled alongside the cruiser and let it have the brunt of her portside omnilaser attack at point blank range.

Even with her shield power intact, the *Freedom*-class cruiser's shields couldn't withstand that kind of firepower at a distance of less than 300 meters. The *Tenacity*'s omnilaser batteries carved out a 50 meter wide groove down the length of the cruiser's port side that left it lifeless like so many other hulks now drifting on the battlefield as the *Tenacity* continued on past the debris.

"Admiral, six of the enemy vessels and a number of starfighters have penetrated our lines and are heading towards the transports."

"Guns, take out the battleship chewing on the *Incorruptible*'s engines, focus on it's port bow," Yader ordered.

"Are any of our ships free to intercept?" Legan asked, turning to the battle ops officer.

"Negative, all of our ships are engaged and the enemy vessels have too large a lead. None of our ships can intercept them before they reach the convoy except the *Goliath*. It's the only warship in range."

"The *Goliath* can't handle six warships," Legan said turning away from the battle ops officer. "Helm…"

"Hold on," the battle ops officer interrupted. "Another ship is moving to intercept the enemy vessels. It's deploying starfighters."

"Identify," Legan ordered.

"The vessel's ID transponder reads as…the *Perseverance*."

Chapter Forty-Eight

"This is General Legan speaking to all fighters. Six of the enemy vessels have broken away from the battle and are heading for the transports. We have to stop them before they get there. Pulsar squadron, assist the *Perseverance* with the capital ships. Quasars, Sentinels, we have the fighters, looks like Centaur II's and III's. Hit'em hard. Legan out."

Alec then switched his comm from intersquadron to his squadron's personal frequency. "Ok Sentinels, listen up. Accelerate to attack speed and drive right down their throats. After you come out on the other side swing back around and try for torpedo locks. Stick with your wingman and watch each other's backs."

Alec switched off the comm and took the few seconds he had before they reached the enemy starfighters that were now angling away from the capital ships and towards the Kataran fighters, to activate his torpedo launcher and quickly reprogram the first projectile. As soon as he completed his task, Alec let it fly at the incoming starfighter formation.

The torpedo crossed the ever-shrinking gap between the fighters in less than two seconds, detonating just before it reached the enemy formation. The enemy starfighters broke formation to avoid the explosion while the fighters nearest the detonated torpedo got a sparkling shower on their shields from dust sized debris as they intersected the edge of the fireball. With their formation now in disarray, the enemy starfighters were left vulnerable to the *Perseverance*'s fighters in their momentary hesitation following the torpedo's explosion.

Quasar and Sentinel squadrons bored their way through what was left of the enemy formation then turned about and fell upon the remaining disconcerted starfighters with a vengeance. Meanwhile Pulsar squadron took potshots at the enemy fighters as they flew through the space brawl and on towards the six capital ships that were getting dangerously close to the convoys. When the starmasters reached their maximum firing range they simultaneously fired a spread of 24 torpedoes at the leading enemy vessel.

When the *Enigma*-class battleship *Validity* saw the incoming torpedo barrage, it immediately reacted with a hail of red laser fire, trying to knock out the torpedoes before they hit the ship. As massive as the battleship's firestorm was it was ineffective against the small torpedoes. Only one torpedo was hit and exploded prematurely, which left 23 torpedoes to hit the battleship.

And hit they did. While not as powerful as the capital ship variety, the starmasters' torpedoes did succeed in bringing down the battleship's port shields and tearing away a small chunk of the hull, but the *Validity* and its five companions continued on in at the vulnerable transports, disregarding the fighters.

Pulsar squadron fell in behind the enemy ships and started chewing at the trailing vessels' rear shields with their lasers and torpedoes, trying to knock out the ship's engines, but their efforts were more or less useless. With a continual onslaught of torpedoes they did manage to take down the two trailing cruisers' rear shields and disable part of their engines, but it was too little too late. The lead ships had already entered firing range on the convoy. The leading ships, followed by the limping cruisers, started to fire sporadic laser blasts in the direction of the convoy when the leading *Validity* came under fire.

Waves of pulsing blue omnilaser blasts and a spread of torpedoes from the *Perseverance* poured into the damaged and unshielded section of the battleship, igniting an internal explosion that ripped the ship apart.

Shocked by the violent death of its sister ship, another *Enigma*-class battleship and the two limping cruisers turned on the *Perseverance* as the remaining pair of cruisers continued on in at the convoy, launching their own barrage of missiles at the weakly shielded transports.

Returning to the *Perseverance* after the Sentinels and Quasars finished off the enemy starfighters, Alec watched in horror as the enemy missiles shot toward the convoy cluster.

"No!" he screamed aloud.

Suddenly, a number of projectiles shot out from the convoy cluster, outnumbering the incoming missiles two to one. The projectiles met the missiles halfway in a series of brilliant explosions that obscured the transport cluster from Alec's view. As he angled in on the three ships attacking the *Perseverance* the fireballs dissipated and a relieved Alec saw one of the ships in the still intact convoy cluster move out of the formation and towards the pair of cruisers.

Alec then dived in at the battleship harassing the *Perseverance* and let it have a pair of torpedoes as his tactical overlay tagged the ship emerging from the convoy as the *Goliath*."

"Admiral, the ship moving to intercept the cruisers reads as the *Goliath*."

"I guess the High Admiral managed to retrieve her after all," Plescal said from the center of the *Perseverance*'s circular bridge. "Lieutenant. Shield status?"

"Bow shields are down to 42%."

"Helm, I want a 90 degree turn to the starboard."

"Aye sir."

"Guns bring the aft weaponry to bear on the far left cruiser. Concentrate fire on the breaches in their shields. All other batteries focus on the battleship. The second cruiser will keep for now."

The *Perseverance* pivoted to the right, bringing all of her port omnilaser batteries to bear on the trio of enemy warships. As the *Perseverance* traded fire with the enemy ships, her starfighters made strafing runs on the enemy's flanks, staying well away from the hot zone between the ships. With the cruisers' aft shields already down and the starmasters exploiting that vulnerability, the enemy ships were quickly losing a war of attrition against the *Perseverance*. After a continued barrage of blue fire and torpedo impacts the, cruiser's shields eventually collapsed.

Once that happened the *Perseverance*'s omnilaser blasts and torpedoes tore through the outer hull, exposing the internal decks of the ship to space. Emergency containment doors helped to contain the ship's escaping atmosphere but slowly the ship began to shut down section by section.

"Guns, target the…" Plescal said as his order was cut short as the cruiser under fire exploded into a shrapnel filled fireball twice as large as the *Perseverance*, "target the second cruiser but keep fire on the battleship," Plescal finished as the fireball darkened, leaving bits and pieces of the ship floating in all directions.

One rather large section of the dead cruiser drifted into the aft section of the second cruiser, punching through its shields and destroying the ship's engines. Eventually the cruiser's interior power readings faded, as did the remaining battleship's until the pair were just a collection of floating junk that vaguely resembled warships.

"Guns cease fire. Sensors, where are the other cruisers?"

"Destroyed Admiral. The *Goliath* took them out."

"Status on the convoys?"

The Lieutenant at the sensor station worked at his console for a moment then responded in a more relaxed tone of voice. "Sensors show no damage to convoy vessels. A few ships are showing weakened shields though."

"Good. We can't afford to loose any of them. What's the status of the main battle?"

"Attackers are fleeing. Sensors show severe damage to four of our warships with moderate to light damage on the remainder. But all of the vessels on the convoy manifests are accounted for."

"What about our fighters?"

"Out of the total 36, sensors show 27 operational with another three adrift."

"Admiral," the communications officer spoke up, "General Legan reports that some of our pilots are EV and need pickup."

"Inform the General to relay their location and we'll retrieve them shortly. Captain, ship status?"

Captain Veske looked over his command chair's diagnostic readouts then turned to face Admiral Plescal. "Bow shields are down to 37%, port shields are at 52%. Minor damage on the port hull. Two omnilaser batteries are offline. The rest of the ship is fully functional."

"Very well. Helm, move us into position to retrieve the EV pilots and the disabled starmasters as soon as we receive their coordinates from General Legan."

Four hours after the battle had ended Admiral Plescal and General Legan had transferred to the Tenacity via shuttle and were now seated in a self-conforming chair and a reversed stiff backed chair respectively in Admiral Legan's quarters. The High Admiral himself had just returned from the bridge and was seated on his comfortable couch as he looked at his two disobedient subordinates.

"If I remember correctly you two were ordered to Alpha Prime to prepare for the fleet's arrival. Care to explain the discrepancy?"

The pair of officers looked at each other for a moment then Admiral Plescal finally responded. "Actually your orders were to prepare Alpha Prime and facilitate the fleet's arrival. Our being here falls under the latter stipulation."

"Oh really, how so?" Legan asked curiously amused.

"You mean besides from the fact that there wouldn't have been much of a fleet left to facilitate if we hadn't showed up?" Alec asked sarcastically.

"Yes, besides that."

"Well, we figured that since you weren't supposed to be at the rendezvous point until another four days from now that we would have enough time to beat you here so we could give you the specifics of our orbit navigation system and offloading schedule. We thought it would expedite the process if the fleet knew what it was supposed to do before it gets to Alpha Prime instead of after," Plescal explained.

"What about the operations on Alpha Prime now? Why did you leave them unattended?"

"Once Supply Core's startup elements were firmly established there was little need for our intervention. The Supply Core Administrators have things running smoothly and didn't need us looking after them."

"So you decided to come here to expedite the fleet's integration?"

"Yes."

"And?" Legan asked, looking directly at Alec.

"Alright already, so I was bored out of my mind. I'm a pilot, not a desk jockey."

"You too Admiral?"

"Guilty as charged."

Legan shook his head in disbelief. "I guess I should be grateful that I have such incompetent officers."

"Incompetent?" Alec asked. "We're not the ones who can't follow their own schedule."

"Point," Legan admitted.

"Why were you here early? We didn't expect to find anyone when we arrived, let alone revert from IS space into a battlefield."

"I was forced to move up my time table slightly after you left. Sorry about that."

"You're forgiven," Alec said. "Lucky for you we arrived when we did. Who was attacking us by the way? I know there were a number of Peace Core vessels in the enemy fleet, but most of the capital ships and fighters were outdated models."

"I have my suspicions, but no hard evidence."

"I didn't ask for any," Alec admonished.

Legan eyed Alec for a moment then continued. "The name on the top of my list is Lena Mian. Her connections to Peace Core aren't exactly a secret, but I must admit it does seem to be a bit of a stretch to think that she'd raise a rogue fleet and have the Peace Core vessels rearmed to come after us, especially since she didn't know we were leaving."

"That doesn't exactly fit with her pacifist philosophy," Plescal commented.

"No, it doesn't. Maybe it was someone outside the Republic with a tie to Peace Core. I don't know. But one thing for sure is that they're not following us to Alpha Prime. I have our warships spread out far enough to detect any vessels before they would be able to scan the convoys. We'll cover them then take evasive routes so our destination will remain a secret. It wasn't difficult to track the convoys here, but this is where we disappear for good."

Standing on the bridge of the *Tenacity*, High Admiral Legan watched through the forward viewport as the last of the fleet's warships jumped to IS space, leaving the *Tenacity* as the last vessel in the F-147 system.

Sufficient repairs had been made to all of Legan's ships to get them to Alpha Prime. Survivors from both sides had been retrieved with the enemy pilots, crew, and officers being held in brigs throughout the fleet. All the cleanup that had to be done after the battle was done, and now it was time to leave.

"Admiral, the IS core is fully charged. We're ready to make the jump," the officer at the helm station informed.

Legan looked out at the stars that made up the Human Sphere and said a final, silent goodbye.

"Take us out Lieutenant."

Seven seconds later the *Tenacity* jumped into IS space, leaving the Sphere's influence behind.

Chapter Forty-Nine

"I respectfully disagree with Senator Mian," Aidos Treckly said after being recognized by President Morrison.

Standing in one of the upper tiers of the Kataran Senate chamber, Treckley, the senator from Persarvis II, raised his voice enough that the recorder probe hovering nearby would be able to clearly relay his words to the senate's sound system.

"We don't have the machinery or manpower to track down High Admiral Legan and repossess his warships. Furthermore, I believe it would be a misjudgment to declare the High Admiral and his men enemies of the state."

At that point Lena Mian interrupted. "So what would you have us do? Let them get off scot free with the Republic's military. Legan stole those warships from the people of the Kataran Republic. We cannot allow this indiscretion to go unpunished."

"On the contrary, High Admiral Legan's actions, while somewhat unorthodox, have aided the Republic immensely. Remember, now that with the military under his control High Admiral Legan could have easily seized control of the Kataran Republic for himself, but he hasn't. It's been 22 days since the reports of the fleet's departure and not a single vessel has been sighted since. Rumor has it that he's left the Republic entirely. Instead of condemning him and his men as traitors we should honor them for their contribution to the new era of peace."

"Do you mean to say that their past heroics outweigh this…this mutiny?"

"No, I'm not speaking of the past, rather the present. High Admiral Legan and his men are soldiers from a past era who are not compatible with pacifism. They strive for peace using the tools of war while we see those very tools as the enemy of peace itself. We both have the same vision of a peaceful existence, but our methods differ. High Admiral Legan is a soldier who won't let his guard down, even if ordered to do so. Both he and the new ear of pacifism cannot coexist. But instead of fighting against the consensus of the people, High Admiral Legan chose to let the Republic continue into its pacifistic future, even if he and his men cannot be part of that future. Furthermore, High Admiral Legan had taken the Republic's military off our hands, saving us the time and expense of dismantling it."

Treckley raised his hands to shoulder height before him in a pleading gesture. "Let us not condemn our brothers for action that have helped the Republic make the transition to pacifism that much easier. Instead, let us wish them well in whatever future they will make for themselves."

When he stopped speaking, Treckley lowered his hands to his sides in the midst of the senate's silence. Then one senator seated on the lowest of the tiers stood and applauded. Slowly, a handful of senators scattered throughout the senate stood and applauded with him. Soon the entire senate was on its feet roaring with approval of Senator Treckley's words with Mian politely joining the overwhelming consensus, grinding her teeth together the entire time.

Standing on the bridge of his newly renamed flagship, Admiral Termel looked out the *Bastion*'s viewports at the mottled, greenish brown world before him that he would now be calling home. Clustered together in geosynchronous orbit, Admiral Termel's 37 warships rode a silent vigil over the surface landing zone that a number of his family's ships and personnel were slowly transforming into a base of operations.

One by one the transports had arrived from various points throughout the Republic, carrying the equipment and personnel that Termel was going to need to start carving out his little empire. As he looked out over the planet below, Termel's gaze gradually shifted to the stars, as did his thoughts.

May you succeed in creating your vision of the future Admiral. And may we survive long enough to see the day of your return.

Chapter Fifty

Sitting on a low couch in his quarters, Treys Legan was methodically rubbing his Anteron artifact between thumb and forefinger when the door chime sounded.

Coming out of his introspective mood, Legan placed the artifact on the 30 cm high table in front of him as he got up off the couch and walked to the door. Another chime sounded before he hit the activation panel, retracting the single door into the wall with Isen Tyrel standing on the other side.

"Do you have them?"

In response Isen hefted a small satchel that he was carrying over his right shoulder. "Right here."

Legan moved to the side of the doorway, letting Isen enter his quarters and closing the door behind him.

"Take a seat," Legan said, pointing in the direction of the table.

Isen chose one of Legan's self conforming chairs and plopped down onto its soft material. "Cozy."

Legan returned to the couch and picked up the artifact off the table and held it up for Isen to look at. "I'm hoping this piece will somehow fit together with the ones you collected, but there's only one way to find out."

Taking the cue, Isen pulled the four artifacts that he had out of the satchel and placed them on the table in front of Legan, one by one. Legan stared at the pieces for a moment then picked up the one on his far left. He adjusted the two pieces in his hands until he aligned the non reflective, black artifacts correctly. Legan fit the two pieces together and found that the artifacts now clung to each other.

After studying the newly joined pieces, Legan picked up another of the artifacts and fit it into its appropriate place as Isen watched quietly. It too clung to the first artifact as the pattern suddenly became obvious.

Legan picked up the next artifact and placed it on the end of the second, forming a rough horseshoe shape. Picking up the final piece, Legan fitted it into the slot between the third and fourth artifacts, completing the pentagonal ring. As soon as the fifth piece was connected, the entire ring of artifacts began to glow red, prompting Legan to place it on the table top.

As Legan and Isen watched, the five artifacts slowly melted together, filling in the center of the ring and flattening out into a 27 cm wide circular disk with a number of tiny gems imbedded on its surface. The two men stared at the newly formed armory key for a moment, then Legan finally spoke.

"I've never seen anything like that before."

"I have," Isen said, still staring at the flat disk.

"Where?"

Isen stopped staring at the key and dug a hand into his right pocket. He produced the biotech vile and held it up for Legan to see.

"Here. This is one of Morning Dawn's newest inventions. I don't think the technologies are the same, but the metamorphoses are similar."

"You lost me."

"Watch," Isen said, standing up. He popped open the vile and poured it into his palm.

"See," he said after the liquid solidified into his biotech suit.

"Impressive. I knew Morning Dawn's technology was a bit ahead of Midnight Star's, but I didn't think the gap was this large."

Isen deactivated the suit and returned the vile to his pocket. "Well, if this key is any indicator, whatever is stored in the armory should far surpass Morning Dawn's technology." Isen craned his neck to the side as he stared at the key. "What are those gems?"

"I'm not sure," Legan said as Isen sat back down.

"The larger one in the center appears to be the focal point of the design," Legan said, picking the disk up and turning it over.

"Looks like a map," Isen said.

"It does at that," Legan said frowning. "I wonder…"

Legan suddenly stood up and walked over to his quarters' computer terminal.

"What?" Isen asked as Legan slipped into the computer terminal's swivel chair.

"I've got a feeling that the top side of the disk is a star chart."

Isen turned the disk over again and studied the top side. "You're saying these gems represent stars?"

"That's the idea," Legan said, typing in one last command. "Turn the holoprojector on."

Isen looked around for a moment, then spotted a control panel imbedded into the table top in front of him. Reaching out, Isen flicked the appropriate switch, causing a two meter wide diagram of the Human Sphere to materialize in front of the color strewn viewports on the far wall.

"Scroll out."

Isen did as bidden, shrinking the map of the Sphere and bringing the new systems into view.

"That's as far as it will go."

"Ok," Legan said, reclaiming his position of the couch, "look for any correlation."

Both of them alternated between looking at the hologram and the disk for a good ten minutes before Isen reached a hand to the projector controls and scrolled in on a small region of space outside the Sphere.

"There," he said, pointing to a specific section of the hologram. "Those three stars. They're all red giants. And look," he said, turning to the disk, "these three red gems are in a similar arrangement."

Legan looked back at the holographic map again, then nodded.

"I think you're right. Now that I look at it, several of these stars match up with the other gems."

"Looks like we've found the armory's location. The *Tenacity*'s computer should be able to give us the exact location." Isen looked at Legan. "Shouldn't it?"

Legan nodded. "I'll have it scanned and the image fed into the ship's computer. It shouldn't be hard to locate the exact position if the disk's star chart is accurate enough."

"I'd bet it is. Something this complex wouldn't have been sloppily designed."

"I agree." Legan looked at Isen. "Looks like we're going treasure hunting in the near future."

Isen smiled. "I can't wait."

"Ten seconds to reversion," one of the bridge officers called out.

Admiral Legan stood on the *Tenacity*'s bridge walkway with Captain Yader on his left and Isen on his right, both of whom stood a half step behind him. Behind them stood Cara, with Gradir and Silas hovering off each of her shoulders. Ketch, Mejal, and Bryen stood off to the side, ignoring their fawning companions. A few senators and governors onboard ship were scattered among the Midnight Star agents as everyone awaited their arrival at Alpha Prime.

"Five, four, three, two, one, mark," the helmsman counted aloud.

The color vortex around the ship collapsed into nothingness, revealing a blue green planet with the *Perseverance* already in orbit, ready to act as traffic coordinator for the convoys that would arrive a few minutes later.

Legan took a step forward as he looked out the viewport, then a moment later he turned around to face the group assembled on the bridge.

"Welcome to Alpha Prime, our new home."